"A great read ... didn't put it down until 1 a.m. ... a full-bodied, compelling espionage thriller. Goodspeed has captured the horror of life in the mud and blood-filled trenches of World War I as only an experienced soldier with a great eye can. On top of that, he's got down pat the cultural differences in the manners, mindsets and methods of the Britons and Germans among whom his Canadian hero finds himself."

JOE SCHLESINGER, *award-winning CBC journalist and foreign correspondent*

Nov. 27, 2009

For dear Utte on her birthday,

    I hope you will derive
as much pleasure from this
"page turner" as I did ......

    With love from Treasa

THREE
TO A LOAF

A NOVEL OF THE GREAT WAR

MICHAEL J. GOODSPEED

Blue Butterfly Books

THINK FREE, BE FREE

Blue Butterfly Book Publishing Inc.
2583 Lakeshore Boulevard West, Toronto, Ontario, Canada M8V 1G3
Tel 416-255-3930   Fax 416-252-8291   www.bluebutterflybooks.ca

Detailed ordering information for Blue Butterfly titles is located on the next to last page of this book.

LIBRARY AND ARCHIVES CANADA CATALOGUING IN PUBLICATION

Goodspeed, Michael J. (Michael James), 1951–
    Three to a loaf : a novel of the Great War / Michael J. Goodspeed.

ISBN 978-0-9781600-6-7

    I. Title.

PS8613.O646T47 2008   C813'.6   C2008-901911-3

Design and typesetting by Fox Meadow Creations
Text set in Adobe Garamond
Printed in Canada by Transcontinental-Gagné

The paper in this book, Rolland Envrio 100, contains 100 per cent post-consumer fibre, is processed chlorine-free, and is manufactured with biogas energy.

No government grants were sought nor any public subsidies received for publication of this book. Blue Butterfly Books thanks book buyers for their support in the marketplace.

This book is dedicated to
my beautiful wife, Shannon,
who has shown immense patience
with all of this.

1

THERE ARE MANY fine personal accounts of the Great War and if I thought I had nothing new to tell, I would not have attempted this narrative. There are others who long ago achieved literary fame and who fought longer and in conditions of more sustained misery than those that I endured. My story differs from previous chronicles of this period. At critical phases of that terrible conflict I saw service on both sides; and, for a brief period, I held the power to alter the course of history. As to the value of this account and the nature of my actions, I have neither the vigour nor the desire to deal with my reader's judgments. The war was a long time ago and I will meet my maker knowing I risked my life and shed my blood struggling to shape events for the betterment of mankind. If along the way I failed, I did so in good company. Future generations will come to their own conclusions on that war. I have made arrangements that this manuscript should only be made public long after I am dead. Although there were things I would like to have changed, I know what I did was right. And now, in my final years, I see no merit in submitting to the constant probing of the curious or the sceptical.

After more than eight decades, I've come to realize that life is a chain and its links are forged from people and events. I will begin this memoir with the event that prompted me to join the army. I had no doubts as to the nature of the war by the spring of 1915; by then, few of us did. The casualty lists had already been shocking enough and it didn't take any great leap of the imagination to realize what conditions were like over there. My first step toward joining the army was taken on a grey day in March. Much of the snow had melted; and, like it always is at the end of the winter, what was left by that time was coarse and granular. The wind was raw, and summer still seemed a long way off. I was in Montreal standing on the curb-side outside McGill University's library with Jeanine Dupuis, with whom I was wildly infatuated although she doubtlessly didn't reciprocate my feelings in anything like the same measure.

The army had a hundredweight motor truck decked out with banners and flags. Perched behind the driver was an officer and beside him was an overweight sergeant with a bass drum. They were trolling through the campus looking for recruits. The fat old drummer was pounding away on his drum with one arm and wiping his brow with a handkerchief with the other. A middle-aged captain with a cardboard loud-hailer shouted at me.

"You, sir, climb aboard with us!" He already had three young men with him who were grinning self-consciously. "Yes, you, sir! You'd do one of our city's regiments proud. Come down to the armouries with me and sign on." He pointed to the drum. Stencilled around its edges were the words "Your King and Country Need You."

I hadn't really thought seriously about joining the army up to then. I was satisfied with my life up to that point; but I had other considerations. My father expected me to finish my education and take a position in the family business. Jack Ferrall was one of the pillars of the English business community in Montreal. Actually he was of Irish descent, but in Montreal's polite society during those days that kind of thing was really a trifling distinction. The real problem was my mother. She was very much a German, born and raised near Hanover. She had met my father while he was on a prolonged business trip to Europe. They were married and almost twenty-one years later, I came to be standing outside the university library.

Without giving it much thought I shouted cheerfully back at the recruiting officer, "Come back in a few months. I'll join up after I graduate." The recruiting officer just shrugged and turned to exhort a group of young men heading off to classes on the other side of the street.

When the soldiers turned their attentions elsewhere, Jeanine looked at me with ill-concealed surprise. "I had no idea you were planning on joining the army," she said in her ever so slight French accent. It was just one of the things about her that half the male population at McGill found heartbreakingly irresistible. She had the hint of a wicked smile playing about the edges of her mouth. "Rory, you're always full of surprises."

"Well, I've been thinking about it for a while now." I shrugged self-deprecatingly, anxious to change the subject to something that would make me appear more decisive than I felt. I looked out at nothing in particular in the middle distance and said with great earnestness, "I've been giving the war a lot of thought. I suppose when the country's at war it's not right to stay home." I don't think Jeanine was any more interested in me after that little exchange, but for a long time afterwards I certainly thought about it a great deal. Looking back on it, I don't suppose my plans really made much difference to Jeanine, but those few moments made a huge difference to me.

Jeanine and I turned into the library and I began to think about where I stood in relation to what was going on around me. The war was something that pained my mother greatly. My mother wasn't alone in this respect. The governor-general's wife, the Duchess of Connaught, was Prussian born, and the malicious gossip going the rounds in the country was that she was drowning her sorrows in whiskey. Mother hadn't reacted like that, but the strain on her was visible to those who knew her.

Like everybody else, I followed the events of the war with keen interest, but until that day I had been a spectator. I was fascinated and more than a little disturbed that Germany and the Empire were at war. Despite my mother's origins and an upbringing that was heavily influenced by my Germanic roots, I considered myself to be both solidly Canadian and a member of the British Empire. For her part, my mother was proud of her new country and revered Canada in a way that I suppose only the recently arrived can appreciate. Even so, I knew the idea of Germany and Canada being at war caused her considerable pain.

It wasn't the way I felt about my country. My country was where I lived and we were proud that it was an immense part of the British Empire. Like the rest of my generation, we took pride in our British connection and quietly thrilled to see the vast shaded expanses of pink on contemporary world maps. It was much like belonging to a family with rich and famous relatives who lived in a different city. It was a part of you but it was also something that was distant and in practical terms didn't make a lot of difference from one day to the next—unless of course, that Empire went to war.

I was patriotic enough, but having spent most of the summers of my boyhood and adolescence in Germany, I never believed the German people or the Kaiser were the menace to civilization that the papers made them out to be. Nonetheless, my thoughts on the war were confused. I felt strongly about Germany's violation of Belgian neutrality, and German militarism was something no responsible person could ignore. The reports of German atrocities in Belgium troubled me deeply. Still, if I'm to be completely honest in this memoir, I must admit that my first serious thoughts about joining the army and going off to war had nothing to do with a sense of duty or right or wrong, or even a yearning for adventure. I was impulsively trying to impress a petite university student with big brown eyes and a captivating smile.

✠

Over the next few weeks, I periodically toyed with the idea of joining the army when I graduated in two months time; but I kept my thoughts to myself. A week after the incident with Jeanine and the recruiting wagon, I stopped by my father's office in Sainte-Annede-Bellevue. I had something or another to pick up. I've long since forgotten what it was I was going for, probably to get money; but I remember the occasion clearly as it was the day before my twenty-first birthday. It was also the afternoon when I realized the war had already begun to change things irrevocably.

The anteroom to my father's office was a dingy sort of place with weak electric lights, few windows, and dark office furniture. About a dozen clerks normally occupied it. They were sober hard-working men who, for the most part, still wore bowler hats, stiff celluloid collars, and black ties. On that day the chief clerk, a very tall red-haired man in his late fifties by the name of Thomas Randall, was instructing two young women in the duties of maintaining financial ledgers. Half the desks that were normally occupied by clerks were vacant. Randall looked me up and down with what at the time I supposed was a cool and disapproving look. "Good morning, Rory. Your father's in his office. Someone's with him just now so you'll have to wait out here until he's free." He gestured to a wooden swivel chair at an empty desk and turned to continue his instruction.

I waited for about twenty minutes, feigning interest in a three-day-old newspaper that had been left on the desk. When Randall took the women downstairs to show them the company files, one of the men remaining at the desks leaned over to speak to me.

"So, Rory, I guess you're probably wondering what's going on today, eh?" He was a cheerful sort and had bad teeth, and as long as I could remember coming to my father's office he had gone out of his way to be nice to me—but only when the imposing Mr. Randall was out of earshot. Before I could answer, he launched into a description of the latest developments in the front office. "All five of the younger lads that used to be here joined the army the day before last. They went out at lunch and didn't come back. I hear they joined the Royal Highlanders. They'd been talking about it for a while. I never really expected them to do it. But yesterday around three in the afternoon one of 'em came back and told Mr. Randall and your dad." He paused and looked around guiltily to see if Mister Randall was in earshot. "I thought they'd be mad, eh? But not at all. The office is going to be giving them a little farewell ceremony and a lunch before they leave to go to training camp next week."

Ducking his head toward the desk he continued, "The girls are new, aren't they?" He grinned broadly as he said it. "Mr. Randall won't hire any men, as he says unmarried men of fighting age should be in the army. The girls are all married, but I think both their husbands are in the army too. There's more coming on Wednesday too. Who would of thought it would come to this even just a few months ago, eh Rory?"

I only saw my father for a few seconds after that conversation. He was busy and we never discussed what went on in the business. I don't know if it was the conversation in my father's office, or perhaps it was a steady accumulation of influences, but driving home to our house in Mount Royal that afternoon, I couldn't help but be struck by the way the war was looming so large in my life.

I was one of the most fortunate young men in the city. I was getting a first-class education; I had already travelled widely; I enjoyed family wealth and had unlimited access to a motorcar. My future was as guaranteed as anybody's could possibly be. Sitting on the leather seats of my father's new McLaughlin touring car made me realize that I was probably amongst the luckiest people to have ever lived. We had no real worries. My home had two telephones, electricity in every room, two motorcars, two maids and a cook, as well as a gardener who came around to keep the flowerbeds and lawn in order in summer and to shovel snow in winter. No one could possibly have asked for anything more. But like most other young men who are comfortable and secure, I was also slightly bored and not wise enough to know what a dangerous predicament that can be. I was still a very young man then, but the days of my youth, like those of so many of us in my generation, were to disappear far faster than I could possibly have imagined.

✽

When I arrived in Mount Royal I parked the motorcar beneath the old elm tree that stood by the roadside. I dreaded what I was about to do; but it was the one thing I had to go through with before I went any further with my plans. I still believe this was one of the hardest moments of my life. I didn't want to hurt my mother. Even then, as I went in to tell her about my decision, I don't think I had fully enunciated my reasoning to myself.

My motives were mixed. Part of my thinking was, I hate to say it, but it seemed the thing to do. There was an undeniable element of following the herd in my choice. But this was only a small factor. I suppose there was also a large measure of genuine altruism in my decision. I knew that I was needed and felt personally obliged to help out the country and the Empire. There was also an element of uncertainty in my thinking. I was not entirely clear about what we intended to get out of the war, but I was keenly aware we were living in dangerous times and I had to make an individual commitment. Doing something and going with my instincts seemed better than doing nothing. All of these notions seem a little quaint almost sixty years later. Now so many have begun to sneer at this kind of reasoning. I'm not saying they're entirely wrong; but those who sneer at youthful magnanimity are foolish and cynical.

My mother was sitting in the drawing room reading one of Edith Wharton's novels. She had her feet curled up under her. On the couch beside her were the devoured remains of three of the day's English and French newspapers. She held her cheek forward for me to kiss her as I came in.

"Rory, you are back early, shouldn't you still be at your classes?" She always pronounced my name with a soft Germanic purr. From the way she looked at me I could tell something weighed heavily on her mind. "What is it?" she said.

"Mother, we haven't really talked about the war." I began to stumble. "I mean really talked. We've said it's a terrible shame and a great tragedy, and we've gone over the causes of the war until we're blue in the face, but we have to talk about how it affects you and me, now."

"Speak plainly, Rory. Are you joining the army?" she asked flatly.

"Yes, I've decided to join ... I wanted to discuss it with you first."

"Is there anything to discuss? It sounds like you have already made up your mind."

"Yes, I have, but I wanted to discuss my reasons with you. That's important."

She nodded her head. "Thank you." There was no sarcasm in her tone.

"I know you are unhappy about my decision for several reasons. You don't want to see your only child go off to war. You especially don't want to see me go to fight Germany and you don't want to see your son fighting your nephews. I know it's very difficult."

"I suppose that sums my position fairly well. So what is there to discuss?"

"Despite being half-German myself, I believe we have to support our country. I don't like it any more than you do when the newspapers refer to us as Huns, but Canada and the Empire are at war and the cause is a decent one." I paused for a moment. "When you married Father and came to Montreal you chose to be a Canadian. I may be part-German and I'm proud of that, but I'm a Canadian first, just as you are now. I don't think there's an easy way around this. This isn't a choice between your views and Father's, and I am not turning my back on the half of me that's German. I believe that stopping the Kaiser from conquering Belgium is the correct thing to do. German militarism as it's developed in the last several years can't be allowed to prevail in this war. We both know the true Germany, but what's happening in Europe now is wrong and we can't ignore that. That's why our country is at war."

I was standing above my mother and my voice was much louder and more emphatic than I had intended. I sat down on the chair opposite her. I drew a deep breath.

"Besides, I think it would be wrong for me to have benefited from everything this country has to offer and not pitch in when there's a problem. Do you see what I'm trying to say?"

My mother had tears in her eyes and her voice was choked with emotion. "This isn't the first time I have thought of this. Your father and I have virtually ignored this subject for many years, long before it ever came to war and long before you were old enough to become directly involved. I have for several months now thought this was a decision you were going to make. I'm not happy with it, but I have no choice and so I am forced to accept it."

Mother was in many ways a German patrician to the roots. She was born into a well-to-do family of German industrialists with large land holdings not far from Hanover. She was entirely a product of her times. For her, our brief conversation was in itself an outpouring of emotion. I had known for almost a year now that the war and the threat of war between Germany and Britain was something that placed enormous strains on my parents' relationship. It was something she would never admit to anyone; she would force herself to endure this problem on her own. For my father's part, I was not so sure that he was enduring any kind of hardship on his own, although to be truthful, I had absolutely no proof that he had been unfaithful to my mother. I had sensed for several years that this chasm between them had grown enormously. Since the declaration of war last August it was very much in evidence.

My mother and I embraced in the formal way we had always done. She got up from her couch and swept me out of the room. "I am sure you have much to do now, but before you go off and join the army I want you to telephone and see about getting someone to fix the doors to the coal cellar. Mary tells me they're leaking badly and unless they're fixed they'll be a problem all summer."

It was her way of telling me the matter was at an end. We were on to discussing the more mundane things in life; whatever rift there may have been between us was now healed. I was relieved at this, but I didn't believe things were fine. That would take a long time, but I didn't choose to pursue the matter further.

With the confrontation with my mother over, I still had to deal with my father. That now appeared to be a larger difficulty than I would have admitted to ten minutes beforehand.

I did not speak to my father about my decision until late the next day. He was off overnight in Ottawa on business of some sort and wasn't expected back until late the following afternoon. I decided that I would go to my classes, say my farewells to my close friends, and then go directly to his office to speak with him. Thinking about it at the time, I realized that the sequence in which I had decided to inform those closest to me about my decision to go into the army revealed much about my allegiances. I felt guilty about this, as I had no particular reason to place my affections for my father behind that of my friends. I also knew that out of a sense of filial duty, I owed him more than being the last to know. Perhaps I feared him more than I care to admit even now.

When I got to the university, before going into my first lecture, I announced my decision to Tom Moore, an old classmate of mine from my days at Loyola, Montreal's Jesuit college. Tom was as good as a telegraph and no sooner had the professor made his entrance than Tom got to his feet and announced to one and all, "Please join with me in wishing our own Rory Ferrall the greatest good luck and a safe return, as he is soon going off to France to serve his country."

I was taken aback by this sudden announcement. The professor grinned broadly, stuffed his hands in his trouser pockets, and flapped his academic gown as if he were a ruffled pheasant. He cleared his throat and asked in a loud voice, "Good for you, Ferrall, what regiment have you joined?"

"I haven't actually signed on yet, sir," I said in a quiet voice. "I intend to go down to one of the armouries later today. I'm not sure which unit I should join. I was hoping the recruiters would give me some advice on that one."

"There's no need to go down to the armouries, my boy," quipped my professor, who was clearly enjoying himself. "Just over in the lobby of the Student Union building, the Princess Patricia's Canadian Light Infantry have set up a recruiting desk." He fixed me with a knowing stare. "I'm sure there's no finer unit you could join. I'm told they're re-building their ranks and they're doing it entirely with university men. You'd do well to join them, be amongst fellow

McGill men, friends." He dropped his chin to his chest and looked at me expectantly as if he had just finished summing up a brilliantly argued case before a jury.

"I suppose I could go over and talk to them. As I said, I haven't given it a lot of thought."

"Go over now, Ferrall. You're a good student, and as far as I'm concerned you've passed this course. There are only a few lectures left until exams, and I have no trouble giving you an exemption." The students in the class burst into a round of applause and I hastily made my exit while thanking the professor and nodding to my fellow classmates.

Outside, I buttoned my coat and straightened my necktie in the glass reflection of the Arts building's doors. The figure that looked back at me in the window pane was well over six feet, had thick curly brown hair, a good open smile, and a nose that was slightly crooked from a hockey injury sustained two years earlier. I should have known I was an ideal catch for a recruiting officer, but I had butterflies in my stomach, and for a few seconds I struggled with one of those foolish adolescent fears that if the Princess Patricia's rejected me I'd never be able to look any of my classmates in the eye again.

On the outbreak of war the "Princess Pats," as the press dubbed them, had been privately raised by a Montreal businessman. At that time, they were extremely choosy and turned away over two thousand volunteers. In the end, to ensure they got into the war before it was over, they recruited only ex-British regular soldiers. It was considered to be a crack regiment, and I was afraid that without any military experience I'd be sent off in search of a unit more accepting of my military experience.

At the Student Union building, which was decked out in flags, I found the recruiting station without difficulty. Behind a desk draped ceremoniously in a red blanket stood an imposing-looking young officer not many years older then I. He was dressed in a beautifully tailored uniform and was leaning on a cane. He smiled at me when I approached. His right arm was in a khaki sling. The officer asked me to sit and then followed suit himself. He lowered himself gingerly onto the chair and appeared to be in considerable pain. He carefully took out his pipe and a leather tobacco pouch and then because of his wounded arm began a very elaborate smoker's ritual of filling, tamping, lighting, and blowing clouds of smoke. When he finished this, he asked me a few questions about myself, confirming that I was in my final year as a university student. He asked about my marks, what courses I had taken, and what I thought about volunteering. He queried me as to what my thoughts were on the war and a few other simple questions. He then asked what sports I played. He was happy to hear that I played both hockey and baseball and nodded vigorously as I answered. "These are good sports for a soldier. They teach team work and they build character." I agreed.

"Right then, Ferrall, you're the man for us." He had me sign a printed recruiting form, handed me a chit with a room number on it, and told me to go next door to the second floor where a doctor was doing army medicals. "I think you're in. You've made a good choice." He shook my hand awkwardly with his left hand, sat back, and the last I saw of him he was staring into space wreathed in a haze of blue tobacco smoke.

✠

That afternoon I returned to my father's office. When I came into the front office, Thomas Randall jumped to his feet. He towered above me, moving quickly to block the approach to my father's doorway. "Rory, what can I do for you? Your father's very busy just now."

"Is anyone with him?" I asked with impatience.

"No, no. But I know he has a great deal to do and he left instructions not to be disturbed."

I rushed past him and headed for the door. Randall was both angry and surprised at my behaviour. I knocked quickly and went in directly.

My father was talking on the telephone. In one hand he held the speaker close to his ear, in the other he tightly gripped the base. His knuckles were white and he frowned fiercely. He looked up at me surprised, put the base of the telephone down, and mouthed the word "Wait." He continued to listen for nearly a minute.

When my father spoke, he sounded confident. "I hear what you are saying and I tell you we can have fifty thousand leather jerkins in five sizes delivered to France or Britain in six weeks. I can have a further fifty thousand every month thereafter if they're needed." He listened for a few seconds and said, "Fine, fine, I'll be in touch shortly. Thank you, goodbye."

He turned to me, levelling his frosty blue eyes at me like a ship's guns. "Rory, what are you doing here? I left instructions with Thomas not to be interrupted under any circumstances."

"He tried to stop me. It's not his fault." I continued without hesitating, "Father, I've joined the army. My professors have given me credit for the remainder of the year. I go to Valcartier in three days, then I'm off to England and then I suppose I go to France."

"Isn't this all a bit sudden?" my father asked, reacting exactly the same way as my mother. "You haven't discussed this at all with me." For the first time in as long as I could remember he looked hurt. I softened my tone.

"I've been thinking about it for a while now. It's not right for me to stay at home when the country's at war. I have to go."

Father didn't say anything for a long time. He got to his feet and walked over to the window, staring out intensely, chewing his lower lip. He was a striking figure, with thick, curly brown hair, a full moustache and, as always, an impeccably cut dark blue suit. It was then, watching him look out the window, that I regretted not telling him of my plans beforehand. I didn't expect him to be hurt by this, and I bitterly regretted I had not told both my father and mother together. In retrospect, it was naïveté rather than lack of sympathy that caused me to make my announcements separately, but my behaviour grieved him all the same and it's one of the things I've always regretted.

My father spoke quietly. "You know, Rory, I was hoping the war would be over in a few months. But in these last weeks, after these battles in Belgium, France, and Poland, I don't think it's going to be. I think the war is going to drag on a lot longer than we ever imagined."

I did my best to sound confident. "It can't go on much longer at this pace, Father. Everybody says that. There'll be a truce sooner rather than later. Both sides have too much to lose, and they're both near the point of exhaustion. It can't possibly last much longer."

My father shook his head sadly. "No, it can go on for a long time yet. Perhaps another year, maybe even a year and a half. I don't know; but I do know both sides well enough to know that it'll get much worse before it gets better." He paused and turned to me. His face looked older than I ever remembered it. "So which regiment have you joined?"

"The Princess Patricias were recruiting at the university today. I didn't think they'd take anyone without prior service. Apparently I'm in."

Father gave a reluctant nod of approval. "Good choice. But I think you'll find their supply of veterans has run out. I'm not surprised they're creaming off the best from McGill. Did they offer you a commission?"

"No, the subject never came up."

My father raised his eyebrows. "Let me make a few calls. You should go overseas as an officer. You're qualified. I'll arrange it. I know several people in that regiment." I was tempted to refuse his offer. I wanted to do this my way; but I realized in a second of unspoken understanding that my father wasn't being controlling. In his own way he was trying to do me a favour. It was his method of saying he wished things had been different between us and I let the matter pass.

✠

Shortly after nine in the morning the next day, we got a phone call at our house and I was asked if I would consider applying for a commission. I agreed.

My last three days in Montreal were spent in a blur of activity. My mother and father insisted upon taking me downtown to have me fitted for an expensive set of new uniforms that in due course would be sent on to me. They spared no expense and had me kitted out in the latest field equipment. By 1915, soldiers' field gear had turned into quite a growth industry. That morning I became the owner of a new trench coat, a shooting stick, and a gentleman's field shaving kit, complete with an assortment of pills and tonics to help me cope with the rigours of field living. In addition, I was provided with an officer's combination rubber ground sheet and poncho, a map case, and a leather correspondence kit. It was an impressive and heavy collection of equipment, and I was more than a little afraid that I would look like the most pampered boy at Scout camp.

On my second-last night in Montreal, my father held a dinner for me at the Saint James Club. It was a rigidly formal all-male affair, attended by both his closest friends and mine. Dinner was excruciatingly correct in every sense. We wore dinner jackets, and the table was laden with heavy silver and cut glass. There were almost a dozen courses. At the end of the meal, one of my uncles on my father's side made a long formal speech about me. My father then toasted my courage and sense of duty, and presented me with one of the latest and most fashionable innovations of the war, a smart Swiss-made wristwatch with an alligator skin strap.

After dinner, we retired to the smoking room, and I for one had too many glasses of brandy. It seemed everyone there came up to me and clapped me on the back to wish me luck and reminisce about the past. Drinks in the smoking room that evening seemed more like a wake, where the corpse was the guest of honour. My father and his friends made their departures by midnight, and my evening ended close to dawn with two of my closest friends and me sitting on the Saint James Club's front steps. We were much too loud and the distressed club porter threatened to call the police if we didn't leave. Before getting a cab to take me home, the three of us promised to meet here again as soon as the war ended. I can still see Tom Moore's and Willie Matheson's faces. Tom lost a leg and his irrepressible good nature at Mons. Willie Matheson went over the top one night leading his platoon in a counter-attack at Passchendaele and was never heard of or seen again. Needless to say, we never had that reunion dinner.

My last farewell was down at Montreal's old Windsor Train Station. I had just embraced my mother and was determinedly shaking my father's hand when Jeanine Dupuis swept onto the station platform dressed in a green velvet dress and a broad-brimmed black hat. I was thrilled. Jeanine, unwilling to intrude for long on a family affair, only stayed a second. She made some small talk and turned to me.

"Rory, I had to come and wish you good luck." She kissed me on the cheek and for a precious second pulled me close to her. "I'll write you." Turning to my parents, she smiled and said, "I wanted to come and wish Rory luck."

The memory of that slender image of fashion and grace haunted me for months afterward. I had no idea of the horrors and trials that lay before me, but long after my chivalrous notions about the war disappeared, Jeanine lingered in my mind as a symbol of what I wanted to return to.

2

ALTHOUGH MY LATTER YEARS of military service was radically different from that of my peers, my introduction to army life was much the same as it was for tens of thousands of others.

As a potential officer, I was given quarters similar to those of men whom I was one day to lead. However, I was treated differently in several respects from the other ranks who did their initial training at Valcartier. I didn't question these dissimilarities at the time. Our disparate military circumstances were really nothing more than the accepted values of our time. And although there were a few young officers who assumed they were intrinsically better than the men we were to lead, there were infinitely more of us who were conscious of the awful responsibilities we were to assume.

As potential junior officers, we were guided largely by attitudes rooted in the army of Queen Victoria's day, where leaders were expected to be culled from a different stratum of society and soldiers were seen as being entirely different. Viewed from five and a half decades later, this certainly seems like a preposterous notion, but it was one most of us unconsciously accepted. I was soon to witness how these beliefs, once thought to be fundamental to our society, were to be violently burned out of our way of thinking. Nevertheless, it was the accepted wisdom of my time, and despite its shortcomings, I still believe that those officers who led our troops in the

field were first-rate men who served courageously and honourably.
They certainly died gallantly—and for officers in the trenches that
was the single trait the system demanded from them above all else.

For my first week, I lived in a rough wooden shack with a pot-
bellied coal stove to heat it. We were later moved to bell tents, with
two probationary second lieutenants in each. This in itself was significantly more comfortable than the men, as they lived eight to
a bell tent. Another comfort allowed us was that even as officers
under training we were assigned a batman to look after our kit. In
Canada, we were much better fed than the soldiers. We dined on
table cloths, ate from hotel tableware, and our mess was richly provided for. Our diet was more akin to that found in a good railway
hotel, while soldiers ate a more monotonous routine of bread, jam,
meat stews, and tea.

Our comforts aside, our commanding officer was determined to
see that we knew our jobs, and we worked longer hours than the
men we would eventually command. Our instruction was seldom
inspired, and in many ways, even at the time, I thought it reflected
the inadequacies of the peacetime militia. While in Canada, I
learned nothing about trench warfare, the employment or handling
of machine-guns, or how to direct artillery fire. Instead, we learned
care of arms. We spent long days on the rifle range trying vainly
to reach the regular soldiers' standards of marksmanship. We spent
endless hours on parade square drill. And we studied and took part
in exercises on minor tactics, physical training, military law, bayonet fighting, judging distance, report writing, map and compass
use, and how to organize and site sentries. Much of what I learned
in Valcartier was useful, but much of it was useless.

As a civilian coming to the army, I was surprised to find that
junior officers were not entirely encouraged to think for themselves
but were instead expected to display initiative only within the confines of a narrowly restricted and largely unwritten doctrine. Perhaps these shortcomings were more evident in hindsight. Like so
many of us who endured the war, I've frequently wondered if the
course of our lives was guided by extraordinarily stupid politicians

and generals, or if it was a case of technology making stalemate and mass slaughter inevitable.

Whatever the truth, I still believe the mental straitjacket imposed on our peacetime militia caused us needless death and suffering, and the fact that larger European armies made similar blunders in no way vindicates our own leaders. The Canadians and, as I was to find out from bitter first-hand experience, the Germans were to rid themselves of much of this smugness as the war progressed. My generation of soldiers paid dearly for the sleepy complacency of our politicians and generals. As a veteran who lived in the mud and watched so many of my fellow soldiers crucified, I have long been troubled by the fact that none of those responsible for the manner in which that tragedy unfolded has ever been called to account for such deeply rooted neglect and stupidity.

My Canadian instructors were for the most part decent older men from across the country. They were men who had militia serv- ice and had volunteered for active duty, but against their wishes were placed in training positions. None of them had ever been to war; and for many, the militia had been a comfortable and highly socia- ble means of performing a civic duty. None of them had expected the kind of slaughter that was going on in France.

My fellow officers were men not unlike me—although few came from as comfortable a background as I did. Most were reasonably well-educated city men, the sons of doctors, clergymen, lawyers, and merchants who had joined out of a sense of obligation. Most were quite intelligent, fit, good natured and resourceful young men. I've often wondered who amongst us survived. I was the only one going to the Princess Patricia's and except for one or two stray acquaint- ances during the war, I never saw most of them again.

✠

I never did get a chance to see my family again before we went over- seas. From Valcartier we took the train down to Quebec City and boarded the *Star of India*. Our ship was a rusting steam-liner that had not long before been employed on more elegant duties. Before being converted to a troop ship, the old *Star of India* ran genteel passengers in first class and a lucrative trade in second class and steerage conveying immigrants from Southampton to New York. She ended her days in late 1917, a day out from the coast of Ireland, when a U-boat torpedoed her.

We didn't see any submarines; but for the first time in my life I saw whales. I was taken by their majesty and their sense of serenity. Early one morning when I was standing on deck, just after a torpedo drill, a very large blue whale surfaced alongside us. It blew a great geyser of water, flapped its enormous tail several times, and rolled cheerfully back into the depths. All of us on deck were thrilled and the men cheered spontaneously.

The only other occurrence of note had to do with our fellow passengers, a company of nursing sisters headed for duty in field hospitals. After my training in Valcartier, the sight and proximity of these lovely creatures was a real reminder of the new life I had volunteered for. Life in the army was much different from civilian life for many reasons, not the least of them was that it was an entirely masculine culture. I managed to chat briefly with some of the nurses before we landed in England, but for the most part we just exchanged smiles and nods.

The day we saw the whales I managed to engage two of the nurses in conversation at the ship's rail. Long after the whales went their own way, we stared out into a steadily rolling grey nothingness. One of the sisters was a woman in her late twenties from Toronto and the other, whose name was Hannah, was closer to my age. She was a petite honey-blonde from Vancouver and she laughed easily. We chatted for almost an hour about so many things, none of which was of any importance and after these years I don't remember any of it anyway; but I do remember the delight I took in her company. Years later, I began to think what a strange thing war was, for apart from its violence, it put us into situations that were completely different from the natural way of things. The ship was very crowded and although I kept my eyes peeled throughout the rest of the voyage I didn't run into Hannah again, but I enjoyed her brief company immensely. On the last day out there was much guffawing and ribald comments one morning when, as part of the normal ship's bulletins, the officer in charge of the trooping announced over the tannoy that the matron had complained of instances of "unseemly conduct and anyone caught embracing a nurse would be charged."

✠

Our arrival in England was something of an anti-climax. We'd all read about the delirious reception given to the Canadian troops when the First Division embarked in England. The papers were full of patriotic nonsense about how the locals were saying it was the largest embarkation of foreign troops since William the Conqueror. As a routine reinforcement troop ship, we docked with no fanfare and came ashore quietly one evening. On the quayside, we were given tea and scones by the Salvation Army. We waited for an hour for our personal kit, and a short time later we found ourselves on a troop train to Salisbury Plain. Our embarkation was a well-organized operation and proceeded with a mechanical efficiency that I found impressive. While the residents of Southampton slept in their beds, we slipped unseen through the countryside to our next stop on our journey to the trenches in France.

England was a much more intense repetition of what we had already gone through in Canada. I was put into an officer replacement training company. Our instructors, both officers and non-commissioned officers, were almost all British. Except for the sergeant major, who was a greying and leather-faced veteran of the Indian army, the instructors we saw the most were sergeants and corporals from the old regular British army. Most of them had received wounds of varying degrees of severity in the earliest days of the war. These NCOs had a cheerful cockiness about them and treated us firmly, but with a kindly good nature.

Our affection for the NCOs of the old army didn't extend to our bayonet-training instructors, who were recently recruited bullies whose mission was to put "fighting spirit" into us. They were all younger, more athletic men, who worked us to exhaustion; and had never been to the front themselves. They took immense pleasure from their graphic descriptions of how to skewer the enemy on the end of a bayonet. Being of German blood—a fact I took pains to conceal—I had more reason than most to loathe these posturing men in their safe jobs.

The few British officers I met at the time were on the whole distant, and they exuded a sense of disdain for their colonial counterparts. It was hard to warm to them, and except for our company officer, a quiet and devout Captain Wallace from the Royal Scots, I never really got to know any British officers prior to arriving at the battalion so I was at a loss to form any kind of useful opinion of them. Wallace was a precise, if unimaginative man with a salt-and-pepper moustache. He had taken a bullet through the knee in October of 1914.

While I was in England, the British army ensured that we received instruction in those subjects that had been quietly glossed over in Canada. I learned how to site and maintain the Vickers and Colt machine-guns, how to remedy their stoppages, and how to clean them in the dark. Because they were still in short supply, we also received a half-day's instruction on the Lewis gun, which was eventually to become our new light machine-gun. The Lewis gun looked like a wonderful weapon—except for the fact that the gunner had to expose himself by climbing on top of it to reload it.

Much to my relief, we studied the developing science of trench warfare. In a wooden hut we were tutored on the design of a battalion's defensive layout using a carefully crafted plaster model. I never saw anything quite as elaborate or as flawlessly designed as our model—but the wire entanglements on the model proved to be child's play in comparison to the murderous belts of wire we were to encounter on sections of the front.

One cold rainy night we spent a frustrating thirteen hours pick-axing our way three feet deep into the chalky Salisbury soil. Captain Wallace half-seriously called us "a pack of lazy dogs" for not completing the trench in our allotted time, but once the captain was out of earshot Sergeant Halstead, pretending he hadn't heard a thing, quietly told us that we'd done reasonably well. Most courses only got a foot down into the rocky soil in that area.

"Remember, gentlemen," he said, "if you are ever planning an operation, you and your men will dig a little faster when someone is shooting at you, but don't expect miracles."

Halstead was a grey-haired Cockney who had spent half his life in distant parts of the Empire. He had a large measure of common sense and I often thought he would have been far more effective commanding a brigade than supervising entrenching demonstrations on Salisbury Plain.

I spent the better part of a day in London on the single day's leave we were given before moving to France. Most of my fellow officers had never seen the city before and we spent most of our time dashing in and out of pubs and sitting on the top of a double-decked omnibus driving about the city viewing the sites. Normally I loved London, but in wartime she looked grey and dismal. Everything was overpriced and I found it a bit disconcerting when the shopkeepers repeatedly asked us, "Ah, Canadian lads, eh? Looking forward to getting over there to have a go at the Hun?" I don't think any of us were wildly enthusiastic about the prospect of battle. We were prepared to go, but deep inside we all wanted it to be safely over. Even then, we would happily have foregone the adventure ahead of us.

✣

After a further two days of training, we were assembled on the edge of the parade square in the pre-dawn darkness under the light of a single weak electric street lamp. There was a steady, cold drizzle of rain and we were informed we were to get our kit ready, for that evening we would be entraining for Portsmouth to catch the night's ferry to Le Havre.

Captain Wallace, leaning heavily on his cane, gave an encouraging and fatherly speech. "You should remember what you've been taught. Make examples of yourselves to the men and make all your decisions as if the shoe was on the other foot. Guide yourself by whatever you would expect as fair treatment from your platoon officer if you were a soldier. Do that and you won't go too far wrong." He assured us we would do splendidly and make our regiments, Canada, and the Empire proud. He sincerely bid us "Good luck and God bless," saluted us, and limped off the parade square.

✠

The train to Portsmouth was late, overcrowded, and reeked of urine and filth. We sat on our kit crammed three to a bench in what had been designated an officers' car. We disembarked in a steady downpour amongst a throng of military police barking directions and indicating our way forward with electric torches. "Canadian officers to the right, Third Division Other Rank reinforcements to the left. Look lively please, gentlemen. Move along now."

After standing around for what seemed like half the night, we were rushed aboard the ferry and ushered into what had was once been a dining salon. It was now emptied of all its original furnishings and was instead provided with a series of crudely made wooden benches. It struck me at the time that the normal comforts provided to the human race were deliberately downgraded and replaced with crude makeshift arrangements when it came to providing services for soldiers. It was not the last occasion I would be reminded of that observation.

The ship sailed an hour later. Our channel passage was a rough one and the ferry rolled and pitched like a cork. For such a short journey, we were a ridiculously long time at sea, and most of us were sick throughout the trip. I don't know what made the crossing more unpleasant, the ship's motion or being confined in close quarters with so many other men who were violently ill.

At Le Havre, our ferry docked shortly after dawn but for some inexplicable reason we were again required to wait on board for several hours. No explanation was ever given for our wait. When we disembarked, we were once again herded into a train station in a roughly fenced holding area and told to await further orders.

Across the yard from us, separated by a wooden fence, were the freshly trained reinforcements destined for the British Third Division. They looked haggard and pale, presumably after having spent an even more wretched night crammed below decks than had we. A British Red Cross refreshment trolley was trundled amongst us. Two pretty young women began unpacking it in order to sell us tea and buns. The two women doing the unpacking were stopped short by a stout, freckled Nova Scotian schoolteacher named Angus Kearsley who demanded in a deep voice, "Are the troops across the fence being served tea as well?"

The Red Cross team leader responded in a very plummy but pleasant English accent, "We have always served this side of the compound their tea first; and then, as soon as that's done we get to the other side."

Kearsley replied, "Unless the Third Division troops get their tea first, they're wasting their time selling tea here."

The men on the other side of the fence gave a ragged cheer and the two tea ladies graciously pushed their trolley around to the other side. We never did get any tea. It may or may not have sold out before it got to us. Kearsley was more than a little brusque and even though he was guilty of grandstanding, I admired him for his consideration.

Some time later, as we wearily shuffled forward to board the trains to take us to our respective forward areas, I noticed the wooden fencing and the warehouse-like structure surrounding us was probably originally built as a cattle shed that had been converted to a troop marshalling area. I wasn't yet a superstitious man, but this seemed a very bad sign.

3

WE DE-TRAINED at a temporary railway siding in the middle of a field with the ugly name of "British Expeditionary Force Picardy Staging Area 3." Shortly thereafter, we were met by a military motor truck that bounced us several miles along a dirt road to the divisional rear area. The lorry lurched to a halt in a motor vehicle compound two hundred yards beyond a cluster of farm buildings. A pair of dirt-encrusted motorcycle despatch riders lounged on their vehicles.

After struggling to gather my kit, I approached the motorcyclists for directions and was mildly surprised when, as I approached, they both stood up and came to attention and the soldier nearest me saluted smartly. I'd been saluted before and I felt no sense of pride in this, but for a brief instant I was startled by the realization that from that point on I really was going to be making life or death decisions on behalf of dozens of men I had never met before. Probably like everyone else in those circumstances, I felt terribly inadequate.

The despatch rider directed us to one of the barns, where a much cleaner but tired-looking staff officer with red tabs on his collar met us and told us we would be joining our units in due course. After a spate of checking and re-checking various lists, we were pointed in the direction of what had once been a small orchard and told to get some sleep because as soon as arrangements could be made, we would be sent forward to our units. We slept under our ground sheets that night but before I finally fell asleep I spent a long time listening to the distant rumble of artillery fire and imagining what lay before me.

Around noon the next day, the staff officer ambled over to the orchard and advised several of us that before nightfall we'd be leaving to join our units. At around three that afternoon, a ruddy-cheeked soldier with a Patricia's cap badge and a thick northern England accent arrived and told me he was there to escort me to battalion headquarters. I said my goodbyes to my fellow trainee officers and as the PPCLI was then still serving with the British Twenty-seventh Division, I was headed north.

The Patricia soldier indicated a waiting lorry and when I made to climb aboard the back of it with him he laughed and said, "No, sir, officers ride in the front. The driver knows where to go."

I asked him, "Is the driver from the battalion?"

The young Patricia smiled and shook his head. "No, sir, these lads never go forward of the battalion rest areas."

"In that case, I want to ride in the back. I want you to tell me about life in the battalion."

The soldier's name was Private Reid. He was originally from a village outside Newcastle. Prior to emigrating to Canada, Reid had served for four years in the Coldstream Guards. He had joined the Princess Patricia's when they were raised in Ottawa and had fought with the regiment since its arrival in the line nine months before. He was a cheerful sort and readily answered my questions. To my great relief, he showed no concern that I was to be in a position of authority. Like every other young officer, I secretly harboured the fear that veteran troops would somehow refuse to accept me because I was so obviously inexperienced.

The trip from the divisional rear headquarters to the rest billets was a stop-and-start affair. More than once we pulled off the dirt road to allow higher-priority traffic carrying wounded to the rear to pass and we waited for almost a half-hour on one occasion to allow a long mule-train laden with artillery ammunition to go forward.

Reid cheerfully answered my questions and, sensing my anxiety, ended his explanations with comments such as, "Don't worry, sir; you'll be fine once you get into the swing of things." Reid told me that the Patricia's had been out of the line for twenty-four hours and that he expected them to be in a rest area for another two or three days.

Reid was proud of his unit and I didn't interrupt him. Men like him were probably in the minority now, as more than two hundred Canadian reinforcements had joined the unit and more were arriving each day. When the lorry lurched to a halt at a shattered hamlet called Loenhoek, Reid showed me the way to battalion headquarters and said, "You've got to report directly to the adjutant, sir. I'll wait and take you up to see the company commander after."

Like Reid, the adjutant was also a British regular soldier. He was a friendly fellow: disarmingly polite and quietly deferential. He greeted me as if I was a long-lost relative. It was obvious he'd been sleeping, but despite the interruption, he was accommodating and helpful. He apologized that the colonel was off at a conference at Brigade, gave me a well-boiled cup of tea, and briefed me on a map of the area, explaining that the battalion was going back into the line again in two nights time. The unit was short of officers and I was to become a platoon commander in Number Two Company. With business over, he nodded and said, "Right then, Reid can take you to see Captain Adamson." He shook my hand and I was hustled off to a barn a quarter of a mile distant.

Number Two Company should have been 170 men strong. That day, it was much less than that. The company was divided into four platoons and a headquarters. Each platoon was divided into four sections with a small platoon headquarters group. There were four such company organizations in the battalion. Theoretically, the regiment could have had any number of battalions. The Princess Patricia's had only one, so the regiment and the battalion were for all purposes one and the same.

Number Two Company was, like the rest of the battalion, still in a state of near exhaustion. There was little movement and men were wrapped in their blankets and stacked like grey cocoons across the barn floor and hayloft. As I was soon to learn, the company was at about two-thirds of its strength. Although they had been in a quiet sector of the line, in the last three days they had had four men killed and three seriously wounded due to shelling. One of the first things I noticed about these sleeping men was their continual coughing and rasping, even as they slept. Colds and flu-like symptoms were chronic, but as I was to see for myself, few men reported on sick parade until they were nearly incapacitated by the onset of pneumonia.

A soldier on fire piquet who was awake and fully dressed showed me the company officers. The officers were only distinguishable from the other sleeping cocoons by the fact that they were off in a corner by themselves and had a field telephone beside them sitting on a web pack. I told the fire piquet not to wake anyone and sat down waiting for my introductions.

Several hours later the company gradually stirred into life, and dirty khaki-clad men could be seen cooking outside, writing letters, or just relaxing, sitting or smoking by themselves deep within their own private thoughts. When my company commander awakened, he too offered me bitterly strong tea that had been brewed some time ago by the battalion's batmen.

My company commander was a bespectacled Montreal businessman and was at least two decades my senior. He had the peculiar name of Agar Adamson. Adamson blearily welcomed me to his company and said he knew my father well. He matter-of-factly advised me, "Rory, you'll be going up the line tomorrow night. I need to send an advance party for our next tour in the trenches. The entire battalion will follow you in twenty-four hours time. We'll be replacing the King's Royal Rifle Corps, and this'll be a good chance for you to get a feel for things, see how another unit operates, and learn how things are done before your own men arrive."

Later, when I thought about this, I was grateful to Adamson. He knew I didn't want to appear the new boy and was positioning me to put me in the strongest possible light before my troops, men who would take a more than passing interest in my abilities and character.

I spent the remainder of that day meeting my platoon, wrote letters home, and, to my surprise, received a cheerful and gossipy letter from Jeanine who disappointingly signed herself "As ever, your true friend." I was still very naïve. Late the next morning, I played a game of pick-up baseball with the newer Canadian-born members of the platoon. For the most part, the British veterans amongst them watched the game and provided high-spirited but unprintable comments about the level of play. By five that afternoon, I was off with the advance party for my first experience at the front.

✠

Going up the line for the first time was an experience I think few men ever forget. In my case, I did it after dark. The night was cloudy and warm but despite the weight of my kit and the fact that I was sweating, I was shivering and my throat was sore. I must have caught a cold during my short stay with the battalion. Three lance corporals and I were to act as guides for the incoming Patricia's. We met up with a British re-supply column consisting of two dozen men heavily laden with sand bags tied around their necks or wearing pack boards with boxes of machine-gun ammunition or several gallon tins of water. The sand bags contained rifle ammunition and rations broken down into section allotments. I was slotted into the column with a guide and men from Number 3 Company of the King's Royal Rifle Corps, the organization we were to replace. Once the column was organized and checked by a young officer, we were on our way.

The approaches to our new position were in low ground and could be observed by day by the Germans sitting on the higher ground to the north of us. As it was, the German artillery had long since ranged in on sections of the road and periodically fired in the dark in the hopes of hitting something. They tried that night, but fortunately no one from our column was hit. I was more than a lit-tle alarmed by my first experiences of artillery exploding in the dark. As it turned out, the rounds landed two hundred yards behind me. But to my overactive imagination it was much closer. The sudden blinding flashes and the violence of those first rounds exploding in the darkness were unforgettable.

In front of me, a short, heavily laden Tommy with an unlit pipe clenched in his teeth grumbled to no one in particular something that sounded like "Let's fucking keep moving then, shall we?" We did. And in what seemed like a short time we were met by a second group of guides and began to break into separate groups; we were then led into the rear-area communication trenches.

These were trenches only in name. In some areas they were just shallow scrapings with mud-puddle bottoms. We splashed on as qui-etly as we could and eventually arrived at a series of deeper scrapings with occasional dugouts tunnelled into the wet earth beside them. Men were occupying some of these tiny reserve dugouts. We could tell they were there because they swore at us when we stumbled over their muddy legs sticking out into the trench. The smell of those trenches and the next line farther forward was unlike anything I've ever encountered since the war. The area around the Ypres Salient was littered with thousands of unburied French, British, and Ger-man corpses in varying stages of decay. I didn't know it that night, but there were also enormous rats in their tens of thousands teem-ing in the fields and trenches surrounding us.

Those churned-up fields had been fertilized for centuries with human and animal waste, and in the trenches latrines were little more than open sewage pits. The effect of those reeking fields was stomach churning. The stench caused me to heave several times as we plodded forward. You never really became used to it; but some-how we managed to carry on with that overpowering and disgusting smell relegated to our sub-conscious. It is the only smell that has invaded my dreams. Dante may have tried to describe the depths of hell and mediaeval artists have tried to paint it. But for me, that murderous odour was the most vivid evocation of hell I can think of. Thankfully, I have never encountered anything like it since leaving those ghastly fields.

The frontline trenches in our sector were deeper, but they were so soggy and shell blasted they were more like an intermittent creek bed than a military defensive works. When standing, our heads were just below ground; but even in the darkness of that first night, there was none of the snug sense of security that I had once imagined trenches would have. I spent the next night and day crawling around what looked to me like a badly maintained ditch. I learned every nook and cranny and peered into no-man's land with a homemade periscope given to me by a British officer. I drew a detailed sketch of the area, marking each dugout, each communication trench, each machine-gun position, each known enemy sniper position, and the routes through our own wire.

That first tour in the trenches was like many others I was to experience. Fatigue and discomfort blurred and overrode the constant strain of being so near to violent death. The overall effect was to create a weary numbness. We coped by developing a crude sense of humour that my family and friends in Montreal would never understand. I still marvel more of us didn't die from sickness. The food was appalling; it invariably consisted of tins of gristly Machanochie stew or fat-encrusted bully beef; it was invariably eaten cold and sprinkled with sand and mud. While in the line, we drank inadequate quantities of sweet tea, which came forward in one-gallon water cans, a good number of which had at some time seen service carrying gasoline.

We didn't really sleep; we were wet and cold for long periods of time and our personal hygiene was as primitive as it could be. All of us were infected with lice. We had lice in every seam of our clothing and in our hair; we itched constantly. Not just soft scratching, but violent clawing at a painful never-ending irritation. Rats overran our dugouts and were forever slithering about the trenches. Great fat corpse-fed rats would come out even by day trying to steal our rations and every night they scuttled across our legs as we tried to sleep hunched against a trench wall. Shooting rats was a hazard to everyone and so the only authorized weapon for rat control was a sharpened spade. Necessity turned ratting into a sport; and with our misshapen sense of humour, we kept our spirits up hunting the wretched animals, turning it into a contest between companies.

The trench's dirt quickly got into everything. We ate dirt. We breathed it constantly. It was in our mouths, hair, and ears. It turned our socks and puttees into sand paper and trickled down our necks whenever we sat down.

I found sleep to be near impossible under those circumstances, although during the days, for an hour or two, I could go back to the company officers' bunker and manage to drift into a periodic kind of half-wakefulness. Nights were, more often than not, frequently times of feverish digging, filling sand bags, and standing to on what passed as a fire step to watch the exhibition of flares and rockets illuminate the sky whenever a suspicious sentry raised the alarm.

We were occasionally attacked by German patrols, frequently shot at by snipers, harassed by machine-gun, artillery, and mortar fire, and on one occasion low-flying German aeroplanes strafed us. Our casualty rate wasn't high, but it was steady. During one of these "quiet tours" the battalion usually lost three or four men killed and many more wounded.

It was for my actions on a patrol during one such "period of inactivity" that I was awarded the Military Cross. Although I will never willingly part with my "MC," I am the first to admit that for everyone who was awarded such a gallantry decoration, there were many more who could have just as readily qualified for one.

On my fifth tour in the trenches, Captain Adamson sent a runner for me asking that I forego conducting a foot inspection of the soldiers in my platoon and come see him.

"Rory," he said in a grave voice. "It's our turn to visit the enemy on his side of the wire. We've been tasked to provide a patrol by Brigade headquarters. I think you should be the man to lead it. How do you feel about that?" I was surprised; I'd never been asked to

agree or disagree with an order before. I was also acutely aware that
I was the only junior officer in Number Two Company who hadn't
yet led a fighting patrol into no man's land. I did my utmost to
appear indifferent. "No, that should be no problem, sir. When's the
patrol scheduled to take place?"

"Tonight. I want you to get back to battalion HQ now. They're
waiting to brief you now."

The battalion headquarters's dugout was centrally located in low
ground about a hundred yards to the rear of our company's reserve
trenches. Although we called it the battalion "rear area," it was
scarcely out of grenade-throwing distance of the most forward sub-
units. I sloshed my way through the communication trenches and
was briefed on the particulars of this specific operation in a dingy
candle-lit hole with a corrugated tin ceiling.

Since arriving in the battalion I'd been "over the top" a half-
dozen times with wiring parties. These were nasty night-time jobs
that entailed stringing barbed wire and marking routes through our
wire so that our own patrols could get in and out. When we were
ordered to put out wiring parties, we watched carefully for signs
of the enemy doing the same thing. Our reasoning was that the
Germans were unlikely to fire on us if they had one of their own
patrols out in front of them as well. We timed our work on our wire
obstacles to coincide with that of the enemy. It was a kind of truce
tacitly arranged between the two sides and in its own perverse way
it worked well.

At the back of the battalion headquarters's dugout, Colonel
Buller was trying to get some sleep on a cot made of sticks and
telephone wire. His second-in-command, Major Hamilton Gault,
briefed me on the general plan. Gault was an imposing-looking
man with penetrating eyes and a substantial but carefully trimmed
moustache. For me, he was still much larger than life, as he was the
wealthy businessman who had provided the money to raise the regiment and then refused to accept being named its colonel. Until that
day, I'd never had a real conversation with him. Gault smiled when

I entered and in a low voice beckoned me over to the map board. He wasted no words.

"Rory, as part of the overall plan to maintain an aggressive posture in this area we've been tasked by Brigade to conduct a raid with a view to bringing back a prisoner and inflicting casualties on the enemy. The enemy to our front is believed to be a Württemberg Reserve Division, but aerial reconnaissance indicates major supply and troop activity in the enemy's rear." He looked at me inquisitively to see if I was taking all this in. I nodded and he went on.

"Division is anxious to confirm as to whether or not the Württemberg troops have been replaced. If they have, it's probably an indication of unusual activity and could possibly indicate a major offensive in our area. On the other hand, if the Württemberg Division is still hanging on here, it probably means Fritz is keeping them in the line so he can concentrate all his resources to resist the French push to the south of us at Artois. Rory, you are to take a patrol out tonight and bring back a prisoner. We need this information. If we're going to be attacked, Division will allocate us more artillery ammunition, and likely more machine-guns. That would make all the difference for our survival. If we are not going to be attacked, I for one want to be the first to know it."

He shifted uncomfortably and tapped a pencil against the board that served as his table. "Anyway I'll leave the details to you." Gault raised his bushy eyebrows and looked at me knowingly. "Oh. Apart from the prisoner, the staff really does want you to inflict maximum damage on the Hun as well." His voice trailed off as he said this. "I'll also leave that aspect to your good judgment." He took a deep breath through his nose and rubbed the back of his neck. "Any questions?"

Once again I nodded. "No, sir. If I could go back and look at the ground and select a route, then I'll come back this afternoon. I'll probably have a lot to ask you once I've thought about how I'm going to do this."

Gault rose. "Very wise, Rory. That's exactly what I'd do if I were you." He looked at me in an avuncular sort of way. "You'll be fine once you get going. These things aren't as daunting as they seem."

I should have resented this kind of talk because with five tours up the line, I was beginning to fancy myself as something of a veteran, but I knew Gault wasn't being patronizing. He'd led numerous patrols himself and patrolling wasn't something normally required of majors.

"Agar tells me you're doing a fine job and you've settled in like an old hand. Keep it up. You'll be fine," he said as I turned away and gathered myself to leave.

I was pleased to hear this and thanked him as I crawled out the muddy doorway of the bunker. My father had written to me a week before this incident and told me he'd received a letter from Gault assuring him that I was in good health and getting on well. Neither of us ever mentioned the connection.

I spent the afternoon squinting through a telescopic periscope and prepared my plan. My sergeant, a sandy-haired Scot named Ferguson, selected the men for the patrol for me. He was extremely disappointed I didn't include him in the upcoming operation.

"I want to try something different on this patrol," I told him. "It should be kept smaller than what we've been used to. It seems to me having too many men out there increases our risk of drawing fire."

Sergeant Ferguson looked down and stirred at the mud between his feet. He didn't ask how it was going to be different and I didn't tell him. Apart from the size of the patrol, I hadn't thought through the details. Even at that stage of the war, we seriously mistrusted much of what came down from the staff. I'm sure in this respect the Patricia's were no different than anyone else. Staff bumbling in the Great War has become a cliché, but in late 1915, as throughout the war, we did our best to accommodate the staff's wishes. But for our own survival, we always interpreted their demands. The pattern had by then become all too apparent; utterly ridiculous orders regularly came down from otherwise sensible men who were out of touch with the reality of life in the forward trenches. I suspected the situation I faced with my patrol was no different. I was going to do my best to get a prisoner, but I sure as hell wasn't going to draw attention to my patrol and draw fire by inflicting meaningless casualties on the enemy for the sake of appearing to be aggressive.

The problem confronting me was the same one that confronted every infantry officer in that war. The Germans had been industriously adding to their barbed wire obstacles in front of their positions. I spent several hours squinting through a periscope but I could see no way to get through their wire. If the staff wanted me to get a prisoner, and at the same time they wanted me to do damage to the enemy, I had to get through the wire. Scores of thousands of men on both sides had already died vainly trying to solve precisely that problem. In their directions to us, the staff typically stated their demands quite explicitly. Get us a prisoner and inflict damage upon the enemy. We were left entirely to our own devices in determining how we were to accomplish these tasks.

Our battalion front was a typical patch of ground in the Ypres Salient. Throughout the Great War, the Ypres Salient was one of the most fiercely contested patches of ground. It was a large bend in the Allied line that jutted into Belgium; and for most of the war, it was the only piece of that unfortunate little country that remained in the hands of the Allies. The PPCLI held eight hundred yards of it. Depending where you were, we looked out at three to five hundred yards of rolling shell-pocked territory that separated us from the German army.

Over this barren scene, a few stunted shrubs valiantly attempted to grow and a half-dozen shattered tree stumps served as reference points. As if this once tranquil bit of farmland wasn't sufficiently desecrated, the whole area was liberally strewn with the rotting corpses of English and German infantrymen. The backdrop on either side of all this was a fifty-yard belt of barbed wire entanglements. This obstacle belt was made up of densely massed wire coils and complex webs of barbed wire windlassed to wooden stakes. Behind this, on the German side, armed with machine-guns, was a battalion of some of the best soldiers in the world. The landscape was utterly evil and I was expected to lead men through its most impenetrable zone, shoot up their trenches, and return triumphantly with a prisoner.

That night I found myself with five men standing on the fire step of our forward trench. With me I had Private Rivers, a Canadian-born militiaman from southern Ontario, Lance Corporal O'Neil from Calgary, privates Jenkins and Grey, both originals from the East End of London, and Lance Corporal Mullin, a quick and aggressively intelligent young man from Winnipeg.

The sky was partially concealed by high-level scattered clouds and the moon was to rise at ten. A gusting breeze stirred the coils of wire, making a slight chinking sound. Last light was at around nine. It could have been worse. I would have liked it to be much darker, but I was grateful I hadn't been tasked, as some men had, to go out on a clear night with a full moon. At 9:15, as I'd arranged, artillery began to fall across the entire front of the trenches opposite me. At the same time, two machine-guns on our flanks began firing rapidly back and forth across the German trench tops.

"This is it, follow me," I whispered in a way I hoped wouldn't convey my fear.

We slipped over the top and wended our way delicately through the wire to our front. The path through our own wire was innocuously marked with bits of sand bag. If we kept to the left of the sand bag strips we found a narrow path that threaded its way through our wire. The path wasn't easy to see and barbs caught at our tunics and trousers. Close to the enemy side of our wire we had to lift two coils and crawl under it. The shelling stopped a minute before we crawled into no man's land. We crawled forward twenty or thirty yards and I made an exaggerated pointing motion to Private Rivers. He gave me a thumbs-up and mouthed, "Good luck." Quietly, he lay down and cradled his rifle, scanning the darkness before him. Rivers' task was to wait just outside our wire and keep his eyes peeled for our return. If we were lost, or heading in the wrong direction, Rivers was to catch our attention and guide us back through our own wire. Rivers would have a long wait lying on cold damp ground, but we all knew that amongst the six of us, he was the one with the most certain odds of surviving to see morning.

I pulled out my compass and took a bearing. We were going to go forward at a crouch for a hundred yards, and at the lip of a series of prominent shell craters on a patch of higher ground, we would push forward on all fours to the enemy wire. The four men behind me were supposed to keep an interval of five or six yards between each of them to prevent themselves from all being killed in a single burst of machine-gun fire. But in the dark, when men are tense, the urge to bunch up is almost irresistible. We'd never really trained for this kind of operation and I'm afraid at times we all followed our instincts and moved huddled together as a small crowd.

We reached the cratered area without incident, went to ground and watched and listened for a long while. The five of us peered into the dark, perched on the lip of one of the largest craters. I scanned the way ahead with my field glasses. The light was getting brighter and the moon was rising behind the clouds. I remember thinking that for some strange reason moonrise was early, and I found it amusing that one of the results of my patrol when I returned, if I hadn't brought a prisoner back, would be to submit corrections to the astronomical tables.

We waited and watched the German lines for an hour. It was just after eleven that I heard muffled sounds from the area of the German trenches. A few minutes later we could hear the whistle of German artillery rounds passing close overhead and almost instantly artillery impacted three hundred yards to our rear. It was exactly what I'd hoped for.

I motioned for the men to get down into the craters and whispered, "Stay here, I'm going forward. For God's sake, don't shoot me when I return. Be prepared to move out as soon as I get back." One of the men, I think it was Grey, made to question me. I silenced him with a wave of my hand. "If I'm not back by three o'clock, go back without me. I'll get back on my own. Nobody's to be caught out here in daylight." I was gone into the night.

I crawled forward as fast as I could without making too much noise. I was moving towards the sounds near the German trenches. Sporadic artillery continued to fall behind me, and somewhere, a long way over to my right, a German machine-gun began shooting at our trench lines.

After crawling for about ten minutes, I stopped and carefully pulled my field glasses out from inside my tunic. Scanning the trench line I could see nothing but the forest of wire and some regular shapes that I presumed to be sand bags piled on the forward edge of the parapet. Near me, probably within a hundred yards of me, were at least a hundred heavily armed enemy soldiers. Despite this, the battlefield seemed as empty and as desolate as the moon. My speculations were interrupted by a dull red glow. Someone was lighting a pipe or a cigarette in one of the forward trenches. I watched intently for several more minutes, totally absorbed in my study of the ground. As my senses adjusted to the surroundings, a few seconds later, directly to my front a man coughed softly. Later I could very faintly hear stifled laughter. Whoever was in front of me was obviously in good spirits. I continued to watch the area before me. Suddenly, very close to me, a footfall and someone grunting almost made me swallow my heart. A German wiring party had come out of nowhere and was moving quietly and steadily across my front.

Two dark shapes in round field caps were struggling with a large coil of barbed wire concertina. A few yards behind them was another figure with a heavy-duty pair of wire cutters and what I guessed was probably a much smaller coil of fastening wire. They stopped in front of me and quietly began to bounce the wire out along the edge of the obstacle belt. After a few seconds the wire became entangled in itself and one of the men began tugging at it frantically. It made a loud metallic scratching noise and the man with wire cutters cursed and hissed in a South German accent. "Hoffart, you stupid oaf! Do you want to get us all killed? Make another noise like that and you will be out here every night this week."

I didn't know whether to be euphoric or terrified. It was exactly what I had hoped for. Despite having put a brave face on it, I knew

I could never find a way to sneak through that thicket of wire and I had imagined us going forward, throwing a few Mills bombs, and then withdrawing empty handed and ignominiously. My best possible opportunity would be to find a wiring party—and truthfully, I didn't expect to do that. Now I had one and they were literally within spitting distance. I watched.

Hoffart slowly untangled the wire and then turned his back to me while he attempted to fasten the end to one of the other concertina rolls. The other two men quietly moved off twenty or thirty yards back to the right and were absorbed in their task of stringing their end of the wire. They must have been standing in a shell hole for I couldn't see them well. I only sensed that their backs were to me. Without giving it any further thought, I immediately stood up, drew my trench knife, and crept up behind Hoffart.

I placed the tip of my knife firmly against his neck, just under his right ear. He startled and made a sharp gasp. I whispered softly and slowly in German with a menace that surprised me. "Don't make a sound, Hoffart, or you die!" I waited a second. The leader made some kind of hissing remark again and shuffled away with the wire coil. "Come with me. One sound, one move to escape and you're dead. Move now."

I tugged him towards the Canadian lines and he glided soundlessly through the darkness with me. We moved off about thirty yards into no man's land and I gently pushed him down into a shell crater. He moved with a grace that I admired. Hoffart, whoever he was, understood the situation clearly. My knife was still pressing hard against his neck. "Lie down and don't make a sound." I increased the pressure on the knife to reinforce my point. With my left hand I pushed Hoffart's face into the mud. I then reached around and gingerly slipped his rifle off his shoulder and placed it beside me. As I did so, my knife came away from his neck. He didn't move and my knife went back under his ear.

A moment later I heard Hoffart's leader hissing for him in the dark. "Hoffart...Hoffart!" There was a pause. "Hoffart, we are going!...Hoffart! Hoffart!" Then there was silence for a good minute. I was straining in the dark to see, but all I could make out was the indistinct shape of the wire before me and the line of the German parapet. "Hoffart, you fool!" The voice sounded desperate. I could hear the steps of the leader as he checked the wire Hoffart had recently been securing. He hissed again. "He has tied off the wire, but where has he gone?"

He walked confidently forward and stood not more than ten yards away from us. The leader slipped his rifle from his shoulder, dropped to one knee, and peered into the darkness. I could see he was wearing spectacles and a round field cap without any peak. He wasn't a tall man and was probably an NCO. "Hoffart! Hoffart!" He hissed again louder than ever. At that moment he chose to leave and turned about. He whispered to the other man, "Hoffart has disappeared."

I fully expected him at this point to scurry back to the safety of his trench line and report Hoffart's mysterious disappearance. My plan was at that point to make best speed back to the crater, pick up my patrol, and move as fast as possible back to the safety of our own lines. This was not to be. Hoffart's leader did something that made me forever more respectful of the calibre of the enemy we faced. The little man with spectacles moved off, beckoned for the other man to come near, and they both sat down not a dozen yards away and waited. I could see the muzzles of their Mauser rifles pointing steadily into the darkness. After a minute I breathed ever so faintly into Hoffart's ear, "No sound." My knife was back pressing at his neck. Hoffart wasn't moving.

I probably waited an hour for the German NCO and his subordinate to leave. The German NCO reminded me of an old Indian hunter I once met at a friend's cottage in Quebec. I was told the hunter could sit stone-still for an entire day waiting in one spot for his prey, but then the hunter wasn't waiting for something that shot back.

I was inexpressibly relieved when they got up. The NCO wasted no time and moved off quickly in the direction he had originally come. I waited a further ten minutes, for I didn't want them to go off a short distance and wait for me to surface. There was no sound. I whispered to Hoffart, "Now, come with me. Try to escape, I will kill you. Co-operate, you will be comfortable and safe, a prisoner. Do you understand?" Hoffart bobbed his head. "Let's go." We moved off slowly and quietly.

I found the shell hole. In fact, I almost walked by it but Lance Corporal Mullin called to me gently and stood up to relieve me of my prisoner. "Lord Jesus, sir, where the hell did you find him?" he exclaimed in a whisper. It was the same admiring tone I'd heard people use when someone brought a good-sized trout home at the lake.

"I'll tell you later," I said. I was suddenly terribly shaky. We frisked Hoffart but he didn't appear to have any other weapons. We tied his hands behind his back and set off stumbling towards our own lines. Thirty seconds after we got to our feet a pair of German machine-guns opened up and began traversing our battalion frontage right to left and left to right. We threw ourselves to the ground and stayed put while rounds cracked closely above our heads and ricocheted around in the thickets of barbed wire.

When the firing stopped, we got under way again and seconds later I could hear Rivers shouting "Over here, over here!" Once inside the maze of our own wire, our machine-guns began to fire rapidly to cover the final torturous and dangerously exposed leg of this short journey. We were back with a prisoner. I was as weak as a baby and trembling like a leaf. I remember leaning against the trench wall feeling very wobbly and thirsty. Within a few minutes, Major Gault and the colonel were up to greet us, and Hoffart and I were hastily escorted off to the battalion headquarters's dugout.

At the battalion headquarters's dugout, we sat Hoffart on an ammunition crate and gave him a hot drink. He cupped it in both grubby hands, sipping it in the light of a flickering candle and looked around at us suspiciously. I spoke to him in German.

"Hoffart, you're a lucky man. Luckier than we are, you're going to spend the rest of the war in comfort. You'll be dry, have good food and a clean place to sleep every night, and most importantly, you're going to get home at the end of this—alive and in one piece. That's a helluva lot more than the rest of us can say. But I want you to answer some simple questions first. Do you understand?"

Hoffart nodded his head doubtfully. He was sceptical as well as frightened. Prisoners of war were protected by international law in those days, but the expectations restricting information to name, rank, and regimental number were not nearly as severe as they were twenty-five years later.

Hoffart looked at me with exhausted innocence. "You speak very good German for an Englishman."

"Thank you, but we're not English. We're Canadians." I tried to be as pleasant as possible. "My mother's German. I spent a lot of time near Hanover as a child. Where are you from?"

At that moment, I turned and asked Major Gault in English if Hoffart might have a drink and perhaps a cigarette. He rustled about in his pack and produced a bottle of brandy. I offered Hoffart a healthy shot in a mess tin. It was only then, in the warmth of the dugout, that I smelled Hoffart's rank odour. The poor man must have fouled himself out in no man's land. I didn't find it funny. Braver men than me casually admitted to losing control of their bowels in the regiment's earlier battles at Frezenburg and Bela-waerde Ridge. Gault lit a cigarette and handed it to him. Hoffart began to weep. It wasn't gratitude; it was relief from the terrible strain he'd been through.

I spoke as gently as I could without sounding patronizing. "It's all right, you're safe." The other officers discreetly left the bunker and Hoffart and I chatted for fifteen minutes.

Hoffart was grey-faced and had a pinched and anxious look about him. He was in his mid-twenties and was a reservist from Allensbach. Before the war, he had worked as a carpenter's assistant in a small furniture factory. He was married but had no children. He was called up in August of 1914; and, with the exception of four days leave in April, had been in a frontline division continuously.

Hoffart was in the Twenty-sixth Württemberg Division, not the Twenty-seventh. "The Twenty-seventh," he said, "had been withdrawn a week ago and were now sitting on their asses doing who knows what." The Twenty-sixth had been in the line for four days and were slated to rotate into a rest position the next night. Hoffart was certain they were going to be replaced by Bavarians. Just this morning he'd seen their officers doing their reconnaissance. After a day's rest, his sergeant told him they were going to be employed reloading artillery ammunition onto train cars in support of a major effort against the French.

I poured Private Hoffart another healthy measure and gave him another of the major's cigarettes. He was a good man and I liked him. I didn't feel that I'd used him. At the time, I took satisfaction knowing I probably saved his life. Hoffart was going to miss the next big offensive—and whatever came after that. I called for one of the headquarters runners to watch over him and ducked out under the hanging sandbag door to use the field phone. The brigade staff needed this information.

4

THE ROYAL FLYING CORPS confirmed Private Hoffart's information the next day. Years later I learned it was corroborated by a sophisticated network of Belgian train watchers who at great peril to themselves reported on the movements of enemy trains. True to the estimate provided to me by Major Gault, the German army was fully engaged repelling a disastrous French offensive to the south of us, which meant, for a time, we were safely out of the major action.

Shortly after my patrol, we found ourselves moved back to decent rest billets. We rotated in and out of a very quiet area of the line and during one of those spells in the rear I was promoted to full lieutenant. I'm sure my German friend, Private Hoffart, had a lot to do with it. The battalion officers were put up in a good-sized farmhouse a mile west of Armentieres, and for once I managed to find a nice dry spot for myself on the dining room floor. It was strange how things had changed. For a few days I actually thought of that patch of farmhouse floor as home.

Our actions during those weeks were minor. Like everybody else in the British Twenty-seventh Division, the Patricia's were employed on quiet stretches of the front. The entire division was still recuperating from its near fatal mauling at the Second Battle of Ypres four months prior to my arrival. Other fresher divisions weren't so lucky. To relieve pressure on the Russians and draw German troops from the east, the French and British armies chose to attack in the areas of Champagne and Artois, as well as around a small village called Loos. We were glad to be out of that one too. What we heard from our own rear-area troops was disturbing. British casualties at Loos were staggering and we were thankful at having been spared the horrors of that bloody campaign. Our stretch of the front was no more comfortable and it was often dangerous, but we felt immensely lucky that it was our turn to be tasked with relatively safe reserve and flank guard roles.

One morning in February stands out clearly during one of those stretches in the trenches. I was on a tour of my platoon area talking to the men, conducting routine inspections of weapons and sanitary arrangements. It was a grey, cold, foggy day and wet enough that we were thoroughly miserable. My boots were sodden and my trousers were caked with wet mud. I was chatting to one of my corporals about nothing in particular when we heard the whistle of incoming trench mortar fire a little further down the line. We threw ourselves against the parapet wall. Several rounds landed in the space of a few seconds and no sooner had they stopped than I heard men cheering and catcalling. The shouting was a good sign; it seemed all the mortar fire landed either in front of or behind our trench lines.

I hurried to the sound of the cheering, but as I rounded one of the bends in the traverse between Two and Three Sections, I was electrified. Private Reid, the young man who acted as my guide on my first night at the battalion, was on his stomach clawing at the duckboard. His face was drained of colour; his mouth twisted in a horrible grimace. Reid lay in a grotesque smear of blood and dirt, his legs shredded into trailing ribbons of mangled flesh and ragged bits of uniform. He died in my arms seconds later.

That morning was the first feeling of genuine hatred I had for the enemy. I wanted Reid to survive the war. He'd been kind to me. He was cheerful, resourceful, and I knew he would have made a difference to those whose lives he touched. For him to die so suddenly, so capriciously and in such agony and filth filled me with loathing and rage.

After Reid's death I continued to be shocked by the closeness of death—but that morning something inside me went numb. I suppose it was what psychologists now call a survival mechanism. Whatever it was, it was another watershed moment in my life, one that fifty-five years later I recall in vivid detail. When the Loos offensive finally came to a shuddering stop over seventy thousand young men like Private Reid were dead. When the war was over, twenty million Private Reids had been slaughtered on both sides.

A week later, the entire British army went onto the defensive and the Patricia's were at last transferred to join the rest of our fellow countrymen in the Canadian army.

✠

When we joined the Canadian army, the battalion was tasked to man the line around the town of Hooges. At Hooges, we received another reinforcement draft from Canada; and for the first time in my experience, the Patricia's were at full fighting strength. Like me, most of the new men were recruited from universities in Quebec and Ontario. Not surprisingly, there were a lot of potential officers in this new draft and, as I was to learn later, senior army planners were angry that the upstart PPCLI had again creamed off more than its share of the available talent. Elitist recruiting didn't help us escape the destruction lying in wait for the Canadian army. Like the rest of the university men, I was soon involved on a section of the line with the deceptively tranquil sounding name, Sanctuary Wood. It was to be horrific and was my last pitched battle. Sanctuary Wood was another link in a chain inexorably dragging me into a new life.

Our arrival in the new sector of the line was ominous. To go forward we had to pass through a patch of ground near Hooges that had once been the intersection of two country lanes. Because the crossroads was directly observable to German troops on the high ground to the north of us, several months earlier British troops nick-named it Hellfire Corner. Anything that moved by day on Hellfire Corner was shelled mercilessly, and at night, the Germans regularly blasted it with speculative shrapnel and high explosive bombard-ments. To get to our new positions we had to pass through Hellfire Corner. On our first tour in the sector, despite moving through the crossroads at night, we lost seven men just getting to the trenches. That month we crossed and re-crossed Hellfire Corner three times.

Our new position was an utterly godforsaken piece of ground. The battalion's trenches meandered across a waterlogged bottom-land and the Germans looked down on us. Because the Salient was Belgian ground, the Allies refused to surrender an inch, and we found ourselves defending a low-lying salient jammed like a pro-vocatively scolding finger into the German lines.

Behind our trenches, the ground was deeply cratered. Over the winter those craters filled with black water, turning the larger shell holes into small evil-looking lakes. On dark nights, men from my platoon frequently crawled back there, cracked the ice, and washed away as much of their filth as they could. We stopped that soon enough.

When the warm weather came, the ice disappeared and the mud at the bottom of the crater gave up the bloated corpse of a long-dead French soldier. Our poor Frenchman wasn't the only unburied veteran in the area. At several points along our trench walls men repairing collapsed sand bag revetments came across the decompos-ing bodies of French and British soldiers who died there months before. God knows what terror and agony those men died in, but their rotting arms and legs routinely fell into our trenches. There was nothing else we could do—we dug through those remains and sealed off the dead with sand bags. The memories of those corpses were less easy to lock up.

On June 1, Number Two Company was manning the "Loop," a semi-circular section of trench that sat like a wart on the very tip of the Salient. The Loop's trenches were deeper and in better repair than those occupied by the companies on either side of us. But although our trenches may have been deep, their approaches were exposed on both sides and we could only get safely into the area in daylight by crawling on all fours for several hundred yards.

On that final stint in the Loop, Number Two Company was stronger than we had been on our previous tour. In addition to our new reinforcements, in our last period in rest billets we'd received two Lewis guns on an experimental basis. The Lewis gun looked like an oversize rifle with a large, circular, pan-shaped magazine on top. I had been introduced to it in England on training and knew it would become a fearsome addition to our weaponry because it increased our firepower several-fold. We needed it.

A year and a half into the war the majority of troops on both sides were only a few months away from civilian life. Few of us were good marksmen. By June 1916, two-thirds of the soldiers in the PPCLI were Canadian; and despite whatever personal strengths we Canadian-born members of the regiment may have had, we had only been in uniform for a few months and couldn't shoot anything like as well as the British originals who'd spent their peacetime years on the British army's rifle ranges. We took great delight in getting this new weapon, little realizing that the automation of war was reducing all our chances for survival.

In late May, there were indications the Germans were going to attack but we'd no idea when their offensive was to begin, or how fierce and determined it would be. The morning it all started was gloriously sunny; larks were singing somewhere behind us. I was in a philosophic mood thinking about home and watching a starling sitting on the trench lip. I'd become superstitious in a half-believing take-no-chances sort of way and I was puzzled whether this was a good or a bad sign. Not that I believed in omens or charms, but some things became a habit. Was the bird a symbol of a more natural life, or did it mean our violent way of life had become natural? A year before I would have scoffed at any kind of superstition. Now, unconsciously, in a world that arbitrarily snuffed out life, I suppose I searched for meaning anywhere I could find it. I wasn't alone. Even the most religious or analytical of us in one way or another saw the course of their lives influenced by good and bad luck. I think we all had some kind of superstitious practice or belief.

On that first day in the Loop I was very tired. My eyes burned. I smoked a cigarette, and sat enjoying the early summer sunshine on my face. The small patch of sky visible from the bottom of our trench was cloudless. When you were in the trenches your horizon was limited to the stretch of sky above you and the sandbagged walls in front of you. It was a strange perspective on the world. In front of me, a sentry peered through his lookout hole scanning the German trenches opposite. In the adjacent firing bay, four of my men prepared lunch. They were laughing and taunting each other. Morale was high. We were well-fed and our clothes were dry. Although we were aware of being in one of the worst places on earth, that morning we were happy. Everything's relative. That morning we were warm and dry.

One of the voices called out, "Don't worry too much if you don't get enough to eat today, Hargreaves. Once Fritzie's done with us this time, there's only gonna be three to a loaf anyway." They laughed enthusiastically, as if it was the first time they heard the joke.

Beside me, Sergeant Ferguson, my platoon sergeant, sat quietly cleaning his rifle. Ferguson was a man of remarkably few words. During my first few days with the platoon, I found his silences a little intimidating and irksome; but the longer I knew him, the more I grew to understand him; and in that halting and formal way peculiar to soldiers constrained by rank, age, and discipline, we became good friends. We sat together in silence on the firestep of our forward trench enjoying the sunshine.

Like most of my platoon, I'd by then taken to smoking cigarettes and used tobacco as a self-rationed reward and a comfort. That morning I was smoking contentedly, reading through a packet of letters that had come up with us the night before.

The letter that my mind kept coming back to was from Jeanine Dupuis. Jeanine was getting married, and as I was one of her "dearest and most trusted friends," she wanted me to be one of the first to know. She was marrying a French-Canadian lawyer at the end

of the summer and would go off to live in Quebec City. They were
going to honeymoon at a cottage on a lake in the Laurentians. She
was deliriously happy.

In those days of constant exhaustion, filth, bad food, and violent
death, soft, warm, feminine companionship was something I dreamt
and fantasized about constantly. I had often thought of Jeanine—
her eyes, the softness of her skin, her figure, her delicate and fragrant
scent, and her soft, husky voice. I'd only known these at a distance.
I had never slept with a woman and that morning I was convinced I
never would. Now my life was unnaturally masculine, brutish, and
harsh, and I only half-expected to survive the war. Just as I'd become
superstitious, I'd gradually come to accept that I might die. And
women were so far removed from my existence that dreaming about
them was like wishing on a star. But as I said, I wasn't unhappy.
For the time being, I was philosophic about these things, and little
things, like dry clothes and sunny skies, lifted my spirits.

It wasn't just violence and hard living that had changed me;
although those two things probably had a profound and irreversible
effect on me. I was now twenty-two, but I felt at least a decade older.
Perhaps my unnatural ageing was in part due to my new position as
an officer and a leader. In this, I recognized I had some advantages:
I was much taller than all my British-born soldiers and had the benefit of an expensive education. As unfair as it was, those things gave
you an edge. Reflecting back on it, I was ideally raised for this kind
of transformation. I was young, strong, athletic, reasonably quick
to learn things, and temperamentally willing to accept a challenge.

My sense of inadequacy regarding my position as a leader had
by then all but disappeared. This was probably not entirely a good
thing. My new-found confidence had come at the cost of boiling
my values down to only those personal qualities and skills I needed
to survive. In my months at the front, I placed enormous importance on trust, physical courage, endurance, cunning, determination, and good humour. Not a lot else mattered. My outlook on life
necessarily became simplistic; but my life was no less complicated.
I had other practical worries that day-to-day living and leadership

imposed upon me. When the Canadian university men arrived, those who came to my platoon looked on me as a veteran. Some of them were several years older than I. They were innocent and treated me with deference and formal military courtesy. I suppose my Military Cross gave me credibility, credibility that I probably didn't deserve, but it helped my confidence and my stature.

There may have been more than a tinge of fatalism and self-pity in all this mellow speculation. That June morning I was curiously detached, as if I was watching things from afar. Jeanine was the only woman I had ever truly been passionate about and I had let her slip entirely away without even telling her of my feelings. Although I've known a number of women since, my love for Jeanine was entirely different from the rest. Now I appreciate that the Jeanine I loved never really existed. She was, however, one of the few women I had ever really known at that point. High school had been a rigidly male and Jesuitical regime of Latin, Greek, French, English, history, mathematics, science, and sports. My three years at McGill University weren't much different; a brief introduction to the army—and now I was at the front sitting in a foul-smelling trench surrounded by a group of men who I was to lead and was prepared to die with. It was all very alien, and at the same time so normal. These trench walls, mud, fatigue, cold, and wet had become my life. The sun made me drowsy and I wanted to crush out my cigarette and sleep.

The first rounds of the German barrage hit us with shattering intensity. It's a challenge describing the effect of a single artillery round exploding nearby. Fifty unexpected large-calibre rounds detonating in the space of five seconds is truly cataclysmic. The German barrage hit us like an eruption from hell. As best I can make out, in that first salvo only two rounds actually landed within the company trench lines, but they killed half a dozen of our men outright. Our position was well registered and the rounds that didn't land inside our trenches were very near misses. They collapsed trench walls, blew down parapets, buckled dugouts, and the shrapnel from them inflicted horrific jagged wounds.

Sergeant Ferguson, with more presence of mind than I, swept up the pieces of his rifle and shouted rather unnecessarily "Take Cover! Take Cover."

He scrambled along the bottom of the trench and scuttled into his scrape carved out of the side of the forward wall. I was momentarily at a loss—the company officers' dugout was fifty yards along the trench line and a further twenty yards to the rear. I had no place to go. Ferguson looked up at me and began to shout something. "Sir..." He didn't finish his sentence. I threw myself into that tiny space, landed on top of him, and dug my fingers into the dirt floor, pulling myself downward as if willing to be swallowed by the earth. The first few seconds of that bombardment are imprinted in my mind as if etched in stone. My remaining two days in the Loop lasted a lifetime.

The initial bombardment on our forward trench line was the most intense part of the shelling and it went on continuously for over an hour. I'd been under artillery fire several times before, but nothing matched the concentration and length of this unforgiving pounding. With each explosion the ground shook. My brain and every bone in my body felt like it was being pounded by a mallet. My head ached with a piercing pain and my nose bled from any one of a hundred close concussions that smashed me into the trench floor and walls. Despite lying alongside Sergeant Ferguson, I was completely isolated. The two of us swore and screamed obscenities until we were hoarse, but still those horrifying explosions smashed and rattled us around the bottom of that scrape like we were insects caught in a jar of fire crackers. One of the early rounds hit the lip of our trench and the blast forced fine sand straight through my tunic. Almost sixty years later my wrinkled right shoulder is still the consistency of sandpaper from the grit embedded in it. The pounding went on for well over two hours. I was frightened the whole way through it but after an hour and a half of that merciless hammering, something changed in me physically. I became cold and very tired, as if my body couldn't keep up with the physical and emotional intensity of the bombardment.

The barrage ended as abruptly as it had begun. One moment

we were writhing in terror at the bottom of our trench, and the next the explosions and concussions stopped. It was like turning off an electric light. For almost a minute Sergeant Ferguson and I lay dazed and mistrustful, trying to get our senses back, waiting and watching to see if this was really the end of the barrage or simply a feint to lure us from our trenches so we could be cut down by a sudden secondary salvo.

After what seemed like an eternity's silence, Ferguson and I crawled out. I sniffed the air. There was no indication of gas. The trench line that had been the Loop was a mess. In some places, walls that had been a full seven feet deep were reduced to four-foot ditches. Across no man's land I could hear indistinct shouting and whistles blowing. The barrage started once again well to our rear.

I peeped over what had been our parapet and saw a long line of grey-clad figures scrambling through gaps in the German wire. I shouted to Ferguson, "They're coming! Get them up and out at your end of the trench, I'll do this half." Ferguson nodded agreement and we were both off. I was screaming, "Get out, get out! They're coming. For God's sake get up, they'll be on top of us in a few seconds!"

I was terrified, but it was a different kind of fear from the one that gripped me lying on the bottom of a trench when there was nothing to do but hope you didn't take a direct hit. I was shrieking at the top of my lungs and running along the platoon line. Men groggily climbed from their dugouts. The roof from one of the platoon dugouts had been collapsed by a direct hit. Ominously from this hole there was no movement whatsoever. Men hauled weapons and ammunition cases up from hollowed sections of the trench wall. We frequently practised this drill during quiet spells in the line and that monotonous repetition was now paying off. Much to my relief, behind me came the rapid mechanical staccato chatter of the Vickers gun as it came into action.

In front of me, Lance Corporal Mullin's gruff voice was calling out, "Jesus, Mary, Joseph! Hargreaves, you get that fucking Lewis gun up here! Move man, move!"

The sound of rifle fire crackled along our line as men found themselves a bit of cover on what was left of our trench parapet. With the Germans a hundred yards away I shouted the order: "Vickers and Lewis guns go on! Riflemen, prepare grenades! Use grenades only when they reach the wire."

The order was passed up and down the line. While the two Lewis guns in my platoon and the Vickers heavy machine-gun continued to do their grisly work, men feverishly primed and prepared Mills bombs. When the assault closed to within thirty yards I shouted, "Grenades!" Three seconds later, a dozen Mills bombs sailed through the air and exploded on the far side of the wire. I could hear the shrieks of Germans shot and blasted in our wire and I could see men's contorted faces as they went down in front of us.

Perhaps I had missed it earlier, but just as the Jerries were on the wire I heard for the very first time the whooshing and crackling sound of a flamethrower. It was the first I'd ever seen or heard of these weapons and it belched a dripping, greasy, terrifying blast of liquid fire out to a distance of forty yards. This new flame device scorched across a part of Number Two Section's trench before its operator was riddled by a long stream of bullets from one of our Lewis guns. The German soldier fell and his weapon shot a huge oily black tongue of smoke and liquid fire along the front of our wire, horribly burning several of his own men. My throat was dry and my heart furiously pumped blood through every fibre of my body.

Impossibly, the Germans in succeeding ranks continued to charge toward us. My men threw a second volley of Mills bombs into the screaming desperate men clawing at our wire. The blast from our grenades was so close it seared our faces and black dirt showered on top of us. In a last desperate effort to kill us, Germans who had gone to ground threw their potato masher hand grenades at us, but in most cases they hit the wire and bounced back at them. I remember seeing Mullin picking one potato masher grenade up and throwing it back when it landed near us. No sooner had one

German soldier been shot down before us than another grey figure in a spiked pickelhaube helmet loomed behind him.

By that time, I no longer tried to control the fight. It didn't matter anyway, no one was listening, each of us was consumed in our own private struggle for survival. I seized a rifle from one of the grenadiers. I don't know how long I fired and reloaded and fired again into those grey shapes. Some time after, it seemed that what was left of the German line in front of us began to melt into the ground. One second they were within a few feet of us and the next, scattered grey figures were fleeing across no man's land. Our machine-guns continued to fire upon them.

For an instant, I was filled with a strange sense of admiration for these men who seconds before had tried so spiritedly to kill us. I remember it vividly, I was seized by the noble sentiment that it was a shame to kill such men and in my innocence I shouted, "Cease fire! Stop!" Again the order was passed down the line and our trench went quiet.

It was then that Sergeant Ferguson gently grabbed me by the elbow and spoke quietly in his Highland burr. "No sir. The ones we don't get now—they'll be back to finish us in an hour." My scruples melted. My decision was instant. "Vickers and Lewis guns go on, rapid fire!"

I've often considered that moment. God forbid, that I should ever have to relive that time, but I'd make the same choice again. The second push that day was upon us in a matter of hours.

When the shooting stopped, I expected a kind of tranquillity to come over the line, but as things died down across no man's land, our trenches were a flurry of activity. Our field telephone had ceased working soon after the barrage started and I sent a runner to report our situation and establish contact with company headquarters. I sent two others to establish contact with the platoons on either side of us. We were taught that when the firing stops, officers should begin redistributing ammunition, repair defences, and oversee the care of the wounded. In our field service training pamphlets, this description sounded so efficient, so neat and rational. It wasn't. I remember the lull in the fighting as an exhausting and difficult time, punctuated with decisions I was not psychologically prepared to make.

I wasn't overcome by conscience, grief, or even revulsion with the slaughter that I had just participated in—that was all to come later—but I was assailed by conflicting emotions. The soldier in me told me to ready ourselves for the next phase of the battle. What was left of Rory Ferrall within me wanted to devote his energy to helping the wounded. As the firing died down, the cries of the wounded increased in intensity and it took an unnatural act of the will to ignore them. The soldier in me prevailed.

In accordance with my training, I knew that if we couldn't repel the next assault, none of us, wounded or fit, would live. I posted sentries on the Lewis and Vickers guns and supervised the redistribution of ammunition. Much as I wanted to tend to the wounded, my most pressing concern was the redistribution of our remaining ammunition as quickly as possible. If we were attacked in the state we were in, we would have been easily overrun. The ammunition for both Lewis gun teams was exhausted and my right-hand section had thrown all their Mills bombs. It was clear to me that despite inflicting fantastic casualties on the enemy, our situation was a great deal worse now than it had been an hour before. There was little ammunition and no hope of immediate re-supply. The Loop was such an exposed position that no one was going to be able to get anything up to us before dark. I made a quick calculation and concluded that if the Germans attacked again before nightfall, we would be able to fire at a rapid rate for no more than four minutes. I kept that conclusion to myself. It wasn't information anyone else could use and it would spook the platoon. When what was left of our ammunition was redistributed, I turned my attentions to the wounded.

In the few minutes available to me, I scrambled up and down our sector of the Loop and counted seven dead and eleven wounded. Half the casualties came from Three Section on the right flank. I re-shuffled men from both One and Two sections. Four Section, I left intact. Men were on their knees applying tourniquets and field dressings to our casualties.

It was then I realized I had to make another unpleasant life-or-death decision. I had six vials of morphine entrusted to my care and there were eleven men with serious wounds. Everyone in the platoon knew I had the morphine. Within an hour, once the initial localized shock wore off, every one of those eleven men would be in agony and each of them would desperately need one of those vials. Instead of making a decision on the spot, I chose to wait. I had no idea how long we would be isolated out on the Loop and never having administered the drug before, I wasn't certain how long the effects of a single shot of morphine would last on a man. What I knew for sure was I didn't have enough to go around. I trusted to my instincts, hoping the decision would become self-evident.

Perhaps I should have explained my reasoning to the troops; but that morning, I didn't think I had time. I'm sure that to the men I must have seemed bloody-minded and pig-headed when I said rather bluntly that morphine would be distributed to the most needy in an hour. To have issued the morphine then would have relieved some of the suffering instantly. To my thinking, waiting until the first effects of shock wore off would ensure the least amount of suffering. From the resentful looks of some of my soldiers, I knew the decision wasn't well-received or well-understood.

With the casualties put under cover, I called the NCOs to my sector of the trench and explained the situation as best I could. With seven of them standing in the trench, I thought they were a representative cross-section of how the regiment had grown. Half of them were British-born originals, half were Canadians. All of them were tired and apprehensive. They stood nonchalantly, smoking cigarettes and pipes, rifles slung over their soldiers almost as if we were on an exercise. I imitated the kind of thing I heard on training. "The entire platoon has done bloody well and you should be proud of yourselves. The leadership in the sections is first rate and we wouldn't have lasted out there without your efforts. Well done."

I looked around at their faces and was surprised to see looks of satisfaction. I continued. "I've no new intelligence, but I can tell you that we're going to stay put here for a while yet. With the approaches to the company position being so exposed, don't let anyone get any false hopes about being relieved, re-supplied, or our casualties evacuated before dark. Our only way out of here is to hang on and drive Fritz back the next time he tries to push us off this ground. To that end, I want to see really tight fire control. Make every round count. I don't think I have time to speak to each of the men individually, but I want you to go back and explain how things stand to them. If I can, I'll be around this afternoon."

It was then I tried to fix things with the morphine. My voice went to a stage whisper. "Tell the men—and when you do this, make sure you're out of earshot of the wounded—there are only six vials of morphine and there won't be any more. I'll personally tell the wounded that we'll do everything possible to get them out tonight. I'm going to go around now and give morphine to the six I think need it the most and have the best chance of surviving. If any of the fit men are bitter about me withholding it, explain my reasoning to them. For God's sake don't let morale sag now. We're going to need all the grit we can muster to get through to tonight. I'm counting on you."

I looked around and half-expected them to roll their eyes. Corporal Yeats, a short, patient little Irishman with a monstrous moustache and unfailing humour, inhaled deeply on his cigarette and then blew smoke upwards. He pushed his forage cap back and chuckled, "Ah don' think the lads'll have much choice, sar. An' besides, there's still a lot more fight in 'em yet. If Fritzie comes callin' back, he'll get the same again."

By noon, the sun was warm and had we been anywhere else, I would have said it was developing into a glorious day. I received word that the platoons to the right and left of us were in as bad shape as we were. Our new company commander, the sergeant major, and two other platoon commanders were dead. Lieutenant Molson, from the platoon on my right, was the next senior officer and had assumed command. There was no telephone communication to anyone as all our cables had been cut. My plan was simply to hang on.

My men dug furiously, hollowing out their protected shelters and rebuilding as much of the trench line as possible. At just before two I was inside a dugout talking to one of the wounded, Private Turner, a dark-haired university man from Toronto. Turner had been hit by grenade fragments and most of his left shoulder was badly mangled. He'd lost a lot of blood and had no morphine. His face was turning pale and waxy; his breathing was raspy. He squeezed my hand with astonishing strength, an indication of his intense pain. I did my best to sound confident. "You're going to be okay."

I looked at his dressing. It was completely inadequate, the best someone could do in a bad situation. "It probably feels a lot worse than it is. You'll be out of here just after dark. In fact, you're probably going to be back at university this fall. You'll be finished your degree long before the rest of us are out of here." It was the closest I could come to a joke.

At that moment the shelling began again. Like the first salvo, this one came upon us without any ranging rounds to give warning. One moment it was quiet and the next we were being hammered. Because I was in another man's dugout I tried to back out. As I did so, I collided with the occupant who was scrambling in. The man trying to crawl into his own dugout actually backed out and apologized for running into me. Once out in the trench, I pushed him into his own hole and went running off to find the hole I had taken to sharing with Sergeant Ferguson.

The barrage we endured that afternoon was even longer and more intense than the one in the morning. It was no comfort to us that we had already survived a heavy shelling that day. This second round was more wearing on our nerves. We were tired and strung out by then. In the morning, we screamed and cursed at the barrage; in the afternoon, we sat on the dirt floor clutching our knees.

I was terrified and more than any other time wanted to be away from this nightmare forever. Beside me, Sergeant Ferguson shook like a leaf throughout the last thirty minutes of the bombardment. Ferguson was a man I had come to rely upon and to trust implicitly. Witnessing his terrors only increased mine. It was clear to me then the truth of something I had been observing for some time. All men are given only a limited amount of courage; and each man expends that courage at a different rate. Ferguson was as brave as any man but he'd been through every one of the regiment's actions, and for the first time I could see the physical effects that this constant psychological grinding was having on him.

I not only respected Ferguson, I truly liked him and enjoyed his company. He was quiet, genuinely a pious Methodist and only spoke when he had something to say. He was fair and intelligent and lived by simple values. Ferguson had been a rock for me in helping me to adjust as a new officer. He had come into the regiment as a lance corporal and was steadily promoted. He'd served around the world for seventeen years with the King's Own Scottish Borderers and emigrated to Canada at the ripe old age of thirty-five. Four years of life as a building construction supervisor in Halifax and enlistment in the Patricia's on the outbreak of war brought him to this trench.

Now he was trembling like a leaf in a hailstorm. Despite the heat of the day, his hands shook and his teeth chattered violently. Just as it seemed the bombardment was letting up, he began to shout. "That's fucking long enough, that's fucking long enough," and he bolted from the dugout. The bombardment wasn't over. As soon as he stood up a shrapnel round exploded behind our trench. I knew it was fatal because I could see Ferguson's legs from where I sat. One moment they were two muddy columns wrapped in putties and the next it was as if someone poured a horse bucket of blood down them. My friend and mentor was hit by multiple fragments in the head and torso and died instantly.

I crawled out of the dugout to help him, but from the volume of blood I knew what I'd see. I was numb and for several minutes lost sensation in my lips and hands. Ferguson's shoulders and head were gone and what was left of him just collapsed onto the duckboard trench floor like a sack of wet grain.

The barrage died down and once again we could hear the cheering and shouting of German soldiers as they got up from their trenches. This time we were much slower to react. It seemed like a long time before I remember hearing our machine-guns go into action. Once again I rushed up and down the line hoarsely shouting at men to get up and fight. Our trench was chaos. Whatever repairs had been made to it were long since obliterated. The trench was no longer a protective fortification. It had become an open sewer that carried the remains of our troops along to some godforsaken cesspit.

As the Germans closed to the wire, we repeated the same bloody choreography. This time when we crawled from our bunkers we could see the shelling had cut several gaping holes in our wire. Minutes after the barrage, my first indication that the Germans had made it into our trench lines was when a young baby-faced Württemberger poked his rifle around from the adjacent firing bay. He looked more curious than dangerous. I shot him instantly in the face with my revolver and then threw a Mills bomb over the trench wall. I rallied two men and we charged in to clear up once the bomb detonated. There was no time to think and all of us reacted on instinct. The trench was a shattered mess with upended duckboards torn and smashed like matches. Between the wooden slats were the contorted bodies of German and Canadian soldiers. From that point on, for several hours, I have no memory of anything that happened.

When I came to, I was at the bottom of a trench that was in deep shadow. Lying on the trench floor beside me was a dead soldier from Four Platoon. He was a freckled, red-haired lad with a prominent gap in his front teeth. He was on his back against the trench wall and looked to all the world like he was in a deep sleep. The firing had stopped and I could hear the sounds of digging and someone moaning softly in terrible pain a few feet from me. At first I felt nothing apart from a burning thirst and dizziness.

From the sounds around me, I realized I was lying in a bay with the wounded. There were several men in this section of the bay; at least two of them were already dead. Moving to prop myself up I was surprised to see that my left hand was bandaged halfway up to the elbow and that someone had tied a field dressing that covered my forehead and left eye. My head throbbed with every pulse. The crystal on my new watch was shattered and its hands were motionless at 2:30. I reckoned from the shadows we probably had only an hour or two before last light. Without thinking, I tried to use my left hand to steady me, and immediately a stabbing pain ran through my arm. Struggling to my knees, I was assailed with the sickly sweet smell of blood and vomit. I retched violently. As I did so, a sleek, heavy rat scurried in front of me from around behind the dead man with the gap in his teeth. It regarded me coolly for several seconds with its sharp little eyes. It looked me up and down, baring its yellow teeth and twitching its nose and whiskers, savouring its good fortune. The loathsome creature was weighing up how long it would be until I was dead and what kind of a feast it could make of me. At that moment, anger and the will to live surged through me. I was determined not to let myself die and allow those evil beasts to devour me.

Rising to my feet, I lurched into the bay beside me and staggered into Lance Corporal Mullin, who was checking the sighting of a Lewis gun. Mullin grabbed me gently by the elbow and had me sit on what had been the fire step. "Jesus, sir, you're one hell of a mess. I didn't expect to see you on your feet again. What are you doin' out here?"

"What happened?"

"We held them off again, sir." Mullin said. "They got into our lines twice and there's only ten of us left to hold the platoon position. It's the same left and right of us. You and Mr. Molson are the only officers left alive in the company and Mr. Molson is shot through the face. He's in the next bay as well. Lance Corporal O'Neill and I are the only NCOs left in the platoon. To tell the truth, sir, I thought you were going to die."

Mullin gave me a drink from a two-gallon tin container with water sloshing about the bottom. It tasted faintly of gasoline. I slurped it greedily and vomited most of it up soon after. I later found out that foul-tasting water was the last reserve in the platoon. Mullin didn't blink or even ask me to go sparingly with it. He looked out into no man's land. "If they come again before we get re-supplied, we can't hold 'em, sir. The Vickers gun is gone and we have less than a hundred rounds for the remaining Lewis gun. We've only twenty rounds left per man. We're out of Mills bombs." He looked around him licking his lips in nervous frustration. "I sent a runner back to company headquarters over an hour ago. I don't think he got through. The Huns started shelling the communication trenches just after he left."

We spent the rest of the daylight hours waiting for a final push but nothing happened. German stretcher-bearers worked openly in no man's land hauling and lugging their wounded. At first they moved around cautiously but when it became apparent we weren't going to shoot them, more of them appeared and they worked steadily. All the while Fritz's stretcher-bearers worked, there was no sniping or artillery fire. Stretcher-bearers on both sides were a plucky group. We had all heard stories of German atrocities committed under the guise of collecting their wounded. Those of us who spent any time in the front didn't believe them. I would be lying to say that we never entertained the idea of shooting these men. We all did. In the last twelve hours, the enemy had killed over half of our comrades in the most violent manner imaginable. You can't go from that kind of intensity and anger to being even-tempered and genial in a matter of minutes. Sporting rules didn't apply. There was nothing noble about holding our fire; it was entirely practical. Tempting as it might have been to shoot down enemy stretcher-bearers, we left them undisturbed. It could easily have been our own men looking for us out there.

I slept on the trench floor beside Mullin's position for several hours after our meeting. I didn't want to go back to the bay that held the wounded. Something inside told me if I did, I'd die, and so I chose to stay with the living. Before I slept again, curiosity got the better of me and I picked at my bandaged hand and saw that the dressing was binding my two smallest fingers by thins strands of flesh and skin. I didn't try to discover what the dressing around my forehead and eye hid.

Shortly after dark, the company was reinforced by a group of cooks, batmen, and clerks from battalion headquarters, and a few grooms from the unit horse lines. These men crawled forward through the communication trenches leading to the Loop with bulging sandbags tied to makeshift pack boards. A further eight men reinforced our platoon. They hauled up ammunition, water, food, and field dressings, and then, once seeing the state of our defences, went back to bring forward coils of wire.

One of the clerks, Private Hendricks, from the University of Toronto, a serious-faced divinity student with thick steel glasses and a raspy voice, confirmed to me that not only was the colonel dead, but that there were only three officers in the battalion who were not casualties. Major Gault had come forward and reorganized things the night before, but he'd also been badly wounded and was awaiting evacuation over in Number One Company's area.

Before he was hit, Gault ensured that cigarettes and a generous rum ration were sent forward with the new men, along with the ammunition, water, food, and field dressings. In the absence of being relieved, the shot of rum did a lot to cheer those still fit to fight. I didn't take any as the thought of it set me to retching. Instead, at Lance Corporal Mullin's urging, I drank some cold tea and ate hard tack biscuits and swallowed a few mouthfuls of greasy tinned Machanochie stew. I don't remember drifting off to sleep on my perch on the fire step.

The sounds of firing and shouting wakened me. My good eye was blurred and gummy but I could see orange light drifting in and out of strange shadows. The enemy fired several flares suspended from tiny swinging parachutes over our position. I struggled to get up. During the night some kind soul had covered me with a rubber ground sheet and sand bags. Even in my groggy state, I could see that we were under attack again. Fritz was trying to bump us out of our most forward position by rushing us in a silent night assault.

Suddenly, on both sides of us, in Number One and Number Three Company areas, the sound and blast of heavy shelling rocked the night air as "coal boxes," the heaviest of German artillery, crumped and blasted the summer night. Dragging myself to my feet, I could see German troops much less than two hundred yards away running forward into the drifting pools of light created by their own flares. They were regularly spaced and held their rifles at the ready.

I reacted instinctively croaking out, "Three Platoon, one hundred yards. Enemy to your front. Rapid fire!"

My head throbbed and sweat seeped from every pore. I was too wracked by pain to be frightened. The response from our line was ragged as the crack and thump of rifle fire gradually increased to be joined by the higher-pitched hammering of the Lewis gun. I was of no use to anyone where I was and set about dragging grenade boxes to the fire step with my good hand. I tired quickly. My pulse raced and I lost my breath. I was hot, clammy, and nauseous.

The light from the flares gradually subsided and men stopped firing, conserving their ammunition for targets they could see. Hitting anything in that light was more a matter of luck than skill and each man knew he would receive no re-supply for at least another twelve hours.

We could hear the Germans advancing and calling out to one another as much for encouragement as to maintain some semblance of alignment. This assault felt substantially different from the others. Without being initiated by a barrage, it seemed almost half-hearted. We weren't as frightened or as desperate as in the other two preceding assaults, and despite their fatigue, my men calmly shot the Germans down as if they were targets on a range. The fight was bleeding out from our opponents, and who was to blame them? God knows where they got those men. Twice before on that day, hundreds of them had been cut down; and to get at us they were now literally clambering over the stiffening bodies of their comrades. I was dumbstruck that they had the discipline and courage to keep coming.

Explosions and sporadic shooting from our left flank indicated when the enemy closed up to our belt of wire. Then, for a few brief seconds under the lights of our own Veery flares, we could see shapes looming closely in front of us. A dozen Mills bombs exploded in quick succession, brilliantly illuminating our tiny patch of battle in a series of brilliant flashes. The Lewis gun raked the forward line of the barbed wire with a withering fire. Then, a few moments later, almost as if on cue, it was quiet again. Whatever was left of the enemy's assault line fled back through the darkness to their own trenches. All of us, wounded and fit, were utterly drained, but for a brief time we were happy and relieved; the assault was over.

It was to be a long night. Just beyond our wire a German soldier was wounded. Somewhere out there, he lay in terrible pain out of sight in a shell crater. This time there was no gallows humour or crude joking. Minutes after the firing stopped, he began to moan and his moans soon turned to screams. He sounded like a young man, and he shrieked and moaned in the most pathetic manner for several hours. As the end came, he called repeatedly for his mother. His shouting became steadily weaker and his voice increasingly hoarse, but those pitiful shrieks pierced our souls. Years later, the smell of burlap and freshly turned earth drags those awful screams into my mind. He died two hours after dawn. On one side of me, Hendricks, the divinity student, sobbed, and on the other, I could hear the profane and bellicose Lance Corporal Mullin repeating snatches of prayer to himself.

Our third day under fire in the Loop was as warm and filled with sunshine as the first two. The two lance corporals left in Two Platoon organized things remarkably well. Dugouts were freshly excavated, sentries were posted, weapons were cleaned, and men were ordered to eat and get whatever rest they could in shifts. I was too weak to protest when Mullin moved me back to the firing bay that held the wounded. There were only four men in there by morning of the third day. Our dead were stacked in the communication trenches running between Two and Three platoons. I remember little of that day. Sometime around midday a German aeroplane zoomed in from nowhere and tried to drop an aerial torpedo on us. He missed by only a few feet and aside from startling all of us and moving a great deal of earth, he did no damage. He then circled back to machine-gun our trench line. He wasn't very accurate with either attempt and only served to give us notice that Fritz was still interested in taking our miserable little patch of ground from us.

Whenever I drifted into wakefulness that day, I saw the divinity student tending to us. He sponged our heads, gave us water to drink, brushed away flies, and kept the rats at bay. It was the best medical treatment available and we were grateful for what little comfort he provided.

Two or three hours before nightfall, a runner from the Forty-ninth Battalion from Edmonton crawled into our position. He informed us that we were to be relieved after dark that night but also that aerial reconnaissance indicated the Germans were continuing to mass fresh troops all along the trench lines facing Sanctuary Wood. It wasn't what we wanted to hear.

At around six that evening, Jerry began to shell us again. He must have anticipated that we were to be relieved as he started pounding our rear areas first. That, along with the aeroplane's visit, was an indication of what was to come. The divinity student shepherded all the wounded into our tiny dugouts and then stoically went to his position carved into the wall of the adjacent fighting bay.

I don't know how any of us who were wounded survived the pounding we took when the Germans shifted their guns onto our position. It is one thing to endure this endless series of bombardments when you are fit; it was quite another to live through one with your strength expended and your spirits bled into the mud. Although I was conscious for the entire barrage, I fully expected to die and cannot remember much of it. It was one of the few horrors of the war that my mind has deliberately erased from memory.

The inevitable attack that followed was different in that when the

German artillery lifted, ours began to pound him. Someone must have been directing our guns from a distance or from an aeroplane. Those who have never had to fight for their lives will probably never understand this, but the sound of artillery falling on my tormentors warmed the furthest reaches of my soul and I was filled with a sense of joy knowing that the men on the other side of that field were now in their turn being horribly mutilated and killed.

As the barrage lifted, the divinity student raced back to our bay and began to attend to each of us in turn. I could hear him as he moved to the first dugout. "Oh, dear God," was all he said and he moved on to the next man. "You're looking chipper, Ford, it'll be dark soon and we'll have you back at the regimental aid post before you know it."

When he got to me he was positively exuberant. "Mr. Ferrall, you look wonderful. You'd think you just had a nap." I felt utterly dejected and lifeless. My hand and head throbbed with a pain I am at a loss to describe now. I was feverish, thirsty, and trembling from lack of food but Hendricks' presence and his sense of purpose gave my spirits a lift. There was an inspiring simplicity to this man and he breathed new life into those of us who were wounded and survived the shelling in our muddy little scrapes.

Private Hendricks secured our dressings, brushed off the dirt that showered over us during the barrage, said a few kind words to each of us, and took up his post with his rifle in front of us on the firing parapet. He was an average man in dire circumstances calling upon extraordinary reserves of energy and vigour. He was about five-foot seven, and sturdily built; in his early twenties, he was fair-skinned with a ruddy complexion. His steel-framed glasses gave him a solemn scholarly look.

He kept up a regular commentary in his gravelly voice advising us on the progress of the battle. "Fritzie's a little slow getting out of his trenches this time. He's probably been badly hit by our artillery. Oh, Oh … Here he comes now."

From my scrape in the trench wall, I had a good view of Hendricks. His red face was sweating profusely. He wore the collar of his tunic buttoned up as per regulations and kept his forage cap squarely on his head as if on parade. Something about him gave him the appearance of being the kind of man who viewed his life's responsibilities as unshakeable obligations. Just the day before, our earnest divinity student had scarcely seen any of us. Now we were lying helplessly at the bottom of a collapsing trench and this stranger had willingly assumed the role of our guardian and rescuer. He possessed a sense of duty that made him the sort of man armies, and when you think about it, all other institutions, can't survive for long without.

Apart from Hendricks, I could see nothing but the trench wall opposite me. Hendricks began firing his rifle, taking very deliberate aimed shots. He would periodically turn and shout to us, "They're 100 yards away now … They've closed up to fifty yards. They've stopped and gone to ground … What's left of 'em are heading back … We're going to make it through this one boys … Now our artillery is falling on their position again. Whew, I wouldn't want to be out there."

Hendricks turned around and stared at the sky behind him. "There's an aeroplane up there, one of ours; I'll bet that's who's direct-ing the artillery fire on the Hun." Hendricks certainly sounded cheerful but I wondered where that bastard in the aeroplane had been two days ago when the Germans were killing us so efficiently.

By nightfall, the German artillery, in anticipation of our being relieved, began to shoot at our rear areas and communication trenches again. Sometime after dark, I was awakened by the pres-ence of dozens of men filing quietly past me through our trench. Hendricks' tired raspy voice cut through my fever and pain. He barked in a subdued voice, "Watch where you're stepping! The wounded are in those scrapes." The Forty-ninth Battalion had arrived to relieve us.

A short while later Hendricks helped me to my feet and I was vaguely aware that we were moving out in some semblance of a line. I was terribly groggy and felt worse than I've ever felt before or since. As we reached the communication trenches, I wanted to know what was left of my platoon. I asked Hendricks, "How many are left? How many are walking out with us?"

He replied, "Oh I couldn't really say, sir. Now don't worry yourself about these things. You've done your job; the important thing is getting you back to the regimental aid post."

Lance Corporal Mullin's baritone but tired-sounding voice whispered in the darkness. "Mr. Ferrall, including the eight replacements who came last night from Headquarters company, there's seven wounded and eight fit men. We held the bastards and we're all going to walk out of this to tell our grandchildren about it. Don't worry about nothin'. We've done ourselves proud."

At that moment our artillery began to explode in the darkness forward of us as our divisional gunners put down a barrage to cover our movement. "We can't tarry any longer, sir. Let's be going. Don't you worry, sir, we've got all the wounded." I remember looking into those hollow eyes. Mullin spoke again in a much more gentle voice. "What you see around us is what's left of us who can still breathe. The Forty-ninth'll be burying those we've left behind. We've gotta go now."

✠

I remember only snatches of that march to the rear. We staggered to the regimental aid post to discover it had been destroyed by a direct hit the night before. Twenty seriously wounded Patricia's and all the medical staff were killed. All casualties had to be evacuated three and a half miles further to the rear to the town of Zillebeke. We joined a stream of shattered men and walking wounded from the other companies.

Hendricks half-carried me all the way. He kept up a constant chatter. "You're safely out of this one then, sir. You're doing fine. It's not much farther." Despite the threat of artillery fire, for ten minutes of each hour we rested. Near the end of that march, Hendricks began to sing music hall songs to me to keep my spirits up. He was imposing his will on me not to let me die and in doing so he frequently changed the tone of his encouragements. "You're an officer, sir, and I don't care how you feel, you're not going to let the others down now by quitting. Ah, that's wonderful; you're doing marvellously... Almost there now... How about another chorus of 'Green Grow the Rushes O'?... Ups-a-daisy, over this embankment... We're here, sir, please sit down, I'm going to get you onto a stretcher." Hendricks sat with me throughout that night until I was taken away by medical orderlies to see one of the divisional surgeons.

My days as a combatant officer were over and from the frying pan I was now heading unwittingly for the fire.

✠

After several hours, my turn came. I was carried into a large tent that was lit by flickering kerosene lanterns. My stretcher was set down upon two sawhorses, beside which sat a folding wooden chair. An exhausted orderly in a blood-stained white coat with a high collar sat himself beside me and gingerly removed my field dressings. He sat back and grimaced. The kerosene light glinted on his bald head. He began swabbing at the left side of my face with a piece of linen soaked in a chlorine solution. The pain was immediate and I hissed sharply.

"Sorry about that, sir. It's gotta be done if we're to see what kind of wounds you've got."

My good eye was tightly shut and I could hear him muttering. "Whatever it was that hit you must have given you one hell of a headache, sir. I don't see any shrapnel lodged in the wound. It looks like you got winged by something. A fraction of an inch over and you wouldn't be here. You're lucky, very lucky, sir."

He prodded and probed and examined my head wound from several angles. "The flesh around your eye is pretty chewed up and it's too swollen and bruised to tell much just now—but I'd guess you've been seriously concussed as well. Where else are you hurt? Ah, someone's tied up your hand." He picked up my left hand and held it up the light. "Not a bad job, not a bad job at all considering where you've just come from."

Less gently, he unwrapped the dressings from my hand and whistled appreciatively. He picked up my hand and sniffed it like a connoisseur sniffs a wine cork. "That's nice, sir. You've been hit three days, living in a shit pit and not a whiff of infection. Someone's looking out for you. This, sir, is what you gentlemen in the infantry refer to as a blighty, kinda like a home run in baseball, isn't it? One good smack and you go round all the bases."

He called out, "Corporal, this one's for the surgeon as well. Have the bearers get him in to see the nursing sister in surgery please! Fresh dressings on the head and prepare his left hand for surgery." He patted my arm. "Don't worry, sir, six to ten weeks you'll be right as rain and heading back to Canada. Good luck." He waved for the stretcher-bearers to move me, smiled a fatigued and kindly smile, and said, "Next! Come on. Come on Bearers, these lads haven't got all day to sit around waiting for dimwits like you. Look alive now, boys."

I was moved to another, more brightly lit tent where a silent nursing sister, who I could make out only in silhouette, cleaned my face and swabbed my eye; she then re-applied clean dressings. She left my stretcher, going beyond our circle of light for a few moments and then came back and set about with a large pair of scissors to cut away the filth of my uniform until I was lying naked. I was long past feeling embarrassed.

Once this was done, a very tired and short-tempered-looking doctor, who looked more like Teddy Roosevelt dressed up as a butcher than a surgeon, came in and checked me over. He had large rimless spectacles, prominent yellow teeth, and a thick bushy moustache. He parted his thinning hair severely down the centre. Instead of a clean white surgical gown, he had a yellowing vulcanized apron that was smeared and stained with wet blood and he wore heavy rubber gloves. The doctor peeled off his gloves, moved around the stretcher, and examined my left hand for several minutes. Like the orderly, he sniffed it and studied it closely. "I think I can save your hand. You're going to lose two fingers, but I'm going to try to save the rest." He turned to the nursing sister. "Let's do it now."

My last recollection was overwhelming weariness and the urge to cry as a rubber face-piece was placed over my mouth and nose.

5

THE UN-REPAIRED cobblestone roads jolted and jarred the ambulance wagon carrying me from the hospital complex to the railhead on the Ypres-Poperinge road. I had been lying in bed for a week in a wooden fifty-man temporary building. My fever had abated and my wounds were showing signs of healing without infection. Now I was certified as "Fit, limited travel/Unfit, frontline duty." I thought it would be the beginning of my journey home. In accordance with Canadian army evacuation policy, I was to be transferred from the forward casualty clearance and holding centre to a treatment hospital somewhere in England.

As bad as I felt, it was a delight to be out of that hospital. I wanted to be away from the climate of death that enveloped Flanders. The nurses and orderlies were kind, but the casualty clearance centre was a thoroughly depressing place. From my bed I was able to see acres of graves covering the countryside and each day the borders of the graveyard spread as fresh crosses sprouted across the landscape. Each morning and afternoon, sombre khaki processions traipsed behind long lines of coffins. I was thankful to be getting away from this gloomy complex of makeshift buildings, shattered men, and its death garden.

My stretcher, along with one other, was lashed to the frame of a rickety commandeered Belgian dry goods wagon. Looking out the back of the wagon with my good eye, I saw low clouds scudding across the sky. Like the rolling distant thunder I had once heard on the prairies, guns boomed and rumbled back and forth intermittently in the distance. The sun was gone the whole time I'd been at the casualty clearing hospital and cold rain spattered intermittently down on the broken Belgian countryside. My thoughts were muddled. As the dangers from concussion receded, the doctors gave me morphine for my pain. At the time, I almost wept with relief; my hand and eye caused me intense pain. The suspension of pain left me blissfully numb, and for much of my time in the casualty clearing station I lay in a trance.

That morning I was lucid enough to realize my lack of sensation was a blessing as the wagon driver repeatedly apologized. "Sorry, lads, sorry. It'll be a lot smoother when we've got you on the train, believe me." I didn't answer him, but I wasn't feeling much. Just before I was transferred to my stretcher, one of the nursing sisters thoughtfully injected me with morphine. The man next to me said nothing. He was wrapped in a blanket and his face stared in blank terror at the canvas tarpaulin above us. I never learned his name or a thing about him; but the sight of him made me grateful I was not more seriously wounded. Whatever physical wounds the poor man suffered paled in comparison to the torment within his mind.

✠

I no longer needed the handrails that lined the hallways of my ward at Number Two Canadian Army Stationary Hospital in London. It was the first time I was walking without feeling dizzy or faint. On my sixth day in London, I was dressed in army-issue paper slippers, blue pyjamas, and dressing gown, and shuffling along with great determination through the corridors when I saw a striking young blonde nursing sister coming towards me pushing a trolley of medical instruments. I wasn't certain, but she looked very familiar. "Excuse me, Sister, are you Hannah? The nursing sister from Vancouver?"

She looked slightly hesitant but quickly regained her composure. "Yes, but I don't think I know you, do I?" she said with a weak smile.

"No, I can't say we actually know each other, but we've met. On the troop ship, the day we saw the whales, we chatted for an hour or so."

"Oh my, yes, it's you. The nice officer from Montreal," she said, bursting into a warm smile. "I've often wondered how you got on." She hesitated for a split second, afraid she had made a gaffe and it occurred to me that now, to some people, I had become an object of pity. This was an emotional change of tack for me. Since coming out of the line, I had been brooding over being undeservedly lucky when so many other good men were dead. Hannah recovered immediately and smiled broadly. "How are you?" She seemed genuinely pleased to see me; or maybe it was just that she was one of those women who illuminate the world with their smile. It didn't matter; I was thrilled.

"I'm getting better," I said with ill-concealed embarrassment. I'd no reason to be ashamed, but I hadn't prepared myself for giving explanations to anyone who wasn't wounded. The few conversations I had about the subject were with other patients and we limited our questions to what part of the line we were in and when we were hit. We never discussed circumstances. "I ran into a little difficulty a couple weeks ago in Flanders. I'm just returning to my ward from the ophthalmologist. He says there's no sign of infection, so I'm quite lucky. How have you been doing for the last ten months?"

"I'm really well. I'm sure you know, we're much too busy here," she said with a grim flourish. "I'm sorry, I really can't talk just now, but please tell me your name and ward. I'll come and see you, soon. I promise."

✠

Two days later I was bitterly discouraged to hear the hospital ophthalmologist tell me I was going to lose my left eye. It wasn't responding to treatment and he was afraid it was now showing signs of infection. It could kill me. If they took it out, I'd be fine. If they didn't, he couldn't guarantee me anything. In a way, I had almost expected that news. Each day the doctors looked a little more anxious when they examined me. And since leaving the casualty clearance hospital, no one had given me assurances that I would ever see with my left eye again. I pinched myself and resolved not to allow the news to dampen my spirits further. I was alive. I knew instinctively things were going to get better; and that afternoon they did. Hannah breezed onto our ward. She loaded me into a wheelchair and cheerfully wheeled me out into the garden.

"We're not supposed to fraternize socially with patients, but if anyone asks, you're my brother's best friend. I do have a brother and he's serving in the Tenth Battalion somewhere in Flanders."

I fumbled for my cigarettes and Hannah looked down at them hungrily.

"I'm so glad you smoke! Wait." She dragged my chair across the lawn behind a large clump of shrubbery that concealed us from the hospital. "Can I have one of those please? They'll court martial me and then shoot me if they catch me smoking." Hannah curled her feet up under her on the grass and took off her starched uniform veil. I was taken aback by her behaviour. I wasn't in the least bit shocked, but I was pleased by her independence and cheerful willingness to break the rules.

"I'm sorry, I couldn't have gotten around to see you earlier. We've been rushed off our feet. I think it's ghastly." I held a match for her as she lit one of my cigarettes and she exhaled a cloud of blue smoke. She paused and looked at me pensively. "I should explain myself. It's not ghastly that I'm working hard. I wish I could do more. There are so many young men here whose lives are totally shattered." She had a faraway look in here eyes and we smoked in silence for a minute.

"You probably think I'm a fool for talking like this. I know I don't really know you, but..." Her voice trailed off.

"No, it's all right. I thought when we talked that day on the ship; well, it seemed so natural." I thought I was sounding sappy and changed my tone. "I need someone to talk to anyway. I've been keeping to myself the last two weeks. It's quite a change talking to someone who hasn't been living in a trench."

I wanted to make her feel comfortable and I wanted our conversation to go on forever. Apart from matronly Red Cross tea ladies and the forbidding-looking but over-worked ward nurse who changed my dressings, I hadn't any kind of a conversation with a woman for months. We stumbled through the weather, laughed about the hospital food, her matron, and talked about Montreal and Vancouver.

During the two days I'd waited for her to come and see me I'd foolishly convinced myself that she was the woman of my dreams. I suppose I was emotionally starved and I let my imagination run wild. I couldn't read because of my eye. Hannah was a beautiful young woman who was coming to see me and all I could do was lie in my starchy-smelling hospital bed and await her arrival. I imagined our life together, what it would be like to make love to her, what she looked like in the mornings, and what kinds of things we'd do together when the war was over. I can't say I really believed any of it, but in the state I was in, fantasy lurked dangerously close to reality and I didn't want to distinguish between the two. Hannah could have been talking in Greek for all I cared.

We grew quiet again and smoked another cigarette in silence. "You know, Rory, I'm glad you're wounded." She held up her hand to stop me from speaking. "I'm glad you're out of that part of things. So many of our boys come back as wrecks. I can't abide watching innocent men suffer and die and rot. If we save them, they're returned to duty at the front or go back to Canada, to become what? Occupy a bed space in a dingy hospital for the rest of their lives. I want it over. And for you it's over, but you can still make a life for yourself, that's something I'm glad of."

"It may be that I'm going home, but it's not going to end for a long time yet, Hannah." I threw my cigarette down and stared up at great masses of puffy white clouds. "What bothers me is I don't even know what we're fighting for any more. Once I believed some of the stories about the Hun and defending the Empire. I don't believe or disbelieve anything any more. I think we're fighting now, because we're fighting."

Hannah looked at me intently. I wasn't sure if I'd gone too far but I continued.

"I'm half-German, my mother's German, and I've seen so many killed, our side, Germans, what's the difference. I'm no socialist revolutionary, but can anyone tell me what's worth this price?" My voice was rising and I felt flushed.

Hannah reached forward and touched my hand. "Do you remember what it was like in Montreal the day war was declared? I was in Vancouver on Robson Street that day. It was an incredible celebration. People hanging off streetlamps, crowds singing 'God Save The King.' You'd have thought we all won the Irish Sweepstakes. I was no different."

"Montreal was the same."

"You're right, though, from where I am now, it seems we're in a trap and we can't get out. The war goes on because we can't end it. I'm certain if it was up to the soldiers in the trenches, it'd be over tomorrow. It sure as hell would be for those of us here in the hospitals."

Hannah looked at me and then looked far away. "You know, Rory, I have a brother in the Tenth Battalion. Jack's in the artillery and I've a cousin who's just joined up in Vancouver. None of us could really tell you what Canada hopes to achieve from all of this."

"No, I don't suppose any one can. Who's Jack?" I said innocently.

"He's my fiancé," she said, pushing her hair back from her face and staring out over the shrubbery.

I didn't hear anything Hannah said after that. It was foolish really, but it showed how I'd changed. I never for an instant thought Hannah had a fiancé. I assumed she was interested in me. I was quite hurt. It wasn't until later I realized she merely wanted to be friends.

I should have known that from the start, but I was so starved for feminine companionship any pretty girl would have appeared to me to be a possible lover. I had so many readjustments to make in the world and at the time I didn't even realize it. In the months I'd been in the trenches, both the rules and I started to change. Women were already more forthcoming with men without being romantically interested. I missed almost all this in my short time at the front. I didn't realize it then, but Hannah was on the knife-edge of that kind of thinking.

Hannah looked at me rather startled. "Are you alright, Rory?"

"Oh, I'm fine, really, Hannah." I was struggling not to appear a complete fool and resorted to self-pity to escape. "I was just thinking that they're going to take out my left eye tomorrow. It can't be saved."

"You poor dear." She grabbed my good hand. "Rory, I'm very sorry." She looked away and then said. "I read your file this morning. I didn't think you wanted to talk about it. It's really the best thing. Your doctor's very good, but you must be concerned."

In truth, I wasn't as concerned as I should have been about my eye. Losing an eye was trivial compared to the isolation I felt. I'd already come to grips with the loss of an eye. The deeper pains I felt were psychological. But like the rest of my feelings, I couldn't exactly describe them. I was terribly lonely and dispirited. I suppose doctors today would say I was clinically depressed. I wasn't feeling sorry for myself. God knows, looking back at it now, I had every reason to feel dejected. I knew instinctively that an eye and half of one hand was a cheaper price than so many others had already paid. All the while I'd been in hospital in England I was angry with myself but I didn't know why. Now I felt even more foolish falling so head-over-heels in love with Hannah, a woman I scarcely knew. Even then, I didn't have the wits to see I wasn't in any kind of emotional state to become attached to anybody. Even to myself I was a stranger. The other thing I hadn't come to grips with, and I suppose I still haven't to this day, was why I survived and so many others didn't. I knew it was a problem with no answer, but the fact that this difficulty gnawed away at me played a big part in sending me to Germany.

✚

I was wheeled into a green-painted operating room. Once again a rubber face-piece was pressed down on my face, and my eye was removed without incident. The anaesthetic made me violently ill for two days and my eye socket gave me searing pain for long afterwards. Hannah looked in on me every day that week. Each time I saw her I wasn't much company. I was too groggy from morphine, or in too much pain when they switched me to codeine to wean me from the morphine. The last time she looked in on me she seemed sad. "Rory, you're going to be moved to a convalescent hospital tomorrow. I don't think I'll be able to see you again for who knows how long." She held my good hand and spoke some more. I don't remember what she said, but it was soothing and achingly feminine. She then kissed me hurriedly on the cheek and left.

✚

The hospital orderly who came to pack me off in the morning was an elderly Englishman. He walked with a pronounced limp and had a ragged moustache and an equally ragged haircut. He gave me fresh pyjamas, a heavily starched regulation blue dressing gown, and new paper slippers. The old gentleman waited patiently, leaning on my wheelchair, and when I had changed myself, he very deliberately said to me in a thick North Country accent, "Aye now, sir, there'll be a delegation of politicians and what not from Canada. They'll be in the lobby in a half an hour. Want to see some of the lads, all junior officers like yourself who are soon to be discharged to convalescent hospitals. We'll get that bit of unpleasantness over with, and then you're off to a country house to rest and mend for a few weeks."

In the lobby I was wheeled into a small assembly of bandaged and broken men all dressed in blue-issue pyjamas and seated in a semicircle to greet our visitors. Behind them stood a small knot of grim-faced doctors and nurses. "Who's all this in aid of?" I asked a man seated beside me with a heavy bandage over the stump of his wrist.

"Sir Sam Hughes, the goddamn minister of militia," he said bitterly. "Last time I saw him was just before we shipped overseas. He kept us waiting on parade in Borden in the heat and dust for three hours to say goodbye. He's come to gloat and get his picture taken with 'his boys' as he likes to call us."

Close to an hour later, a cluster of portly and greying lieutenant colonels and majors arrived. To a man, they were dressed in magnificently tailored uniforms. I was quick to notice that although they were all wearing regimental badges of famous Canadian militia units, there wasn't a field service medal or a wound stripe amongst the lot. One of them cleared his throat and addressed us. "Gentlemen, the honourable Sir Sam Hughes, the minister of militia and member of Parliament for Haliburton County will be here momentarily. Sir Sam will address you collectively and then he will sit with you for a group photograph and perhaps a few individual photos for any of you who might care to have a photograph sent home to your families to let them see how you're getting on. Now, Sir Sam is sorely pressed in his schedule; so, I'm afraid there'll be no time for questions."

This announcement generated a hostile buzz. Before it died down, one of the ranking attendants drew himself to his full height and crashed his foot to the floor, calling the room to attention. "Room! Our minister of militia, Major General Sir Sam Hughes."

At this point, a fit-looking man in a major general's uniform burst into the room. I'd seen pictures of Sam Hughes before and I instinctively distrusted him. His jaw was extended aggressively and he slapped his riding crop against his trouser leg. He strode purposefully across the hospital lobby. Hughes was fleshy faced; nonetheless, he was a tanned, physically powerful-looking man. Despite the fact that Hughes exuded energy and vigour, his bright blue eyes had a glassy, over-focused look. My immediate impression was that he was slightly insane. He glared down at his audience; not one of us sat to attention in accordance with the standard courtesy demanded by military discipline. Some men pointedly slouched and lolled casually. Poor Ernie Gillespie, who was missing a foot and was plainly shell-shocked, sat slack-jawed and vacant-eyed near the middle of the group. He was shivering and weaving his head from side to side.

The minister stood before us, looked down distastefully at Ernie, rocked on his heels, and licked his lips. "Gentleman, I want to say to you how proud all Canada is of your sacrifice. You've displayed the kind of leadership and commitment that we have come to expect from our troops." At this juncture the minister paused, clearly irritated by two men to my right who were talking loudly. "If I may go on please, gentlemen!"

"Oh don't let us stop you, Sir Sam, we've been waiting for a long time to hear what you have to say," the culprit closest to me said loudly. The audience tittered and some men clapped.

Someone called out, "Go ahead, General, we're honoured by your gracious visit. We've been waiting a very long time indeed." There was more laughter.

On the other side of the room, a man leaning on a crutch chimed in. "We're as happy seeing you as we were getting your Ross rifle, the one that jammed after three rounds. You do remember the rifle you forced us to use? We're anxious to hear what you have to say." This was greeted by "Hear, hears," ragged clapping, and pounding of canes and crutches.

Sam Hughes was regarded by most serving soldiers as a posturing clown, and those forced to use the Ross rifle despised him with an intensity not normally attributed to bland Canadian politicians. We regarded him as a war-profiteer and a murderous buffoon. He had long been a focus for my anger and I suspect that of everyone else in the room.

One of the senior officers jumped in. "Gentlemen, in all my years I have never seen a general officer or a minister of the Crown treated in such an insulting and offensive manner." To which some-one at the back of the room drawled, "Yeah, well then, Sir Sam isn't exactly a real general is he? More like a Kentucky colonel, don't you think?"

At this point, I got unsteadily to my feet and gestured with my bandaged hand to the enraged minister. "Sir Sam, I do apologize on behalf of these men. Please let's skip the speeches and get right to the photographs. I'm sure you'd love to have your picture taken with Ernie here. His family would be delighted to know you cared." The audience broke into applause and Sir Sam turned on his heel and stormed from the room with enthusiastic but unprintable heckling ringing in his ears.

As Sir Sam's entourage wheeled from the room, a tall, mous-tached colonel poked a generously proportioned major in the chest. "I want their names. I want the names of the ringleaders. There's no excuse for this kind of behaviour."

✠

Minutes after the incident with our minister of militia, I was wrapped in a blanket and trundled aboard a touring car by my ward's English orderly. As he folded and tucked the blankets around me, he whispered reassuringly, "I'm glad to see you'll be out of here, sir. This won't be the last we'll hear of that incident. I don't like the looks of that politician general fellow. Mark my words, you Cana-dian gentlemen will be hearing from him again."

I was driven south for an hour or so out of London's clouds and drizzle. Spitting rain turned to watery sunshine as we motored into the Sussex countryside. Woods, fields, and villages rolled by. Out-side the automobile, suspended closer to the windowpane, the face of an unwelcome ghost kept pace with me like a shadow. My reflec-tion in the window stared sullenly back. I had a heavy bandage over my left eye; my right eye was hollow and sunken. My skin was coarse. The man hovering outside was much older and more sinister than the Rory Ferrall I remembered on the day of my enlistment. I was startled by the image. I'd never before seen that face glowering back at me.

We motored through the old village of East Grinstead. There was a donkey cart in front of a pub. Children on bicycles and women with wicker vegetable baskets under their arms stared at us. It was as peaceful and rustic as a post card; and unlike London, there wasn't a uniform in sight. We turned past a line of half-timbered mediaeval buildings onto a lane and drove through a stand of beech trees. The road twisted abruptly and we were at my new residence, Hammerwood Park. Hammerwood was a decaying mansion which, I was later to discover, was built by the architect who designed the White House. The manor's stately but scruffy looking rooms housed a hundred convalescent officers. I was assigned to the wing for officers who were missing hands and arms.

My room was on the second floor. The room was large, with high, ornately patterned ceilings and dark paintings of arrogant eighteenth-century aristocrats hanging from the walls. In each of the four corners was a bed, only one of which was occupied. I stood in the doorway and stared at a young man sleeping on his back. The stumps of the man's arms were bandaged from his elbows to his shoulders. I walked over to my bed and stared out the window at the manor's grounds. I was doing my best to look on the bright side of things. I'd no reason to feel sorry for myself. The poor fellow sleeping opposite me was going to have a much tougher adjustment than I was, and I would only stay here for a few weeks at most. None of this really cheered me up, but it didn't depress me either.

After a few moments of sitting quietly in that dismal space, the door burst open and two men dressed in blue pyjamas and dressing gowns swept into the room. One of them was short, dark-complexioned, middle-aged, and had a huge moustache; the other was in his late thirties, red-headed and clean-shaven. The moustached man beamed at me and in a rapid fire stage whisper said, "McLeish, look what we have here, another roommate." He gestured towards my bandaged hand. "My goodness! This young man seems to be a disarmingly charming fellow as well! Splendid. Good for you. Colonial or Imperial?" I looked at him uncomprehendingly.

The red-headed man spoke up in a Canadian accent. "Captain Redvers wants to know where you're from. Are you British or from one of the enlightened dominions beyond the seas?"

"I'm Canadian. Who are you?"

"I knew it, Redvers! Listen to that accent. Another free man from the land of ice and snow. His eyes have far too much intelligence and sparkle to be one of your sort. It's what happens when you have clean air and room to grow."

Captain Redvers approached and offered me his left hand. Both men had an empty sleeve pinned to their dressing gowns. "I'm disarmed by your charm, sir." He bowed his head in mock solemnity. "I am Captain Jeremy Redvers, late of the Royal West Kent Regiment, and later than that, assistant headmaster of Brixham Grammar School. To whom do I have the pleasure of addressing myself?"

I was being cautious, not certain if I was the butt of some kind of a practical joke. "I'm Rory Ferrall, Princess Patricia's Canadian Light Infantry, pleased to meet you."

The red-headed man proffered his right hand. "I'm Harry McLeish, Royal Canadian Engineers. I used to be a mining engineer in northern Ontario. Now that I have only three limbs, I can't paddle, can't dog sled, can't swot mosquitoes, and I'm going to be of no use to anyone in the field any more. But, like I say, forewarned is forearmed." The two men began to chuckle and the sleeping man stirred.

"What time is it? Have I been asleep long?"

McLeish answered: his tone changed completely. "Sebastian, it's not yet tea time. You've been asleep for a few hours now. Sebastian, we have a new roommate."

"I don't want to talk to anyone. I want someone to take me to the bathroom and then I want to be fed and then I want to take more codeine and go back to sleep." The man's voice was angry and had he been somewhere else and in a different condition, I would have described him as petulant.

Redvers jerked his head toward the door signifying we should leave. "Not to worry, Sebastian, we'll get someone for you now. Won't be a minute."

Out in the hallway with the door closed, the three of us walked beyond earshot and Redvers whispered, "Sebastian's in a very bad way. He's lost both his arms and a foot as well. He used to be a regular cavalry officer. A smart mess life, polo, riding to the hounds, expensive parties. Not any more, I'm afraid. He's always in great pain and he's rude to everybody; so don't take it personally. I'm not sure I'd be much different if I was in his circumstances." Redvers went off to find an orderly and McLeish took me on a tour of the grounds.

The three of us were to become great friends. I eventually became fond of their insane humour and looked forward to their relentless punning on anything to do with the word arm. Like the others, I did what I could for Sebastian, but each day he seemed to shrink further into himself.

My days at Hammerwood Park consisted of rounds of restorative exercises, long walks, and sitting several times a day in a room with a dozen other men while civilian volunteers read to us. I was still forbidden to read because my doctor felt I would strain the severed muscles in my empty eye socket. What was left of the workings of my injured eye tried to follow my good eye over the page and put too great a strain on the damaged muscles. He was right of course. Twice I became bored and disobeyed his orders and tried to read. I only succeeded in giving myself a terrible eye ache.

After my second week at Hammerwood, I began to have nightmares. There was nothing unusual in that. Most of us there had them at one time or another. In fact, I probably had bad dreams every night since being out of the line. Each night, the halls of Hammerwood Manor echoed with the groans and night terrors of wounded men. It was not unusual for men to wake up sweating and

terrified in the middle of a barrage or find ourselves being smoth-
ered in a dugout or re-living any of the thousand horrors we had
experienced. My bad dreams were different. When I was at Hammerwood I dreamed and shouted aloud in German.

Jeremy and Harry were amused by the fact that their roommate
was "secretly a Hun." They both threatened to "take up arms against
me," and amongst the three of us, I was always cheerfully referred to
as "that damn Hun." None of this bothered me in the least. Sebastian, on the other hand, hated me for it. His hatred for me seemed
to grow with each day he lay helplessly in his bed. I felt sorry for
him. It was almost as if his soul was going gangrenous as his body
wasted away. On the nights I shouted out in German, Sebastian
would begin to shriek at me, and invariably an orderly would show
up and things would eventually settle down. After the fourth incident of this sort, Sebastian was moved to another room and I never
saw him again.

However, in my fourth week at Hammerwood I did meet Sebastian's uncle. I was surprised by his visit. Sebastian Ryeford's uncle
was a pleasant man. He was dressed in the uniform of a Royal Navy
captain. He had a kindly round face and carried a stylish malacca
cane. He smoked cigarettes in a gold cigarette holder, wore a gold-
rimmed monocle, and walked with a pronounced limp. On our first
meeting, he walked straight into my room and introduced himself
as Captain Mansfield Cumming. He spoke softly. "I'm afraid my
nephew has been very rude to you and I'd like to apologize. Sebastian isn't normally like this at all. We're all very worried for him."
He asked me how I was getting on, made small talk, and then delicately got round to the matter of my dreams in German.

"I should imagine you must be very fluent in German if you
dream in the language?"

I admitted that I spoke German as well as I spoke English and
that I had spent many summers in Germany visiting relatives.

"That's terribly interesting." Cumming seemed absorbed in everything I had to say. "How did you feel about fighting the Germans if
you have so many German relatives? Does it bother you?"

He framed his questions in a calm, non-intrusive voice. He was very convincing and in the state I was in, I was glad to have someone to talk to about it. Redvers and McLeish were forever making jokes about my German roots, and although they didn't irritate me, I was nevertheless glad to talk to someone about the subject.

Cumming suggested we walk outside. He offered me a cigarette and listened to me ramble on about my feelings. I don't remember all that I said that day. Cumming kept my conversation stoked by asking politely after each of my relatives, what I had heard of them, and how my family felt about me volunteering. I stopped in my tracks when he asked, "How did your Mother react to you being awarded a Military Cross? That must have been an awkward time for her." He was looking at me steadily.

"How did you know I won an MC?" I replied. "I don't wear a uniform and I've never told anyone here I have one. Who are you?"

"That's observant of you, Rory. I'm very sorry. It must seem rude of me. I really am Sebastian's uncle and godfather, but I'm also connected with military intelligence. In fact, I'll be quite open with you. You deserve it. I'm head of British military intelligence and when I heard that Sebastian had a roommate who was dreaming in German, I decided to drop in to see you when I next came to visit him.

"Poor Sebastian's not doing well. I'm worried for him. He's my favourite sister's only child. But I'm digressing."

He sighed and much to my astonishment pulled a short thin sword out of the end of his cane and began slashing aimlessly at fluffy dandelion heads on the lawn. "I had your file sent to me before I came here. I've read it and I know officially what there is to know about you. That's not much.

"By the way, your minister of militia wants your head. There is a damn fool investigation apparently about the way you Canadian chaps behaved towards him. Personally, I think that kind of spunk is what makes you colonials such good soldiers. If it were some of the Australians I've met, they probably would have taken the silly old bugger out on a rail. The New World doesn't seem to respect authority in the same way as we do in the old. Anyway, I hear Sam Hughes is a self-serving, rotten little man. It's too bad, you fellows deserve much better. The hospital and the medical authorities are stalling him and he's furious." He swung around dramatically. "Did you know there's almost as much in your file about your run-in with a politician as there is about your war record? Extraordinary amount of correspondence."

I said nothing and stared at him.

"I'll come to directly to the point. I'm looking for help. I need people who can get by in Germany. People who can help us win the war. There are too many Sebastians, and God knows, I suppose I'm preaching to the choir with someone like you. You've been through a lot more of this than I have. There's been too much suffering and killing. We're deadlocked and who knows how much longer this can go on? Throwing more men and material at it won't do anything.

"We can't afford to lose, either. Whoever loses this war is going to be in a hell of a mess for decades after. Look at the Russians. It's not impossible that we could end up in the same sort of fix they're in now. So, the simple story is we need your help, Rory. I want you to come down to London and meet some people later this week."

He put up a hand and shook his head. "You don't need to give me an answer now, but I'll need to know where you stand on this after you've heard what I have in mind. I can't tell you the details just now; but I must emphasize, everything I've said to you today has to be treated with the utmost secrecy. We've sent a few chaps like you into Germany. Not nearly as many as we need, nothing like it; but you cannot under any circumstances tell anyone what I've just told you."

He paused and sheathed his sword-cane, looking self-satisfied at having laid waste to the lawn. He pulled what was left of his cigarette out from his holder and threw it away with surprising vigour. "I'll send a car up here to bring you to London in three days. I'll explain more to you then. Of course you are completely free to refuse this request, but I don't think you will, Rory. Quite simply, we need you badly. I think you're the sort we can count on."

He limped off leaving me dumbfounded and gawking after him.

6

DINNER in the hospital's dining room was always noisy. The manor's not-so-large great room was packed with tables and chairs and a hundred hungry convalescents. I approached my two roommates. Redvers picked up a spoon and brandished it defiantly. "McLeish! Quickly, it's the Hun. Let us arm ourselves against a common foe."

McLeish looked up from his bowl of watery soup. "Oh, Rory, you'll love the food tonight, sawdust bread, turnip jam, turnip soup, and a magnificently grilled but mysterious sausage. The maître d' felt the wine list doesn't do the rest of the meal credit so he has kindly substituted an unpretentious but wholesome cup of Bovril to accompany tonight's table d'hôte. Who could ask for more lad?"

I waited for the waitress to bring my tray and ate in silence for several minutes. "What do you suppose is happening in Russia these days?" I asked. "I haven't read any papers for a while and someone just mentioned to me that things are pretty grim there."

"The place is a mess," Redvers said. "Russian casualties have been astronomical. The army's hanging on by its teeth. The Germans have just re-established Poland as a country made up from conquered Imperial Russian territory and this month they've captured most of Rumania. The Russians and their army are on the brink of starvation and the home front is turning into chaos. You don't need to be a genius to understand that they're losing the war. We'll likely see them switch from fighting the Germans to a bloody great episode of killing each other. Ever since things started going badly for them, the place has been infested with political radicals. They're losing their side of things hands down."

McLeish looked dourly at his plate and then chipped in. "Mind you, nobody is saying that publicly yet. But you can figure it out for yourself from the newspapers. If the Russians do collapse, the Germans will be able to turn their entire army against us. What you see happening to dear old Mother Russia will probably happen on the western front. If the Boche brings all his divisions from the Russian front and lets them loose on us, France will cave in or we'll go under, or both of us will buckle. In which case, you'll probably have the same kind of anarchy here that the Russians now have. My guess is that the Russians' troubles haven't even begun yet."

Redvers became sombre and stared glassily ahead of him. "If that happens, we'll think of these times in this mangy old hospital as the good old days and this meal will look like a king's banquet. Just pray that the Russians hang on, Rory."

I said nothing and chewed my vegetable sausage.

✠

Three days later a smart black touring sedan driven by a lance corporal from the Royal Marines pulled up in front of the hospital. The head nursing sister from "Arms and Hands" advised me that I was to go up to London to be seen by an ophthalmologist and be fitted with a glass eye. I'd be back in a couple of days. They changed the dressing on my hand and I was given a hospital inmate's blue cardigan, fresh pyjamas, a clean dressing gown, extra socks, and a small canvas valise to carry my shaving gear.

My trip to London was uneventful. The driver had seemingly been given orders not to talk to me and we journeyed together in a strained silence. Not surprisingly, I wasn't taken anywhere close to the Canadian Army London General Hospital. In the early afternoon, I was deposited in front of a small group of expensive-looking apartments in Whitehall Court. The lance corporal ushered me into the building and to a lift at the end of a wood-panelled hallway. On the fourth floor we alighted to a carpeted and well-appointed corridor. The lance corporal beckoned to me to sit and wait in a chair. He turned the key of a doorbell in the middle of a heavy oak door and seconds later Cumming limped out into the hall.

"Rory, good to see you. How was your trip?" He turned to the driver. "Thank you, Lance Corporal." The driver saluted and turned about without saying a word.

Cumming ushered me into a spacious, stylishly furnished apartment and motioned me to a chair. "How are you feeling, my boy? The doctors protested at you leaving the hospital under any circumstances. You know I wouldn't be doing this if the stakes weren't so awfully high. As I said, we need you." He stuffed a cigarette into his gold cigarette holder, struck a wooden match and inhaled noisily. "I'm sorry, would you care for one of these?" I took one. He lit it and settled back into a chair opposite me.

"What I propose to do is give you some lunch and then we can start with the more formal briefing. There are some people I want you to meet in the next day or so and I want you to feel free to ask any questions you like, anything at all that strikes your fancy. If I don't know or can't tell you the answer, I'll say so. But first, lunch."

He tinkled on a small hand bell and for a few moments we smoked while Cumming explained to me that his flat in town and his office were one and the same place. Upstairs, he explained with a wave of his hand, were some "other offices," and he lived here because he was happiest when he was working. He was the only one in his line of work who actually lived here. "Everyone else has to go home at nights. Do you know that foolish socialist, George Bernard Shaw? He lives on the floor downstairs from me. He has no idea who we are. I have a good mind to throttle the silly bugger if we ever meet in the lift."

He laughed at this thought and without pause immediately began telling me the stories behind the naval bric-a-brac that graced his bookshelves. "Do you see this? That was the compass from the forward gun of the *Agamemnon*, my first ship, quite a story here."

He was a charming man with a natural facility for conversation. Against my will, I found I liked him immensely. He did, however, have a few disconcerting habits. One of the most alarming was, when he sat in his armchair with his wooden leg straight out before him, emphasizing whatever point he was making by vigorously stabbing himself just below the knee with a sharpened letter opener. I pretended not to notice.

A few minutes later, from a room somewhere at the back of the flat, an elderly servant with long, grey, wispy hair and a dark funereal suit pushed out a trolley with linen napkins, thick roast beef sandwiches on fresh rye bread, crisp pickles, and beer. Cumming then behaved very strangely. He screwed his monocle into his eye and stared at me as if I had offended him. His tone change abruptly. "Just so I've got this right and we aren't wasting one another's time, tell me again why you decided to join the army and come to France."

"It was my duty," I said simply. Cumming didn't answer but continued to scowl at me. I grew uncomfortable and continued. "So many others had joined, I couldn't very well sit around and enjoy the benefits of everything I had without doing anything. I know I'm half-German, but I think Germany was wrong to invade Belgium and, while you're asking, I don't believe all that nonsense about German atrocities. My country was at war and it was my duty to go." I could feel myself becoming flushed. "Why does everybody keep asking me that? Do I have to be dead to prove my loyalty?"

Cumming changed his tone. "No. That's fine, Rory," he said quietly. "We don't have a lot of time. I'm just testing you. Oh, and Rory, if I may, let me advise you. When someone asks you something and you give them an answer, don't fall for the trap of giving more information just because they're silent. It's the oldest trick in the book. That was a test too, a silly one I suppose. Let the other person make the next move. Learn to hold your tongue. Measure your responses. You'll be fine."

Cumming's change in tone didn't appease me. I was still angry and said, "With respect then, Captain Cumming, perhaps you should explain to me why you think I should be going to Germany?"

"A very fair question considering the circumstances. I think I said something to that effect previously. I believe that whoever loses this war is going to be in a terrible state. We've lost so many men, expended so much national treasure that whatever terms are decided upon will be very harsh. We have to win. We're no longer fighting for the original causes. I believe we are now fighting to maintain the very fabric of our societies. There has never been anything like it before. The losers will suffer enormous social and political upheavals; and on top of this, the winners will exact a terrible revenge for their losses. I don't know what sort of society will come after for the losers, but it will not be anything like either side now knows and it will not be pleasant. This war has gone on too long and been too costly to end in any kind of sensible accommodation. In its simplest form, we cannot afford to lose and that is why we need you to go to Germany.

"Now, tell me about yourself, Rory," he said, changing his tone yet again. "I want to hear everything: your likes, dislikes, family, schooling, sports, reading habits, absolutely everything. I hope you don't mind, but this is necessary. I want to get this right, because if you do go to Germany, I've got to be certain you have the temperament to pull off the kind of thing I have in mind. Tell me about your schooling. What were your favourite subjects?"

Lunch proceeded at a leisurely pace, and for each morsel of information I gave him, he regaled me with some new humorous story of his own. He did his utmost to put me at ease and succeeded remarkably well. I didn't think of it at the time, but he frequently enjoined me to "Drink up, we'll have another." The crafty old fox was testing me for any weakness with alcohol. To tell the truth, I wasn't accustomed to drinking in the middle of the day and was already feeling slightly woozy from just one beer. I declined his offer of drinks but asked for seconds on the beef sandwiches and pickles, adding pointedly, "I haven't seen that kind of food for over a year."

"Oh, Rory, come, come now," he said. "Don't be a prig and don't be too hard on me. I don't usually eat like this. I pulled a few strings here and there intentionally to give you a good meal. It was the least I could do considering I've yanked you out of your convalescence. Like the rest of the country, I'm living on a ration card too."

I acknowledged that that was very good of him and helped myself to another plateful of sandwiches. At the end of the meal, Cumming regaled me with further stories about his navy days until the doorbell rang, at which point he ushered in a portly little man in a dark brown suit clutching his hat and an umbrella. He wore the thickest pair of glasses I have ever seen and he carried his head upward on a strange angle as if trying to catch as much light as possible. He looked like a mole or some other scurrying creature that was used to dark tunnels and was stressed by sunlight.

"Rory, please meet Doctor Gustav Bronau from Cambridge University. Gustav is a don specializing in modern German literature. He also happens to be one of my close advisors on matters concerning German politics and German society. Despite the name, Gustav is Polish by birth, but he has spent most of his life in Prussia."

With the formal introductions done, Cumming excused himself from the room and left me with Dr. Bronau. I didn't like Bronau. The more I looked at him, the more I saw there was something officious and self-important about him. It was hard to see his eyes through his enormously thick glasses, and he had a permanent predatory smirk that made me distrust him. Once Cumming left the room, Bronau settled into an easy chair and began to speak as rapidly as he could in German.

"So, Rory, I understand you want to go to Germany and serve out the rest of the war as a spy. Why would you want to do that?"

I bristled at Bronau's inference that I was looking for a safe place to "serve out the war."

"Since you're asking, I didn't volunteer for this. As I understand it, things are being explained to me in an attempt to persuade me to go to Germany. I was pulled out of a convalescent hospital."

Bronau nodded his head. "So you don't want to go?"

"I didn't say that. What exactly do you want to know, Doctor Bronau? If you're suggesting I'm trying to get a safe ticket out of the war, forget it. I've already got one." I held up my bandaged left hand.

Bronau sniffed at my anger and changed the subject. "Where did you learn your German? You speak the language extremely well, even when you are angry. Oh, by the way, I apologize, but before going too far with this, I had to be certain your German could hold up even when you are under pressure."

I was still irritated. "I learned German at home. My mother is German. I grew up speaking both languages."

Bronau nodded. "Have you read anything by the German writer Thomas Mann?"

"Some short stories; my mother had them lying about the house."

"Are you familiar with any contemporary German musicians?"

"No, I don't think I could name any."

"Tell me, who is Prince Guaiacum?"

"He's the Kaiser's youngest son. All I remember about him was that the press hated him before the war. They thought he was spoiled."

"What is Siltfleesch?"

"It's head cheese. It's pickled and eaten with raw onions and fried potatoes. I hate it."

Bronau continued to pepper me with disparate rapid-fire questions, constantly changing topics in an effort to catch me off guard. He finally shifted in his chair as if he were acutely uncomfortable. "Your German is excellent. You seem to be up to date on most things. I believe with some simple coaching you could easily pass as a German officer."

My ears picked up at the mention of my future role.

As if on cue, Cumming stepped into the room, which seemed very odd at the time, because we were in an apartment and he left the room behind me and re-entered from a door on the other side. I remember thinking at the time, he must be some kind of wizard.

"Well, Gustav, I've overheard what you've just said to Rory. I'm not in the least bit surprised. Rory is an intelligent and resourceful young man."

Bronau vigorously brushed dandruff from his shoulders. "Captain Ferrall's German is grammatically excellent and his use of German idiom is like a native. If I didn't know his background, I'd say he was an educated Berliner."

"Thank you, Doctor Bronau, but I'm not a captain, I'm a lieutenant and my relatives in Germany live near Hanover."

Bronau merely smirked and nodded. Cumming said to me solicitously, "Rory, just as I told you when we first met, you may choose whether or not you want to accept this task. You speak the language well. You're young and quick-witted, and I know you are a capable man. You've also sacrificed already a lot for your country. I'm asking you to accept this task and go into Germany to work for us. We desperately need to find out what the Germans are up to. If you accept, only then can I tell you more about the plan we have in store for you. You'll just have to trust me. If you choose not to accept, you can walk out of here and you will be driven back to the hospital. You will never hear a word from us or about this matter again, I promise." He paused and lowered his voice. "What will it be, Rory?"

I had every intention of stalling for time. I wasn't ready to commit myself. While Cumming was working himself up to pop the question, I had been mentally preparing to delay him, but I didn't. Years later, I try to convince myself that I agreed because I still felt a sense of guilt for surviving when so many other good men died. That may have been true, but the uncomplicated truth was that I wasn't thinking fast enough, and for whatever reason, I simply replied, "I'll go."

"Thank you, Rory," Cumming said, "and Gustav is quite right; although he let the cat out of the bag early." He frowned at Bronau. "I arranged to have you promoted to captain once you are attached to us. The job is going to be hazardous enough. You might as well get paid decently for it."

*

I spent the next hour deep in conversation with Cumming and Bronau. Once I'd agreed to go along with the plans they laid out for me, Bronau became relaxed and friendly. His tone changed dramatically. I didn't like him or trust him any more for it though. Despite this, Bronau was a fountain of information about life in Germany. We sat in easy chairs and the two men brought me up to date on Germany's political and domestic situation.

Cumming was emphatic: although the Germans were going through hard times, they were a very long way from being defeated. "Rory," he said, "I don't for a minute believe any of this drivel we hear in Parliament and read in the press. Germany's not about to throw in the towel, not by any stretch of the imagination. I have never agreed with any of that. The War Office puts out that sort of rubbish. People have lost so much; the politicians feel they have to hear that the Boche is ready to collapse. Things may be tough for the Germans, but then they're tough people. You know that from your family, and you certainly know that from your time in France."

He fiddled about putting a fresh cigarette in his holder. "I'm afraid they have something up their sleeve. I don't know what it is. They've already surprised us with U-boat warfare, bombing London from zeppelins, poison gas, and, as you know, flame throwers. Mark my words, they're up to something new. I need you to go and find out what it is."

I didn't say anything. Everything suddenly seemed absolutely ludicrous and I struggled to keep from laughing aloud. How was I, half-blind and maimed, a twenty-two-year-old Canadian infantry officer going to go masquerading into Germany and discover the Imperial German army's most important secrets? This wasn't war; it was more like some schoolboy fantasy out of the *Boy's Own Paper*. I did my utmost to stare blankly at Cumming; and then in a chilling split second, I realized that this wasn't nearly as absurd it sounded. I was the one being foolish. Like hundreds of thousands of others, I had already been given tasks that were far more insane, and every day, highly intelligent, rational people were devising suicidal plans that were promptly and disastrously implemented by equally reasonable men. These two were serious. "How do you propose I do that?" I said.

Bronau and Cumming looked knowingly at one another. Cumming inhaled deeply on his cigarette. He sat back and blew smoke at the ceiling. "Last month on the Somme, during part of the same offensive that you were wounded in, the German Ninth Landwehr Division attacked a battalion of the Gordon Highlanders. They took a wounded German officer prisoner. Nothing unusual in that. He was about the same age as you. Now I suppose we've probably taken several hundred young German officers prisoner, but this chap is quite different. He's very much like you. He's an American from upstate New York. His name is Alex Baumann. Both his parents were German immigrants. He speaks perfect English, perfect American English, anyway."

Cumming forced a tight little smile at his joke and continued. "The Gordon Highlanders used him to help carry wounded to the rear. One of our officers at the casualty clearing point, after hearing his English, had the good sense to have him sent up to divisional intelligence for immediate de-briefing. Baumann was sent on to army headquarters; and, as I was in France at the time, I interviewed him. This was two days before I heard about you and Sebastian. No one outside our own chain of command knows that Baumann is a prisoner. We've withheld all his documents and he's been kept segregated from all the other prisoners. He's been well looked after. I knew we could do something with him at the time, I just didn't know what. Later, when I heard about your nightmares, the whole plan fell into place." He stopped and looked again at Bronau.

"I'm going into Germany as Alex Baumann?" I said.

"Exactly, Rory." Cumming paused. "Do you know that Baumann's identity card has no photograph on it. When I saw that, I thought it gave us some possibilities. Baumann has told us that before he was taken prisoner, his battalion was reduced to three officers, all of whom went over the top with him. There's an excellent chance Baumann is the last surviving officer of his unit. Which probably means there is virtually no one in Germany who you would run into who knows what Baumann looks like, or who knows him.

"He left New York and joined the German army several months before you signed on in Canada. Did you know that there are at least ten million people of German descent living in the U.S.? Over a thousand German-born Americans left America to join the German army in August and September of 1914. A lesser number of German-born Canadians did the same. Our North American friends have kept very quiet about that. That's probably a good sign. For America it's another indication they're probably going to come in on our side, don't you think?" He didn't wait for me to answer.

"I would imagine Baumann had some of the same misgivings you had about joining." He thought about this for a few seconds and qualified himself. "No, that's probably not correct. America's not at war and certainly wasn't even contemplating it when Baumann enlisted. At any event, things have changed and Baumann's quite concerned that America may come in on our side; and if she does, that's going to leave friend Baumann in a bit of a sticky wicket if he ever chooses to go home."

Bronau squirmed in his chair, anxious to get a word in. "How do you feel about all this, Rory? Does the morality of espionage bother you? I'll be frank. There are men who feel being a spy is morally reprehensible, not something suited for gentlemen."

I tried to smile. "I've spent the last year doing everything I could to kill Germans in every imaginable way. I've been on a patrol when we threw grenades into a trench of sleeping men. I've lived through bombardments and shot at attacking men as close as you are to me, and you're asking me if I have any moral reservations about reading other people's mail and impersonating someone else. No, Doctor Bronau, believe me, any reservations I have aren't moral ones."

Cumming tapped me on the knee encouragingly. "Well said, well said. I tell you what, Rory. You must be tired, and I don't want to drive you into the ground. I've had a room prepared for you upstairs. I think you should get some rest this afternoon. Tonight I've arranged for all of us to have dinner at my club. Not to worry, Rory; I've also arranged to have some suitable clothes sent round for you. I tried to get you a uniform made, but I wasn't able to get the proper regimental accoutrements. I'm afraid you will have to make do with civvies. Now, we're off to show you your new room and you, young man, must get some sleep. After that there is another chap I want you to meet."

Bronau, chimed in cheerfully. "Yes, Rory, you are going to have to keep your wits about you in the days ahead. How thoroughly you do your job over the next three weeks will determine whether or not the Germans put you up against a wall and shoot you."

Cumming rolled his eyes as we left the room.

CUMMING walked me upstairs and into an apartment that seemed to occupy the entire floor. Unlike his flat below us, the floor above was cheerlessly furnished with wooden desks, metal filing cabinets, and heaps of files. A smiling and arrestingly attractive woman greeted us at the door. She was introduced to me as Mrs. Chaver. Mrs. Chaver was efficient looking and in her late thirties. Despite smouldering brown eyes, high cheek bones, a flawless complexion, and a perfect smile, she had an aggrieved aura of menace about her. Her dark auburn hair was tied back in a bun and she wore a black dress that demurely revealed a hypnotically proportioned figure.

"Mrs. Chaver is our office manager here, Rory," said Cumming with a touch of pride. "We couldn't possibly get along without her. She will show you the room we've set aside for you at the back of the offices and explain any arrangements that you may require for the next day or so. I'll be back at eight and we'll go to my club for dinner. See you then." Without waiting for an answer he backed out towards the door.

Mrs. Chaver shook my hand and said, "I've been expecting you, Captain Ferrall. I don't know exactly what it is you will be doing and I don't want to know. Amongst other things, I am looking after your living arrangements for the next several days. If there is anything you need or require, please tell me." Once the door closed and

Cumming was gone, Mrs. Chaver's demeanour instantly became frostier and more business-like. "I work here every day between eight and six. Whatever it is you are going to be doing, I am led to believe, is to be of the utmost secrecy and I have been directed to help ensure that whilst you are living here, your behaviour is both discreet and your whereabouts are undisclosed." She looked at me sternly as if I was a disobedient child. "If there is anything else you need or anything you want to do, you must ask me."

"That's very good of you," I replied in my most military manner. "Now if you'll please show me my room, I believe there are some clothes for me. I'll also be requiring some pocket money. Five pounds will be fine for now. I need a haircut and a few other items."

I had no intention of getting a haircut. I just wanted to get out, walk about a bit, perhaps go to a pub, but I wasn't going to tell this beautiful dragon that. I just wanted to get away from here. She was a strong-willed woman, and I sensed if you came off second-best with her in your first meeting, she'd forever exercise the upper hand. Before she could answer, I added, "I'd like to go out in the next ten minutes, so if we could please view the room and my change of clothes, you can make arrangements to find me my pocket money. That will be all for now, thank you, Mrs. Chaver."

She nodded in reluctant agreement and I followed her to a small bedroom at the back of the flat. It was set up with a metal army cot, fresh linen, and had an expensive-looking wool suit, shirts, neckties, shoes, socks, underclothes, and two felt hats in the clothes closet.

"I've taken the liberty of guessing your shoe and hat size. There is a range of shoes, hats, and shirts here for you to try from."

"That's fine. Thank you. I'll try them on and then I'm going to go out and stretch my legs and get a haircut. I should be back in an hour. After that, I'd like to get some sleep before I go out this evening."

Mrs. Chaver was flustered. "I'll—I'll have to check with Captain Cumming."

"That's fine," I said. "As far as I'm concerned you are free to advise him of my plans. Oh, and Mrs. Chaver, I'm a commissioned officer and a veteran, and under no circumstances will I have my private comings and goings dictated to me. Is this clear?"

She allowed me a surly and barely perceptible nod.

"Thank you."

✠

Out in the streets of London I felt completely invigorated. The shoes were a touch large, but the rest of my civilian clothes fit comfortably. Mrs. Chaver had also chosen for me a very nice felt hat with a rakish brim. In addition to being beautiful, she had style. I felt as if I'd been released from prison. I hadn't worn civilian clothes in months, and I hadn't been free to walk about in non-military surroundings for ages. It was a few minutes after three and I set out at a brisk pace. To my surprise and dismay, I soon tired. I walked to the nearest large intersection and waited vainly for a taxi. A bus eventually came along and I asked the driver directions to a good public house, some place crowded, with real beer. After a short ride, the bus driver dropped me at the Three Bells near Earls Court and I took a spot in the corner.

I ordered a half-pint of bitter and sat back, happy enough just to watch the world go by. I knew instinctively that even for a short time I had to get away, to be on my own for an hour or two. I needed to make some distance from the institutional confines of the last eighteen months.

Despite my assurances to Cumming earlier in the day, I wasn't at all certain I'd mentally agreed to this scheme of espionage that had been set out for me. There were other things. Bronau and Mrs. Chaver irritated me intensely, out of all proportion to what they should have. Before all this, I was fairly tolerant. I could ignore people who bothered me. Not now. I was agitated. To my superstitious mind, I saw Bronau and Mrs. Chaver as some kind of forewarning; but more than that, they were a part of the world I hadn't accepted—a world that was being pushed down my throat; and in addition to this, for the first time in my life, I was beginning to get some real sense of who I was. I was no longer someone who drifted along with life's currents and tides.

Up until then, I'd never given much thought to my character, my personality, or my position in the world. But in those last few days at the convalescent hospital, and now in London, I felt a sense of distance from the rest of the world. I wasn't isolated, just distant. I was determined to be in control from now on. It was a new sensation for me; and Cumming, Bronau, and Mrs. Chaver all seemed bent on manipulating me. They didn't try to conceal their purposes. Cumming was a little different. I liked him. It was hard not to; but he was definitely one of them. Cumming had the virtue of being personable and charming; or, maybe I was deluding myself. For all I knew, Cumming was the most dangerous of the bunch; but I didn't think so. I wanted to accept that he was a decent man and truly believed in what he was doing. But then I reasoned, no matter how sincere Cumming was in his beliefs, he could still do me enormous harm if he was wrong.

Sipping my warm beer, I reckoned that with no other reference points to guide me, Cumming's character was probably the only indication I had. If I was forced to trust people like Bronau or the lovely but poisonous Mrs. Chaver, I'd have told them where to stuff all this spy nonsense at the outset. The members of Cumming's supporting cast were unpleasant and dangerous. They knew what they wanted, but in my life they were second-rate players. Both of them knew it and it bothered them, and to compensate they were aggressive and malicious. If I was going to survive in this league, I had to be a lot more like Cumming, someone who took the longer view of things.

In between plotting my own destiny and admiring one of the pretty bar maids, I stood up to order a second half-pint. At the bar I leaned forward. The prettiest girl behind the counter had cut her hair straight to her shoulders in a bob and was wearing a short dress with a hemline that came up well above her ankles. No doubt things were changing; happily, some of them were for the better.

I took my seat back in the corner as perplexed as ever as to what I was doing. I'd never before tried to identify the borders that defined my life. It was a kind of introspection that was new to me. At twenty-two, I was neither particularly self-absorbed nor suspicious of the world. In retrospect, I could honestly describe myself as being "innocent," but that's not how I thought of myself. I was simple and trusting; and for the most part, over the years, I had swum along with whatever currents were moving me: family, school, university, the army. Forces and institutions over which I exerted no control had largely governed my life.

Looking out across the room, my eyes were pulled repeatedly to the pretty bar maid straining at the draft beer pump. I tried to be discreet, but my instincts pulled me like the needle on a compass. They were beyond my power to manage and I was constantly drawn in pre-determined directions. In this case she was young, attractive, and fashionable, and she made me acutely aware of the fact that I had never slept with a woman. In so many ways my life was incomplete.

During my months at the front I'd listened to all the army horror stories about venereal disease. The truth was, I was convinced somehow I was going to survive the war, and if that was to happen, I wasn't going to go home painfully infected and crippled from syphilis. I had heard they could partially cure it, but even so, I wasn't interested in finding out just how far along modern medical science had come. Probably the truth was that even in my most drunken moments on leave I was too shy about sex and women in general to consider paying for a prostitute. I could never have lined up along with so many others at those filthy little brothels or waited half-drunk for my time upstairs with some wretched farm girl in a grubby little estaminet. My sexual inexperience bothered me, but I resigned myself to wait for a risk-free opportunity for that initiation.

There were other holes in my life. I still had no idea what I wanted to do when the war was over. But that afternoon was the first time I had ever acknowledged the fact that when this was all over I didn't have to go tamely and work in my father's business. Things had changed, and when I went home I would do it on my terms. In the space of that smoky hour in the Three Bells, I knew that over the course of the last year something deep within me had changed.

As to my current situation, for whatever reasons, I'd committed myself to going to Germany. But as far as I could see, I still held most of the trump cards. I could go over there and, if I chose to do so, I could go to ground. I could find something safe, and, however the war turned out, I could emerge at the end with what was left of my skin and my reputation intact. No sooner had I considered this option I dismissed the possibility. Faces from the battalion reared in my imagination, dead faces of men like Sergeant Ferguson and Private Reid. If I went to Germany, I wasn't going into hiding.

I was angry with myself for that. Something had been etched into my nature. I'd always do the "right thing." In that respect, I thought people weren't a lot different from dogs. Some dogs were naturally bred to work; others were lapdogs. I smiled at the thought. With my shattered face and my experiences in the trenches, I made a pretty awful lapdog. I was more likely some kind of carefully bred retriever, one who would go on fetching every time someone threw a stick.

Cumming saw the retriever in me. The cagey old beggar could see through me and he could afford to be charming. Neither Bronau nor Mrs. Chaver had that ability. That was the difference between them and Cumming. Cumming was decent because he was perceptive. He had a much clearer appreciation of things and the mental clarity gave him control. It was how the world went around. Instinct and circumstance guided us. Those who figured out the nature of the circumstances and were able to identify people's characteristic instincts ran things. The rest of us were trained and bred to our duty; if we never understood what kind of breed we were and how to compensate for it, we perpetually spent our lives retrieving and running for those who did. Sometime toward the end of my canine deliberations, a heavy-set man in his early thirties lurched over to my table.

The man weaving above me was glassy eyed and belligerent. "All those bandages you've got wrapped around you. I salute you." He raised his glass and slopped beer on himself. "You've just come from Flanders then, have you?"

"A month or so ago." I didn't like his tone and was wary.

One of the bar maids, another cheerful-looking woman, in her late forties with bleached hair and dramatically shadowed eyes, sensed trouble and moved quickly around to my table. "Come on now, Alfred. This lad's minding his own business." Good naturedly, she pushed Alfred aside and said to me, "You look like you've been there and back, luv. What can I get you? It's on the house. Alfred has managed to get himself a protected job in the Ministry of Munitions. Very proud of it, he is," she said scornfully.

"So then, what was it like?" Alfred continued. I nodded and said "Thanks anyway" to the bar maid and slipped out from the bench and headed for the door. I didn't want a scene. Behind me, I could hear Alfred calling after me, "Don't think because you've served in the army you're too good for the likes of me now. I'm doing me bit too."

I walked aimlessly about the streets for a spell. For no good reason this encounter with Alfred left me feeling hollow and worthless. I thought my first foray into civilian life was a disaster and was depressed by it. Despite all the wartime talk about everyone standing shoulder to shoulder with one another, in my gloom I was convinced the war wasn't going to change anything. Anyone could see that when the fighting was over there would be a huge gulf between those of us who'd served and those who stayed home. The retrievers would be pushed aside in favour of the show dogs. Those who stayed home would have a huge lead on those who went overseas: businessmen, politicians, professionals, everybody but the poor bloodied wrecks who came home with bits and pieces missing.

I stuffed my hands in my coat pockets and quickened my pace, heading nowhere in particular. The shrewd homebodies who stayed comfy all these years were going to benefit from an even greater advantage from those who would never return. A whole generation of Alfreds would fare better than they had any right to because most of their toughest competitors in life were cold and decomposing in squalid patches of France or Belgium. The incident in the bar left me discouraged. Today, they say these feelings were normal, but at the time I was haunted by anger and the survivor's false sense of guilt. I've long since come to deal with survivor's guilt, or at least I think I have; but then, as now, it seems that those who risked the least gained the most.

When I got back to Whitehall Court, I lay down on my cot and fell into a deep sleep. I was awakened by Cumming knocking at my door to take me to his club.

✠

In the back seat of his car, Cumming rattled on cheerfully. "Oh, not to worry about Lance Corporal Reagan," he said, pointing to the driver. "He's a very good man, utterly dependable, and besides," he said cheerfully, "he has a hearing problem. He was badly shelled in the defence of Antwerp. When he got back to England, he didn't want to leave the service. A good thing too. Reagan has a Distinguished Conduct Medal. I'm told his unit put him in for a Victoria Cross, but they weren't giving any out. The Marines found him the ideal spot with me. Unless he's looking at you, he can't understand a word you're saying." Cumming looked out the window and tapped his empty cigarette holder on the glass pane for emphasis.

"Now to answer your question: aside from myself, Bronau, and the fellow you are going to meet tonight, nobody else is going to know where you are. Your family, your regiment, and the convalescent hospital will be told you have been seconded to service in German East Africa. I'm afraid we are shortly thereafter going to have you listed as missing in action when you arrive in Africa. This may all sound a bit harsh as far as your family is concerned, but then, Rory, I fully expect you to come to life when this is all over."

I thought about this for a few seconds. "Can't you do something for my mother, give her some hope that I've been taken prisoner? It'd be devastating for my parents."

Cumming paused and stared at me. "Yes, I suppose we could do something like that. But you know, the less said the better. You of all people know this is a brutally serious business. I don't want anyone to suffer, least of all your family. I can't emphasize it enough: we desperately need the information you're being asked to collect. Now, if for any reason you don't come back, you'll continue to be listed as missing in action in East Africa." He looked at me very strangely.

"Fair enough." I paused. "Are you worried about me? Do you think I'm not up to this?"

"No, I'm not worried about you, not in the least; but I'm concerned." For a second, Cumming looked completely out of character. He started fiddling frantically with his cigarette holder, took hold of himself, and then continued. "I want you to leave for Germany in three weeks. In that time you have to cram in several months of recuperation and train yourself to become a German officer. Tonight you are to meet Major Crossley. He is assuming the direction of your case. I'll keep an eye on it from a distance. We'll give you the very best preparation we can; after that, it's your wits and good fortune that will bring you home safely. And yes, I think you're up to the job."

✠

Whyte's was one of those historical St. James Street gentlemen's clubs I'd read about in novels. I must confess, considering the circumstances, I was more than a bit taken in by the theatrical feel of the place. My surroundings made me feel far more important and capable than I should have. I was young, and conspiring on near equal terms with one of the Empire's most powerful eccentrics. My suspicions of the afternoon vanished and I felt ridiculously confidant.

I wasn't the only one affected by the club. You could see Cumming passionately believed in the virtues and trappings of being a gentleman. It was written all over him. Central to his view of life was his club. Whyte's was a bastion of privilege and authority, one of the places where fortunes and national destinies were still determined by stout grey-haired men over port and the cheese tray. Cumming looked supremely at ease there. In view of the nature of our discussions, I was surprised he chose such a public place to conduct sensitive official business. He treated the club's servants as confidently as he treated Lance Corporal Reagan, and throughout the evening our conversation never paused. It's been suggested that kind of faith in the world died with the war, but I don't believe it. The locations and the faces may have changed, but the rich and powerful have gone on behaving as if their management of the world's affairs was entirely in the natural order of things.

We joined Bronau and Major Crossley in one of the private rooms upstairs. The whole affair began as a cheery get-together over drinks before sitting down to dinner. Major Ewen Crossley was a regular army officer in his early thirties. He was a powerfully built man with sandy hair, a ready smile, and an easy laugh. Seen from his right profile, he was strikingly handsome. Sadly, Crossley had been hit in the face with shrapnel at the First Battle of Ypres while serving with the Royal Horse Artillery. From his left side, he was hideously disfigured. I couldn't help but smirk, thinking that British Imperial Intelligence was purposely being staffed by a collection of maimed invalids. I liked Crossley immediately. He was supremely confident without being overbearing or full of himself. At the first opportunity he pulled me aside and elaborated on his plans for my future.

"I've been assigned to help you manage your preparations, Rory. I've got to be honest. I haven't done a lot of this sort of thing. Like yourself, I'm recently out of a convalescent hospital; although I suspect I was given a bit more time to mend than you." He took a long drink and looked at me over the edge of his glass. "If you've any ideas or suggestions, please let me know."

Crossley's revelation quickly brought me back to earth. Dabbling in the role of the talented amateur was all very well for sports and dramatic productions, but when it came to playing with my life, I wanted to trust in a system that at least had the veneer of being professional.

"What's the plan so far? I'm still a little sketchy on the details," I said, trying to keep the apprehension out of my voice.

"We've got Baumann here in London. We transported him from France along with five or six of his fellow POWs the day before yesterday. In anticipation of you accepting this task, Baumann and other lightly wounded prisoners have been brought to a military hospital here in London. This has all been C's doing up to now."

I had never heard Cumming referred to simply as C before. Later I was to learn it was the moniker his department and history was to use for all intelligence chiefs thereafter.

Crossley continued. "All of them have been given some kind of a drug in their food. It makes them feel quite sick as long as they continue to be administered it. You're to be put into the hospital tomorrow. Baumann will be trundled into your room. After that, he will begin to recover. We'll keep the others ill for a few days so things don't look too contrived. We've told all the Germans that they have some mysterious kind of influenza and we want to keep them isolated. The plan is the two of you will stay quarantined for a few weeks after your recovery. So far, all of them are so sick they haven't had time or energy to question the diagnosis.

"Once you're in with Baumann, we want you to find out as much as you can about who he is. During the day you will be given physio-therapy exercises and have your eye looked after. To ensure we don't lose anything, we'll have a special hidden microphone in the room and on the other end a shorthand clerk transcribing everything Baumann says. You'll get notes to confirm whatever pertinent information Baumann tells you.

"In between your physiotherapy sessions you will also be taking lessons from some of our German experts. German weapons, organizations, staff procedures, and training methods—everything you would expect to know if you really were a German infantry officer. I want you to have as firm an understanding of the background and detail of German army life as any junior officer in Baumann's situation would have. We have one of our pre-war military attachés and members of our intelligence staff working with a couple of talkative German prisoners who are telling us a great deal about their army. Anything you can think of that you might need to know, don't hesitate to ask me. We'll try and get you whatever information you need."

"What happens when my training session is over?"

"I'm still working on the details. Essentially, Baumann will escape and make his way back to Germany. Once you get to Germany, I think it's best you take over and figure out things from there. Both C and I believe you're better off exploiting whatever opportunities present themselves to you. If we send you over with a predetermined plan, it's likely you'll get caught out trying to pattern your behaviour to match something we've dreamed up here in London. No, you'll be the man on the ground and you will have to insinuate yourself as best you can into the German Army's confidence. We can give you an alias and a background; after that, we're looking for you to come up with the game plan. Just keep your ears and eyes open. When you've found out what it is they're up to, make your way as quickly as possible to a British Embassy in The Hague, Copenhagen, or Stockholm. Identify yourself with the code name 'Landslide' to the military attaché in any of these places and we'll bring you back for de-briefing from there."

I didn't say anything for a few seconds. I twirled my drink around in the bottom of the glass. "Sounds like you'll get me into Germany all right. Staying there's going to be the problem. Will there be a hue and cry raised here in England when Baumann goes missing? I think it's something that might help provide cover for my story if the Germans have some sort of proof Baumann actually went missing."

"What are you suggesting?"

"A police manhunt in Britain, newspaper coverage, something

the Germans could read about or have listened to on our wireless to verify my story."

Crossley looked thoughtful for a moment. "Yes, I think that's a good idea. We can do it." At which point an elderly club waiter announced that dinner was served in the next room.

I sat down next to Crossley to a disappointingly bland meal. Whyte's may have been a sanctuary for the rich and powerful, but it hadn't escaped wartime rationing. With the exception of the wines and the cheese tray, the food was as appalling as could be imagined in rationed wartime London.

Across the broad mahogany dining table from us, Bronau and Cumming were deeply involved in their own animated discussion about watching ports and keeping tabs on German shipping. Crossley leaned back and began to tell me what he knew of Cumming in a hushed voice.

"C's quite a fellow," he said. "I can't think of a man I admire more. Do you know anything about him?"

"Not much, just what I've seen today and a brief meeting at my convalescent hospital. He's a cagey one, I'll grant you that."

"No, cagey isn't the word for it. He's brilliant, inexhaustible, and a good man to boot. Bronau thinks he likes you because you remind him of his dead son. I don't suppose you know, but that's how he lost his leg. Several years ago he rolled his open saloon car. He was returning to his country house from a party, driving much too fast. His son was with him. Both C and the boy were trapped beneath the car. In order to get out from beneath the wreck and rescue him, C tied a tourniquet around his thigh and tried to cut away what was left of his own leg with a pen knife. Didn't help though, the lad was dead anyway. Since then he's thrown himself into his work. Lives at the office. Do you know he has secret passageways and doorways built into his headquarters building?"

I must have looked at Crossley suspiciously for he became defensive. "I'm not gossiping. The reason I'm telling you all this is that if I were in your shoes, I'd be highly suspicious of this whole venture. C likes you. That's obvious and he wouldn't be sending you off on a harebrained scheme if he didn't think you had a good chance. He's like that."

I thanked Crossley for his candour and he quickly changed the subject. We made small talk for five minutes or so and when the conversation dwindled we pretended to study the prints of the English countryside on the wall opposite.

After a few moments, Cumming finished his discussion with Bronau and leaned forward across the table. "So, Rory, how do you find the food? Not much, is it? I'm afraid it's the best we can get in London without breaking the law."

He winked at me mischievously. "Do you know that Mrs. Chaver tells me she doesn't like you? She thinks you're much too aggressive and stubborn. I think that's a very good sign. A very good sign indeed. I use her to intimidate people. A sweet and sour test, if you will." He smiled mirthlessly at his joke. "If she wins, then I don't use them. In this business I want people with strength of character. So far you've passed all the tests, Rory." He raised his wine glass at me in a private toast. "Well now, since Ewen has explained everything to Rory, here's to a successful outcome to all this. To your very good fortune, Rory."

8

MY NEXT PERIOD of hospitalization was in the East London
suburb of West Ham, in a gloomy, soot-stained, red-brick Victorian hospital. The hospital had been converted to a British army
institution and held upwards of six hundred men in various degrees
of trauma. I was placed on the fourth floor in a locked wing of four
rooms. The wing was signed in bright red: "Keep Out. Influenza
Observation Area."

My room at the end of the hallway was lit by a single naked
light bulb hanging from the ceiling and was painted in a hideous
shade of yellow. There were two steel beds, one bedside table, and
a stained canvas privacy curtain between the two bed spaces. The
single curtainless window looked out onto a landscape of red-brick
buildings and a distant patch of street with small shops. Alex Baumann, looking like death under a blanket, was wheeled in on a gur-
ney the morning after I arrived.

Baumann looked alarming. He was conscious but his face was
waxy and his breathing was laboured. Four other Germans in a similar state were put into the room beside ours. Baumann proved to be
a less than charming companion on that first day of our acquaintance. He was violently sick to his stomach and looked to me like he
would die at any moment. I genuinely felt sorry for him and bathed

his forehead with a damp cloth and gave him sips of water. He was at first too miserable to be surprised by the fact that I spoke to him in German. By mid-afternoon, he began to show faint signs of feeling better. By seven that evening he was well enough to sit up for a few moments. I introduced myself in German.

"I'm Rory Ferrall. Welcome to the quarantine wing. They seem to think you have the same sickness I had last week."

Baumann looked at me suspiciously. "So why are you in here with prisoners and why do you speak such good German?"

"Because until you five arrived, I've been the first and only case of influenza in this particular hospital. I was moved from the Canadian Army General Hospital last week to get a new glass eye. Half the patients there have come down with the flu. A week ago I didn't show any signs of it. They thought I was safe and I was shipped here. The glass eye's been put on hold for a few days yet."

"So how is it you speak such good German?" He asked again with obvious persistence.

"My mother's German. I'm Canadian, from Montreal. Where are you from?"

Baumann collapsed back onto his bed. "Montreal," he said with disbelief. "Do you speak English or French?"

"English mostly, but I get by in French. I went to a French school."

Switching to English, Baumann said, with only the faintest trace of a German accent, "You're a German from Montreal. You won't believe this: I grew up in Albany, New York, just a few hundred miles from you." He sank down onto his back.

"So, if you're an American, how'd you end up here?" I said.

"It's a long story." Letting his head fall back into his pillow, he closed his eyes. "I'm too sick to get into it now." A few minutes later I could hear his rhythmic breathing. I remember thinking at the time that even with my eye bandaged I didn't remotely resemble Baumann. He was shorter and stockier than I was, and much fairer, with long blond hair, brushed straight back in the German style without a part. He also spoke German with a slightly different accent than mine. If I ever met anyone who knew him, the game would soon be over.

In the morning when I awoke, Baumann looked rocky but was sitting on the edge of his bed gazing out the window. "We're locked into this ward. There's a guard outside in the next hallway."

I nodded. "I knew they were going to do that. They told me yesterday they were transporting infected German prisoners here. It doesn't matter; I wasn't free to come or go either. They want everybody who has it to be isolated. So far the influenza bug we have has infected half the First Canadian Division and much of the French Second Army. Our hospital's out of bounds to everybody. They're trying to contain it. If it spreads much further they're afraid we'll lose the war. That's why we're both in the isolation ward." I looked at him to see how he reacted to this. Baumann showed no expression, so I continued. "I didn't know it had spread to the Germans as well. Maybe Mother Nature will end the war for us?"

"I didn't have it when I was captured," he replied dryly and lay down again.

Baumann slept for most of the day. He was asleep for breakfast and lunch. When an orderly with a gauze mask over his mouth and nose brought dinner trays, Baumann was looking better. "You should try to eat," I said. "I didn't want to either, but it'll help you get your strength back. If you're like me, you'll be much better in a day or so."

After a dinner of beans, vegetable soup, bread, margarine, and some sort of revolting rice pudding, Baumann complained of a headache. He was retching violently again within the hour.

It wasn't until mid-morning of the next day that Baumann began to revive again. This time he showed more colour in his cheeks, and by noon he tried taking a bit of Bovril and dry bread. By lunch the next day, he was weak but noticeably mending. Over the next few days we talked in a desultory sort of fashion but our relationship grew slowly. Baumann was reluctant to engage in conversation at first. He spent a lot of time looking out the window and sleeping.

When I was taken across the hall to an empty room for "physio-therapy," Ewen Crossley in a doctor's lab coat urged me to "get him talking."

"He will," I replied, remembering the crushing black mood that gripped me for weeks the last time I left the line. "Give him time."

On Baumann's fifth day he began to open up. The other four German prisoners had been maintained on their venomous dosage and were showing no signs of "improvement." I was impressed with Baumann's genuine concern for them when they were moved to an "intensive care unit." It was a good move. Within a few hours, he began to loosen up. "You know, Rory, I'm glad to see those boys move out of here. They show no signs of getting better. Do you think they'll be all right?"

I was as reassuring as I could be. "It's hard to say. I've heard hundreds have died already from this epidemic. They'll get the best treatment possible here, though, and the hospital will keep you advised how they're getting on."

Once the other Germans were gone, it was almost as if Alex needed to reconnect with someone. That night we began to talk about our backgrounds. He was born in Germany but emigrated to America before he was three. Both his parents were German immigrants from the town of Sonneberg. His father had done well for himself and now owned a bakery shop in Albany. He had no brothers or sisters, and since joining the army, his mother had taken seriously ill with a crippling form of arthritis. Like me, he was a hockey player and had played for his high school. Baumann had other talents. He played the flute and was about to enter his third year in civil engineering at Rensselaer Polytechnic Institute in Troy, New York. When the war broke out, along with two other friends, he sailed for Germany to enlist. He was commissioned as a replacement subaltern in the Fourth Landwehr Battalion of the 153rd Thuringian Infantry Regiment, Ninth Landwehr Division.

I told Baumann everything about my background; and for a time, I completely forgot we were enemies. Thinking back on it, in spite of the circumstances, there was something therapeutic about those hours conversing about home and our shared interests. I felt better for it and realized that I had more in common with Alex Baumann than most people I had met since leaving Canada.

After a few days, a serious-looking Welsh doctor in a white lab coat visited Alex and me. He advised us that he thought that we were both out of danger, but the War Office's Department of Preventive Medicine wanted to keep us under observation for at least another week to develop information on the sickness. The doctor gravely measured all of our vital signs, took blood samples, and answered Alex's questions with a straight face. He explained that the other four POWs were showing some signs of improvement, but they weren't yet out of the woods.

After that day, I was allowed to leave the ward supposedly to be fitted for my glass eye and to join in physiotherapy classes for my left hand. I actually did do some physiotherapy, but I was never fitted for a glass eye as the doctors who examined me felt that there had been insufficient time for my eye socket to heal. I would go into my new life as a spy with a black eye patch. I was disappointed to hear this, as it seemed to me to be a detail that would prevent me from blending inconspicuously into my new surroundings.

Each morning, I went to a room in the hospital's basement and would be met by different instructors who tutored me in an astonishing array of subjects. I learned German army ranks and customs. I studied German military organizations as well as practical training on all of the weapons and the German names of their parts. My training was quite thorough and even extended to a daily review of flash cards so that I would never stumble on some simple military term. Ewen Crossley was maintaining a dossier on all the information we were compiling and dropped in periodically to prompt me on information I should get from Alex. In the afternoons, Alex and I played cards; and, as I still was not allowed to strain my eye socket, he read articles to me from magazines. Our conversation naturally drifted to our own experiences on either side of the trenches in France.

Alex spent much of his time opposite the French army near Verdun, although for a short spell he served across from the British near Cambrai. We agreed that we were never in the same sector. We talked of the routine in the trenches, the food and the discomfort, some of the personalities in our units, and how we spent our short periods of leave. Our conversations were spontaneous and I can't remember ever having to prompt him for information. For both of us, talking about our lives in the trenches helped in a small way to cast out some of the demons that lurked in our subconscious. Each day I began to feel a greater sense of energy and self-reliance. It was almost as if I was becoming more like myself again.

I couldn't be certain, but I thought Alex was more seriously affected by the fighting than I was. Unlike my experiences, where I spent my entire period of service on the defensive, Alex, in addition to his periods manning frontline trenches, had participated in the strategic offensive at Verdun as well as in two divisional assault operations before being captured on the Somme. He was incredibly lucky to be alive. He'd been lightly wounded by shrapnel in the first days of the German assault on Verdun, and after his evacuation, came down with a fever that turned into pneumonia. He was out of the line for several months. He returned to his unit a virtual stranger. Being taken prisoner during the British offensive on the Somme was probably an enormous relief for him.

Despite this, Alex was still worried. The possibility of going back to Albany caused him concern. He never expected America would even consider becoming involved in this European war, and he hoped his adopted country would remain neutral. He was homesick and the newspapers he read in the hospital were full of news about American outrage at unrestricted U-boat warfare. From the British perspective, American participation was a foregone conclusion. Alex was legitimately concerned that when he returned few people would understand why he had chosen to go and fight as he had.

One morning near the end of my stay in hospital when I went down to the basement for my training, Ewen Crossley was waiting for me. On the table in front of him was a bottle of brandy. "Bit early for that don't you think," I said.

"It's not for me. I think you and friend Baumann still need to cover a few points to flesh out your background. Tell him you saw it sitting in a glass case in the doctor's office. You scoffed it."

That afternoon I shuffled back into our fourth floor wing in my cardboard slippers. Under my arm was my customary batch of newspapers and old magazines. Hidden under the papers was a very fine bottle of Chateau Paulet brandy. Alex and I uncorked it shortly after lunch and by mid-afternoon he was teaching me German army marching songs and regaling me with tales of his fellow officers from his unit. My shorthand clerk listening on his headphones in the room beside us scribbled furiously throughout the afternoon and managed to assemble a convincing roster of names providing me sufficient background detail on the personalities of Alex's old unit.

Two days later, Ewen Crossley, dressed in a lab coat and sporting a stethoscope, appeared with our solemn Welsh doctor. Ewen seemed to enjoy his impersonation immensely and threw himself into the part. "Captain Ferrall, your period of quarantine is over. I think you're fit now and you won't infect anyone. You're going back to Canada. As for you, Oberleutnant Baumann," he shook his head with mock solemnity, "I'm afraid we'll have to keep you for a few days yet. The good news is your friends who were so sick when you arrived are all recovering very nicely. After that, when you're released from here, we'll send you to a prisoner-of-war camp in Yorkshire; and hopefully, not much longer after that, we'll have won the war and we can send all you lot home."

That afternoon was the last I ever saw of Alex Baumann. We both promised we'd get together back in North America when the war was over. I'd go to down to Albany and he'd come up to Montreal when all this killing and destruction was at an end. I'd like to have seen Alex again, although I'm not certain he'd have been happy if he were ever to hear the truth about our relationship. Alex Baumann was a good man and I suppose in a ridiculous sort of way, if

I was going to go into Germany as anybody, I might as well have gone impersonating someone like Alex who I liked. It seemed to make it easier for me. He was laughing when I left and he called out to me, "The next time, I'll bring the brandy!"

9

FROM THE HOSPITAL, Ewen Crossley took me back to Whitehall Court and deposited me at my makeshift room in the anonymous offices of British military intelligence. He told me I'd be leaving for Germany in three days time and thought it would be a good idea if I had two days leave before I went. There was only one condition: I was left on my honour not to try to contact anyone; officially, I had already been listed as being seconded to Headquarters British Forces East Africa.

Upon arriving at Whitehall Court, we were met by Mrs. Chaver, who looked as stunning and as disagreeable as ever. Much to her dismay, she had been instructed to leave me more money and keys to the office. I was to come and go as I pleased.

I would like to be able to say that I spent the next two days dissolutely having the time of my life, but unfortunately, I didn't. On my first day I didn't do much of anything. I went to an inane music hall theatrical, which was really little more than badly written propaganda. I ate a surprisingly nice dinner of sole and grilled vegetables at the Savoy and rode around aimlessly on the top of the omnibuses. On my second day I got up late and in the afternoon went to the cinema. I saw the film *Birth of a Nation*. I couldn't see what all the fuss was about. It was a disjointed endorsement of an extremist view of American history, but these were strange times everywhere.

I took a bus across town to Soho to see a much different sort of twin feature, *Fickle Fatty's Fall* and *The Village Scandal*. They were ridiculous bits of slapstick featuring an overweight buffoon, but I needed a good laugh and found them funny. My eye socket hurt from the strain of sitting in the darkened smoke-filled theatre for so long, but it was worth it. On the cab ride back to Whitehall Court, I made up my mind: if I survived the war, I'd go to the movies every week. I was back in my room by eleven.

I'd love to describe myself as being completely self-assured in those days before setting out as a spy, but the truth was, I was frightened and tense as a drum. I was anxious to get going. I was restless and edgy and just wanted to get on with the damn thing.

✠

Crossley was at my door by eight the next morning and took me downstairs for my last interview with Cumming. We breakfasted together and throughout the meal Cumming only obliquely alluded to my coming operation or the fact that I was going off to Germany. At the time it irritated me. I thought Cumming fancied himself playing a gentleman's game of some sort. One of the rules of the game was to conduct all business over meals and the other was to pretend it was extremely bad form to discuss any of the particulars in any great detail. After breakfast he shook my hand and wished me the best of luck. "Rory, I look forward to seeing you when you get back. I know you're going to do splendidly."

Ewen and I went back upstairs and in my room another change of clothing was laid out. The mysterious Mrs. Chaver, I thought. "This, Rory," Ewen said, "is your disguise. Alex Baumann escaped from hospital last night and stole the clothes of a civilian orderly. Tomorrow morning the police will announce to the papers that in North London he was believed to have accosted an elderly shopkeeper when he was locking up his store and robbed him of over a hundred pounds. He's thought to be trying to make his way to Holland.

"Once you're gone, there'll be a terrible outcry in the papers and the member of Parliament for North Glasgow has kindly consented to raise a question in the Commons as to why the government allows dangerous German prisoners to be at large with virtually no escort. By that time, you will be safely aboard a Norwegian fishing boat headed for Larvik. From there you will make your way into Sweden and across to Germany, all the while pretending to be an American journalist should anyone ask you your business. I shouldn't think you'll have any problem until you get to Germany."

I packed the clothes in a cloth valise that was provided and we drove to Victoria Station, catching the 10:30 train north to Newcastle. We sat in first class, sharing our compartment with an exhausted-looking captain of the Royal Engineers. As soon as the train started to move, the captain almost immediately fell asleep and I felt an overwhelming sense of relief. The whole thing was at last under way. The train chuffed through London's suburbs and out into the late summer countryside. I stared at the fields and farms, thinking how far behind me now were those relatively carefree days at university. The Royal Engineers captain got off at Milton Keynes and left the compartment to us. Ewen immediately pulled my dossier from his brief case.

"Rory, we might as well go over these details a few more times before we get to Newcastle. After this, you'll be on your own." I answered all his questions without hesitation and he seemed satisfied.

"Yesterday, I spoke to an inspector from the London police," Ewen said almost apologetically. "He told me that when one is interrogated and has an alibi, the thing to remember is only to tell them the absolute minimum of information. Be relaxed but keep all your answers to the very minimum. If you start going on, trying to dress things up, you'll be caught up. They'll almost certainly try to test your story, so for God's sake don't try to embellish things if it feels like you are in trouble."

Once again he had me review my story and he began to probe me for any weaknesses in it. It was a useful exercise, but I wished

I could have gone through my tale with Bronau in German. After a half an hour of examination, Ewen stopped and said, "There is one other danger I do have to tell you about. The Norwegian boat you will be escaping on, it has to run the North Sea and it could be attacked by submarines."

I had already assumed that this part of my journey would have some degree of hazard. I wasn't particularly surprised. I showed no expression and said nothing, staring at him, trying out Cumming's advice.

Ewen began to stammer. "It's not a great danger, but when the weather is good some of these men fish in the North Sea and then bring their catch into northern English and Scottish ports. They get paid far more than they would at home. The only problem is, there's a very slight danger from German U-boats. If they catch them heading for our waters, they sink them." I still said nothing. "It—it hasn't happened often ... But you should know," he stammered.

I nodded my head, enjoying my new trick. "That's fine," I said.

Just before our train pulled into Newcastle, I slipped into the lavatory and changed into my new clothes. They were baggy and a touch short. Evidently the hospital orderly I stole these from was shorter and stouter than I was. I felt like the ridiculous Fatty Arbuckle from the films I'd seen the night before.

When we got off we were met by a lantern-jawed Tyneside police inspector. He had grey hair, wire spectacles, and wore a heavy wool suit and felt hat. He looked as if he were ready for a day's shooting on a grouse moor. "Would you be Major Crossley and the other gentleman, then?" Ewen acknowledged we were. "Aye, then follow me, please."

Without speaking to us, he shepherded us into a tiny motorcar and drove us to the dockside. Pulling up a hundred yards away from a long pier, he pointed with his briar pipe. "She's down there. That's her, the one you'll be lookin' for, beside the tug. We get one like that in here every odd week or so in the fine weather."

The boat the policeman was indicating was a small craft. I was disappointed. I'd been expecting some sort of ocean-going tugboat, something with a small private cabin where I could hide away from prying eyes. Instead, the *Grunnhild*, as she was called, was a motor-sailer, forty-five feet at the water line and with a beam of twelve or thirteen feet. She had high gunnels and looked double-ended, like a Newfoundland dory. She was a schooner, rigged with two masts and a boom extending over her stern for trawling. The cabin was little more than a protected cockpit for the boat's wheel.

"Well that takes care of that," I said, doing my best to sound cheerful. "I won't have to worry about getting lost trying to find the galley at meal times."

The policeman stared impassively at the boat. Ewen smiled. "Not to worry, the weather should stay fine and the sea will be calm at this time of year. If there's even a slight breeze, she'll get you into Larvik in a little under four days. And if it's overcast tonight, the U-boats will never see you. I think she'll do splendidly. All you've got to do now is get them to take you aboard. I'm not going forward with you. If the Germans ever make inquiries, we want the skipper to be truthful and say you came alone. This is it." He extended his hand. "I'll see you shortly, my friend. Best of luck."

✚

I walked up to the *Grunnhild* and called out, "Hello there! Is anybody home?" Nobody answered and for a few seconds I sheepishly walked up and down the jetty and then climbed aboard. About an hour later, two men approached, one in his twenties and the other in his early fifties. They were fair-haired and tall, and dressed in heavy dark sweaters. I stood up and waved. They looked at me suspiciously.

"Hello," I said, "are you sailing tonight?" The younger one nodded suspiciously. "I'd like to go with you, if I may? To Norway." They exchanged apprehensive glances. "I can pay. I have to get to Norway and only you can help. Please?"

The older one looked at his son, who spoke rapidly in Norwegian. The father shook his head. I thought this wasn't a good start. I pulled twenty pounds from my pocket and thrust it forward towards them as they clambered aboard. It suddenly dawned on me they probably thought I was a deserter and if they were caught helping me, they would be accomplices. Not a very appealing prospect in wartime Britain.

"I'm an American," I said. "I'm not British. It's all right." I proffered the money again and the son translated.

His father spoke briefly in Norwegian and reached out and took the bills from my hand. His son said haltingly. "We leave in ten minutes, please stay inside." He jerked his head toward the cockpit.

"I really am an American," I said again, pointing to my chest. "I'm not British. This is okay."

The two looked at each other, and the older man smiled at me. I don't think they believed me for an instant. No matter what I said, my eye patch and bandaged hand screamed veteran to them. They were taking no chances. "Please stay inside until after we are sailing."

Once we were under way and clear of the Tyneside harbour, the son introduced himself to me. He was Arne Knudson. He and his father, Peder, lived in a small fishing and farming hamlet ten kilometres from Larvik on Norway's southern coast. "We aren't going directly home. We must fill the boat with fish first," Arne said. "You will have to be very quiet about this when we get to Norway. We are not allowed to be here. What we do is against the law. Norwegians are neutral."

We sailed northeast all night, headed for the extreme south end of the Bjørndalbanken fishing grounds. The night was cold, and dressed as I was in the cast-off suit and cotton shirt, I shivered. Seeing this, Peder draped me with one of the heavy wool blankets that he kept stored in the locker at the back of the wheelhouse. There wasn't much of a wind up and we motored along using their strange little twenty-horsepower kerosene engine. Under power with the sails and the engine, we chugged forward at a good clip. As a landsman, I had no real means of estimating our speed, but I reckoned judging by the speed the occasional bit of flotsam floated by us, we were moving along at a respectable pace.

The kerosene engine on the *Grunnhild* was something I had never seen before or since. It worked like a charm. Peder had installed it several years earlier and they normally only used it in a tight situation—such as getting away from English coastal waters in wartime. Arne proudly told me it was an old experimental design from Denmark and his father often repaired it with homemade parts.

At dawn, we flew a large Norwegian flag from the mainmast. In these waters, we were once again a neutral vessel. We reached the Bjørndalbanken two days later in the late afternoon and spent the rest of the day and most of the evening trawling for herring. Throughout that first day on the fishing banks the sun shone and the weather was magnificent. Most of the time I was at the helm while Arne and Peder worked the nets. In an effort to make myself useful, I tried pulling nets for an hour, mostly with one hand. I had to give it up because I had trouble keeping up and succeeded in shredding my bandages and aggravating my wounds.

The effort wasn't entirely in vain. I sensed that Arne and Peder were more willing to accept me for having made the effort to help out. Neither of them asked me throughout that first day how I came to be in such an injured state, although I suspect when they chattered to one another in their sing-song Norwegian they were no doubt discussing who I was and what I was doing wounded, with no baggage and ill-fitting clothes. Whatever they thought, they treated me well.

We motored in large circles and hauled in nets of struggling, gleaming black herring. The hold filled rapidly and the small boat rode lower and more steadily on the water. In a way, I was in awe of these men. For all their initial reluctance to take me on, out at sea, Peder and Arne Knudson treated me as if I was a long-time crew member. They had a practical outlook: quiet, capable, and matter of fact. Late on our fourth day out, Arne could see I was enjoying myself. The sun shone warmly on my face and a light breeze kept the sea at a comfortable swell. "It's not always so nice out here. My father lost two brothers fishing in such waters. That's why I speak English. My father wanted me go to the Normal School and now I am a teacher at the Collegiate in Larvik. I only do the fishing in summer. Life on the boats is not so good in the autumn and the spring times."

As the day progressed, I discovered Arne and Peder were grateful Norway was out of the war, but both were anxious to see the Germans defeated. Norway had already lost half her merchant marine fleet to the German policy of unrestricted U-boat warfare, and every sea-going family in that most maritime of nations had a relative listed amongst the dead and missing. For the more intrepid amongst them, running the U-boats became a bit of a game, albeit a deadly one. Norwegian fishermen could sell their catch in England for far higher prices than they could ever fetch at home, but they bitterly resented the inherent danger of being cold-bloodedly sunk by a U-boat for going about their lawful business. Feelings in Norway, I was told, ran high against the Germans. Sweden and Denmark, Arne said disdainfully, "were not so inclined," as they both prospered through much higher levels of trade with Germany.

Having heard all this, the talk very guardedly got round to my circumstances. "Why do you want to get to Norway so much?" Arne said with a sceptical look on his face.

I was careful in describing my situation. I told them my name was John Harker. I was an American journalist working for the *Boston Globe* newspaper. I had been wounded covering the British defence of the Somme and I had been convalescing in a military hospital in Newcastle. I wanted to get to Germany to cover the war from the German side as well. The British knew of my intentions and refused to let me go. The British government cancelled my visa while I was in hospital and rather than go all the way back to the United States and to try to make my way into Germany, I decided to escape from hospital and get to Germany as best I could. "That's how I ended up in these stolen clothes hiding on your boat."

Arne translated all this for his father. Peder's leathery face lit up at the explanation. He obviously liked my account. Even though he wasn't keen to have me report the German side of things, he was an independent sort and it was obvious he was partial to my disregard for authority. Following this explanation, Peder talked rapidly in Norwegian to Arne for several minutes.

Arne turned to me. "My father says he will take you to Sweden in a few days after we get home. He thinks you are a good man. People should know both sides of the war. He says if you go and write about the Germans, it will help make America want to join the fighting and the war will end soon."

We sailed into the Skagerrak, keeping well south of the Norwegian coast as the wind turned on us, blowing strong and driving cold spray from the north. Low iron-grey clouds and rain soon followed and the tiny *Grunnhild* pitched and rolled in alarmingly steep seas. Peder and Arne grew quiet but didn't look unduly concerned. I shivered in my blanket and was glad when we changed course and headed north into the wind, on a direct course for our harbour south of Larvik.

Larvik appeared as a cluster of lights off our portside. Within the hour we glided into a protected anchorage and tied up to an ancient bollard alongside an unpainted fishing shanty. The smell of the land was richer, earthier, and sharply different from the sea air. From a building not far off, lights and happy voices came tripping down through the drizzle and the darkness. Laughing women and children in their nightgowns holding kerosene storm lamps surrounded the *Grunnhild*. There was a dog barking and racing up and down the pier. Farther along the cove, a house began to flash its lights at us and someone away in the dark began banging furiously on a pot. For these men, homecoming was a time of triumph and uninhibited joy. I stood on the deck of the *Grunnhild* watching the hugging and cheering and mirth. A safe homecoming was clearly a cause for major celebration. With so much of the world facing hardship and loss as part of their daily lives, it was insane that the rest of us so readily tolerated war.

I spent the next four days at the Knudsons'. I was put up in a loft in "the new building," next to one of the grass-roofed outbuildings attached to the farmhouse. I slept on a straw-filled palliasse under a goose-down quilt. Peder's wife, Annalise, gave me an old sweater of his to wear and I took my meals with the family. At dinner on my second night, I met Arne's fiancée. She was a tall blonde woman with high cheekbones and piercing blue eyes. She was such an astonishing beauty that the sight of her made me seriously think about staying put in Norway. She curtseyed to me when we were introduced, and had she not been blushing, I'd have sworn she was mocking me with her formality and old fashioned manners.

It was a healthy four days. The air was fresh and the food was plentiful and nourishing. I felt entirely relaxed and completely at home on that farm. I'd be a liar if I didn't admit that the thought of staying here for the rest of the war crossed my mind. Here, life had a cosy certainty; and compared to dreary, dirty old London or the murderously squalid trenches of France and Flanders, this Norwegian fishing village was the Garden of Paradise. The farm buildings and fishing shanties sprinkled along the coast were unpainted but scrupulously clean. The people in their own quiet way were matter of fact, friendly, and accepting. Today, these men women and children would be categorized as living in poverty; but it would be nonsense. For in their vigorously simple lives they found strength, dignity, and pride. They harvested and caught their own food; their woodsheds were filled and they were all in robust good health. It was a fairy-tale picture of a peaceable kingdom. The Knudsons, and many like them, worked hard and lived their lives to a rhythm that must have been unchanged for centuries—except I suppose for those centuries when their ancestors took it upon themselves to rape, murder, and plunder their way across much of France and England. It was difficult to imagine such serene and peaceful people ever having been the scourge of anything.

My four days at the Knudsons' farm were spent emptying herring from the *Grunnhild* and filling barrels that were taken by horse and cart into Larvik for processing. Nets were dried and mended; the boat's hold was scrubbed and sluiced clean and a hundred chores were done around the farm.

The morning we set sail for Sweden, I pulled Arne aside and asked him if he had any Swedish currency. I showed him the rest of my money and told him it was of no value to me. "Arne," I said, "you should have all of this. There's sixty pounds here; I won't be needing English money and I know you and your family can use it. If you give me enough Swedish money so I can get something to eat and to get me to Germany, I'd be very grateful."

Sixty pounds was a large sum of money in those days and I'm sure it would have a gone a long way for him. He didn't look in the least bit surprised or greedy. He seemed appreciative and rather formally said, "Thank you, John. We shall do whatever we can to help you."

When we pushed off from the jetty, there was a crowd of Knudson women and children as well as a small army of neighbours to see us off. In the morning's brilliant sunshine, the farewells were cheerful but restrained: good-natured and optimistic as opposed to the exuberant greetings when we arrived. I was sorry to go. I wanted to melt into their way of life and never be heard from again. I told myself it was my duty, I owed it to my dead comrades, and that I was motivated by a sense of adventure and pride. But I lied. I tried to console myself thinking that Norway mustn't have been that wonderful, or a quarter of a million Norwegians wouldn't have emigrated to North America in the last thirty years. I waved good-bye with my good hand and wondered what Sweden would be like. It couldn't be any nicer than this little windblown patch of coastal paradise.

10

THE GRUNNHILD motored out into the waters of the Skager-rak and promptly ran into a brisk wind coming out off the Baltic. The instant Peder and Arne raised their sails we were swept into a choppy sea with an irregular swell. Within the hour I became violently ill and was clinging to the starboard gunnels for dear life. It was a long, wearying journey to Sweden. Despite keeping the mountain-tops of Norway and the Swedish coast in sight for all of the ninety-mile trip, I was sick for the entire time. Unlike our trip across the North Sea when we didn't see another vessel, on the crossing to Sweden the war and the blockade of Germany were very much in evidence. To starboard, off on the horizon we could see two lines of smoky plumes indicating what I presumed was the Royal Navy's screen of cruisers and dreadnoughts as they steamed back and forth maintaining their chokehold on Germany's Baltic approaches. I was so sick, I didn't care. The British ships, if they were remotely interested, could see we were a fishing boat flying a Norwegian flag and they left us to ourselves.

After seven hours of constant tacking in the face of a strong easterly wind we sailed into the harbour at Göteborg. I lay on the deck feebly holding onto the gunnels. I'm certain my face was green. Two stern-looking, grey-coated Swedish policemen with theatrical side-burns and moustaches were waiting on the quayside. They called out to us and Arne and Peder both answered. I was surprised to see they could converse so easily in Swedish. Arne and Peder pointed at me and guffawed uproariously at my sickness and the Swedish harbour police, after a good laugh and cursory walk about on our boat, moved on. I got up to my feet rather unsteadily and climbed ashore on to the quayside. Except for my eye patch, I suppose I could have passed easily enough for a Scandinavian fisherman.

Wearing the old fisherman's sweater and with my jacket draped over my shoulder, I walked the streets of old Göteborg with Arne and Peder. Arne insisted that we get something to eat; and then, after we had "some good Swedish food," they would help me buy a train ticket to the Swedish ferry port of Trelleborg.

Climbing off the *Grunnhild*, I was too sick to feel like eating, but after walking about for a short time, my balance and later my appetite returned. We ate in a dingy, low-ceilinged tavern with dark wooden furniture and smoke-blackened beams. The tavern had probably been there for three hundred years. The food was delicious. I wolfed down a huge bowl of some kind of thick soup made from fish and potatoes, and Arne and Peder consumed monstrous portions of reindeer stew. At the end of his meal, Arne looked up at me impassively and wiped his mouth with his sleeve. "It is good that you have eaten as much as possible here; there's not so much to eat in Germany. Now, let us see you to the train."

The train station was just a short stroll from the tavern. When the time came to bid goodbye to Arne and his father, I was certain they both wanted to say something more than they did. Arne shook my good hand and said, "Good luck and God bless," while his father looked on worriedly. I was touched, but also alarmed. I hoped they hadn't seen through my alibi. Once Arne said his farewells, his father, with something halfway between a hug and a clap on the back, let me know he was anxious for me. Then they were gone.

I felt completely alone on that platform and wanted desperately to go with them back to their hamlet near Larvik. More than any other time since I met Cumming, I genuinely considered skipping out on Germany. For a few seconds I pictured myself in Norway: leading a healthy normal life on the sea and farm, herring suppers by a warm fire, laughing blonde children, and blue-eyed, blushing women. It was an idyllic and vivid possibility; and much more appealing than my harebrained future, a future that had an excellent chance of ending propped up against a brick wall and shot for a spy. Returning to Norway was more than tempting, and staying on the platform was an act of the will. I waited apprehensively in the station's gloom for about an hour. As dusk fell, the train for Trelleborg came steaming and chuffing into sight. Once again, I had a chance to escape from a fate not of my own choosing, and for reasons I've never fully understood, I carried on with what I'd committed to do.

The coach I climbed onto was empty and the whole trip to Trelleborg was in the dark. I hoped it wasn't some kind of an omen.

✠

That night the train stopped at several towns as well as a number of small villages. Some time in the night, it pulled over for an interminable length of time at a siding that seemed to be inexplicably placed in the middle of a forest. There was a lot of shunting and banging of cars and the conductor officiously walked back and forth through my compartment. Throughout the trip, nobody spoke to me or seemed to take much notice of me, and I was content to sit as inconspicuously as possible doing my best to sleep. We pulled into Trelleborg just before dawn.

When I got out of the train I was famished; but as the sky was still grey in the east and it was a long time yet before any shops or restaurants would be open, I made do with walking about and looking as purposeful as it was possible for a stranger to appear at five o'clock in the morning. I walked for several hours and became familiar with the docks, and twice made my way into the adjoining farming areas. In 1916, Trelleborg was a long, winding coastal town of brick and timber buildings on the south coast of Sweden. As towns go, it was pleasant, tidy, and efficient looking, and I'd have liked to have spent more time there if things had been different.

By eight o'clock, Trelleborg was coming to life and I made my way back to the docks to buy a ticket to Germany. Trelleborg, as Arne advised me, was a Swedish shipping centre with numerous ferries linking it to Denmark, Finland, Germany, and the Baltic states. I walked to the nearest wicket and asked as confidently as I could in German for a ticket for the next ferry to a north German port. The elderly man behind the screen was smoking a large meerschaum pipe and seemed to be hard of hearing. He began to shout and pushed an incomprehensible Swedish timetable at me. Looking at the matrix before me, I recognized the names Trelleborg and Lubeck and asked to be given a ticket on the next ship to that port. I repeated my request and the old man began jabbering again at the top of his lungs.

I was alarmed; he was drawing attention to me. I was considering giving up buying a ticket and returning later in the day, when a stylish and very pretty young woman with shingle-cut blonde hair and a broad-brimmed feathery hat explained to me in halting but clear German that the next boat to Lubeck did not leave until late the next afternoon. I explained that this would be fine and through her good offices managed to purchase a ticket for the two o'clock departure on the SS *Konung Gustav V*. I asked her if she could advise me of a place where I could stay that was "nearby, cheap, and clean." She pointed me in the direction of the Skateholm Hotel, not far from where we were. I thanked her profusely and watched forlornly as she smiled at me, tucked her purse under her arm, and sashayed gracefully out of the ticket office.

I spent my time in Trelleborg in the hotel reading German newspapers. I only ventured from my room to take my meals. I was grateful to Arne and Peder. In exchange for my pounds, they left me a generous sum in Swedish kroner. At 1:30 the next day, I was standing in a short line of commercial travellers on the *Konung Gustav V*'s gangplank. I was easily the scruffiest-looking man in the queue. Despite my appearance, my trip to Lubeck was uneventful. The usual passenger service had been severely curtailed by the war and the ship's upper decks were largely deserted.

I kept to myself and found a forward seat with a good view in the second-class lounge. I buried myself reading old copies of the newspapers *Berliner Zeitung* and *Vorwärts*. Looking up from my papers, I saw the skyline of Trelleborg recede on our port side and several hours later the lights on the coast of Germany loomed up from the horizon over our bow. From where I could see, a flock of sea gulls on the ship's railings played a never-ending game of swirling and squawking while bumping one another off their perch at the front of the ship. There wasn't much news in the two newspapers and what was reported was depressing; both were full of rationing, casualty lists, and lurid accounts of drama and valour at the front.

When the ferry docked, I became very conscious of not having any luggage. To give myself some credibility, I carefully folded my two newspapers under my arm and officiously strolled off to descend the gangplank. My heart was in my mouth. The other travellers all looked rather bored, but my pulse was racing and my palms were sweating heavily. Underneath an electric light, two German sailors stood guard at the bottom of the gangplank. They had rifles with fixed bayonets slung over their shoulders and they suspiciously scrutinized the papers of everyone getting off. I shouldn't have worried that I didn't have papers, but I did. My stomach was in a knot. The tallest sailor, with a big black moustache and a badly pitted face, demanded, "Papers! And where's your luggage?"

I heaved a sigh that was only partly an act and pulled myself into my most commanding posture. "I have no papers or luggage because I am an escaped German officer. I am Oberleutnant Alex Baumann. I've made my way here from England. Now, please take me to the nearest German military headquarters. I have had a very long journey."

My heart sank. I hoped the sailors would greet me with admiration; but instead, they fixed me with a disbelieving stare. "What do you have in those newspapers. One of them yanked the papers out from under my arm and glared up at me. "*Vorwärts*? You read the socialist papers? Are you a socialist, my friend?"

"I'm not your friend. I am Oberleutnant Alex Baumann and I am an escaped German officer. These papers were left on the magazine tray in the second-class lounge of this ship and I read whatever I want to, without permission from you. Now, take me to the nearest German military headquarters."

"How do we know you aren't a radical socialist from Russia?" The youngest sailor snarled.

"If I was a socialist subversive, I'd hardly be demanding to be taken to the nearest military headquarters, now would I?" I hesitated for a second and then chose to get angry. "What's going on here? Take me to your officer now. You'll see things are as I say."

I was led off to the guardroom and locked into a small cell. Twenty minutes later, a bearded petty officer appeared and began the entire routine once again.

When we finished, he looked unconvinced and said, "You will stay here. I must confirm some things yet."

An hour passed and the small guardroom remained plunged in silence. I was hungry and had to go to the toilet. I was sure I'd been forgotten. Finally, the doors opened and the petty officer appeared with a short vizefeldwebel of the military police behind him. The military policeman was about six inches shorter than I. He wore a forage cap and had a dark complexion, prominent ears, and a round pumpkin-like head. He may have been no beauty but there was nothing funny about him. His brown eyes had a frightening intelligence in them. I felt like a bird in the gaze of a cobra. "So, you claim to be an escaped German prisoner of war? I am afraid until we can prove your identity you will be kept under close security. Once you prove who you say you are, you will be treated as an officer. Now you must come with me."

I was handcuffed and led away to the front seat of a waiting lorry and crammed between the driver and the military policeman. We drove out of the seaside town. The vizefeldwebel didn't speak to me throughout the drive. "You will talk to one of the staff officers at North Central Military District Headquarters. He'll decide what he'll do with you next."

We drove steadily through a series of towns and villages for under an hour and turned into a fenced military Kaserne. Inside the barracks, the lorry stopped on a short avenue lined with magnificent chestnut trees before a large three-storey headquarters building. I was later to learn that I was taken to the village of Kritzmow, a Headquarters garrison town near the city of Rostock. Inside, I was taken to what I presumed was some kind of orderly room and deposited on a wooden chair in the middle of an empty office filled with clerks' desks and filing cabinets. The vizefeldwebel smoked a cigarette in front of me and flipped through a magazine. He certainly left the impression that I was unwelcome and that he disbelieved my story.

"This is a wonderful reception I'm getting. I risk my life to escape and I'm treated like a criminal," I said. The NCO merely looked up from his reading and shrugged. "There will be an officer here shortly."

Twenty minutes later, a tall, dark-haired, middle-aged Guards captain in a well-tailored field-grey uniform walked into the room. He was broad-shouldered and athletic-looking, and would have appeared healthy if he didn't have the face of someone who consistently works too hard. He had a nervous habit of compulsively brushing his rather long hair back over his scalp. He had an open face, but the eyes were sunken and spoke of extreme fatigue. I noticed he was wearing the red collar tabs and striped trousers of the General Staff. He clicked his heels and gave a slight stiff bow. "Forgive me for keeping you waiting, Oberleutnant Baumann. My name is Captain Von Lignow. As you can imagine, we were not expecting you." Turning to the NCO he said, "Vizefeldwebel Kleer, please remove this gentleman's handcuffs. Now, Oberleutnant, you must begin your story from the beginning if you please?"

I began the catechism I'd rehearsed fifty times with Ewen Crossley. Von Lignow offered me a cigarette and did his best to sound

encouraging. Both he and Vizefeldwebel Kleer took notes, although
Kleer said nothing throughout the interview and whenever I looked
at him, he stared back impassively. Von Lignow asked several questions. He struck me straight away as being intelligent and observant. I expected that. Seeing the red tabs and red-striped trousers, I
was in no doubt the German army was taking my arrival seriously.

Staff officers from the Greater General Staff were recruited from
the nation's intellectual elite, and to be a member of this small body
of men was enormously prestigious. General Staff officers numbered
fewer than two hundred officers at the war's outset. They were unof-
ficially the intellect and creative nucleus of the German army. General Staff officers, quite unlike similarly designated officers in British
or French armies, were not at all the same as those officers who
merely did staff jobs. As I learned in my briefings in the hospital
basement, General Staff officers served only in the most vital operational, logistic, and intelligence posts within the Imperial German
Army. They all possessed authority that vastly exceeded their rank.
General Staff captains and majors on behalf of their commanders
routinely assumed responsibility for the day-to-day running of divisions, corps, and in some cases even armies. As the war progressed,
within their own fraternity they made virtually all major decisions
affecting the German wartime economy.

Junior Staff officers on the Greater General Staff were rigorously
selected. To get around the army's propensity for promoting on the
basis of seniority, they simply took on the authority of the senior
officer on whatever staff they belonged to. Captains and majors on
the General Staff not infrequently, in the name of their superior
commander, overruled commanders of much higher rank. On my
arrival I'd not expected to be met by one of these men. Nor, to tell
the truth, had I expected any of them to be as personable as Von
Lignow. I'd never met one of these men before; and even though I'm
half-German, I fully expected a double-chinned, arrogant Prussian
tyrant. Von Lignow, on the other hand, was a fit, mild-mannered
aristocrat of the old school. As well as exuding a penetrating intelligence, he had charm, infectious energy, and a flattering sense of

concentration that made you feel he was fascinated with everything you had to say. As I told him the story of my capture and escape, he stopped taking notes and listened appreciatively while Kleer scribbled away furiously.

"Your story is fascinating in every respect, and I must say, Alex, I have nothing but admiration for you. But just so we are clear on a few points," Von Lignow said to me, "can you please tell me again who your commanding officer was, and tell me once more, precisely, where and how you were taken prisoner? Of course, we shall have to confirm this; but be assured, as soon as we do, we can stop all this questioning and suspicion," he said with a sweep of his arm. In contrast, Kleer nudged his chair forward and leaned closer across the desk towards me.

"Certainly, sir. My unit was the Fourth Landwehr Battalion of the 153rd Thuringian Infantry Regiment, Ninth Landwehr Division. Major Schreiner, a regular army officer, commanded my unit. In my last days before capture, I was temporarily commanding Number Three Company. There were no other officers left alive. My company commander, Captain Becker, had been killed the day before.

"On the evening of the 2nd of June, after our third attempt in two days at penetrating the English lines, we broke into their forward trenches near the village of Auchonvillers. The final thing I remember was moving down an English communication trench to re-group and reorganize what was left of my company. I was told my wounds were probably caused by the shrapnel from an English Mills bomb. I can only suppose I was knocked unconscious and wounded in the English counter-attack. I don't remember anything else until I came to in a trench with other wounded English and German soldiers. Our objective had been recaptured and I had become a prisoner." I looked wearily at the two men opposite me.

Von Lignow nodded his head. "Thank you. We shall contact the Ninth Landwehr divisional headquarters; and, as soon as we confirm things, we can end this interrogation." Von Lignow stood up, clicked his heels, and taking Kleer's notes left the room.

Vizefeldwebel Kleer leaned back in his chair and looked at me suspiciously. "Oberleutnant, tell me, where did you do your officer training?" he asked, sucking on a tooth. "I too find your story fascinating." He looked at me coldly as if trying to intimidate me. "I have heard of some of you Americans who came over at the beginning of the war."

"I'm flattered you know about us. I don't believe there were so many of us, Vizefeldwebel. Not more than a thousand I'm told. My family was German and I have always considered myself as German as you are. The answer to your question, however, is the Landwehr Officer Training School and Depot outside Schönebeck. I was in Number Two Wing. Now tell me something, Vizefeldwebel. Were you a policeman before the war?"

Kleer was not in the least bit put off by my condescension or aggression. "Yes. Very good of you to guess. I was a policeman and it's my job to be suspicious. When I first saw you I thought that there was something—something, not quite right here. Is there anything you're not telling us, Oberleutnant?"

I was alarmed with this turn in the conversation and to conceal my fear, I pretended to be angry. "Don't be ridiculous! There's nothing to tell other than what I've said already. When Captain Von Lignow returns he'll be able to prove I'm who I say I am. At which point, you, Vizefeldwebel, will stop calling me Oberleutnant and begin calling me sir. I'm tired of having to demonstrate my loyalty to every one I meet in the army." I raised my hand to display my tattered bandages. "If you want evidence of my dedication I can show proof." I flipped my eye patch up to reveal a gaping eye socket.

Kleer was unfazed. He took a long drag on his cigarette. "As I said, my duty is to be suspicious. Are you a radical socialist, Oberleutnant? Do you know Germany is seething with radical socialist agitators? Why would you choose to come ashore from Sweden attempting to surrender to the navy with a socialist newspaper tucked conspicuously under your arm? You won't be the first socialist deserter that has come over to us from Sweden and tried to corrupt the navy. Do you know, your newspaper, *Vorwärts*, it should be banned? It's a front for Marxists, pacifists, socialists, and every other defeatist in Germany. What do you expect to do now that you are back in the Fatherland?"

"Something worthwhile to help win the war, Vizefeldwebel." I was rattled and uncertain how to deal with Kleer. As a policeman, he was much better at this game than I was, and I have to confess, his steely manner frightened me. Instead of trying to throw him off my trail, I made the foolish mistake of insulting him. "I'll probably do something a lot more substantial than sitting safely around a dry, heated office trying to catch pacifists."

Kleer was stung by my remarks but he kept his cool. "That's fine. We shall see how your story checks out, but in the meantime, I do have more questions I want you to answer." Kleer peppered me for ten minutes. He asked me about my family, my unit, the locations my battalion had been garrisoned in when we were out of the line, and a dozen other aspects of military life. He then reviewed my capture and escape in painstaking detail. I wasn't stumped by anything he said, but I did try to drag out each answer by protesting vehemently as to my treatment.

When Von Lignow returned I was shouting. "I don't have to put up with this, Vizefeldwebel, I am a German officer and I did not fight and escape from the English to be badgered and insulted by a village constable in uniform!"

Von Lignow looked amused. "Vizefeldwebel Kleer, we owe our guest an apology. He is indeed who he says he is. In addition, I have the pleasure of informing you, Alex, that for your actions in the first few days of June of this summer, the Ninth Landwehr Division awarded Oberleutnant Alex Baumann what they thought was a posthumous Iron Cross Second Class. Alex, I am truly sorry for having put you through this interrogation and I apologize. For reasons I know you will completely understand, I instructed Vizefeldwebel Kleer to be as tough on you as possible. But you are obviously an officer who knows the meaning of the word duty and we have been forced to distrust you. You will forgive us; and please, allow me to be the first to congratulate you on your escape and your Iron Cross."

Imitating the Prussian gentlemen I had seen so often in my summers in Germany, I bowed my head and clicked my heels in response to his apology. I was astonished. Alex really had gone down fighting like a lion. Not that I ever doubted the man's courage, but the ribbon of the Iron Cross sticking out from my buttonhole was a godsend. It would not only make me much more believable, but my new-found credibility guaranteed me an extra measure of safety. I needed that, for under Kleer's insistent interrogation I was frightened. In the few hours I'd been in Germany, Vizefeldwebel Kleer had as much as told me he thought I was some kind of a fraud. I was terrified there would be a thousand others like him who would grill me constantly about my background—but as an escaped POW, with visible wounds and now with the ribbon of an Iron Cross on my tunic, I instantly became unassailable. The Iron Cross would act like a charm to ward off evil. With such credentials, one would have to be an absolute boor to cast doubt on my credibility.

Von Lignow clapped me on both shoulders. "We need more men like you, Alex." He was beaming with pleasure. "With leaders like you, Germany's going to win this war. You are going to come with me over to the Headquarters officers' mess. There we'll feed you, give you something to drink, and then get you back into a proper uniform." Turning to Kleer. "Thank you so much, Vizefeldwebel. As always, you have done an excellent job. We could not have known. You know, Alex, Vizefeldwebel Kleer here happened to be at our headquarters for the last several days. He is working with counter-intelligence in Berlin and today he happened to be up doing some routine liaison work. We have no counter-intelligence troops here at District headquarters and so we thought he might as well respond to the navy when they called about you. This is one for your stories back at your Berlin mess, eh, Vizefeldwebel?"

Kleer, ignoring the implied rebuke, looked blankly at Von Lignow. He stiffened to attention and nodded knowingly towards me. "I have no doubt we will all hear more from Oberleutnant Baumann." He turned and fixed me with his unnerving stare. "Sir! I'm sure our paths will cross again." He put on his cap, saluted, and left the room.

When the precise clicking of Kleer's steel-cleated heels faded from the hallway, Von Lignow laughed. "You know these counter-intelligence types? In peacetime, Kleer was a Berlin police sergeant, spent his time bullying pimps and small-time crooks. He's angry, trusts nobody and never will; I'm sure he feels badly he couldn't have you shot. It's the closest he'll ever get to fighting. Now, let's go to the mess. You need something to eat and we'll have a drink; your escape is the only good news I've heard in a month."

WITHIN THREE DAYS, I was packed off on the train to the Zweiberg veterans' hospital to see a series of doctors. There I was prodded and poked and put through a regime of physiotherapy exercises for my hand. But the real reason I was sent to Zweiberg was because it had a reputation for doing first-class work on men with a wide range of eye wounds.

My first day at the hospital was disturbing. I'd never before seen so many men who were blind or partially blinded. One whole wing of the hospital was filled with silent men, sitting straight up and straining to recognize the world around them. It wasn't at all like the atmosphere of Hammerwood Park's convalescent hospital. In many of the rooms of Hammerwood there was a sense of hope. Most men at Hammerwood had lost a limb and were steadily learning to cope. Zweiberg was filled with men who, through the loss of their sight, were imprisoned for life. They couldn't see the world around them and their futures were much harder to visualize. For them, adjustment to the world was more profound. Most had their heads cocked backwards or to one side, all of them straining to force their ears to compensate for the loss of their eyes.

I was fortunate: I could see perfectly with one eye. Zweiberg was like witnessing an unpleasant dream. I was lucky enough to be referred to an ophthalmologist by the name of Dr. Uvar Krittinger.

Long before the war, Dr. Krittinger had been a pioneer in the field of ocular prosthetics. He had a small staff at the hospital, and on the strength of a phone call from a General Staff officer he agreed to see me as soon as I could get there. At Zweiberg I was fitted with a glass eye, and if I was staring at you face on, it looked remarkably real. But most of the time I chose not to wear it. It was uncomfortable to put in; and once I had it in, I could only stand wearing it for a few hours before the edges of my eye became inflamed. I carried it in a leather pouch wrapped in a piece of silk and returned to Kritzmow wearing my black eye patch.

✠

Two days after my return from Zweiberg Hospital, I was sitting beneath an ancient stuffed stag's head in the foyer of the East Prussian Military District Headquarters officers' mess. I was fed, rested, and clothed in the field-grey uniform of a landwehr junior officer. I felt at ease in a German officer's uniform. The handmade officer's jackboots they issued me were of excellent quality and were as comfortable as a pair of old slippers. The only thing that I found myself a little self-conscious with was the hat that I held in my hand. I'd hoped to be given a forage cap. Instead, I was issued with a "pickelhaube," the spiked leather helmet, which was the trademark of the Kaiser's Imperial Army.

Despite my reservations about my headgear, I was pleased with myself; I'd successfully spent the previous forty-eight hours in debriefings with officers who were interested in Allied morale and preparedness. No one was surprised, or happy, with my descriptions of canned meat and fresh vegetables served to POWs, or, that from the little I'd seen, the British civil population was unlikely to rise up in rebellion. The officers debriefing me merely shook their heads and muttered that the navy's submarine blockade of England wasn't working.

After those debriefings, I was unjustly smug. Playing the role of Alex Baumann was simpler than I'd imagined. I sat in the foyer

while staff officers and officers from nearby training establish-
ments filed past me on their way to lunch. Several of them, men
I had never seen before, nodded to me and smiled good naturedly
in greeting. My acceptance in my new surroundings was virtually
complete; and, except for the questioning of Vizefeldwebel Kleer,
my transformation to a German officer was astonishingly smooth.

My new-found mentor, Captain Von Lignow, treated me like
a younger brother. On my second day back at the headquarters,
when he realized I didn't have a watch, Von Lignow reached into his
desk and gave me a fob watch of his own. He said it had belonged
to him when he was in school and I shouldn't worry; he owned
two others. Von Lignow was an interesting character. As the middle son of a titled but not-so-well-to-do rural Thuringian family,
Captain Wolfgang Von Lignow was a bit of an oddity amongst the
land-owning Prussian Junkers of the Greater German General Staff.
He spoke German with a slight but noticeable rural Thuringian
accent. As I was to find out later, he also spoke excellent English
and French with a thick accent. He played the piano brilliantly, was
an exceptional horseman and fencing master, and was an amateur
astronomer who before the war had been regularly called upon to
lecture to learned societies.

Wolfgang Von Lignow was an enormously capable man; and,
as I was soon to learn, was suspect in a General Staff that despite
its rigorous intellectual traditions, prided itself on being single-
minded and brutally clever in the engineering and mechanics of
war. A graduate of the military academy at Lichterfelde, he had
seen service in several Guards regiments. He was accepted into the
General Staff as an oberleutnant, an unusual occurrence as most
junior General Staff officers were captains. He was married, from
the photograph on his desk, to an obviously very pretty woman.
They had two infant daughters.

On the outbreak of war, Von Lignow was serving as a company
commander in a Guards Shutzen Battalion on the Russian front.
After the winter battles on the Masurian Lakes in 1915, he was repatriated in order to put his considerable intellectual talents to the

task of mobilizing Germany's home front. When I arrived at his headquarters, he was reorganizing and coordinating civil transport for most of northern Germany. I was waiting for him as we were to have lunch together in the mess and he was to advise me of my new employment.

"Alex, I'm afraid our friend Kleer has been making his presence felt since returning to Berlin," Von Lignow said. "There's a telegram from the office of the chief of staff of counterintelligence. It says you should not be employed in any sensitive position until such time as you have been thoroughly vetted and confirmed as absolutely reliable. Can you imagine the impudence of such a man? We'd have won this war a year ago if people who knew better didn't listen to fools like him in Berlin. Now clerks and imbeciles are dictating to us. I'm sorry Alex, with your language skills I had arranged a very useful job for you in Intelligence. Instead, I'm afraid, I would ask if in the meantime you would accept a position on the staff of this headquarters? It's not so much, but it's important. I need someone with brains and resourcefulness to work on the strategic transport desk for North Central District." He looked at me steadily. His offer reminded me of my company commander in the Patricia's asking me if I would "care" to take out a patrol. It was excruciatingly polite, but it wasn't really something I was in a position to refuse.

"I've no problem with that, sir," I said. "I came back to do whatever's asked of me."

"Excellent. Again, I'm sorry. Fools like Kleer are forever making our lives difficult; now let's eat and I'll explain to you the details of the new position."

Our meal was much as I expected: a thin slice of cheese, watery vegetable soup, heavy, tasteless bread, coffee made from acorns, and wrinkly apples for desert. Breakfast had been identical. The mess waiter was an elderly civilian from the local neighbourhood and the linen on the table was threadbare. We ate at long tables decorated with polished candelabra flanked by small pewter statues of German soldiers from past battles. The mess maintained its traditions of gentility, but the atmosphere was one of bleak determination. No one tarried for conversation after eating. Germany was besieged and hungry; and, as Von Lignow explained, the country now needed men to keep things moving.

He put his cutlery down and spoke quietly. "Alex, as a Headquarters officer with responsibilities in transport, you'll need willpower as much as brains to be successful in what you do. I want you to serve as a Staff officer of strategic transport. You are to keep an eye on all civilian road and rail transport in the lines of communication and rear area of the German Eighth Army. This is a big job. Your area of responsibility stretches from Koningsburg in East Prussia to Augustow in Russian Poland. You will command nothing, but you will be the eyes and ears of this headquarters and ultimately responsible to ensure that things happen on behalf of the army. If you come across a problem you can't handle, call me. If I can't solve it for you, I will advise the North Central District chief of staff, Colonel Von Steiger. He has absolute authority in all matters of military-civil concern and that's just about everything at this point. Your authority to make things happen stems directly from General Groener, director of the Army Food Supply Office, and from there through the Staff chain to General Ludendorff, Eighth Army's chief of staff."

Von Lignow toyed delicately with his silverware. "So, believe me, you will not lack authority; you won't be a General Staff officer, but you will operate with my confidence in these areas. You will need to have authority. With ever fewer resources, you will have to keep things running smoothly and you must ensure no one quits on us. There will be no one to teach you your job. I've no fear that will be a problem. A volunteer officer from America with the Iron Cross who has been seriously wounded and has single-handedly escaped from England will have no difficulty figuring out how to make a few motor trucks and wagons run smoothly. We'll win this war as much in the Fatherland as we will in the trenches of France and Russia; and you, Alex, will help us do it."

I thanked him for his confidence and when he got up to leave the table he said, "Oh, I almost forgot. Tomorrow the Grand Duke of

Saxe-Weimar will be here. He visits us every so often. I've arranged for him to present you your Iron Cross before lunch. I'm sorry, there'll be no parade; we've no time for that here. We'll do it in the mess salon. Come by this evening and see me for a more detailed briefing on your new responsibilities. In the meantime, get yourself some maps of the area and talk to the commanding officer of the district transportation battalion. He'll give you an idea what kind of civilian and military resources you will be responsible for."

✠

I never did get a chance to speak to Von Lignow that evening. When I went to his office, I was told by a clerk that he was in conference with the District chief of staff and would not be free for many hours. The next day I presented myself at the adjutant's office prior to being awarded the Iron Cross. The adjutant was a plump, cheerful, older man with a gravelly voice, silver-rimmed glasses, and the Kaiser's long-service medal; he was probably in his early sixties or late fifties, and, if he was out of uniform, could easily have passed for a country butcher. He was jovial and came around from his desk to check over my uniform for me.

"You look well turned out in that new uniform, Alex. It's not every day we get a District headquarters officer presented with an Iron Cross."

We walked over to the mess and waited for ten minutes with a handful of other officers who I didn't know. All of them had been detailed to provide a respectable crowd for me. Captain Von Lignow ducked in at the last minute and was momentarily followed by a pair of anaemic-looking aides-de-camp who preceded a stout, bearded man who looked like he was dressed as an extra in an Italian opera company. He wore thigh-high cavalry boots, a chest full of medals, and a marshall's field-grey uniform.

Wilhelm Ernst, Grand Duke of Saxe-Weimar and cousin to the Kaiser, was introduced to me by one of his aides. I stood ramrod stiff at attention as he pinned an Iron Cross Second Class to my tunic and read a brief citation. He then turned to the small cluster of officers present and gave a short speech praising the army and extolling the virtues needed to win the war. Most of it was sonorous drivel and the only thing I clearly recall was at the end when he said, "We are all called upon to serve the Fatherland in different ways, so let us all follow the example of this fine young officer and victory shall be ours." He then toddled off for drinks with the district commander. Von Lignow whispered in my ear, "Come with me. If this silly old fart starts talking to you, no one will ever be able to shut him up and he will waste your entire day."

Von Lignow led me across the barrack square to a second-floor office in the building where he and Kleer interrogated me. He looked exceptionally tired. His eyes were bloodshot and his face was drawn. He motioned me to a wooden chair in front of his desk. For a captain, his office was a large one. There were several Bakelite telephones on a table beside his massive desk and the walls were covered in large-scale maps of northern Germany and the western and eastern fronts. There was a tiny window that opened to a clerk's office and beyond it a small tabletop telephone exchange manned by a corporal.

"Alex, things have changed since we spoke yesterday. I've been in conference with the chief of staff and Colonel Von Steiger from Eastern Front Headquarters. We've received new orders from Berlin. As you know, unlike our situation in the west where we're stalemated, the war in the east is going well." He stepped up to one of the large maps and I could see his energy level visibly rise. "Our troops now occupy a line running from the Latvian border in the north to Sevastopol in the south. Behind this line, North Central Military District Headquarters has been tasked to ensure that the resources of whatever territories we occupy are exploited with a view to providing maximum support to our war effort."

He brushed his hand over the map of Poland, Byelorussia, and Russia's eastern regions. "As General Staff officer for North Central Strategic Movement, in addition to my normal duties, I'm now charged with providing assistance for the exploitation of all civilian resources in rear area sectors five, six, and seven. We've got to extract all the war material and manpower we possibly can from these regions. Agricultural produce, metal, timber, chemicals, industrial equipment, and labour—all of it is to be mobilized to help us win the war. We've no choice. If we don't exploit these lands, we're going to starve. Last night I was given clear directions. To conduct this task, nothing is to be taken from the eastern front's field armies. We'll have to do it entirely from within our own resources. Poland, White Russia, and Russia itself must become factories for us. Do you have any questions?"

"Yes, one that springs to mind right off," I said. "What exactly are you talking about when you say 'exploit' these territories?"

"A good point. I thought you might raise it." He allowed himself a brief smile. "No one has spelled that out specifically and everyone I talk to becomes extremely vague on the subject. The predicament we find ourselves in is going to pose a serious moral problem for us. I think that is what you are getting at?" He paused momentarily. "My views are straightforward. I'm a German soldier, not a murderer or a common thief. I recognize these are difficult times and if we don't take drastic measures, we're going to be defeated. Defeat is unacceptable. I'm also a realist and I know what resources we have and how long we can continue to fight. This is a matter of survival; and, I think in the circumstances, we are fully justified to appropriate material and take such measures to ensure our survival. That is not a licence to commit murder, but it changes how we deal with our own population and that of neighbouring states. You know what military defeat will mean for Germany? Never mind losing whatever overseas territories we have left, the war's gone on for so long and been so bitter that whoever loses is going to be crushed unmercifully. There is no possibility of an honourable armistice. Therefore, we must win; and to do that demands extraordinary measures." He stopped and lit a cigarette with a wooden match. Wolfgang Von Lignow's assessment of the war was a mirror image of Cumming's British version, but Von Lignow's appraisal was much more desperate.

He continued. "I think you understand the decision we face.

We've got to exploit these territories; but we must do it as civilized men. We can't iniquitously plunder them. I won't have any part of that. We'll win this war, and we won't turn ourselves into jackals doing it. Having said that, it's not going to be an easy thing to do; I need officers to work with me on the ground who can help me put together a plan to exploit our occupied territories—but at the same time ensure we don't slaughter the inhabitants through starvation. I don't know how we're going to do that yet; and Alex, that's where I need you. I can't drop the management of all railways and internal transport. There is no one right now I can hand my work to, so I need you and several others to be my eyes and ears, to go east and conduct a reconnaissance of what's there; I want you to help me devise a plan to turn the entire region into a productive military asset. I told you yesterday you were to be the Staff officer for Rear Area Transport. Change that title; you are now to be Staff officer, Rear Area Productivity—Polish Sector, Rural Bialystock."

He turned to the map and swept his hand over a large map festooned with pins. "This is Bialystock. It's an area named after the Polish city. The Bialystock area is within the first sector we are to turn into a 'Productivity Zone.' The area has been divided into three zones: The City of Bialystock, East Bialystock, and what we call Rural Bialystock. You will be responsible for Rural Bialystock. You will have two weeks to analyze it, assess it against pre-determined quotas that you will be assigned, and then formulate a plan for its ongoing exploitation.

"Finish that, and you will probably be given the remaining two new territories to develop. Four days from now there's a conference in Berlin. I'll be going to it and so will you. The director-general war production will be briefing all staff officers associated with both western and eastern front rear-area productivity on goals, quotas, and methods. We will attend the conference and from there you will probably go directly to Poland and begin your reconnaissance. You can stay in touch with me on an as-required basis by telephone, and as I said, I would appreciate it if you advise me of your findings and recommendations."

I was dumbfounded. "That's an enormous task."

"Enormous, yes. Unmanageable, no. Other officers, once we find suitable ones, will be tasked with sectors further south in support of the Austrians in Galicia. They'll also report to director-general war production. Your first sector, Rural Bialystock, will probably become one of the models for a productivity zone in the east."

"Why me, sir? Why did you select me for this task?"

"I would think that's obvious. I've told you. I need someone who can think for himself, someone who is determined, has initiative and leadership; and someone who has an original turn of mind. I could get an experienced major or even a reserve lieutenant colonel to do it, but I'm looking for someone with imagination—I also want people who will do this without turning Poland into a graveyard. I don't care about rank or age. This war may last several years yet. We'll have to get more than one crop from our territories. I trust you won't disappoint us."

I didn't say anything. The whole proposal sounded so completely beyond anything I had ever contemplated before, I was a bit stunned by it all and it must have shown on my face.

"It sounds like a lot," Von Lignow said. "I imagine it may seem overwhelming considering what you've just been through." Von Lignow leaned against his desk and seemed to unwind a little. "The conference doesn't begin for four days, so before you begin, I want you to take some leave. Relax. Enjoy yourself. It's not much, but in the circumstances it's the most we can do."

"That'd be wonderful, but there's nowhere I really have to go just now; and I've no money," I said.

"I've thought of that. The adjutant has had a new pay book and your service and leave records forwarded from Ninth Landwehr Division. See him, he'll arrange for you to be paid and issued with a new identity card as well as leave and travel warrants. If you want, you're welcome to travel to my family home in the Thüringer Wald. We have a small country house south of Jena. My father and mother live there. You're welcome to stay with them. It'll give you somewhere to go. I'm sure the food in a farming village is better than anywhere else. You can go for long hikes, get your strength back. You'll need it. I can't go with you, but I'll meet you in Berlin on Tuesday."

Von Lignow's thoroughness astonished me. "That's kind of you. I'd like that. Thank you."

"Don't thank me too much. I have ulterior motives. These days I never get to check in on my parents and I want you to do that for me. Besides, I need you refreshed and ready to work when you return. There's nothing for you to do here before Tuesday. After that, we will both be busier than you can imagine."

12

I WAS DELIGHTED to get four days leave. I hadn't expected it. To be truthful, despite an occasional surge of confidence, my nerves were a mess, and for every hour of feeling sure of myself, I suffered ten in teeth-gnashing despair. Most of the time I was on edge and tense, and in any given day I found myself swinging erratically from being complacent about my situation to a state of obsessive anxiety. I don't think I showed it, but most of the time I was even jumpier than I'd ever been at the end of a long spell in the line. When I thought seriously about what I was doing, I became unnerved. My mind incessantly played out scenarios where I'd be discovered and unmasked in front of everyone. I daydreamed and imagined a thousand settings in which I'd be caught. My most vivid fear was someone would call my name and I wouldn't answer. To guard against this I took to repeating over and over to myself "My name is Alex Baumann." The crazy repetition of that mantra only left my nerves more ragged. So, the opportunity to travel and be by myself was a stroke of luck for which I was profoundly grateful. I knew, if I had just a few days to adjust mentally to my identity and circumstances, I could survive. Despite Von Lignow's congenial nature and apparent acceptance of me, I needed time to become comfortable in my new skin.

At the adjutant's office, I found the "village butcher," or "Old

Fleischer," as I'd nicknamed him, already had money, new pay documents, a railway pass, travel and leave permits, as well as a new identity card for me. Fleischer also advised the quartermaster stores to issue me a second uniform and set of personal equipment. The thoroughness and efficiency of these officers impressed me immensely and it made me proud that I was half-German. That pride was confusing and didn't make my task easier.

Von Lignow sent a telegram to the post office nearest his family advising them of my arrival, and two hours later, I was on a train heading south. The German train system has always been a marvel. But in the early years of the century, Germany unquestionably had the most developed and efficient rail system in the world. Throughout the Great War, it ran like a Swiss watch. German railways were run by the best minds on the General Staff. Men like Wolfgang Von Lignow literally worked themselves into early graves co-ordinating and revising timetables, routes, and manifests. Now, I enjoyed the benefits of their efforts. My train rolled into Rostock's central station right on time and rolled out precisely five and a half minutes later. From the swaying comfort of my first-class carriage I watched the countryside fly by.

Journeys always make me introspective. On a long trip you are a prisoner of time and motion. There's not much to do but watch the world go by and to think. And invariably, in those circumstances, I find you mull over where you're going and what you're doing. That day was no different. Germany looked as I remembered: scrupulously cultivated fields, tidy woodlots with trees planted in precise military files, picturesque mediaeval villages, and a rural road system that was as organized and trim as if it had been lifted at Christmas time from a department store's toy train display. I was at home here. And while it was reassuring not to have to agonize about the culture or the language, more than ever before, I struggled with my purpose.

I shared my compartment with a fellow junior officer from a Hanseatic Jager battalion, an athletic-looking chap about my age with a blond goatee and an intelligent, friendly face. His uniform was worn and discoloured and he had that resigned look about him that indicated he was heading back to the front after a spell of leave. After a few pleasantries, we both became absorbed in watching the landscape roll past. By unspoken consent, we left one another to our thoughts.

A few short months ago I would have shot this fellow had he appeared in front of our wire. Even now, I was risking my neck so my compatriots might kill him and tens of thousands like him. There was nothing particularly original in my thinking and I know my insights were commonplace—but my doubts about what I was doing were genuine. The other thing that troubled me was the lieutenant looked like someone I knew in high school. He could just as easily have been a cousin of mine, or one of the people I played with as a child in my grandparents' village. One sleepless night I'd calculated the odds of that happening. It was not only unlikely, it was astronomically unlikely; nevertheless, I worried about the possibility of meeting someone I knew. The Jager officer looked like the sort of fellow I'd have gotten along well with. It was a foolish world and I didn't pretend to understand it.

At one point, while I was thinking about all this, the Jager lieutenant, lost in his own troubles, was gazing out at the countryside. I allowed myself to stare at him closely. He turned and caught me watching him. I immediately shifted my gaze out the window. It was then I decided to grow a short goatee like the one he wore. I'd never worn a beard before; in fact, before I joined the army, I doubt whether I could have grown one, but a beard seemed to me one means of making me look more German. In the unlikely event that I should stumble across someone from my past, it might prevent some acquaintance from recognizing me. I didn't feel any better about what I was doing, but my decision made me feel safer.

My train rumbled through the fields of Mecklenburg and onward to Neubrandenburg, where I caught a series of connecting trains that took me through Berlin and on to Jena and Eulenfeld, and from there onward by foot for three miles through wooded hills and vineyards to the Von Lignow estate. The Von Lignow's place was a half a mile from a tiny mediaeval hamlet called Bösendorff. The family house was situated on a pine-covered hillside overlooking the road and the Saale River. The grounds consisted of a modest slate-roofed grey stone and timber house with a large vegetable garden. When I knocked on the door, the Von Lignows seemed to be waiting for me for they answered immediately.

Herr Doctor Von Lignow was an elderly and frail-looking man with a large grey moustache. I would have guessed his wife to be ten years his junior. She was stout, had a ready smile, and peered out at the world through thick glasses. They had only received Wolfgang's wire an hour earlier, but they greeted me like a long-lost relative and seemed genuinely delighted to have me stay with them. They put me up in Wolfgang's old room, and apart from the occasional odd job that I could find in an attempt to make myself useful around the house and grounds, I spent the next three days hiking in the forest and reading from Herr Doctor Von Lignow's considerable library. The Von Lignows were something of an oddity. Although possessing an aristocratic name, they were a solidly middle-class family. Their land holdings were confined to their three acres of Thuringian hillside. The title was one that had been bestowed on a soldier from the Napoleonic Wars and the family had never possessed much in the way of property or wealth. Doctor Von Lignow had only recently retired from his full-time country medical practice, but since the war he had been frequently called upon to travel to outlying regions as most doctors of military age were off serving with the army.

Like my few days in Norway, my brief stay with the Von Lignows was a marvellous interval. In the brilliant sunshine of those early autumn days you could smell the grapes maturing in the vineyards; the nights were cool and clear and a thousand stars shone above the Thuringian countryside. The doctor and his wife were terribly proud of their only son, who had been accepted for the General Staff at such an early age. And, I also guessed, they were quietly delighted he was no longer serving in a frontline unit. The Von Lignows were unstintingly generous hosts and while I stayed with them I ate as well as at any other time in my life. I had no idea if the shortages that afflicted the rest of Germany were as severe for them. At all events, we ate rabbit and pork, both of which were raised in hutches and pens behind the house, as well as potatoes and fresh vegetables from their garden.

My stay in the Thuringian Wald was notable for one thing: I finally came to grips with my incessant wrestling with the morality of what I was doing. When I was in England I had no doubts that my mission was entirely honourable, but as I had got to know Von Lignow and the remainder of his staff, I began agonizing over what I was doing.

It was late one afternoon during one of my forest walks that I turned a sharp bend on an uphill trail and ran across a band of gypsies. There were at least seven or eight of them several yards off the path, clustered around a small cooking fire. Four or five of those dark brooding faces were men of military age. They didn't have to say anything. The one furthest from me, without ever breaking eye contact, smoothly reached down and cradled an antique-looking rifle. The others looked at me with a sudden expression of guilt, which turned immediately to implacable hostility and suspicion. I'm certain they were illegally hunting deer.

I did my best to look pleased to see them and called out a cheerful "Good afternoon," only to be met by a cold silence as I continued walking upwards and towards them. I felt exposed and vulnerable as I was unarmed and wearing my uniform. Not very convincingly, I shouted out, "Are you hunting too? We must all do what we can to survive these days. I'm from this area and I know at this time of the year you can find good deer tracks on the high ground near the crest of this hill. Go at dusk, you'll get a good shot." I winked and strolled past them waving and saying, "Good luck."

I felt like an idiot and fully expected to be fired at or attacked from behind. At the slightest sound I was prepared to run. If anything, their silence made them seem even more menacing than they were; for apart from poaching deer, the gypsies would have been deadly anxious to keep their men away from the clutches of the army. Nobody followed me; and when I strolled a few hundred yards further down the trail, I ran as fast as I could until I came out a mile or so from a main footpath that led to another small village. I had no intention of reporting the gypsies; it was unlikely they would hurt anybody. After all, they had more to lose than I; and, no doubt after seeing me, they probably packed up camp and were fleeing as fast as possible deeper into the woods.

Despite feeling threatened by that gypsy band, I identified with them. I didn't fit into my surroundings either, and had anyone actually known who I really was, I would have been hunted down much more ruthlessly than any itinerant band of poachers avoiding military service. After that fleeting encounter I was more than ever convinced I was locked in a struggle for survival. The look of calm menace in the eyes of the gypsy with the shotgun convinced me of that. Here was a man who understood what it took to survive. That gypsy had a sense of survival bred into him over hundreds of years of being an outcast. Consciously, I knew once and for all I had to stop fretting about things like duplicity and civility. Survival has no etiquette. You do what it takes to stay alive. When I returned from that walk I was determined to become Oberleutnant Alex Baumann.

In many ways after that, I was no longer conscious of being a spy. For one thing, it was too wearing on my conscience and my nerves. I couldn't be forever agonizing over my deception and worrying that I was half-German. The gypsy's eyes told me as much as anything I'd seen before that life was a struggle and only the strong survive. I would become Rory Ferrall only when I discovered what I was sent here to find. Surprisingly, this thinking worked. After that encounter, I simply stopped worrying and for a long time began playing my part as if I had been born to it.

I left Thuringia late the next day. As I made my farewells to the Von Lignows, I caught sight of myself in a small gilt-edged mirror that was hanging in the hallway. I was wearing my uniform and my new beard was growing in nicely. It was several shades lighter than the hair on my scalp, but it gave me a Germanic look. I was pleased with myself, utterly convinced I had finally crossed that psychological threshold and actually become Oberleutnant Alex Baumann. A few days earlier, when I first put on a German uniform, I felt slightly ridiculous wearing my pickelhaube. That afternoon things were different. As I caught sight of myself in the mirror, I confess I thought that with my pickelhaube, goatee, and eye patch I looked rather rakish. The old doctor insisted I take with me several volumes of books I had shown an interest in reading and Mrs. Von Lignow had tears in her eyes. She pressed upon me a small package of pork sandwiches carefully wrapped and tied in brown paper as well as a small packet of letters for Wolfgang. I promised to write them, and slinging my pack over my back, set off down the road to the train station at Eulenfeld.

✠

The staff conference in Berlin was an intriguing experience. I'd never done any kind of staff work before, and I certainly never imagined I'd go to my first staff conference as a German officer. The planning session for the development of occupied productivity zones was to be held in the "Red House" on the Konigsplatz. The Red House was the German nickname for the drab brick headquarters building that housed the Greater German General Staff. It was fenced off with coils of barbed wire.

To get into the building, I had to go through two checkpoints manned by soldiers wearing the new steel coalscuttle helmets and the metal necklace insignia of the military police. It wasn't surprising to me that the inspections were thorough and professional. At the final check point, my documents were taken into a sandbagged bunker and verified by telephone against the conference nominal roll. As the sentry handed my documents back to me with a brisk flick of the wrist, he barked, "Oberleutnant Baumann, you are fifteen minutes early. You go to the third floor, second room to the right. It is forbidden for you to go anywhere else but that room as well as the washroom on that floor and other rooms designated by

a member of the staff. Do you understand, sir?" I nodded in agreement and he had me sign a list certifying my arrival and briefing.
He crashed to attention and saluted smartly as I left.

Upstairs, I took my place at a large wooden conference table
behind a handwritten place card for Oberleutnant A. Baumann.
The room had a high ceiling and, at the front, supported by easels
on either side of a speaker's podium, were maps of the rear areas of
the western and eastern fronts. The air was dry and my eye socket
was swollen and painful. Over the next ten minutes the room filled
with about forty officers of varying ranks. With the arrival of General Groener the conference was called to attention. Groener rushed
into the room, removed his hat, and put on his reading glasses. He
was a man I'd heard a great deal about in the short time I'd been in
Germany. Tasked with gearing the German economy to wartime
production, he, like Von Lignow, was considered an oddity on the
General Staff because he held views that were considered "liberal"
in comparison to his peers. I was to learn later Groener was one of
the few senior General Staff officers who opposed the use of unrestricted U-boat warfare. He was nonetheless a brutally efficient individual and not a man to waste his words. He spoke without notes.

"Thank you for coming to Berlin this afternoon, gentlemen. You
all know the purpose of this conference and I assume you have all
been briefed on the importance of the tasks ahead of you. What
you are to hear today is to be treated as secret and sensitive information. This information is not to be divulged to anyone. We do not
want the press, our own troops, our enemies, or any of the peoples
in occupied areas to be aware of what we are planning until such
time as we implement specific aspects of the plans that you will
devise.

"You gentlemen who are not members of the General Staff, and
that is the majority of the people in this room, have been selected
for these tasks not on the basis of your rank, but on your assessed
ability to cope with uncertainty, your imagination, and your dem-
onstrated commitment to the Fatherland. We cannot afford to have
you fail as the war will almost certainly be won or lost on Germany's

ability to sustain itself materially over long periods of intense combat. Without substantial strengthening of the German economy from the occupied territories, I believe we only have the capacity to fight for a further eight months. Exploitation of productivity zones will significantly enhance our fighting ability and our stamina as a nation. I cannot stress how important this is."

Groener then paused and looked at the audience over his glasses. After a few seconds he continued. "I would ask that each of the officers seated at the table who has been assigned to a sector rise and identify themselves."

Most of the "sector" officers were captains and majors, and Groener frequently added appreciative comments such as "Captain Kaufman is in civilian life a regional director of The Fördern Bank; Major Breckner is an assistant mathematics professor at the University of Heidelberg."

When my turn to rise came, I identified myself as "Oberleutnant Baumann, Ninth Landwehr Division."

General Groener raised his hand theatrically and came around from his podium. "Oberleutnant Baumann is the youngest and most junior member of this staff. His presence as a sector officer deserves some explanation. He was born in Düsseldorf, raised in America, and returned to the Fatherland on the outbreak of war. He fought with distinction in Belgium, was awarded the Iron Cross Second Class; and after being seriously wounded was taken prisoner by the British. He then escaped from England and made his way back to Germany. He is an officer of initiative, resourcefulness, and daring; and despite his age, he richly deserves a place on this staff team."

The officers present stood up and began clapping and cheering. I knew instinctively that to remain a "grey man," I didn't need this kind of attention. I was blushing, and even though I knew the Alex Baumann they were cheering didn't exist, I enjoyed the attention. I nodded humbly and sat down.

With the introductions finished, Groener continued. "Now, gentlemen, each of the regions on the eastern and western front has been subject to a preliminary assessment as to how it can contribute to the war effort. Your tasks will be to confirm that assessment, and then develop and implement a comprehensive range of plans in your specific sectors to exploit the resources of those areas."

Groener went on to describe in some detail the manufacturing, supply, transport, and security rationale behind creating the economic productivity zones. He rattled off statistics and facts at an alarming tempo and then invited another officer to speak. When the subject got around to productivity operations in Belgium and France, my mind began to wander. I looked around the room and noticed that except for Von Lignow, all the General Staff officers were red-faced and overweight, with an unsightly roll of fat bulging over the high stiff collars of their uniforms. I assumed this was because in their unnaturally work-oriented institution they rarely got any physical exercise. A major from the staff followed Groener and gave a long briefing on the economic potential of Belgium.

An equally stout major with glasses, a deep voice, and an Iron Cross Second Class followed him. "The situation in the rear area of the eastern front is quite different," said the deep-voiced Staff major who went on in great detail to explain what material could be squeezed out of Poland and occupied Russia. "There is no need to take notes on any of this," he said as he flourished a thick typed document. "Typed copies will be given to each of you. You gentlemen will have more work cut out for you, as we have not done the same intensity of analysis to date as we have on the western front. You will be required in most instances to start from scratch."

The briefing went on in tedious detail outlining the specific areas we were responsible for, the resources to be allocated to us, and a thousand other details. My eye continued to hurt with a scratchy, throbbing intensity. It wasn't until we broke for dinner shortly after six that evening that I got my first chance to talk to Von Lignow. I approached him and clicked my heels.

"Sir, I had a very relaxing few days at your house and your parents were extremely hospitable. Thank you very much. They're a charming couple and they gave me a packet of letters for you." Von

Lignow beamed; he seemed genuinely pleased for me. "One thing," I said. "Your father looked at my eye and he suggested I see a doctor here in Berlin for some ointment for it. It hurts like hell. How do I go about seeing someone at this time of the evening?"

"That should pose no problems. St. Marten's hospital is only a short distance away. I'll make arrangements."

Von Lignow went off and came back a few minutes later. "I'm afraid I can't go with you, but go to the front desk. A driver will be waiting for you and he'll take you to the hospital. They're expecting you. We shall resume here tomorrow morning at 7:30. I'll see you then, Alex, and thanks so much for the letters."

✝

St. Marten's Hospital smelled of antiseptic. It was a drab, cheerless place, not a lot different than most of the institutions I had been in over the last several months. After a wait of ten or fifteen minutes, I was led down a series of corridors and down a flight of stairs to what I supposed must have been an out-patient clinic. In fairly short order my eye socket was being examined by a gruff old doctor who was assisted by an attractive young nurse. The doctor mumbled something about having to examine a pharmaceutical reference and left the room.

The nurse was tall, slender, and in her early twenties. She was friendly looking, with auburn hair done up in a bun beneath a starched blue-bordered veil. She had a fair complexion, a disarming smile, and bright blue eyes. I fidgeted and sat on the edge of the examination table. I wanted to say something, but anything intelligent eluded me. I was tongue-tied. I forced a smile and she smiled back. This went on for a few uncomfortable seconds when she said, "Your driver tells me you're the officer from America who escaped from England. Is that true?"

"How did you know about that?" I asked with unfeigned surprise.

"Why shouldn't I know it? Your driver told me," she said laughingly. "And besides, it was in the papers yesterday. Haven't you seen them?"

"No. No, I haven't." I was startled by this news, as I hadn't expected it.

"You look surprised."

"I am. I—I just thought they'd keep it quiet, in case others tried to escape using the same means; that's all."

"No, well it seems you're a hero once again," she said, nodding towards the ribbon of my Iron Cross.

At that moment, the doctor came back into the room with a small blue jar of ointment in his hand. He deftly salved the rims of my eye socket. The relief was almost instantaneous.

"Keep the edges of your eye socket moistened with this. Use it sparingly when you cover the socket with your patch but use it liberally when you use your glass eye. You should have sufficient in this jar to last you for a month or two. I think that will be all." He turned abruptly from me as if I was a piece of furniture. As he left the room he said, "Nurse Richter, please show our young hero to the front door. Good evening, Oberleutnant Baumann."

The nurse smiled quietly, but looking at her eyes I had the impression she was laughing at me in a cheerful sort of way. It didn't bother me. She seemed bright and natural, and as we walked through the hospital corridors I lost my reticence. I turned and touched her lightly on the arm. "Will you go out with me for a coffee or a drink after? I'm sure it'd be all right. I don't know anyone in Berlin and I'd like someone to talk to. Just for an hour?" I felt foolish, as if I was soliciting her sympathy.

She smiled again and I remember thinking she had magnificently animated eyes. "That's very forward of you," she said, but continued to smile. "And I don't get off duty for another forty minutes. Would you be willing to wait, in the front reception area?" She hesitated and went on. "You know it's not allowed. But this one time, I'll do it. Oh, and I should tell you, you won't find coffee for sale anywhere in Berlin. But there's a little café at the edge of the Tiergarten where we could get a nice cup of acorn tea."

I dismissed the driver and went into the lobby to wait. She kept me sitting on the hard benches of the hospital foyer for over an hour. When she swept into the room she was wearing a navy blue cape lined with scarlet. It billowed out behind her. I stood and she offered me her arm. Without breaking stride she propelled me along with her across the tiled floor and out the front door. "Don't linger. Act like I've known you for years." She smiled and bobbed her head like royalty to the porter behind his desk.

When we were thirty yards away from the front door she stopped, let go of my arm, and curtseyed. "Oberleutnant Baumann, my name is Gabriele Richter; now, may I have the pleasure of knowing your Christian name?"

I bowed in mock courtesy. "Madame. I'm Oberleutnant Alex Baumann at your service, but please, for tonight, simply call me Alex."

"I had no intention of calling you anything else," she said.

We walked for about twenty-five minutes before we reached the Tiergarten, the huge park that dominates central Berlin. Gabriele was an easy person to talk to. She radiated happiness and pleasure. We chatted away as if we'd been friends for a long time. We talked of the war and life in Berlin and her job at the hospital. She was a marvellous companion and I found I didn't have to contribute much. As long as I steered the conversation and dropped in questions from time to time, she continued to talk. If she hadn't been so cheerfully confident, she might have appeared scatterbrained. But behind her breezy manner, I had the impression she was clever and self-assured.

She led us to a small café at the north end of the Tiergarten, and as the evening was warm, we sat outside at a table in the small front garden. It was a charming little place that sold cakes and tea. After we ordered, I remarked on an impressive coat of arms above the front door that indicated the establishment sold its wares to the Royal Family. "Oh yes," Gabriele said with mock solemnity. "The Kaiser's servants buy his cakes and baumkuchen from this establishment. It's nice to know the Kaiser is so well taken care of, isn't it?"

"You don't like the Kaiser?" I said cautiously.

"It doesn't matter much whether I like him or not. But no, I'm not keen on him or the system that has gotten us into this hideous mess." She paused for a split second and her manner became icy and severe. "How do you feel about him?"

"I don't know the Kaiser, or very much about him—but I'd like to see us end this war. We're all going to lose far more than we'll ever gain by it, no matter who wins."

Gabriele sipped at her tea and tilted her head to one side. "I don't know if you approve of it, Alex, but I'm a socialist. I don't believe we should have gotten into this war and it would be wonderful if we could sue for peace." Her tone changed dramatically in the last few seconds. She looked at me as if she were challenging me.

"No argument from me. I've seen more than I want to of fighting and killing; but the war won't go away because we dislike it."

"No, I know you're right," she said. "And neither the French, nor the Russians or the English will give us a fair deal in the event that we sue for peace. We've gotten ourselves into a terrible stew. I just wanted to let you know where I stood on things."

"That's fair." I offered a cigarette and she shook her head.

"Not in public in uniform, thank you."

I lit mine, inhaled deeply. "May I ask you two questions?" She nodded. "Why do you have such a good sense of humour if you're a socialist? Aren't they all supposed to be intense and brooding, out to change the world?"

She laughed. "Not all of us. What's your next question?"

"Number two. Why would such a pretty and intelligent woman like yourself be free to go out with me at a moment's notice? I'd have thought someone like you would already be spoken for."

Gabriele smiled softly and looked down at her teacup. "I was. Until three months ago I was engaged to be married to an architect. He's been off in the army for the last two years. He's in the artillery." She paused and looked directly at me. Again I began to feel uncomfortable, wishing I'd never raised the subject. She looked at me strangely and began to chuckle. "He came home on leave in

June. I was deliriously happy to see him. I wanted to go away with him for his leave and he told me he couldn't because he'd contracted syphilis. I sent him packing and you're the first person I have agreed to go out with since then—Here I am," she said with a flourish. "And you?"

I wasn't used to this kind of candour in a woman; but I was far from repelled by it. I liked it. "Me? Nothing much to tell. I was at university in America and came back to Germany when the war broke out. I'm single. Always have been—Here I am." She laughed. "Oh, maybe I should add, I don't have syphilis," I said.

Gabriele laughed again. I was mesmerized by her cheerfulness and the way her eyes sparkled when she laughed. It was one of the defining things about her. Her laugh was soft and feminine but it was at the same time vigorous. Unlike most of the very few women I'd known in my restricted upbringing, there was nothing tentative or apologetic about the way she laughed. She was someone who, without being foolish, found most things amusing; and quite aside from her looks, I found her unconcealed enjoyment of life devastatingly appealing. Then again, looking back on it, around women I was not the most sophisticated of men—but had I met Gabriele again today, I'd be equally captivated.

We lapsed into silence for a few moments and watched people walk by on the Tiergarten's pathways. Gabriele spoke first.

"You know, before the war there were always a lot of men in uniform strolling about this park. It's different now. People's faces are different. Before the war, men looked confident and full of life. Now, the men, even the young ones, look tired and the women are apprehensive." She turned to me and asked suddenly, "What will you do when the war is over?"

"I don't know. I suppose I'll finish my degree. I was studying engineering. I don't think I'll go back to America. From what I hear, it sounds like America has begun to side with the British and French. If they join the war against us, I won't be able to go back. I won't be a German-American any more. I'll be a German who was raised in America."

"That's not so bad, you know," she said with another of those dream-like smiles and she reached out and gently squeezed the back of my misshapen hand. "You've had a difficult time of it for the last few years. Your wounds are terrible, but they mean you will probably survive this war."

"Yes," I said philosophically. "I'm lucky."

"I wasn't being sarcastic," she said.

"Neither was I. I'm lucky." We stared at our cups and Gabriele kept her hand resting on mine. She suddenly pulled her hand away.

"I'm sorry, you must think I'm very direct, I don't know what came over me."

"Oh, that's fine. Nobody's done that in years." I didn't give her time to dwell on it. "Tell me something about yourself. Have you always lived in Berlin?"

She sipped carefully at her tea before answering. "Yes. My father is a journalist and a businessman. He publishes several small magazines. My mother is from Potsdam. I have a brother who was in medical school until last year and is now in the army on the Russian front. He has been missing in action for over a year. We hope he's a prisoner, but I don't think so. I have a sister who is a student. We're all socialists. Tell me some thing about yourself now."

I shrugged self-deprecatingly. "I was born in Düsseldorf. Before I can remember we moved to America. My father worked at a bakery shop in Albany, New York. Now he owns three of his own. My mother works at the bakery, so do my brother and two sisters. I did well at school and won a scholarship to the Rensselaer Polytechnic Institute to study engineering. The war broke out and along with a couple other Germans in my class we left school and sailed for Germany to enlist. They made me an officer and two and half nasty years later, here I am. They've given me some kind of a staff job and I expect I'll spend the rest of the war pushing papers around. Between you and me, that suits me fine."

"Do you regret leaving America?"

"To be honest, yes. I often regret coming over here to fight. But at the time I thought it was the right thing to do. I suppose if I thought it was the right thing to do, I shouldn't regret it. I can't say I've enjoyed myself in the last two years. I never thought it would be like this."

"Nobody did," she said quietly. "Will you spend much time in Berlin?"

"I hope to. They've given me a staff job that will take me back and forth from Poland. I don't know much about it," I lied. "Today was my first day. It looks boring, something to do with supply, but boring is fine just now."

Gabriele looked at the watch she had pinned to her blouse. "It's getting late," she said. "I've really enjoyed our talk."

"So have I." I was doing my best to sound nonchalant, but I blurted it out. "Can I see you again sometime soon?"

Gabriele touched my hand again. "Oh yes, of course." She sounded mildly astonished, almost as if she fully expected I should call her again.

I was exuberant. She reached into her handbag and took out a stub of pencil and scrap of paper. "You can telephone me at this number. It's my home. I live with my father and mother. I'll tell them I'm expecting your call." She smiled and rose from the table.

I walked Gabriele to her stop and waited until the electric trolley-bus squealed to a halt at her tram stop. The trolley-bus was packed with weary Berliners standing in the aisles hanging on to leather straps, heading home to the suburbs from a long day's work. Gabriele wouldn't hear of me escorting her home. I watched as her trolley rolled down the street away from me with its wires sparking and crackling overhead.

It was after, when I walked back to the officers' quarters near the Konigsplatz and I stopped to look in a shop window, that I seriously began to think about the snares I was likely setting for myself. I was on a narrow cobblestoned side street staring into an expensive tailor's shop window. The headless tailor's dummies were all outfitted in the uniforms of smart regiments: Prussian Dragoons, Guard Artillery, and Foot Guards. The best-dressed German men of that age group had been wearing field-grey for several years now. In the corners of the window display were large pre-war photographs of young officers wearing finely tailored uniforms hand sewn by the firm. They were handsome men, probably the sons of well-to-do families. They looked confident, almost smug. They struck dashing poses, standing beside their well-brushed mounts. Some of them self-consciously smoked cigarettes while others stared determinedly out somewhere. All were posturing manfully for the photographer. I wondered where those young men were now. The odds were good that several of them were probably festering corpses in some unmarked shell hole in Flanders or Russia. As I looked into their faces, I wondered if perhaps I might have had a hand in any of their fates.

When I stood up from inspecting the photos, I once again caught sight of my reflection in the window's heavy glass. I looked the part. My beard had grown in. It made my face thinner and longer and my spiked pickelhaube helmet accentuated the whole effect. The uniform accentuated my height and I was much fitter looking than when I first came out of the line. My eye patch, far from making me look gruesome or invalided, gave me a distinguished look, or so I thought. My uniform was an army-issue one. It wasn't like the fine wool ones displayed in the shop window; but still, the German army didn't do a half-bad job when it came to uniforms and equipment. Not like the Canadians, who sent their troops off to fight in whatever clothing could be made by the manufacturer who submitted the cheapest bid to the Department of the Militia. I smoothed my tunic and turned to catch myself in the most flattering angle. I straightened the Iron Cross ribbon looped through my buttonhole and thought to myself I may not have won this particular decoration, but I had actually won a Military Cross, which was just as well regarded.

Compared to my situation of a few months ago, I was in a relatively comfortable position. If I chose to do so, I could sit out the war. And as intoxicated as I was at just having met Gabriele, the idea of risking my neck to ferret out the German army's most closely guarded secrets and then attempt an ill-considered escape to

Britain was not something that was at that particular moment high on my list of priorities.

I turned away from the tailor shop and resumed walking. I was becoming involved with Gabriele and that would hopelessly complicate my task—I knew that. I also knew I had no intention of disengaging from the relationship. I couldn't express it at the time, but I was drawn to her by an irrepressible force as compelling as whatever caused wild geese to fly south in the autumn, or trees to burst into leaf in the spring. Gabriele was soft and feminine, pretty and intelligent, and she was fun to be with. She was everything I dreamt about on those shivering wet nights in the trenches. Whenever my head ached from fatigue, when my nose ran and my toes were numb and deadened from cold, I thought of soft, warm bodies and better times. I was close to having that now, and something primeval in me wouldn't let me consider losing it. I didn't want to think about how meeting Gabriele affected my life; and so I didn't. Somehow things would sort themselves out. I could manage Gabriele and I could do what I set out to do. It would take care of itself. There was no conflict. As I turned into The Prenzlaur, a small hotel that had been commandeered and turned into an officers' mess, all I wanted was some dinner and the chance to re-apply ointment to my eye. I would slip away from the conference and phone Gabriele tomorrow.

13

THE SECOND DAY of my staff conference was much like the first. To tell the truth, I have difficulty remembering most of what was discussed. It was all very boring. I was deluged with information, most of which didn't remotely apply to the sector in which I was to be assigned. On my second day as a Staff officer, it became apparent to me that the much-vaunted German staff system had some serious weaknesses.

From what I had heard and seen, the system was superbly designed for fighting wars, but once the army began to stray from the areas of its unique expertise, Germany's elite military planners were out of their depth. In coming to these conclusions, I don't think I was being superior or brilliant. In fact, I don't think the Allied armies would have been much different. Given the quality of most of our generals, we probably would have been worse. From my briefings and from what I had seen with my own eyes, the German army was unmatched at mobilizing large numbers of high-quality reserves and moving large numbers of troops. They could supply them and support them and fight them through thick and thin. And any units they deployed were superbly trained, well led, and steadfast. But over the next two days of that conference I was to be given a unique insight into how specialized expertise and genius is unlikely to extend beyond its own particular discipline.

The war the Germans found themselves in was not a short-lived
series of brilliant manoeuvres by large armies. It had become a
static, brutal slugging match; and as I could testify, the Boche could
hammer it out with the best of them. But this war had proven to
be different from all those preceding it. The Great War demanded
mobilization and administration of the entire society; and sitting
around that table, I got the very distinct impression that the German General Staff, despite its fearsome reputation, was not nearly
as adept at this as circumstances demanded of it. They were taking
a short-sighted military view of what was clearly an area of non-
military expertise. There were insufficient trained men to fill critical manufacturing jobs, and Germany was running short of nearly
every important commodity needed to continue the fight.

As an outsider, it was clear to me that instead of people like General Groener and Von Lignow making decisions as to how best to
keep production going, it should have been senior civilians who
were experienced in running factories and chains of businesses:
people like my father, not army officers directing university professors and middle-grade bank managers. Groener and Von Lignow
were brilliant; but they weren't businessmen or industrialists, and
to make things worse, there was nobody there who challenged their
opinions. In other contexts outside the army, I was to witness, much
later in life, leaders with unconditional authority making decisions
on matters they didn't understand and supported by a chorus of yes
men. It's an absolute guarantee of calamity. Since the war, I have
discovered that this situation is not uncommon; and it is by no
means confined to the military.

Around that polished oak conference table on the Konigsplatz,
we found ourselves discussing issues at an absurdly high level. At
the time, I wrongfully thought this was an act of desperation. We
were earnestly discussing the employment of the nation's manpower and the allocation of its vital resources to industry; and as
we did so, the country's key industrialists were virtually excluded
from all of our deliberations. Much as my two eccentric friends
McLeish and Redvers at Hammerwood Park had described to

me, the war's larger material problems had become its central and deciding issues.

From everything that was said at the conference, it was evident the German army was running into critical shortages. No one had expected the war to turn into this kind of bloody endurance contest, and the General Staff gave every impression that they had not thought enough about the problem until late in the game. It was evident from the tone of our discussions that Germany's generals were making all the country's key decisions. As I was to appreciate later, the German General Staff assumed the direction of the German economy as well as the economies of occupied territories not because the country was in serious trouble but because they were convinced they could do it more efficiently and more rapidly than anyone else. And to make matters worse, they were highly suspicious of everyone outside their own circle. Their primary inadequacy was not lack of ability, but arrogance.

Despite their undeniable strengths, the German officer corps and, most specifically, the General Staff, had an exaggerated opinion of its abilities. Men like Groener, and to a much lesser extent Von Lignow, were unblinkingly convinced of their own aptitudes. Several years later I came to realize that this vanity was one of the major contributing factors leading to the war. Much later, I came to grasp that such arrogance wasn't exclusively a German or a military trait; it was generously distributed amongst the ruling classes on both sides. And to my chagrin, it's taken me almost an entire lifetime to realize that insular thinking and self-importance are predispositions that are characteristic of our species.

I slipped away from the conference and managed to make a telephone call to Gabriele's house from a signals exchange on the first floor. Even as a member of the non-combatant economic planning conference, I was struck by the deference and discipline that the support troops who worked in the building showed towards their officers. The signaller at the phone exchange sat rigidly to attention when I asked him for a line. He remained sitting at attention while I placed the call. That would never have happened in our army. Our men would have addressed you politely as "Sir" but there would not have been such a stern sense of regulation and authority in the encounter. It alarmed me because, until then, I had assumed that everyday things in the German army would be almost identical to what I was used to. I'd been raised thinking that people were the same wherever you went, and I suppose in many ways that was true, but in many ways people can be fundamentally different. This routine incident caught me off guard and made me anxious about being found out.

I don't know whether my heart was pounding for fear of being caught out or because I was nervous telephoning Gabriele at home. Whatever the reason, I was tense. As it turned out, Gabriele wasn't home. Her father answered. Our conversation was remarkably informal. I shouldn't have been surprised; after all, this was Berlin and things here were supposedly freer than anywhere else. In Montreal in those days, courtship, in polite society, still had a rigid set of protocols. Men didn't just telephone women and ask them out. It was much more circumscribed than that. All that changed irrevocably in a few short years; but back then, according to my understanding of things, couples first got to know one another in the company of others. Gabriele's father was like his daughter: uninhibited and highly communicative. He spent several minutes chatting with me; perhaps he was trying to get my measure, but he seemed genuinely pleased I telephoned.

Gabriele and I met that evening outside her hospital and again we walked to the Tiergarten. At once Gabriele slipped into the role of a trusted old friend; she was animated and funny and easy to get along with. We chatted freely about a million different things. But looking back on it, our second time together was really more of a meeting of the minds than a romantic encounter. That was important to Gabriele. It was also one of those things I found captivating about her. She had a first-class mind and wasn't shy about expressing her opinions. Her sense of determination and independence also captivated me. I knew she was probably two or three years older than I, but that didn't bother me in the least. Her composure and experience added to her allure. Gabriele radiated a sense of confidence and intelligent self-assurance; and with her healthy good looks and my innocence, I fell head-over-heels in love with her.

Gabriele had been encouraged by her family to have her own views on things, although I vaguely suspected her opinions did not stray far from those of her bohemian parents. At one point, as we were strolling arm-in-arm down one of the Tiergarten's gravelled paths, she turned to me and said, "You seem to shy away from any conversation about the war. Why's that?"

I replied, "I don't think I deliberately avoid talking about it. It's hard to be objective about the war when you've been so involved in it. What do you want to know?"

"How do you feel about it?" She withdrew her arm from mine, stepped back and stared at me.

"I don't like it. I wish it would end, but…" I was picking my words carefully. "We can't lose it. That would be a disaster for Germany."

"Why do you say that?" she said.

"Because, at this point losing the war will mean appalling hardship inflicted upon us. We'd never recover."

"Greater hardship than we've gone through so far? You really believe that?"

"Yes, I do. I think whoever loses this war will suffer terrible civil disorder. The upheaval will be catastrophic. If one side declares an armistice, no one is suddenly going to become nice or fair. This is a fight for survival."

She put her arm back in mine and steered us along the path. "Reluctantly, I agree. We had quite a discussion about this last night at home. We have decided to continue to support the war effort."

"Did you not before?"

"No, not really. We aren't pacifists, but we don't support the Kaiser. That's not a popular position these days, but we have to go along with things until the war is over. When the war is over we'll be fighting vigorously for a more representative government in Germany. The Reichstag and Bundesrat are scarcely the kind of democratic institutions that will prevent us from ever getting into this kind of war again. You've experienced a more modern form of democracy in America. Germany's democracy doesn't extend to the Kaiser. It's fine to have town councils and provincial legislatures, but for Germany, a clique of aristocrats, army officers, and the Kaiser rule our central government. That's got to change."

"That's not a very popular position these days. People aren't fighting for the chance to change things; they want to preserve what they have," I said.

"No. It's not popular, but after the war I think we're going to see a freer and more enlightened Germany. We have the world's most advanced system of social security for our workers, we have the world's best education and medical systems, and soon our workers will have more say in running their own lives. Women will vote and we won't be forced to live by the rules imposed upon us by industrialists and capitalists. We'll do it all democratically, but we will do it." I raised my eyebrows and gave a non-committal shrug. Gabriele gave me a good-natured poke in the ribs. "You forget, Germany was forged in war by a pack of sclerotic princes and generals. The rest of Europe and America aren't like that. We have to make some changes."

"I wasn't raised here, so I won't disagree with any of that. But for now, I think you've got to keep those opinions to yourself. It'll be much safer to express them when the war's over."

She laughed. "Of course, I'm not a fool."

I didn't think much more of Gabriele's political opinions after that. Our conversation drifted on to other matters. She was passionate about jazz; from the little I'd heard of it before the war, it sounded like noise. She painted, she loved the theatre and the outdoors; and for a stuffy socialist, she loved fashion.

I suggested we go somewhere for dinner. This completely natural suggestion was met by an incredulous stare. She laughed again. "You really don't understand, do you? Half of Germany is close to starving. Dinner out will cost us a fortune."

I felt sheepish. "No, it's my treat. We can get something to eat somewhere. Besides, I still have all my back pay from being a prisoner. I'm off to Poland tomorrow, so we may not see one another again for a while."

Gabriele guided us through a maze of crowded cobbled streets to an inexpensive gasthaus. The place looked like something plucked off a Bavarian mountainside with a huge cuckoo clock, stag heads on the walls, massive hand-carved wooden mouldings, and cavernous wooden booths for intimate conversation. Despite the war, the place was crowded and every table was decorated with a small vase of fresh-cut flowers. The proprietors of the gasthaus made ·heroic efforts trying to disguise the inevitable plate of turnips but they also brought us excellent fried mushrooms and spicy potato cakes. The beer was marvellous and the cheese tray, for all it cost me, was bland and rubbery and the portions were microscopic. Although I spent more than a week of Alex Baumann's wages, I didn't mind at all. It was one of the best evenings of my life.

As the evening drew to a close, I insisted that I should see Gabriele to her door; but she wouldn't hear of it. We left the gasthaus and walked arm-in-arm to her trolley stop, and as we waited for the last trolley of the evening we chatted, about what I don't recall. I told her I wasn't certain when I'd be back, but when I returned to Berlin I wanted very much to see her again. She simply laughed and just then her trolley appeared in the distance down the street. Gabriele pulled me towards her and wrapping her arms around me she kissed me long and dreamily on the lips. I was surprised and overjoyed. If anything good could possibly have come from that war, it was that women by then were becoming much freer than they had been a few short years before. She got onto the trolley and took a seat with a window and waved to me. I stood on the cobbled street side and waved goodbye. As the white splash of her veil in the tram window receded into the night, I thought how profoundly the war was changing all of us.

✠

The conference wound up early the next morning. General Groener concluded the formal presentations with what was really an encouraging fact-filled harangue. Germany needed us desperately and we were being packed off to our respective sectors to squeeze the economies dry. That was simple enough. I was issued a new travel warrant, a train ticket, and joining instructions for my new unit. After General Groener left, the staff major with the gravelly voice went around the table and individually saw each one of us off. As he went slowly from officer to officer he clicked his heels and gave a crisp bow. Alternating his patter at each man, he either extended his thanks or wished them good luck. When he came to me, I suppose because of my recent celebrity and my youth, he grasped both my hands and wished me the very best of luck. "You will do well by Germany. Germany and the army are grateful for men like you." He looked genuinely moved and there were tears in his eyes.

At Berlin's Central Train Station, it was raining and low clouds scudded out of the north. Cold drops of rain spattered under the platform's roof. I stood a few feet back from the edge where it was dry. What little equipment and personal effects I had I slung over my shoulder in a field-grey haversack. Tied around my pack was my great coat. With today's unseasonable chill, I knew I would need that coat in a few months. Earlier that morning, my great coat became a great source of worry for me. I realized when I was packing my things that I didn't know exactly how the German army wrapped and tied their coats around their packs. It was not a big matter, but it was one of those things that a German officer would have done hundreds of times and anyone who did it incorrectly would stick out like a broken tooth. I did my best to imitate a picture I had seen the day before in an illustrated magazine. Looking around me, I thought I did a reasonable job of it and I was pleased with myself.

I was also in high spirits thinking about how comfortably I had slipped into my new life as Alex Baumann. A week earlier I was jumpy and frightened, expecting every moment some eagle-eyed policeman or soldier to pick me out as an impostor. Things had changed at a bewildering speed, and in this manic life I was once again riding a wave of confidence. I had a safe, not-too-demanding job, an unshakeable identity, and a pretty girl to dream about while I was gone. Living a spy's life was a delusional existence. Most of the time I actually thought of myself as Alex Baumann. I wanted it to be that way; but the truth was, the rise in my spirits was largely because of Gabriele. With Gabriele in my life, I felt transformed from someone constantly swimming against the current to someone who enjoyed life. I'm certain of it now. The elation I felt had little to do with the success of my role-playing. Gabriele's effect on me was like some strange chemical, that once added to a solution transformed its properties entirely. As short-sighted as it was, I exulted in the change. She was a few years older than I and a lot more experienced in some things, but I wasn't threatened by that. She was exactly what I had been seeking for a long time. When the elderly railway policeman came up to me to check my papers I smiled disarmingly. "Corporal, I hope I'm on the right platform for the train to Seventh Corps?"

"You are, sir, but that train won't be here for another forty-six minutes. Make sure you don't get on the next two trains or you'll find yourself in Belgium." We both laughed and I thanked him. He saluted, clicked his heels, and turned to the next officer on the platform."

The faces on the train platform looked grim. I didn't feel out of place, but I felt out of character with my fellow travellers. I had good reason. All the other men on the platform were almost certainly heading back for frontline duty. They didn't like it, but like millions of others in Europe, they were going back, as they would always go back. Whatever brought them to Berlin, whether it was leave or furlough or training, was over now and they were returning to violent death, wounds, horrific living conditions, and crushing responsibility. On the other hand, I was off to scour the Polish countryside for whatever I thought we could steal to aid the German war effort. I was my own master and certain that I would be returning to the arms of a beautiful woman. I walked farther down the platform. It was cold standing in one place and perhaps because I felt so cheerful and contented, I didn't want to engage any of my grim-faced companions in conversation.

I strolled all the way down the station and stood near the far end, where the passenger platform abuts onto the goods yard. Behind barbed wire fences and protected by patrolling armed guards, I could see vast stockpiles of supplies of every description. Stretched out along the railway line beside me I could see piles of coiled barbed wire. Farther out, towering over blast parapets, were huge tarpaulin-covered structures made out of stacked wooden crates: box upon box of rifle and machine-gun ammunition, grenades, flares, and trench mortar and artillery rounds. Stretching out farther beyond the soot-stained brick railway marshalling sheds were even larger crates and metal boxes of every description: replacement weapons, field rations, clothing, spare parts, medical supplies, and God-knows-what.

As I gazed out over this vast landscape of marshalled ordinance, across the tracks from me I could hear the approaching tramp of hobnailed boots on concrete. In a few seconds a column of freshly raised replacement infantry marched smartly into sight from the station yard and onto the opposite platform. These men would have been the draft of '98. German soldiers had long ago begun to refer to themselves by their birth date and the class of their call-up. They were wearing full marching order: packs, great coats, and blankets. Wherever these men were going, they planned to be gone for some time. Their new grey steel helmets gave them a sinister look of uniformity. The company nearest me came crashing to a halt. Someone shouted an order and the long files turned sharply so that the troops were facing me. They looked formidable, staring determinedly into space. As freshly trained recruits, they were putting on a show for the veterans standing on my platform. They succeeded and I was suitably impressed. When their feldwebel stood them easy, they relaxed, chatting with one another, un-slinging their rifles, adjusting straps, stretching and getting the blood flowing to stiff muscles.

With these fresh troops in front of me, acres of ordinance to my right, and scores of determined veterans to my left, I had a hard time believing Germany was running short of men or supplies. The spectacle before me was one of overwhelming power, yet I knew this was only a minuscule fraction of Germany's military might. Were this scene to be reproduced tens of thousands of times over, it might begin to approximate something of the scale of the German national effort being expended to fight the war. Yet in spite of all this, Germany and her allies were heavily outnumbered. It was fearsome, but it also made me think what an immense waste it was: the energy, the national genius, and the commitment that went into bringing these troops and materiel together for the purpose of going out to destroy other men—men like me or the fellows opposite. It seemed utterly pointless.

For a while I reflected on the futility of all this. If this effort had been put into better housing or medical research or increasing agricultural yields or a thousand other more profitable uses, how much better off the world would have been. But then for a split second, as I locked eyes with one of the young men standing opposite me, I realized; I wasn't just a detached bystander who had the option of musing philosophically about the war. Coming to the easy conclusion that the war was wicked and reprehensible may have been true—but it didn't change the situation in the least. I was as much an active participant as anyone in the ranks of men opposite me, and trite observations about the senselessness of war altered nothing. To sit back and do nothing, to pretend to take the moral high ground without offering any reasonable solution to the problems at hand, seemed a spineless and vacuous response. The time for moralizing on the evils of war had passed. The world missed its chance in the summer of 1914, and now we were locked in a fight to the death. No amount of reasoning or wishful thinking could or would change that.

I had made my decision to fight almost two years ago. My country was at war and I'd chosen not to stand by doing nothing while other men put their lives at risk. Nothing had really changed, except that now I was in a position to do something to influence the war's outcome; and despite my exuberance of just minutes before, I knew I was tired to the depths of my being. There were times I felt my soul had been drained of every ounce of energy. My time in the line had been more gruelling than I admitted to—but something within me, something I could not repress, told me I could never in good conscience withdraw my services once I'd committed them. I would keep going forward as I'd committed to do so long ago. I was no hero. The men on both platforms, the veterans and the recruits, were exactly the same, as were the millions of others who served on both sides month after month in the trenches.

I looked steadily at the ranks of young replacements opposite me. This would have been the class of boys who, according to the German census, officially became men in July 1917. Now in October, they were trained and ready to take their place at the front. I wondered how many would be alive in a year, and what role, if any, would I play in bringing about the deaths and maiming of those unfortunates who would never see a return trip to this train station. I wanted a cigarette. I wandered away from the supply dump and back inside the station where smoking was permitted.

✠

My trip into Poland was uneventful. I shared my compartment with several other officers, all of whom travelled farther up the line than I did. We hardly spoke, and for my part I kept my nose in one of the volumes given to me by Von Lignow's father. When the porter called out, "BIALYSTARY, Seventh Corps Rear Headquarters Command Centre," I reached for my haversack on the shelf above me. One of the other junior officers in my compartment scratched his beard, smiled thinly, and said, "Oberleutnant, you're a fortunate man." He said nothing else, but I knew exactly what he meant. The other officers, all of them about my age, merely stared at me. I knew what they were thinking. As I stepped from the railway carriage I turned and waved to my fellow travellers and simply said "Good luck."

Waiting for me on the railway platform was an unteroffizier from the Second Uhlan Regiment. He was a massive, ginger-haired man with huge ears and hands the size of a Clydesdale's hoof; well over six-feet six, he was heavy set with teeth spaced like fence posts. He had an enormous red moustache that reminded me of my shaving brush. I guessed he was in his mid-thirties. He wore his round cloth cap pushed down over his forehead. He saluted and introduced himself as Unteroffizier Brickner and then led me to a horse-drawn wagon.

"Sir, I'm from the Lines of Communication Cavalry Squadron. I speak some Polish and I've been assigned to your protection. I've been told to have things ready for you by morning."

I threw my pack in the back of the cart and Brickner and I drove for about thirty minutes through a drab town made up of grey stucco and timber buildings. Bialystary looked like a long time ago someone had thrown up a village as fast as they could. Nothing was painted. The main street was narrow and made out of irregular field stones packed in mud. The few side streets running off from it were unsurfaced packed dirt. The place had a damp, unhealthy smell to it, like a basement after a flood. There were only a few electrical lines in the centre of town, and even though it was still light out, most of the windows and doors were shuttered tight.

Of the few people I saw on the streets, most were old women in shawls, tottering along oblivious to us with wicker baskets under their arms. There were a few very young children, with runny noses and ragged clothes. They seemed curious about us and some called out mischievously at us in Polish. Brickner pretended not to notice. He wasn't a very talkative man. Half a mile outside the town we stopped at a small unpainted wooden farm complex. Brickner pulled up on the reins and our tired old nag shuffled to a stop. The farmhouse was a single-storey, weathered building with wooden shingles hammered recklessly over a sloped roof. On one side there was a wretched little vegetable garden protected by a falling-down unpainted picket fence. A few stunted lilac bushes struggled near the back.

Brickner sat in the cart smiling; he made no move to help me get my pack. "Bialystary is one of those places that wasn't burnt to the ground when the Russian army retreated through here last summer. The rear-area commander has put all Lines of Communication troops into billets around here. If you'd gone on to the next stop up, you'd be at the new station, the one outside Bialystock, where the big supply dumps are located. It's guarded better than the Kaiser's jewels. This farm's where the officers from the rear-area security detachment and rear-area signals company live."

He stopped speaking and gave a great retching, hacking cough and spat. "S'cuse me sir. I was gassed last winter at Bolimov." He hacked again in a great painful spasm. "Our own gas too; it blew back on us from the Russians, it still bothers me." He took a few seconds to catch his breath again. "This place, though, it's quite safe. The Poles don't like us, but then again, they don't hate us either. Maybe that'll change. I've been told that you've been sent out to strip the countryside of whatever's left?" He looked at me inquiringly as I pulled my pack from the back of the cart.

"Something like that, but we intend to pay for whatever we take." I paused. "But I'm sure you're right, we won't make ourselves popular. This doesn't look like the most prosperous place, even without the war."

"Sir, you'll be trying to squeeze blood from a stone, believe me. If it's food or forage you want, anything you take will mean the Poles starve. When that happens, maybe then you gentlemen will have to move out of here and into quarters that can be more easily protected." He chuckled softly at the thought. "Tomorrow I've booked a staff car for you. You have priority use on one of the automobiles from the corps transport pool whenever you're out in the rear area. With petrol rationing as tight as it is, you getting an automobile raised a few eyebrows, I can tell you that, but that came down from Berlin. What time would you like me to come round for you?"

I wasn't at all certain as to what I was going to do first thing tomorrow, but I answered confidently. "Come at 0830. We'll go to the main command headquarters in town. I'll let you know what we'll be doing after that."

Brickner nodded, gave me an airy salute, and tugged at the reins. "Eight-thirty then, sir. I'll be here."

✠

I entered the farmhouse without knocking. The place was dim and smelled of boiled cabbage and pipe smoke. I could see a rough table with an army-issue oil lamp on it, some rolled maps, papers, and a few camp stools and chairs. The walls were unfinished and whatever valuable furnishings that were once here were long gone.

From within a cloud of smoke, a voice from a back corner called out in a nasal drone. "So you're the new officer from Berlin come to join us then, are you?" A figure in a half-buttoned tunic lurched up from the only comfortable looking chair.

"I'm Captain Ebersbach." He was a bald, paunchy man in his late forties, about medium height with thick steel-rimmed glasses and a pallid pock-marked face. As he held out his hand he said, "You will be sleeping over by the wall. There's no mattress here for you but behind the outbuilding you can find some boards to make a bed. There are dry boards at the bottom of the pile. Don't go bringing in a lot of bugs with you either when you do it."

I was a bit taken aback and merely said, "Oh, no, that's fine. Thank you."

"Oberleutnant, when you talk to me, you end your sentences with 'sir'! Do you understand? And the other two officers that live here, you will find they are junior lieutenants; you will have them refer to you as sir. Just because we are in the rear area I will not allow sloppy discipline, no first names. Do you understand? Now, isn't it customary that you salute senior officers when you walk into a room?"

I gave a lifeless salute, dropped my things, and went outside to

find the boards to make my bed. I found out later we had an elderly Polish servant who came around about noon of each day and
cooked and cleaned for us. Ebersbach told me that the two "junior"
roommates usually found pressing business that kept them overnight in the rear area's administrative section. I nodded, thinking
that my travels throughout the region would likely make it difficult
for me to get back most nights as well. Nonetheless, I persisted
in making conversation with Ebersbach, if only to get information
from him.

He was a reserve transport officer who spoke Polish. Before the
war he lived in Astadt, a town near the Prussian and Polish frontier.
He ran a small dairy and green grocer's delivery business. When he
was called up, he was promptly transferred to the military police
and tasked with rear-area security and internal affairs throughout
the Seventh Corps Lines of Communication, from the rear headquarters back to the Prussian border. His military police company
was billeted two miles away; and like me, he spent much of his time
travelling throughout the region. When he wasn't travelling, he was
back at this miserable little farm drinking himself into a stupor and,
from what I could gather, making life a misery for the junior lieutenants from the Signals company. It was soon obvious that despite
his posturing, he knew almost nothing about the rear area except
for what could be seen from the window of a train carriage.

I asked about the residents of this farm and where they had gone.
I got an earful. "They're Jews. This whole area was filled with Jews."
He waved his hand dismissively at me. "The Russians burnt their
farms and most of the Jews in the countryside were herded back
into Russia. The town of Bialystary and the city of Bialystock are
still filled with them. Why do you care anyway?" I shrugged but
that night Ebersbach lectured me on the new ideas he had picked
up on his last leave in Prussia.

"When the war's over, we'll take all these lands from Russia. Germany needs 'lebensraum.'" It was the first time I had heard the
word. Unhappily, it was not to be the last. "Make no mistake," he
slurred, "we're entitled to it. We don't have to move off to Amer-

ica like your family; our ancestral lands are here in the East. What the Russians call Poland was part of the German Fatherland over a thousand years ago. It's ours and always has been ours. We have a legitimate historical claim to it. When this war's over we're going to keep it. We fought for it and we won it. It'll be part of the Fatherland. Believe me. Russia will be sorry she attacked us, I can tell you that." Ebersbach went to bed that night muttering about lebensraum and Germany's entitlement to the East. I dismissed him as a drunken crank.

14

THE MORNING dawned crisp and clear with enormous clouds floating in a blue sky. Brickner arrived in front of the farmhouse, his round face beaming from ear to ear. He was driving a mud-spattered Benz touring car painted in field-grey with the Seventh Corps shield fixed to its grill.

"Good morning, Oberleutnant. Your unteroffizier got to the motor pool early this morning, and so we go in style, eh!" He raised his hands cheerfully. "No more horse and cart for us." He began to cough and hacked violently for almost a minute. "The automobile works better than your unteroffizier, sir, but don't worry, both driver and automobile will make it all right." Brickner put his head down on the steering wheel, relaxed his whole body, and willed his lungs back into working properly. "I'm fine now sir. Now we go?" We drove back through Bialystary and up to the Seventh Corps's rear headquarters.

The rear headquarters of an army corps is a massive complex. As we drove into the restricted area, a military policeman in a helmet and gendarme neck plate stopped us at a checkpoint. Our motorcar was shunted off to a siding and I showed him my authorization. He scrutinized it carefully, politely asked me to wait, and went into his shelter to make a call on his field telephone. A few minutes later he re-appeared and gave me a printed sketch map of the headquarters area.

The rear area was bigger than anything I had imagined. It covered many square miles and consisted of train sidings, horse lines, farrier shops, mechanics' sheds, dozens of supply points, ration, fuel and ammunition points, cobblers' shops, railway repair yards, lumber sheds, bakeries, vehicle parks, maintenance huts, field hospitals, training areas, barracks, laundry and bath units, as well as bivouac areas that went on for miles.

Our first stop was next to the aerodrome, After that, we had to drive to the Headquarters military police compound and from there we were directed to the supply offices that were housed in requisitioned buildings in the town. I was surprised at how efficient and disciplined things were. Despite the sprawl, there was no confusion or waiting. From the air it must have looked as if someone had stirred up an ant hill, but on the ground things were purposeful; there was no sense of excitement or tension. The Germans ran their headquarters like a massive, well-organized factory. I was shuttled around from office to office and received my travel warrants, passes, maps, field rations, fuel authorization tickets, and fuel. By 10:30, with Brickner and me in the front seats and an escort of two perpetually silent Uhlan troopers sitting in the back, we were off.

My intention was to drive around the perimeter of my area and after that to follow my nose. I had seven days to make my initial report to Berlin. The area temporarily called "Rural Bialystock" was as dismal a piece of real estate as you could find in Europe. There were dozens of farms; most not much different than the one I was billeted in. During the morning, I didn't see a single head of livestock, and in many places, the farm buildings had been burned to the ground. While I was stopped in front of a rotting wooden bridge over a small creek, I looked out on a patch of gently rolling open countryside and studied the map to confirm our location.

Brickner pointed at the blackened timbers of one the gutted farms. "I told you they hate the Russians more than they hate us. The burned-out ones you see are part of the Russian army's scorched earth policy. The farms that aren't destroyed are the ones where the peasants had something of value to bribe the Tsar's officers. I guarantee you, sir, there's not much in any of these now."

"I suppose you're right," I said. "Let's go see one of these just for our education." The Benz lurched forward over a cart track and we pulled up in front of a stone and unpainted timber cottage and its ramshackle outbuildings. Brickner began to shout something in Polish and presently an old man, unshaven and wearing a peaked cap and high boots, came hobbling out the front door. As he approached us, he pulled off his cap and bowed his head. He was trembling and I tried to sound friendly.

"Unteroffizier, tell him we mean him no harm."

Brickner turned to me. "I know you won't hurt him, sir, but may I suggest, it's best to let him stay frightened of you. Otherwise he won't tell us the truth."

"Don't do that. He's probably been bullied enough. Treat him kindly. I need information from these people. If he hasn't got anything to give us, we can't take anything. Go on, tell him we mean him no harm."

While Brickner translated, I noticed a small boy's head peer out at us from the window and a woman's hand pulled him by the collar out of sight.

The old man began to talk haltingly.

Brickner turned to me. "Sir, he says the Russians took all his livestock last year; the Germans took his cart, and his only son-in-law was conscripted into the Russian army when they retreated through here. He has nothing to give and he and his daughter and grandson are on the verge of starvation."

"Tell him I'm not here to take anything from him. Ask him what they're living on."

Brickner spoke haltingly and made signs to indicate he was eating. After a lengthy reply, Brickner said, "Potatoes and beets from last year's crop. He says they haven't much left. German troops pulled up most of their garden in August. Sometimes they catch perch from the stream back there—but that's all they eat."

The peasant was the picture of poor health. His clothes hung loosely on him and he had large black circles under his eyes. "Tell him we're going to look around his farm. We aren't taking anything. I just want to see what the conditions are like for these people. Tell him we want to help them."

"That's a good one, sir." Brickner laughed cynically and spoke rapidly to the peasant.

The old man's eyes widened and he dropped to his knees and began to shriek and plead with us.

"What did you tell him, Unteroffizier? The man's terrified."

"What you told me to say, sir. I don't think he understands. My Polish, it's probably not so good. Honestly, I didn't say anything bad."

I got out of the motorcar and took the old man by the hand, speaking as soothingly as I could. I brought him to his feet.

"Tell him again, we won't hurt him."

Brickner spoke again, imitating my tone, and we led the old man back to the farm house. I opened the door. Against the far wall, a young woman of about eighteen or nineteen wrapped in a red shawl and wearing a faded blue dress cringed beside a table. In one arm she held a small blond boy. Her other arm was behind her back, and despite her fear, I could see she was grasping a heavy-bladed carving knife.

I spoke as soothingly as I could and raised my hands. "We will not hurt you." I turned to Brickner. "Unteroffizier, go back to the staff car. Bring them some of our bread." Brickner's jaw dropped and he stared at me incredulously. "Do it now! Go!" I said. He returned in a few seconds looking hard done by with a loaf of dark rye bread torn in half. "Do you want me to give them both halves sir?"

"Yes, don't be greedy."

"Our rations have to last us all week, sir."

"We'll survive."

There was nothing more to see. The small farmhouse was empty. The eyes of its inhabitants were frightened, hollow, and dull. I nodded and said thank you in German. "Let's go, Unteroffizier. I've seen what I need to know."

Back in the staff car, Brickner wasted no time. "With respect, sir, we can't go around giving food away like that. We give a loaf of bread every time you want to look at something; you and I, we'll be dead in a week. Sir, I had to do some fast talking with the Headquarters bakery to get what we have." Brickner sounded sincere, but I said nothing. A few seconds later he started again. "Sir, I know you've been at the front. I see your Iron Cross ribbon. Those aren't given away with the mail call, but it's not the same back here. I don't like it, but it's different, honest."

I spoke sharply. "What are you getting at, Unteroffizier?"

"Back there at the farm, I don't like to see these people go hungry any more than you. But here, it's not the same as when I was at the front. At the front we just had to fight. You know that's not easy, but we didn't have to make the decisions we do back here."

"What do you mean?"

"What would you rather do, sir, shoot an enemy soldier or force Polish peasants into starvation?"

"I don't want to do either, to tell you the truth, Unteroffizier. But I suppose I'm more prepared to shoot someone in battle. I'm a German soldier. I don't make war on women, children, and old people."

"Neither do I, sir, but when they sent me back here we had orders to round up whatever we could take from the countryside that we could use for our war effort. Just like the Russians, we took what they left behind and that wasn't much—cattle, carts, motorcars from the towns, petrol, forage, grain." He shrugged his shoulders and steered the staff car into a stubble field around a huge mud puddle. "Doesn't leave a lot for the Polish. These people are dying now. I've been here six months. I see their little funerals out in the country. Not something I'm proud of. Nobody at home or at the front sees that."

We said nothing for a while and the car bounced over the dirt road. The road grew wetter and the big wooden-spoked tires splashed water and mud back at us. We both donned driving goggles.

I was the first to speak. "So we'll do our best, Unteroffizier. I don't know the answer, but whatever decisions I make, I'll try not to be hard on the Polish. Can't do more than that."

"No, sir, we can't, but you'll see, if we don't put the screws to the Poles we may lose the war. If we lose the war, the Russians, the French and English—they'll destroy us. You know what a plundering Russian army would do in Prussia or Berlin? So, the way I see it, it's us or them. I wouldn't stay here if it wasn't like that. I'd insist I go back to the front, and if I did I'd be dead of pneumonia inside a month, but that's what I'd do. We don't have a choice here." After a split second's pause, he added, "Sir."

"Fair enough, Unteroffizier, I know what you're saying. Thanks for your opinion."

We drove in silence past farms and hamlets until we came upon the village of Wyzgorice. We slowed to a crawl as we entered the village and stopped at the edge of what was probably the village square. It was nothing more than a large unpaved intersection with an elm tree and a small shrine to the Virgin Mary in the midst of two muddy roads. On one side of the square was a church, and across from it were a tavern and what was once a general store. The rest of the village consisted of a dozen brick and peeling stucco houses, each with a barn on the ground floor. You would be hard pressed to think up a more uninteresting and dreary location. It wasn't desperately poor, but it was colourless, and had neither warmth nor charm.

I got out of the motorcar and walked into the tavern. The place was empty, and except for a few scattered tables and chairs there was no evidence the building had ever seen better days. I don't know what I was looking for really. I took my pickelhaube off and wiped my face with the back of my sleeve. A few moments later a young girl of about fourteen came out from the back room and began to speak rapidly. There were several other children who followed her but stopped at the doorway. I had no idea what she said, but I raised my hands and shook my head. I turned to leave and bumped into Brickner. "Let's go, there's nothing here," I said.

As we emerged into the sunlight, a very elderly priest, who I assumed came from the church across the square, hobbled over to us. He was wearing a long black soutane and a wide-brimmed black felt hat. He was bent over his walking stick. He spoke in clear Viennese German. "What do you want here, gentlemen? There's nothing in this town."

I sympathized with him but his hostile tone put me on guard. "I haven't come here to rob you of anything, Father. I'm merely doing a survey of this sector and I'll be making a report." I looked him squarely in the eye and said, "May I introduce myself. I'm Oberleutnant Alex Baumann and this is Unteroffizier Brickner."

He was icily correct. "I am Father Krusinski." He didn't offer his hand and glared at us.

"You have good German, Father, where did you learn it?"

"I'm sure you didn't come here to discuss my German. I studied in Vienna as a seminarian. What exactly can we do for you?"

"Nothing, Father, I'm simply passing through, observing the countryside. I'm to make a report on my findings next week."

"Tell them we are on the brink of starvation. Tell them all our men of military age have been taken from us to serve in the Tsar's armies. Tell them the country has been looted by the Russians and by the Germans, and the result is that people such as this family are burying their infant children and their old people. Tell them just to leave us alone. We have nothing else."

There was not much I could say to this. I saluted politely and said, "I'll do whatever I can, believe me, Father. Thank you." We made as graceful an exit as we possibly could under the circumstances.

In the staff car, Brickner waited this time before he started at me. "I know you come from America, sir, and before the war you were a civilian, but no one should speak to a German officer like that. Not ever. Next time, sir, leave it to me. I'll give the old dog a good thrashing for you."

Brickner caught me off guard. I couldn't believe he was talking like that. An hour earlier he had been agonizing over the morality of plundering occupied territories and now he was insisting he be allowed to beat elderly priests.

"Priest or not, sir, we can't put up with that kind of behaviour. Never mind making the rear area productive for the war effort, let them talk like that and we'll have to fight a guerrilla war behind the front. I won't hurt him, but they'll learn to hold their tongue in the presence of a German officer."

I'd had enough. "Listen, Unteroffizier, that's it. I do this my way. You drive, translate, and act in whatever other capacity I tell you to. No more lectures. When I want your advice, I'll ask for it." We drove in silence for the rest of the afternoon.

By dinner, Brickner began to come around. "I'm sorry, sir. Earlier today, I was only trying to help."

I wasn't letting him off. "I appreciate your efforts but from here on in, wait until I ask for your advice. Now, what shall we do about getting us somewhere to sleep? There should be another small village beyond this next ridge line."

Brickner, his guards, and I spent four days much like that first one. We drove around the perimeter of the Rural Bialystock sector; and periodically, where the roads permitted, we explored the interior. The actual city of Bialystock was on the extreme southern edge of my area and was the responsibility of another, more senior officer. So for me, there was very little to report upon. The farms were all completely impoverished. All able-bodied men had long since been conscripted by the Russians and there was nothing I could see that I could include in my report to the Economic Planning Staff that this godforsaken bit of rural Poland could provide to help the war effort. In this I had a serious problem. I had made up my mind not to inflict hardship on the Poles, but somehow I still had to come up with a list of items to be extracted from the area.

On my second-last day, we drove through a very large forest. I'd resolved to make the most of this. The Bialowieza Forest would provide timber. The area on the map was intermittently shaded, and I thought that if I was sufficiently enthusiastic I could convince the staff that extensive logging operations would be a viable source of war material. I would ignore the peasants. Nothing could be taken from them in their wretched state without causing even greater loss of life and suffering. I was determined to do my utmost not to have any part in this.

As dusk began to fall, we found ourselves clutching the sides of the Benz Tourer. We lurched and bounced steadily upwards through a stretch of hardwood forest. The trees were massive: mostly oaks and maples, with bushy pines growing close by the road. The night was as black as I'd ever seen it. Thick pine branches seemed to be reaching out at us, scratching at our faces and trying to shove us out of the car. The whole area had never been logged and I wondered if this whole high feature we were climbing was some kind of royal game preserve that the Tsar or his family used for hunting—that is, if they ever condescended to come here.

We pushed on for an hour and the trail became steadily more narrow and indistinct. The lamps of the touring car threw unnatural jagged shadows in the undergrowth, leaping and shrinking like firelight gone mad. Cold rain soon began to spatter down upon us and I could sense Brickner and his guards were becoming impatient and annoyed. By now they expected to have eaten their suppers and be billeted comfortably under some hapless peasant's roof. As the rain picked up, the guards in the back seat periodically began to mutter under their breath. I told Brickner to stop and turned to him and the men.

"I know you're thinking we're lost. We're not," I said in a level tone. "The map shows the trail through here and I'm certain the map's right, it's just old. Another five miles up here and over this high feature, we come to another village. We'll stop there for the night."

Brickner sniffed self-righteously and looked straight ahead. I expected him to say something, to make a joke or pretend to be fatalistic about it all. I wanted him to support me, but his silence in front of the men was damning.

I was frustrated, and as I waited and listened to the silly old fool's silence I became angry, very angry. It was time to play my trump card. "So if you men think you're badly done by tonight, I can guarantee you that fifty miles east of here it's probably raining too, and there are a lot more men who are lot closer to the Russians than we are. Each one of you know they're having a much more uncomfortable night of it than you are. If I hear any more muttering or complaining, or if I sense any one of you are unhappy with what we're doing, I can arrange for all of you to join them. If you think your rear-area duties are too difficult, I'll give you an option." It was my turn for silence. Nobody spoke. "Good. Now let's get a fucking grip. Keep going, Unteroffizier!"

I didn't enjoy this kind of outburst, and even at the time I thought it seemed out of character for me. I tried to be the sort of officer who led in a more quiet, persuasive style. When I was commanding my platoon, I never had to threaten or intimidate. Sergeant Ferguson had always been ready to step in as the disciplinarian, and when he did, he rarely raised his voice. I was certain German frontline units operated much the same way. Soldiers like the German troops I'd seen in Flanders didn't fight as courageously as they did unless they were well led; and good leaders, I thought, rarely resorted to bullying.

Brickner was probably a rear-area misfit and perhaps, because it was safer, things were different here in the rear area. The quality of the non-commissioned officers wasn't as high, but I still didn't like the idea of alienating the only non-commissioned officer assigned to support me. My position was precarious enough. I didn't want to incur suspicion or hostility needlessly and from the uneven performance I had seen, I had no reason to trust Brickner.

The track we followed continued to deteriorate and turned from a poorly defined rut into an overgrown pathway, scarcely large enough for a single horse to pass. Our progress slowed to a crawl. The road, if it was a road, had not been used for years. In many stretches it was so overgrown we took turns walking before the car to identify where the path led. Every hundred yards we had to back the staff car up and take a run at the undergrowth to get through, and five or six times we got hung up on brush and had to get out and push that monstrous motorcar forward. It took us hours to get over that hill. During one of my spells breaking trail, I remember thinking what I'd say to these men in the morning if it turned out the trail led nowhere. We would be wet and exhausted and I'd look like a bloody fool. Would I apologize or bluff it out? I decided that even in the unlikely event that we were lost here for days I wouldn't grovel. I'd admit my mistake and keep going. None of them could read a map to save their life and they were a hell of a lot safer here than if they returned to their regiment at the front.

During one of my turns at pushing brush aside and searching for the path, we crested the high ground; the road levelled out; the bushes became thinner and the track more defined. A half-hour later we burst out of the undergrowth and came upon a dark clearing. We almost bumped into the tiny hamlet of Dabreeskow. There were no lights and several low, black, square buildings sat darkly at the edge of the tree line. The windows were shuttered and rain dripped steadily from the wooden roofs. A dog barked. I didn't know it then, but Dabreeskow was the answer to my prayers in more ways than one.

As our staff car pulled up in front of the nearest building, a crack of light flickered behind a shutter and a few seconds later the front door opened. An old man with a dim candle lantern stood in the doorway. He held a hatchet in his hand. The dog behind him was barking and snarling furiously.

"Tell him we're looking for a dry place to stay for the night. We won't hurt him or his family, nor will we take anything," I said to Brickner in a none too friendly tone. "Keep a polite tongue in your head while you're at it."

Brickner said nothing to me and broke into Polish. The old man muttered, closed the door, and re-appeared seconds later wearing a coat and floppy felt hat. He led us through the rain across the track to another building. It was a half-empty woodshed with some kind of large mechanical saw in the centre. The floor was covered with sawdust and freshly sawn pine boards were piled against the wall. The building had a fresh, reassuring smell to it.

"This'll do fine," I said, nodding and smiling to the old man. "Thank you." He smiled and raised his finger as if I was to wait for a moment. A minute later he returned with an old wine bottle. I pulled the cork and sniffed it. It was half-filled with something sweet and alcoholic like plum or apricot brandy. He smiled and chuckled, his grey-bearded, gap-toothed face delighted we had not turned him and his family out of their beds. I thanked him again and he backed out smiling and bowing to us.

I raised the bottle cheerfully. "Something to go with dinner. Unteroffizier, you will please divide this evenly amongst us. Now, let's get something to eat."

Brickner came to life once he was in the dry shed. One of our guards began to pile kindling on some bricks as if to start a cooking fire and Brickner quite rightly berated him at the top of his lungs. "Do want to kill us all you fool? No fires inside here, no matter how small. Build your fire outside the door."

He turned to me. "You see, sir, we have idiots for troops here in the rear area. They don't know when they're well off and then they try to kill us out of stupidity. If this one doesn't smarten up, I'll have him sent up to the front myself. Do you think this idiot deserves to have plum brandy, sir? He's dangerous enough to us when he's sober."

I could see the two guards exchange glances behind Brickner's back. One of them may have been a bit simple-minded, but it was obvious they both hated him. I was right not to trust Brickner. He was trying to ingratiate himself with me at the expense of his men. "Give him his share." I turned to the Prussian and said, "Next time keep your wits about you."

We toasted our sausages and ate our dried bread ration as the first grey glow of dawn began to break over the woods to the east. I was cold and stiff. The plum brandy was excellent, although it was powerful and burned my throat. The rain let up. Brickner made a sentry roster for the two guards and put the tall Prussian on watch first. The three of us curled up in our blankets inside the shed and I fell instantly into a deep sleep.

I awoke late in the morning; it must have been near noon. I could see in the doorway that the big Prussian guard was back on watch and he was shouting at someone I couldn't see. The voice that replied belonged to a man and he spoke in very good, but strangely accented German. "Tell your officer I'll wait for him here. I'll wait until he wakes up."

When I crawled out from my blanket, I slipped on my boots, belt, and pistol. Outside, sitting on a log stump quietly smoking a briar pipe, was a little man of about sixty years of age. He had a grey goatee and wore a stylish dark-green homburg. He was dressed in a heavy wool suit and tie. He wore an expensive overcoat around his shoulders like a cape. He was no woodcutter.

"I overheard you. You want to speak to me?"

"Oh yes. Allow me to introduce myself. I am Jacob Lazarowicz. I live in Bialystock. I rode up here to see you." As he spoke he indicated his horse, a sleek bay tethered at the edge of the clearing. I wondered how a horse like that had not been appropriated by the army.

I was taken aback. "You want to see me, whatever for?"

"I have heard from some people that you are doing a survey of the area around here for the army. I have some information that may be of interest to you. May we talk inside?"

We walked to the woodcutter's cabin and sat at the table. Jacob Lazarowicz spoke cheerily in Polish and the woodcutter poured some kind of dark tea for us and brought out more plum brandy. He grinned and motioned me to drink.

"As I said, I am Jacob Lazarowicz. I live in Bialystock and before the war I ran a large textile firm and a chemical plant. I made clothing, industrial dyes, and patent medicines. We traded a bit with Germany and Austria but mostly with Russia, until the war broke out and the Russians retreated from here. The Russians looted my factory and warehouse before they left, and since then I have been working with the German army. In exchange for their leaving the people of Bialystock in peace, I have organized a number of services for the Germans. With German help, I now have a small factory running again. It's not much, we make cloth bandoliers for ammunition, field dressings, pouches for signal wire, that sort of thing. It's not much. I do other things as well. The servant that cooks for you, stable hands, mess servants, orderlies at the field hospital, labourers at the railhead, translators, that kind of thing, I organize them for the German army." He looked at me steadily with clear brown eyes. "It's not much, but it keeps us from starving. Up to now the Germans haven't treated us too badly, much better than the Russians did. And so, we survive. I am trying to make sure that that state of affairs continues."

"So what can I do to help you, Mr. Lazarowicz?" I sipped my plum brandy. It was excellent but hardly what I was used to at breakfast.

"I have information that will help with whatever report you have to make to Berlin. I'm sure you've found that the area you've been travelling in is destitute." He waved his hands at me airily. "I'm not a spy, Oberleutnant. I'm a businessman. I got my information about you from the cook at your house in Bialystary. Your captain talks a lot and I sell him his schnapps. From him and many others like him I get information that we can use to provide services to the Germans. I turn information into opportunity and opportunity becomes profit and profit means people don't starve. Personally, I'm not making any money on this. I heard through the priest you met a few days ago at Wyzgorice, you remember the little village you stopped in, the one with a very old priest?" I nodded. "Well, he told me he thought you were headed this way. I guessed you would come on this track because it's the only inhabited place around here and I rode up hoping to meet you."

"What is it you have to tell me?"

"The priest tells me you are a decent man. Is that so?"

I shrugged.

"I'll get to the point. I have heard that the Germans plan on moving large numbers of Poles into Germany as forced labour to run their factories. That will release manpower to be re-deployed for the front or for other higher-priority industrial tasks."

I must have looked surprised.

"Oh, it's true. It's already happened. Last week near Warsaw, three thousand women and their children were shipped to the Ruhr. Apparently those who don't work in the factories are forced to look after the children, and the conditions aren't exactly comfortable. Now, the only thing your area has to offer, as I am sure you have already deduced, is people. They're all close to starvation; there isn't enough to keep them through the winter, so maybe being shipped to Germany would be a blessing in disguise. After all, they will have to be fed if they're going to work in factories." He stopped and looked at me.

"A week ago I attended briefings in Berlin on the new economic measures. I didn't hear anything about forced labour."

"Of course not. I believe you. But think about it. Would you advertise measures like that? I suspect the war is entering a much more critical phase than we can even begin to guess. Anyway, I believe that even with the best of intentions, it will be better to keep people here on their farms and in the villages. We have to get food shipped here because when you start to ship people around like that, things will go wrong. People get sick and they die in large numbers. That's just my opinion. You are a smart man, what do you think?"

"What do you want from me?"

"Two miles from here I can show you a deposit of nitrogen-rich rock. Germany desperately needs a secure source of extractable nitrogen compounds for its war effort. Before the war, the Germans were dependant upon Chile for its supplies of manufacturable nitrogen compounds. You had huge war reserves, but the British blockade has meant your stockpiles are shrinking to dangerous levels. Your scientists have done a remarkable job synthesising the process and reducing your consumption rates, but you still need a core source of useable nitrogen compounds. The mineral deposit I'm talking about can be used not only to make TNT, but also, I'm told, to manufacture detonators, artillery fuses, and flares, and there's still no synthetic substitute for these. Simply put, Germany is running out of the nitrogen compound stockpiles she has come to rely on. Your army must have this ore if it is to continue fighting."

"How do you know all this?"

"I'm a businessman, and as I said, before the war I was in the chemical business. I should know such things."

"So why doesn't the army just take it?"

"Because they don't know about it. Only you do. And I'm gambling that you are a decent man. If I help you find this, you will make sure that the army employs the people here to mine and refine the ore. Nobody is shipped to Germany. Nobody goes to a labour camp." He stopped and took a small sip of his brandy. I could see there was a slight tremor to his hand.

"This is monstrous. I really don't believe it," I said.

He took off his hat and wiped his forehead. "Yes, it's monstrous. But it's true. This morning I'll show you the rock deposit. I heard about it four years ago when an engineer who used to work for my chemical firm told me about it. He was a Jew too; his family had been forced out of Russia in the pogroms and he didn't want the Tsar's army to get it. We both understood the potential significance of this find. I didn't need the rock for my textiles or chemical manufacturing, and so we agreed to let it sit there. In September of 1914, my engineer was called up into the Russian army. I've since heard he was killed at Tannenburg. Now, you and I are the only ones who know about this. When the war broke out, I had no intention of telling anyone about it. I didn't want to have any part in the killing. I have no choice now. Now the rock is valuable to us. If I show you the deposits, will you promise to help us?"

"Yes, of course! Of course I will."

I believed the man. His story was too fantastic not to be true. So many of the staff officers I'd met in Berlin would unhesitatingly resort to enforced labour to prevent Germany from losing the war. That, I was sure of. We probably would have done the same ourselves. But more than that, I wanted to believe Lazarowicz. His offer gave me the opportunity I was looking for. I needed some means of extracting my tax from the region without harming the population. This was a chance to solve a problem that had been smouldering within me for days. In truth, I'd had no idea how I was going to get out of this one with a clean conscience. Lazarowicz was a godsend. In my mind's eye, I could see the woman with the carving knife holding her child, the young girl in the tavern, and all the other frightened faces that peeped out at us as we drove through their countryside. I'd been thinking about those people all week and I didn't want any of their deaths on my conscience. I swallowed the rest of my plum brandy in one draught. It burned pleasantly.

"Let's go see your rock deposit now."

Back at the woodshed, Unteroffizier Brickner was awake. He had his blanket wrapped around him and was convulsed in one of his violent coughing fits. It hurt to listen to him. When he stopped, I told him, "Get the car ready, Unteroffizier, I want to see something."

Lazarowicz sat in the back, crammed in with the two guards. He seemed to know his way around the forest trails. When we were well down the eastern side of the high feature, he told us to stop at a large rock outcropping. I noted that this part of the hillside was covered in pine trees with dense underbrush. I told Brickner and the guards to wait at the automobile and we walked into the woods. It was wet, and every few feet we blundered into hanging branches. The water cascaded down our necks. Lazarowicz was oblivious to the discomfort; he seemed to be searching for markings left on trees. After a half an hour of searching, he stopped at some deadfall and said, "This is it. I'm sure this is it. All around us, underneath us— nitrogenous rock. Look, scratch the surface."

We both scraped about with sticks and after a few moments Lazarowicz pulled up a small rock. "Look here. You see this, this dark streak in the rock. Take some of this with you. Mark my words, you'll be a hero. But you must allow the people from this area to run the mine and process the ore, no forced labour from this region. Do we have a deal?"

I agreed with him again. We scraped at the rock and gathered fifteen or twenty pounds of it, carrying it back to the staff car in our arms. Brickner was lounging beside the road. He looked scornful. "Rock collections, gentlemen? Oberleutnant, don't you know there is a war on? We have real work to do, sir."

I ignored his comment. "We've got what we need. Unteroffizier Brickner, let's get the staff car moving again."

I had seen all I wanted to see and I had sufficient information on my area to put together a credible report. We motored with Lazarowicz back up to Dabreeskow to let him get his horse, and then we went by the southern route back to the rear-area headquarters.

15

I ARRIVED AT BIALYSTARY long after dark and made my way directly to our farmhouse. I entered gingerly. As I hoped, Captain Ebersbach was sleeping. There was no sign of the junior officers from the Signals Battalion. They must have taken up permanent residence elsewhere. Propped up on the table by the oil lamp were two letters. I lit the lamp and turned the wick down low. One letter was from Gabriele and one was from Wolfgang Von Lignow. It never failed to amaze me: the post offices in both Germany and Britain were marvels of efficiency. In the midst of the most terrible war in history, their mail services continued to run with clockwork precision—a talent the modern world seems to have lost.

I sat down and lit a cigarette. The letters on the table were a reminder of why I was sent here. I'd worked my way into the part I was playing, and in the last week I'd been completely focused on doing my job as an Economic Productivity officer. The lives of hundreds of people in the rural Bialystock region would be affected by my report. Happily, it seemed I was on my way to realizing my objective of maintaining my cover and not causing injury to the local population. With luck and my best efforts I could still manage it. I held Von Lignow's letter in my right hand and Gabriele's letter perched in the glove that covered what was left of my left hand. There was no question; my duty lay with Von Lignow. My connec-

tion to Von Lignow was probably the surest and only means of finding out what the German army's master plan was; and I knew that
if I was doing my job as I should, I'd read his letter first. Gabriele
should never have become anything more than some kind of elaborate camouflage to conceal my real purpose. But that wasn't how
things had developed. I dropped Von Lignow's letter onto the table
and tore open Gabriele's.

After a long day at the hospital she was writing late at night from
a desk in the front room of her house. Gabriele's letter was posi-
tive and cheery, but I could sense the fatigue in it. There was no
news to speak of. She told me of her rounds and the people she
tended to. Her mother was doing volunteer work at an orphanage
and whatever time was left after that she spent her time queuing for
food. The magazines her father published were all in trouble; these
days almost nobody was subscribing to them and there was a serious paper shortage. She was glad I was safely out of the front line
and longed to see me back in Berlin again soon. She signed it "Love
Gabriele."

I read Gabriele's letter a second and a third time before I picked
up Wolfgang Von Lignow's. Von Lignow's letter was much more
difficult to read. He scribbled furiously in a crabbed, impatient
style and it was difficult to make out each word. His letters were
small, and like all Germans of that period he wrote in gothic "Sut-
terlin" script. It was one of those things I never really mastered.
Whenever I wrote in German, my penmanship looked juvenile. My
mother, despite her efforts, was appalled by my German handwrit-
ing. I smiled at the thought of her and felt a pang of guilt for the
sorrow my parents must be going through.

Wolfgang asked how I was getting on and came straight to the
point. He was certain America was going to come into the war
sooner rather than later and they were not going to be on our side.
There was something about a submarine base in Mexico which I
didn't understand and several other lines that were illegible. It was
apparent to him Germany had to win the war quickly. There was a
whole paragraph that I could not read and then he wrote that I was

to call him as soon as I got back to Berlin as he might have a more important job to match my unique talents. Oh, and by the way, did I remember that impertinent little policeman Vizefeldwebel Kleer? He had been around asking for me. He had questions for me and wanted to talk to me about what I knew about officer survivors from my battalion in Ninth Landwehr Division—probably something to do with information on other prisoners. He signed his letter, "Best Regards, Wolfgang."

I sat back in my chair and lit another cigarette. I had almost forgotten about Vizefeldwebel Kleer, the sleek-headed self-important little policeman from Berlin. He was the only one who up to now even suspected I might not have been everything I said I was. Kleer could make everything much more difficult, especially if he had gotten hold of someone from Baumann's old unit. I clenched my fist, crumpling the letter, and cursed under my breath. Ebersbach stirred across the room but he didn't wake up.

I sat in the dark smoking for a while. I had to do something about Kleer or he was going to expose me. Something was fuelling his suspicions and he obviously had no intention of going away. I sat and smoked in the dark for an hour. There were only two choices. I had to do something to get Kleer off my track, to convince him I was who I said I was—or, I had to stop him permanently. As the oil lamp burned down, I started thinking about plans for both eventualities.

✠

I was up early in the morning. Ebersbach tossed a few times and continued to sleep, so I took the liberty of rummaging about for something to eat. In a cupboard in one of the rooms I found a fair quantity of hard black field-ration bread and dry sausage. Ebersbach should never have had this much food for himself. The belligerent little thief was drawing rations for those of us who didn't stay in these quarters. I found on one of the shelves that he had also squirrelled away some apples and pears as well. I also found, concealed high on one of the shelves in the room, two bottles of schnapps behind some old books and field manuals—almost certainly the illegal black-market schnapps Lazarowicz referred to. I put most of the fruit in my pack along with three loaves of the dense bread, but I put the bottles carefully back where I found them. For a second, out of spite, I was tempted to leave the bottles out on the table just to send a message to him. I decided against this. I didn't need more enemies just now.

At 6:30 sharp, I could hear the jingling of a harness and the clopping of hooves. Brickner was outside, this time with his old horse and cart. I gathered up my rock samples, closed the door carefully, and we were off to the rail transport office.

My pass and travel approval, both of which were authorized by a Staff officer on the Greater General Staff, secured me an immediate seat on the 9:30 train that ended at Berlin's Zoologischer Garten Station. It was a mixed train, with several cars allocated to convalescent wounded on stretchers; there were a dozen empty box cars and behind them, nine or ten passenger cars, two of which were marked Officers Only. I got onto the last car.

There were already a half-dozen frontline officers in the car. Although they must have been cleaned and de-loused at a field laundry and bath unit, they still had the stamp of the trenches on them. Their uniforms were patchy, with old stains, and the wool was worn as smooth as canvas. Their eyes were black and hollow, and the flesh on their faces hung limply like rotting fruit. Most of them were sleeping and those who didn't stared blankly out the windows. Not so long ago, I'd known that kind of fatigue.

I took a seat at the back of the last car and busied myself preparing my report. A smiling round-faced major from the Medical Corps climbed aboard, sauntered up the aisle and, after inspecting me up and down, sat opposite me. I nodded politely and energetically continued writing my report.

As soon as the train began to move the major said, "I see, Oberleutnant, that you are busy writing. Is it a letter or a report?"

"A report, Herr Major. I have to submit it this evening at the Red

House." I tried to sound irritated and mentioning the General Staff headquarters was an attempt to put him off with my importance.

"The Red House! You don't wear the insignia of a General Staff officer?"

"No Herr Major, I work for one." I put my head down again. The major stared out the window, obviously irritated at my refusal to engage him in conversation. As I pretended to write, the thought occurred to me that I was getting on the bad side of too many people here in Germany. Vizefeldwebel Kleer neither liked nor believed me, Captain Ebersbach didn't like me, Unteroffizier Brickner didn't like me, and now I had just insulted this major. I wanted people to accept me, to allow me to become invisible.

"Is your job here with the Eighth Army Headquarters or do you travel?" The major wasn't as easily put off as I thought.

I put my pen down and smiled at him. "I work here and in Berlin, Herr Major. I'm an Economic Productivity officer now. After I was wounded ... well, let's say that's what I do now to contribute to the war effort. And you, Herr Major?"

The major rambled on for almost an hour. He was a surgeon and a lonely soul. He had never married, and in the autumn of 1914 left a lucrative practice in Berlin to become an army surgeon at the newly established Kaiser Wilhelm Convalescent Treatment Hospital. Now he not only had no time for a wife and family, he had no time at all. His caseload was depressing. He had just been forward to lecture a group of surgeons at the Eighth Corps General Surgical Hospital on some sort of new post-operative treatment he had developed. Now he was going back to Berlin and a new draft of shattered bodies to mend. I made several efforts to get back to my report, but he kept interrupting. At length, he began to show professional interest in my wounds. "Where did you have your surgery done?"

My mouth went dry. I normally tried to avoid talking about my past. That morning I was caught off guard and began to stammer. "Actually, Herr Major, I was wounded in France with the Ninth Landwehr Division on the Somme. I was captured by the British.

They tended to my wounds. I escaped from hospital in England and now here I am."

The major was fascinated. He had read about an escaped German officer. Was I that one, the American officer? I nodded, and he insisted I let him look at my eye. I gave up. He peeled back my eye patch and peered at my eye socket from all angles. "You're a lucky young man. This is coming along nicely. There was never any serious infection and it's healing beautifully." After, he made me take off my glove and pored over my hand. "Oh yes, this is good work, very good; but you know, I think we do as well. In fact, we would have done a better job on your hand. I'm sure of that. Do you still get a lot of pain in your eye?"

No, I told him, only when I became very tired; but I agreed it seemed to have healed very nicely. As I spoke, I noticed two of the frontline officers were turning about, staring at me. An hour before, I was worried I was drawing attention to myself by not getting along with people. I could never win at this game. Now, I was liked and accepted—but I was even more conspicuous. Eventually the major let me get back to work, but before I got off the train he pulled out an expensive tortoiseshell pen and wrote out for me his name, address, and telephone number. I promised to look him up sometime. He would take me out to dinner and "really show me Berlin." Glancing down at the scrap of paper, I said, "I'll look forward to that, Herr Major Doctor Gehlen." I stuffed the paper in my billfold and promptly intended to forget all about him. That paper would save my life.

✠

When I got to Berlin, I knew I hadn't done a very good job on my report. But I wasn't fooling myself. I hadn't hurried back to General Staff headquarters to impress anyone with my brilliance at creating a summary of the economic potential of the Rural Bialystock region. I wanted to see Gabriele.

I checked into the Prenzlaur Hotel and was given a tiny but

tastefully appointed room on the third floor. In the lobby, I asked the corporal at the desk for use of a telephone and he directed me to a row of booths along the opposite wall. "Take booth number four, sir. Watch me. When I signal, you'll get a connection. Ask the operator for your number."

It seemed to me the army had a queer method of running a hotel phone exchange. I did as I was instructed and sat beside a rugged-looking Bakelite field phone waiting for my signal. I waited for a very long time. The corporal finally re-emerged from somewhere and shouted "Number Four." My line crackled and came to life. I was connected to General Staff headquarters and was given an appointment with a Major Bernhardt the next day at ten. When the operator came back on the line to ask if I was finished, I placed a call to Gabriele. Her mother answered. Gabriele was probably on her way home from the hospital and would arrive shortly. I promised to call back.

I went upstairs to my room but in minutes became impatient and decided to go unannounced to Gabriele's and meet her at her house. I gathered the fruit, dried sausages, and loaves of black bread. Other than my issue pack, I had nothing to carry the food in so I took the pillowcase from my bed. I wasn't at all sure how to get to her address. I walked to the trolley stop and jumped on the first one that came along. I showed the elderly driver her address and he waved his hand at me dismissively. "No, no. I'll call out when we get there. Take a seat sir, please." When I dug into my pocket and pulled out coins to pay, he gave me an exaggerated wink and pointed at my Iron Cross ribbon and said, "For you, Oberleutnant, it's free."

Gabriele was already at home. She was overjoyed when she found me standing at the door of their apartment. She flung both arms around me and kissed me on both cheeks and again full on the mouth. The scent of her perfume and the fragrance of her hair were intoxicating. I was dragged into the front room and intro-duced to her parents. Her father had long Edwardian sideburns and was pale looking, while her mother was petite, with the same intelligent piercing blue eyes. I stammered my way through presenting them with the food in the pillowcase and to their great credit they made me feel completely at ease. They were grateful for the food. Fresh fruit and any supplement to their stringently rationed diet was much needed and deeply appreciated. Gabriele's mother made a great joke of returning the pillowcase. I instinctively liked these people but I was completely tongue-tied around them. I felt cheap and inadequate. I was an impostor in their house and they interpreted my confused feelings as a kind of charming youthful modesty. Gabriele excused herself and left to change out of her nurse's uniform.

I was left to talk to her parents in the sitting room. For a family of radical socialists, they had a remarkably traditional apartment. The front room was large with high ceilings. There were books along the walls, photographs of relatives in silver frames, and lace curtains on the windows. The room had that cluttered Germanic Victorian look that I had grown up with. I was surprised to see that tea on a silver tea set was served to us by a middle-aged maid. The maid was a kindly looking soul, red-cheeked, smartly turned out, and cheerfully courteous. Having a deferential maid as household staff seemed to be at odds with my image of a militant socialist mindset, but I kept my thoughts to myself.

Gabriele's father politely asked me how I found things in Poland and I told them of the shortages there and my fears about what winter would bring. I quickly steered the conversation around to what they were doing and we remained on topics of my choosing.

Gabriele emerged dressed in a dazzling ankle-length navy blue dress. She had on a shawl, and wore her hair down with pale blue ribbons dangling at the sides of her face. She had stylish black shoes with elevated heels and carried a large hat with long rakish feathers on the side. I was spellbound and breathless. I hadn't realized she had such panache. She was mesmerizingly beautiful. Her mother broke the silence. "Well, why don't you two go out for a walk or go to a gasthaus. I'm sure you don't want to be here all night with us."

We bid our goodbyes and when we were on the landing below

her apartment she pulled me again into her arms and kissed me. "Why didn't you tell me you were coming home? Alex this is wonderful. Can you get home often? Did you get my letter?"

I grinned sheepishly and held her awkwardly. The fact was, I had no experience with women and I was still painfully shy. Gabriele sensed how awkward I was but something about her made me feel completely unashamed. We instinctively understood she was more at ease in these situations than I, but it made no difference. We genuinely delighted in one another's company.

That night we walked all around her neighbourhood and she pointed out to me the landmarks of her life. When it grew dark we went to the local gasthaus and laughed and drank Berlin's excellent beer. Gabriele had to be at work before seven, so shortly after midnight I walked her home and promised to call for her at the hospital when she finished.

✠

I walked the three miles back to the officers' hotel that night and slept until after nine the next morning. I luxuriated in the room's private shower, missing any chance for breakfast. I ended up running to the Red House. The military policeman was puzzled and amused at my pack filled with rocks. "Oberleutnant, I have a nephew who has rock collections, but he's six years old." He laughed at his humour and motioned me with a nod of his of his steel-helmeted head. "Go on up, sir, don't drop those on yourself."

I arrived at Major Bernhardt's office at the stroke of ten. Bernhardt was a big man in his late thirties. He was dark-featured, balding, with pale grey, watery eyes, and rimless glasses. At his office door I came to attention in the German manner, head flung back, hands flat along the seams of my trousers. He pushed his chair away from his desk. "Come in, Oberleutnant Baumann. I've heard a great deal about you. You have a report for me about the Rural Bialystock area? You know, you're the first to return with your task completed. These other officers, they ought to be kicked. They outrank you, but most of them have never served anywhere near the sound of the guns, and not surprisingly, we haven't heard from any of them yet, not one. You're the first. What've you got for me?"

I spent ten minutes going over the map and describing the results of my reconnaissance. Bernhardt was not impressed. When I finally got to my descriptions of the Bialowieza Forest and then spilled the rocks over Bernhardt's desk, he sat on the edge of his chair. "Baumann, if this site has the right kind of nitrogenous rock, even a small amount will help us with one of our most pressing industrial problems. Virtually all our explosive ammunition has TNT as the explosive component. Without a new source of nitrogen, it's only a matter of time until we're forced to go to a synthetic ammonium nitrate-based explosive. That will cause us huge problems. Ammonium nitrate has much different explosive properties than TNT. That means we'll have to redesign our ammunition, and if we do that, we then have to re-engineer most of our weapons. That would be a logistical and engineering nightmare. Do you have any idea what that would involve in the midst of a war?" He looked at me disbelievingly. "I hope you're right." He picked up the phone on his desk and made a series of calls.

Minutes later Major Bernhardt and I were on our way to the IG Farben Industries Chemical Research Laboratories on the north side of Berlin. We turned the rock samples over to one of their top chemists, and like expectant fathers, waited on a bench in the hall for the analysis results. Forty minutes later, a pleased-looking chemist confirmed, "This grade of ore is almost as rich as the Chilean nitrogen; it's not as good, so we shouldn't get our hopes up too much, but if there's enough of it, it could potentially solve our problems."

Bernhardt clapped me on the back. "Baumann, this is marvellous. This evening we'll get you back out to your forest with some engineers. I want a feasibility report tomorrow night."

As we drove back to the Red House, Bernhardt looked like a man who had been saved from the executioner. It was a good time to tell him about my promise to Jacob Lazarowicz. "You know, Baumann, you had no right to make such a promise. Help-workers are a critical part of our industrial strategy. We already have several thousand Belgians and Poles working for us right here in Berlin. They're confined to their factory sites, but they're not slaves."

I wasn't certain what the difference between a "help-worker" and a slave was, but I didn't interrupt him.

"Let me tell you, Baumann, help-workers have already made a huge difference for us. We take good care of them. They are no good to us dead or sick. But I'll tell you what I can do. I have no one to work that mine when it gets in operation, so if you organize a work force, a real work force from the local population, I'll do what I can to keep the Labour Board from recruiting in the Rural Bialystock Sector. The work won't be easy; but if your peasants are mining this rock, believe me, they'll be fed. Is that fair?"

I agreed. When we got back to his office, he made a few more calls. "I can't get you out of here until tomorrow morning. The engineers and geologists we need won't be available until then. So until tomorrow, you are a free man, Oberleutnant—Oh, there is one other thing. A policeman is looking for you, an intense-looking little man by the name of Kleer; he came around two days ago wanting to talk to you. I told him you were on a priority mission for the economic staff. Maybe you could call him today."

My mouth went dry and I stammered, "Herr Major, this man, Kleer, I know him. He interrogated me when I returned from England. I think he hates Americans. He's also a little crazy; he thinks I can help him find American and English spies. I've been through all this before with him and I have things to do this afternoon. I've only had three days leave in two years. I am sure you understand. Can you please speak to him; get him off my back, please. He's a pompous, nasty little shit. You can ask Captain Von Lignow; he was there."

Major Bernhardt winced at my vulgarity and nodded. "Ah yes, I almost forgot, Von Lignow—I was saving this until last. Von

Lignow's not a captain any more, you know. He's coming back to Berlin to work as a section head in our newly expanded American Intelligence Section. He's asked that you be transferred to him. We don't want to give you up, but considering your background, I don't think I'm going to have a choice.

"As for your policeman, I'll make a phone call. I'll call our field security officer; let him deal with him. The security troops will arrest him if he shows his face here." He chuckled. "The old guard military police hate the civilian police in army uniform. Neither of them trust each other. To tell the truth, I didn't like the looks of him. I had to speak sharply to him. A vizefeldwebel doesn't give orders to a General Staff major in this army.

"But one other thing." He paused and looked at me wearily. "Watch your language, Baumann. The better class of German officers don't swear or cuss. What else can I do for you, Baumann? You've done good work here."

My heart leaped, and despite the rebuke, I felt I could push my luck. "One other thing, sir? If I may, when I get back from Bialowieza Forest, may I have a few days leave, please?"

"A few days! With such a find, take a week, Baumann. I'll sort it out with Von Lignow. He won't be here for a week or so anyway. So, let me make some calls. You're free to go until tomorrow. Good work."

✠

That night, as we arranged, I met Gabriele and over a glass of beer at our café in the Tiergarten I told her of my leave. She was delighted and began to make plans: where we should go and the things we'd see. As I listened to her, I realized I'd never seen her angry or moody. I wasn't really paying any attention to what she said. She was a robust, capable kind of person. There was nothing fragile about her; but she was still totally feminine. I liked that. As she talked and described the favourite places she wanted to show me, I was trying to imagine how she would react when she learned I was Rory Ferrall of Montreal and not Alex Baumann of Albany, New York. Some day, when this was all over, however it turned out, I was going to have to tell her the truth. I wondered if she'd understand.

I went home on the trolley with her and had supper with the family. Dinner was a simple affair of lentil soup and black bread. Her parents were gracious and thanked me for the food I had brought the night before. I left the Richters before ten as I had to be up early, and I knew Gabriele was tired.

The next morning was grey, blustery, and cold. My instructions were to be waiting at 0730 on the sidewalk outside the military police checkpoint at the Red House. I was there blowing warmth into my fingers when a small crowd of well-dressed civilian men rounded the corner. They wore homburgs and suits and carried smart-looking leather suitcases and Gladstone bags. I was surprised at the numbers. I only expected two men to show up, an engineer and a geologist. Instead, apart from myself, there were nine men in our party. It came as a bit of a shock to see the age of some of them. Several of them were healthy-looking men in their early twenties. My disdain that they weren't in uniform was evident. We regarded each other coolly.

Major Bernhardt joined us with a clerk in tow and muttered under his breath to me, "You come from America to join the army. Look at these assholes hiding behind their deferments." I kept a straight face hearing Bernhardt's crude language. For an instant he came close to smiling and nodded at me before he called out, "Which two of you are the leaders here? My clerk has two tickets for you for officer-class carriages. The remainder will travel in soldiers' carriages." Two of the younger men grumbled and muttered inaudibly. Bernhardt replied cheerfully, "Don't whine. Travelling with honest soldiers will be good for you. You can tell your grandchildren about the experience.

"Now, Oberleutnant Baumann will be in charge for this trip. You will respect his authority and there will be no complaining or whining like I've just heard. Should any of you have a problem with that, speak up now." He paused and looked around him like a falcon on a fence post. No one dared meet his stare.

"This is a very high-priority tasking for the war effort and we expect absolute co-operation. I do not want to hear of any foot-dragging whatsoever. Anyone who gives the oberleutnant any sort of problem will find it will go very hard with him. Each one of you will do your utmost to co-operate at all times. This is part of your wartime duty; if you don't like it, I will personally arrange to have other employment found for you."

On that happy note, our detailed reconnaissance for the nitrogen mine began. Our trip back to Seventh Corps rear area was remarkable only insofar as the senior engineers were reserved and excruciatingly polite to me. Upon our arrival at Bialystary Station, instead of being met by a horse and cart, Unteroffizier Brickner had three touring cars and a lorry-load of helmeted Uhlans to act as guards and orderlies. We motored directly to the Bialowieza Forest, and after dark set up a tented camp at the roadside where Jacob Lazarowicz had led me a few days earlier. As soon as our tents were set up, I directed Brickner to send one of the touring cars to Bialystock and to bring Lazarowicz back the following day to meet the engineers.

The next day the engineers and geologists scratched around for most of the morning and confirmed what I already knew, the site was a rich deposit of nitrogenous rock. While they examined the site and tested rock and soil samples, I went for a long walk. I wanted to keep apart from these men. I sensed they resented me, but more than that, I wanted to clear my thinking as to what I was going to do.

Overnight the temperature dropped steadily and the occasional spatter of rain turned to scattered snow. The ridges of mud at the edges of the forest tracks froze into sharp spires and the few leaves remaining on the deciduous trees tinted the woods yellow and orange. In Montreal, the maples would have already lost their scarlet leaves by now. The changing of the leaves made me think of home. If it weren't for the war, I'd have been well into some sort of comfortable civilian career; but there was no point in fretting about what could have been. There were other problems to worry about.

Gabriele complicated my life now. She made all my previous moral predicaments insignificant. I'd wrestled with my conscience before joining the army, and my thoughts about spying had never hardened into serious resolve. Even at that point, I still suffered from radical mood swings. Some moments I was confidently determined; other times I had to force myself to get on with what I was doing. Occasionally, I experienced a black, paralysing uncertainty. Gabriele only made matters worse. I was seriously troubled at the prospect of what I was doing to her. In any novels that I'd ever read, men of action were utterly self-assured. Whatever mental torment they went through had more to do with how they were going to accomplish their task. I was stumbling as to why, or even if, I should act.

On top of this, I surprised myself because I was also concerned for Wolfgang Von Lignow. He'd stuck his neck out for me; and although he certainly didn't know it, I owed him my life. He took me in as a friend, and based partly on that trust, he was bringing me in to work in one of the Germany army's most influential organizations. If I was ever given the chance to find out what the Germans were planning, I was going to betray him as well. God knows what would happen to him. I'd break Gabriele's heart and I'd probably get Wolfgang killed. That'd be quite a set of accomplishments.

I pulled out a cigarette, and in the protection of the trees found a dry patch of ground and sat down. What difference was there between Von Lignow and the baby-faced German soldier I put a bullet into during my last moments of consciousness in the Loop? Not much really, only that I knew and liked Von Lignow. I'm sure I'd have liked the baby-faced German. He had the misfortune of peering round the trench at the wrong time. I didn't want to harm Von Lignow; but, I told myself, he was a soldier; and I suppose, I'd do him in if I had to. I didn't like it, but under similar circumstances, Von Lignow would probably do the same. Gabriele was a different matter altogether.

It was cold sitting in the woods, and I pulled my collar around me. From a practical point of view, my espionage assignment was going well. If Kleer really had anything on me, he'd have simply arrested me. He was still fishing; and the fact that he was still keeping a good distance from me meant that he probably didn't have much to go on. Apart from that, I'd been incredibly lucky.

Cumming deserved most of the credit. It was his idea to send me into Germany. Sitting there in the chill rain I had to admit it was a clever plan, a brilliant perception of the risks involved. Cumming deserved the credit; he had the wits and imagination to dream the plan up in the first place. On top of that, it was my astonishingly good luck that Alex Baumann had won an Iron Cross Second Class. That little bit of metal and ribbon opened so many other doors. The rest was just happenstance.

If I stayed put with Von Lignow, sooner or later I'd be in a position to discover what the Germans had up their sleeves to win the war—if they had anything. I wasn't entirely convinced they were much further ahead than we were. But, if as Von Lignow mentioned, it was a matter of time until America came into the war, the Germans were going to have to act sooner rather than later. If Germany didn't win the war before the Americans arrived in any numbers, she was dead. You didn't have to be strategically brilliant to see that. I lay back and exhaled smoke skyward. I looked up through the branches. The Germans that I knew weren't going to sit back and wait to be ground down by an Allied strategy of attrition. They were going to try something, and the chances of me being able to sit this one out were just about zero. I needed to start thinking seriously about my escape plan; and that inevitably brought Gabriele back into the equation.

I finished my cigarette and ambled back to the campsite. As I arrived, the touring car with Jacob Lazarowicz pulled into view. When Lazarowicz got out of the staff car, I noticed he was limping, and for the first time I realized the sole of his left shoe was built so that it was taller than the right one. I liked this man. He had courage and character. I took him into one of the tents and poured him a cup of the acorn tea that had been brewing on the paraffin stove all morning. I sent one of the Uhlans to bring the two senior engineers down from the dig.

Once they'd arrived, I introduced Lazarowicz. "This Is Jacob Lazarowicz from the city of Bialystock. He's the man who is going to furnish you with the labour to run this mine. You, gentlemen, will provide the senior supervisors and the mine manager, and will also create the design plan for the mine's operation. Lazarowicz will ensure you have the people you need to keep it in operation. Don't ask for German miners, they're not available. The only people you will likely get are a handful of specialist army engineers to do your blasting. So, before we head back to Berlin tomorrow, I want you to give Mr. Lazarowicz your best estimate of what your manpower requirements will be and when you will need them. Remember, the mine is to be in operation as soon as possible. One last thing: stay close to Mr. Lazarowicz; he can solve a lot of your problems for you. Don't make life difficult for him or you will find yourselves with bigger problems than you can imagine. Lazarowicz can get you a lot more than labour on this project. I'll leave you three to discuss things now. You have a lot of planning and a report to finish before we get back to Berlin. I want to go over your preliminary reports with you on the train tomorrow."

We arrived in Berlin late the next night. I can't say I really understood or cared about the details the engineers and geologists put into their reports. The mine was initially to be an open-pit affair, with improved road access, a transport compound, a few makeshift buildings, and several pieces of heavy machinery; beyond that I didn't care much about it, as I knew I wouldn't be responsible for implementing their recommendations. In fact, I enjoyed questioning and prodding these men about the workings of the mine.

The two senior men were ten years or so older than I, and to tell the truth, I didn't like them. I resented their protected and comfortable lifestyle. I told the senior engineer, a fair, ruddy-faced man who wore a perpetually aggrieved look, that their report looked good, but unfortunately, it was incomplete. Before morning, they had to prepare an additional contingency plan, one that included a much more detailed, labour-intensive option. I threw this in, knowing it would keep them working late into the night. They were whiners with cushy jobs and they had spent the war safely eating hot food and sleeping between sheets. I'm sure they resented me as much as I detested them. At the time I was certain they would be given whatever heavy machinery they asked for.

I wasn't entirely pleased with my behaviour. When I look back on it, I knew that a year before I wouldn't have done something petty like that. But a year before I was a much more passive and forgiving individual. Making them write an extra report was mean-spirited, but even now I have mixed feelings about having done it. It didn't matter what side I was on; in a small way, I thought it helped even the score between those of us who suffered in the trenches and the slackers. It was a ridiculous attitude to have about your enemy, but I identified much more closely with Germany's soldiers than I did with those on both sides who stayed comfortably out of the war. At any rate, I was cheerful. Lazarowicz was happy because we'd saved his peasants and after my meeting with Bernhardt, I was off on a week's leave. Things could have been a lot worse.

My meeting with Bernhardt the next day went well. Before I left Seventh Corps, I telephoned him from the railhead and advised him that it certainly appeared the mine was viable. Unknown to me, he had already tasked the project over to the army engineering officer who was responsible for the rear area. By ten the next morning, he dismissed me. He shook my hand, thanked me for my efforts, and clapped me on the back. After a visit to the paymaster's office I was on my way to Gabriele's.

I arrived at the Richter's apartment in high spirits, only to find Gabriele was angry and upset. She told me a military policeman named Kleer had been around an hour earlier and was asking questions after me. She was furious. "He said you're the centre of an ongoing investigation; and if I held back any information about you, I'd find myself in serious trouble. He did his best to bully me," she said, visibly trying to regain her composure.

I thought to myself that Kleer might in some ways be clever, but he certainly misjudged the approach needed to make this woman co-operate with him. Gabriele took a deep breath. "I told him you were a decorated frontline officer and that he had no right barging in here making these kinds of accusations. He wanted to know why whenever you returned to Berlin you never tried to contact him as he instructed. I told him to contact you directly if he had any concerns and to stop sneaking around."

I listened to what Gabriele had to say and explained that Kleer was almost certainly some kind of obsessive. He was mad. It wasn't the first time he had done this and he was under orders to leave me alone. I apologized if he'd caused her any trouble, and in her presence, I placed a telephone call to Major Bernhardt. I couldn't get through to him and so I dictated a message to his clerk.

"Despite the major's explicit orders to the contrary," I said, "Vizefeldwebel Kleer is still harassing me and now he has been interrogating and upsetting my civilian acquaintances. Can something please be done? The man is making a serious nuisance of himself. He is maligning an officer and he has deliberately disobeyed a lawful command. Formal disciplinary action must be taken against him."

I wasn't nearly as confident as I sounded. Whatever information Kleer had, he was never going to go away. Now that my preferred plan had obviously failed to deter him, I had no choice but to fall back on my second, much riskier option. Kleer had to be removed. My problem was that I was at a loss as how to do it without bringing the world down on my head. I decided to try to put it out of mind for now. If I was going to be risking my life again, I'd enjoy what could well be my first and last chance to spend a holiday with Gabriele.

16

AFTER I TELEPHONED Bernhardt, Gabriele and I walked leisurely to the trolley stop. She wore her large feathered hat, a fur-trimmed coat, and long grey gloves, and carried a small valise. The few things I owned, I had stuffed into my pack. I was calm despite the realization that I had to kill a man in cold blood. I suppose I was composed because I'd really understood this for some time, and now, I'd consciously accepted it. At any rate, through some sort of mental gymnastics I managed to drive the thought out of my mind. On that day I didn't want to bother myself with the war or my part in it. I wanted to be with Gabriele.

We walked in silence for a short distance and I turned to her. "This is all very strange for me, Gabi. What did your parents say when you told them you were going on a week's holiday with me? Weren't they shocked?"

She laughed. "Good God, no! My parents encouraged me to go. They don't believe in the kind of stuffy morality that makes hypocrites out of respectable people. They don't want me to be promiscuous and I most certainly am not; but this doesn't trouble them, nor should it. They like you, and so do I. In fact, I'm very much in love with you, Alex. You know that."

I stammered in response, "I—I am too. It's just that I've never been involved with a woman before. You know that, don't you?"

"You're a klutz, Alex. You're an adorable klutz. Of course I know that. It's written all over you. I don't think you have any idea how to be deceitful and that's what's so endearing about you. There should be nothing unnatural about a man and a woman who love each other sleeping with one another. I don't need some law to tell me what's right. I don't sleep around with men. In fact, since we're counting, you'll be the second one, Alex."

I thought about what Gabriele had just said. "I've never met anyone who is quite as matter of fact about sex as you are. I guess I naturally tend to side with the hypocrites; not because I don't believe what you're saying is true." I was flustered and struggling for words. "Actually, I haven't really given it much thought; it just goes against everything I've been taught. I'm not embarrassed talking to you about it, but with anyone else I would be."

"No, and I won't advertise the fact that we're going on a holiday together. I'd lose my job at the hospital. You could be called up in an officer's court of honour—but with all the loose living the war has produced, that's not likely, unless you run off with your commanding officer's wife. Even so, it's just not the same for men as it is for women. That's why I hate all these conventions; they hide a double standard."

We walked in silence for a few minutes. "We haven't known each other for very long though. How do you feel about that?"

Gabi laughed again. "We know each other, Alex. We share things as if we've known each other for years. I think the war does that. With so much sudden death and separation, everything's compressed. Knowing a person isn't necessarily a function of how long you have known them; it's how well you know them. I think I've thought that one through. Don't you want to go away this week?"

"On no, I mean, of course I do. I'm still a hypocrite. I want to go. But something inside tells me you should never really enjoy this sort of thing. I guess I haven't quite come to grips with this like you have, Gabi."

We lowered our voices as a middle-aged hausfrau carrying a large wicker shopping basket joined us as we neared the trolley stop.

Gabriele didn't miss a beat and with a mischievous grin she leaned forward on her tiptoes and whispered in my ear. "So where do you want to go first, the theatre or a nice gasthof?"

"A guest house? I thought we were going to a hotel?

"Alex, you are so sweet and trusting; we can't afford a hotel. Berlin has lots of very acceptable gasthofs. We'll just have to become hypocrites. Do you mind pretending to be married?"

The woman with the shopping basket looked disgusted and glared at us. "Since the war, nothing works the same. The trolley is late again." Gabriele and I both laughed.

Gabriele already had a place in mind. It was a monstrous Victorian building in a tree-lined suburb. It had been divided into private rooms and apartments years ago. One of her friends at the hospital mentioned to Gabriele that a cousin of hers stayed there with his wife while he was on furlough. They thought it was very nice. When we got to the guesthouse the proprietor was delighted that an officer and his wife should choose to stay there. He wasn't in the least bit ashamed to say he thought it was good for business. Much to his dismay, we advised him we would only be taking our breakfasts there.

In recent years, it's become the practice for some autobiographical writers to provide salacious details of their most intimate moments. I can't do that. Then, as now, I'm constrained by a deep-rooted sense of privacy. To write in detail about those moments would be to betray the trust of someone I loved, someone who was close to me and with whom I shared the closest bonds of intimacy. Suffice it to say, Gabriele and I enjoyed a magnificent week together. It was unquestionably one of the happiest and richest periods of my long life. Throughout that week we laughed and revelled in one another's company. She was the most natural woman imaginable, and where I began the week as a self-conscious late-Victorian prude, she was as carefree, merry, and uninhibited as any war-weary soldier could possibly hope for. With Gabriele, I truly cast aside the fears and worries that had assailed me for so many months. I don't think at any other point in my life I've ever felt so free or so content.

It was only on the last day of our holiday that I began to allow the future to intrude upon our time together. Gabriele saw the week as the foundation of a long and idyllic relationship. I hoped things would ultimately turn out that way, but I also knew I'd reached a point where I had to act to save myself. Things couldn't drift any longer.

My jolt back to reality came at around ten in the morning. It was a crisp grey November day. You could see your breath and the grass in the Tiergarten was still frozen from the previous night's early frost. The trees were bare. We were taking a brisk walk on our way to our favourite café when ahead of us amongst the crowds I saw a tall military policeman approaching on one of the gravel footpaths. Like Kleer, he was middle-aged but he had a weather-beaten face. He wore a leather pickelhaube, a greatcoat, and high boots. He appeared to be searching for somebody. He scrutinized the faces of everyone who passed him.

My first impulse was to steer Gabriele by the arm and turn around. Instead, I chose to brazen it out. I took a deep breath and headed straight for him. Gabriele looked at me, slightly confused as to why we should change our direction. The military policeman studied me carefully and passed by. I called out cheerfully to him. "Sergeant, you look distracted, but you must still salute officers."

He smiled and saluted smartly. "My apologies, sir; I'm looking for someone. You're right, I am distracted." He tipped his head toward Gabriele and with great charm said, "Madam," and turned on his way.

"What ever did you do that for?" Gabriele asked.

"I'm sorry. I thought I recognized him from my time in Ninth Landwehr Division. I thought it might have been the military police feldwebel from my old battalion. He was quite a character. I was wrong though."

For the next two hours I had trouble keeping my thoughts focused. The policeman had rattled me. Gabriele noticed it and during lunch I pleaded the onset of a terrible headache. After our meal, we caught the trolley back to the rooming house and I asked to lie down for an hour in the dark. I'd be fine in an hour. Gabriele was her usual understanding self and went downstairs to read a book in the sitting room.

I lay on our bed thinking furiously about what had to be done. That solitary hour in the darkness of a Berlin rooming house was one of the few times I've experienced absolute mental clarity. I was neither frightened nor anxious; my mind was clear and focused and I sifted through the issues and possible courses of action open to me like some kind of mechanical adding machine. I've never experienced such lucidity; it was probably some kind of survival instinct. When I went downstairs to Gabriele, I knew exactly what I had to do.

✠

In the late afternoon, we went to the Altes Museum on the Bodestrasse to see the national collection of German Romantic paintings. The breadth of Gabriele's knowledge left me astonished. When I mentioned it, she chuckled. "Alex, with my upbringing, it's only natural. As children, men play sports, and women, because we're the weaker sex, we have to cultivate our minds." She squeezed my arm. "Don't be embarrassed."

We ate dinner at Gasthaus Zum Hauser and shared a large bottle of white Mosel. I wasn't enthusiastic about what I had to do, but I was determined. I sipped at my wine and kept Gabriele's glass refilled whenever she wasn't looking. She was a trusting soul and soon became chatty. We sat at a corner table and as the evening went on Gabi began to talk about the Germany she envisaged at the end of the war. While she talked, I discreetly motioned for a second bottle of wine.

Germany would become a country without the Kaiser. Gabriele was a puzzling contradiction. Like so many Germans of the period, she was anxious to see the war over and have a just peace imposed, although she had little time for the Kaiser, Germany's industrialists, the country's class system, or the leadership of the German army.

Unrestricted U-boat warfare was a cruel necessity to bring the war to a rapid end. It was entirely justified, and as she said, "We didn't start this kind of warfare against civilians."

Like most other Germans, Gabriele felt sinking ships bound for Britain on the high seas was completely acceptable in light of the British blockade. The blockade was starving innocent civilians and causing untold suffering to Germany's children. I listened quietly; and while I didn't agree with much of what she said, I honestly sympathized with why she thought as she did. I ordered ersatz coffee and a round of brandies. Taking my brandy with me, I excused myself. "Gabriele, I have to make a quick telephone call; tomorrow I assume my new duties with Wolfgang Von Lignow and I've promised to contact him before my leave is up."

There was no public call box nearby but the proprietor advised me that if my call was official, he would happily allow me use of the phone in his apartment at the back of the gasthaus. I thanked him. "I have to make three or four calls, if that's okay?" He waved his hand. "No problem, sir, no problem. My son is in the army. For you gentlemen, it's no problem."

He led me through the gasthaus's kitchen into a spotlessly clean apartment. On the hall table was a shiny black Siemens telephone, one of the new models with a stylish single earpiece and microphone sitting on a separate cradle. The telephone, like a shrine to modern technology, was on a starched linen runner beside a vase of fresh flowers. I asked the operator for the Berlin District Military Police Headquarters. It took two other calls to get Kleer on the line.

I covered the mouthpiece with a handkerchief. I didn't know if this would work or not, but I'd seen it done once in a play. I did my best to disguise my voice with a rural Bavarian accent. "Listen carefully. The man in your most frustrating case isn't who you think he is. You'll be interested in what I tell you. You're asking questions of the wrong people. But I want a reward. Come alone, tonight at 12:30. Take a seat by the door at Zum Fliegerhof. I'll approach you and give you the information you need. You must pay me fifty marks but don't try to follow me. If things work out, I can get you more information about these people. Tell no one of our meeting. If you do, there'll be no further information."

Kleer tried to stall me. "I can't do that. Where are you calling from? Who is this?"

I hung up and immediately rang the operator and placed another call to the Prenzlaur Hotel. If Kleer tried to ring the operator in an attempt to trace my call, the connecting cables would have been moved amongst the dozens of cables on the operator's call board and there'd be little chance of identifying the source.

I poured my brandy into a potted plant in the hallway and returned to our table. Gabriele was looking slightly flushed. She smiled up at me. "You were gone a long time."

I leaned over and kissed her on the forehead. "I'm sorry; I promised I'd check in before going back to work tomorrow morning. They had to dig around to see if there were any messages for me. There weren't. You've finished your brandy. It's the last night of our holiday. We'll have one more before we go home."

Poor Gabriele's eyes were glassy, but she had a happy serene look on her face and looked incredibly sexy. "Oh all right." She wagged a finger at me drunkenly. "One more, but only one."

When we left the gasthaus it was raining. We hailed a cab and went back to the gasthof. Gabriele slipped on the stairs and collapsed in my arms. We both started to laugh. In our room she fell onto the bed giggling. "Alex, what've we done? I've never been like this in my life; the whole room's spinning. I'm sorry; we can't make love tonight. Tomorrow. I promise." She giggled and after lurching about the room managed to wriggle out of her clothes. In seconds she was under the covers sleeping soundly.

For over an hour I lay beside Gabriele, listening to her breathing and the sound of the rain on the roof. When the clock downstairs struck 11:30, I slipped out of bed and got dressed. On the dressing table I fumbled for a few seconds until I found Gabriele's green silk scarf. I put it in my trouser pocket and turned to look at Gabriele.

She was sleeping heavily and didn't stir. I eased the door shut and padded down the carpeted stairs. The house was in total darkness. On the coat rack next to the guest's door were several coats and hats. I helped myself to someone's heavy tweed coat and a floppy flat cap; both were slightly large on me. I let myself out and walked briskly through the rain-darkened streets.

By 12:15, I was in position deep in the shadows of an alleyway across from the front door of Zum Fliegerhof. The rain had eased and I turned up my collar and put my back against the wall. I was partially sheltered from view from the street by a large wooden trash barrel and the tin drainpipe that ran down the side of the building.

Zum Fliegerhof was a raucous, smoky beer hall. Inside, some kind of ensemble played drinking music and polkas. Whenever the door opened, I could hear music, laughter, and the buzz of a hundred conversations. The club was illuminated outside by a half-dozen low-power light bulbs that encircled a crudely painted beer stein above the front door. The only streetlights were dim ones a hundred yards away at the junction of side streets. Zum Fliegerhof catered mostly to soldiers on leave. Soldiers and their girlfriends, all in varying states of sobriety, lurched in and out every few minutes.

By 12:30, I was soaking wet and shivering. There was no sign of Kleer. I was dying for a cigarette. Several months before, as I lay on my hospital bed, one of the things that I took comfort from was knowing that, with my wounds, I'd never again have to spend another night outside, exposed to the wind and the rain like a wild animal. I flexed my arms and shoulder muscles to keep warm.

As the minutes crept by, I become despondent thinking the whole scheme was lunacy. I didn't have to wait much longer. By 12:45, I saw a figure in a civilian overcoat and homburg walk to the front of the club's door. He wasn't like those who went in or out before him. He was impatient and business-like. Earlier arrivals looked hungry for a good time. This man was predatory. Before walking in, the figure in the overcoat looked both ways down the street and threw his cigarette onto the pavement. In that movement I was sure it was

Kleer. I didn't get a good glimpse of his face, but no one else would have had that same forbidding sense of self-assurance and determination. He was wise to show up in civilian clothes. A solitary military police vizefeldwebel would have attracted the unwelcome attention of quarrelsome soldiers. I waited.

At 1 a.m., people started to leave in large numbers. None of them was Kleer. At 1:30, the club's lights flashed on and off, signalling last call. There was a collective groan from inside and a few moments later the music stopped. At 1:40, people began to drift out of the club again. As if on cue, the rain and the wind picked up. Kleer wasn't amongst the early departures. At two o'clock, the club's windows became bright and the noise level inside increased. From my alley, I could hear the groans and protests of drunken men who didn't want to leave their drinks. This was the time bouncers earned their keep, if Zum Fliegerhof even had bouncers after so many years of conscription. The doors opened and another flood of revellers poured into the street. This time Kleer was amongst them. He stood out from the crowd. Aside from being the only male in civilian clothes, he carried himself stiffly, more like someone leaving a funeral than a beer hall. Kleer turned up his collar and, without looking about, headed back the way he came. His hands were in his pockets, his head down against the wind.

I let him walk for thirty seconds, and then left the shadows and crossed the street. There were two couples between Kleer and me. Two teenage soldiers and two pretty blonde girls were singing some sad song with a repetitive chorus begging "Inge please, Inge please come back to me." The singers weaved back and forth in an exaggerated motion in time to their own voices. They leaned on one another as they sang. As Kleer walked past the streetlight and into shadows, I quickened my pace and made to step around the party-goers. One of them grabbed at me good-naturedly and I pulled his arm off, joining in their drunken chorus, "Inge please, Inge please come back to me." They all laughed and I saw Kleer turn around and look behind him. I waved my arms at the two couples like a music director and belted out again at the top of my lungs, "Inge please, Inge please come back to me." Kleer carried on into the darkened street and I waved a cheery farewell as I eased past the singers. I walked faster.

For well over a mile and a half I trailed a hundred yards or so behind Kleer. He was walking steadily but not quickly. He didn't turn around or give any indication he knew he was being followed. We walked along a street of rundown shops and small offices and then entered a more respectable area of town made up of broad boulevards lined with linden and chestnut trees. The buildings were massive brick three- and four-storey apartment blocks. In the German fashion, all the windows were shuttered for the night. The cobblestoned streets and leaves in the gutters had a glossy varnished look.

When Kleer turned down a darkened side street I lost sight of him and ran to close the distance between us. As I rounded the corner he was crossing the street thirty yards from me. I thought he was going to enter the apartment facing us. I figured he must have been carrying a pistol and if I attempted to charge him, he'd certainly draw it on me. I had to act instantly or he'd vanish inside the building and I'd have lost my last chance to save myself. I lurched into the street and clutched at my stomach shouting in a distressed voice, "Help! Help me, please! I've been stabbed!" I staggered toward him with my head down so he couldn't see my face, clutching at my belly with both hands.

Kleer turned and raced over to me. He put his hand on my shoulder and bent over. He spoke rapidly, "What happened? Are you hurt?"

As he leaned forward, I grabbed his coat and pulled him toward me; in the same motion I stood up, launching a powerful kick into his groin. He began to fall and as he went down I smashed him in the face with a right-handed uppercut. I was desperate, hitting him with every ounce I could possibly muster. I can still hear the crunching of my fist dislocating cartilage and bone. Kleer straightened up and fell back. I was around behind him with Gabriele's green silk headscarf looped around his throat. I wrenched on the scarf as hard as I could; at the same time I forced my knee deep into his back.

Although I'd hit him solidly twice before, Kleer continued to struggle. He was a much tougher man than I imagined—but like me, he was struggling for his life. Kleer's arms flailed about for a few precious seconds and he tried to reach for his pocket, but as he did so I increased the pressure around his neck and jerked him violently back over the cobblestones toward the sidewalk. As I pulled him backwards, his hands instinctively went to his throat in an attempt to loosen the choking silk band crushing his windpipe. He made a quiet gurgling sound. For a few seconds his shoes scratched and thrashed wildly at the wet cobblestones. His hands weakened and he made one more attempt to go for his pocket. I lifted him into the air with my knee and dropped him down on his back, all the while wrenching the scarf ever tighter and then repeatedly jerking him back across the street into the shadows on the sidewalk. By the time we reached the sidewalk Kleer was limp.

I was fairly certain he was dead, but I kept the pressure on for what seemed a long time after. There was no sound except for my laboured breathing and the patter of rain on rock and dead leaves. As I released my death grip on the neckerchief, I realized that in my excitement the scarf had dug deep into the scarred tissue of my left hand. It hurt as intensely as it had several months before when I was in hospital.

I loosened the scarf from Kleer's neck and went through his pockets. As I guessed, he had a small police revolver in the right-hand pocket of his overcoat. I took his billfold, some coins, a set of keys, his fob watch, and some papers he carried in the inside pocket of his jacket. His face was contorted: eyes open, bulging, and sightless. There was no question now. He was dead. Apart from the rain, there was no sound in the street. I pocketed his effects and pulled the body into the shadows at the base of the nearest tree, turned, and began running at a slow jog in the direction I came from.

I ran for several minutes, keeping a few blocks south of the street

I followed Kleer up on. Several blocks away from the area of shops and offices I stopped under a street lamp, beside one of those old tubular red German mailboxes. My breathing was in ragged gasps and my pulse was racing. I was winded, as much from nervous tension as from the exertion of running.

I sorted through Kleer's effects. He had a lot of money with him. His billfold had over three hundred marks in small bills. I pocketed those and the coins—vowing to use the money when the time came to escape. Kleer had the usual identification: police association card, driving certificate, military identification card, military police identity card, a Berlin Public Library card, a military health card, old receipts, an official letter from someone; and curiously, a handwritten file card with a quotation from Saint Paul to the Corinthians.

As I flipped through Kleer's identity cards, I came across a dog-eared photograph of a laughing woman in a straw hat and summer dress. She had a pretty smile and was hugging two small chubby pre-school children. The picture was old and worn, a favourite taken somewhere at the seaside on a long promenade. I didn't want to dwell on the photograph, and for a few weeks it worked. I told myself that I wouldn't let myself be affected by this; but the image of those laughing faces and Kleer's dead swollen eyes have haunted me scores of times since.

Kleer's papers were innocuous enough: some police forms requesting permission for access to files and another personal letter from someone. I bunched all the papers together and stuffed them down a storm sewer on the other side of the street. I set off running again; and when I found another drain, I threw away his billfold, keys, and fob watch. I noticed just before I threw the watch away that it was ten to three. I was tempted to keep the revolver; it was a beautifully balanced little weapon; but I'd been issued a nine-millimetre Luger. Kleer's pistol would be a liability. The revolver made a hollow splash as it landed at the bottom of the sewer.

At the gasthof, I let myself in through the heavy glass door, taking great pains to turn the key in the lock so there was no sound. I returned the borrowed coat and cap to the coat rack; both were now quite sodden and I buried them under another lodger's dry ones. I crept as soundlessly as I could upstairs fearing every creak and groan from the old stairwell would betray me. They didn't. Gabriele was still sleeping, and although when I let myself in, she stirred and thrashed about in her sleep, she didn't wake up. I stripped off my clothes and lay down beside her. I didn't sleep at all that night. When first light brought fissures of grey sunlight to the edges of the curtains I was replaying in my mind for the hundredth time how I would react to the news of Kleer's death.

✠

At six, I nudged Gabriele. "Gabi, we can't sleep the day away. I've got to start my new job in a few hours."

Gabriele rolled over and groaned. "Alex, I'm sick. I've never felt so wretched in my life." She was grey-faced. My head hurt looking at her.

We skipped breakfast and I walked Gabriele to the trolley. The rain was still falling in a cold drizzle. I offered to see Gabi home, but gallantly, she refused. "I'll be fine. You can't be late; call me tonight." I took a trolley in the opposite direction to the officers' hotel, cleaned up, and reported to the Red House by eight.

Von Lignow had been at work since before seven, but he still seemed pleased to see me. He sat behind a mound of papers and brown files. "Did you have a good leave, Alex? I hope so. I've been going over my list of tasks, and we've an enormous amount of work ahead of us." He seemed very pleased with something. "But first, come with me. Because it's our first day, I have something I'll share with you." We walked down the hall to a small kitchen manned by an elderly orderly in a starched white jacket. Few offices in those days had conveniences like kitchens, but in this case it spoke more about the General Staff's propensity for gruelling hours rather than any indulgence to comfort. "Coffee, real coffee. Don't ask me where I got it," he winked theatrically, "but I have a cousin who commands a submarine and he puts in at Portugal from time to time."

With my coffee cup in hand, I followed Von Lignow to a small windowless office with a sturdy wooden table, a hard-backed chair, and a reading lamp. "This will be your home for the next while, Alex. I want you to read in for two or three days, then I'll describe in detail what I have planned for you."

For the rest of the day, Von Lignow had me reading files and staff papers on the implications of America's entry into the war. I wasn't sure there was anything I could do to add to the comprehensive mass of information stacked before me, but I dutifully plodded through assessments of American industrial potential, mobilization scenarios, strategic transport capabilities, and qualitative evaluations of American fighting potential. It was a grim picture for Germany. Within eight months of an American declaration of war, all the official estimates pointed toward a dramatic and decisive shift in the balance of power toward the Allies.

I was tired, but it was different from the deep fatigue I'd known at the end of a punishing spell in the trenches. By early afternoon, I was becoming drowsy and was almost nodding off when one of the military policemen from the front desk appeared at my doorway.

"Herr Oberleutnant, there is a police officer downstairs who wishes to speak with you. He says it's urgent."

I grunted and sat back. "Do you know what it's about?" I did my best to sound indifferent. "I'm very busy just now."

"No, sir, he asks that you come downstairs immediately."

As I passed Von Lignow's office, I poked my head inside and said, "There's a policeman downstairs who wants to see me about something. I'll be back in a minute."

"You didn't have too wild a time on leave did you, Alex?" he laughed. "Now the police are catching up with you for troublemaking in the red-light districts, eh!"

"More likely Vizefeldwebel Kleer again. He was phoning a friend of mine before my leave."

"Oh no, it won't be our friend Kleer. Major Bernhardt spoke to his supervisor personally. I believe you phoned him. That's all been taken care of."

I nodded. I had a sinking feeling in my stomach and my mouth went dry as I went downstairs. I stopped at the second floor and had a long drink of water from the fountain in the hallway. When I got downstairs, I felt composed and alert. There at the front desk was a uniformed police officer: late middle-aged, thin-lipped, ferret-like eyes, and a note book in his hand. I introduced myself. "I'm Oberleutnant Baumann. I've been told you are looking for me?"

The policeman looked at me intensely for a second, saluted, and clicked his heels. "Thank you, sir. I am Detective Sergeant Hulseimer. I am following up on a tragic murder. Last night, you know?" He peered at me intently for a second. I turned my head slightly to the side and looked at him as impassively as I could. "Vizefeldwebel Kleer. He was murdered."

"Kleer, my God! I didn't know. What happened?"

"That is what I am trying to find out. Outside his apartment, some time last night he was killed. Where were you last night, sir?"

"I was on leave, staying at a guest home, here in Berlin. Why?"

"Where you there all the time?"

"No. Up until about ten o'clock we were at dinner at Gasthaus Zum Hauser. We came back at ten. I was there until eight this morning."

"Who is 'we,' Herr Oberleutnant? Who were you with?"

"Gabriele Richter. She's a—a friend. We have been together all week."

"A friend, Herr Oberleutnant? What kind of friend?"

"She is a very close friend. What does this have to do with anything?" The clerk and the military policeman behind the desk both smirked and looked at one another and then made a point of studying the papers on their desk. "Can we discuss this over there?" I said, nodding towards the other side of the foyer.

The policeman followed me out of earshot of the front desk. "We are romantically involved."

"Are you planning on marrying this woman?" he asked disapprovingly.

"Yes, but what does this have to do with Kleer? Can we please stick to the issue?" I did my utmost to sound restrained and civil.

The policeman sniffed and scribbled something in his notebook. "What is her full name and address?"

The policeman questioned me at length about my relationship with Kleer. I told him everything, excluding only the details of the last night. I asked several times what had happened to Kleer, but he told me nothing beyond that he had been murdered.

He looked thoughtfully at me. "Yes, you know Kleer was difficult, and at times he could be persistent to the point of being fanatic; but he was an excellent police officer and a good man. You know when he volunteered for the army he took a big drop in salary; he thought it was the right thing to do, but I am afraid he had many enemies." He sighed and snapped his book shut and said, "I regret if I have inconvenienced you."

"No, not at all; I hope you catch the person who did this. Please call me if I can do anything to help."

The policeman saluted in a tired sort of way. "I have many inquires to make today. Thank you for your time, sir." He looked utterly expressionless.

I stopped at Von Lignow's office door. "I was right. It was about Kleer. He's dead. Someone killed him last night."

Von Lignow's jaw dropped. "Kleer dead? How?"

"I don't know. The policeman wouldn't tell me. Apparently he was murdered outside his apartment last night."

"Do the police think you had anything to do with it?"

"No, not at all. I think they're talking to everyone he had a file on. He said Kleer was not a popular man."

"I can believe that. He was our counter-intelligence man for a while when I was in Northern Headquarters. From what I could see, the man was slightly mad. But still, it's too bad. Did he have a family?"

"The policeman didn't say."

"With so many men dying every day at the front, it seems so

pointless when someone is murdered here in Berlin." He shook his head. "Oh, by the way, while you were out I was just talking to someone on General Groener's staff. Apparently your find of nitrogen-bearing rock, I'm afraid it's not nearly as large as we hoped. The rock varies in quality. That's disappointing. It's useful, no question; but it won't come close to solving Germany's supply problem. It's still good work you did. They want you back. Those other officers aren't working out so well. But don't worry, you aren't going back to Poland. I'm keeping you here in Berlin on my staff." He looked at me knowingly and chuckled.

"Could you please read those files in my out tray? Once you finish with those, we can start having you get to work on your real job. I want you to be my primary analyst. You will go through everything that comes out of the United States: diplomatic cables, newspapers, western front wireless intercepts, English newspaper summaries, agent reports from neutral countries, and embassy intelligence assessments; on top of all this, you will spend a lot of time monitoring wireless communications transcripts.

"We don't have many people in America that we can rely on, but for the people we have, you will be the first level of review to consolidate their reports. Each day by nine you will provide me a verbal briefing and after, by noon, you will prepare a daily intelligence summary for distribution to the chief of intelligence. His staff will incorporate your work in preparing the daily strategic intelligence summary. You will have a clerk and two wireless operators reporting directly to you. All three men are fluent in English."

I walked slowly back to my office. I wasn't thinking about my new job. My mind was filled with images of a wet coat and hat hanging in the hallway.

17

I DIDN'T LEAVE the Red House until after nine that evening. I slipped out just a few minutes after Von Lignow. When I got to the officers' hotel, I went straight to the lobby and made a telephone call to Gabriele. She was embarrassed and profusely apologetic about getting so drunk and told me that Detective Sergeant Hulse-imer had been around to see her late in the afternoon. "He told me he had already talked to you. I'm sorry about that policeman, but you know there was something very strange about him. I'm afraid I wasn't at my best, I still felt shaky but he was very rude and without saying anything he made me feel cheap."

I reassured her she wasn't cheap. There was a long pause in the conversation and I said, "Gabriele, you know when this is all over, we'll get married."

Now it was out there. I meant what I said, but I had no idea how I could ever work it out. Despite our intimacy and trust, it was the first time we had broached what was such an obvious subject, something that had been tacitly understood but always avoided. I've often thought that indicated there was something seriously wrong with our relationship, but at the time I chose to ignore it. I was foolish; of course there was something wrong with our relationship, I was lying to Gabriele and she sensed it. She didn't understand it, but she also didn't want to believe it. The mutual deceit that allows mutual suspicions to fester unspoken is one of the most insidious forms of dishonesty.

"Why not now?" she asked impassively. "Why should we wait, Alex?"

"Because of the war, there's still so much uncertainty."

"I would've thought the war would force us to hasten that decision, Alex. It has for so many other people."

"I don't know. For me there're so many other things I just haven't considered. I've no idea what I'm going to do after the war. I haven't finished university. I can't have you support me."

"Why not?" There was no anger or malice in her voice.

"I don't know. Women shouldn't support men. It's not right." I was fumbling and it showed in my voice. "You know that I love you, don't you?"

Gabriele laughed. "Of course I do, but really, Alex, you think so conventionally. What does it matter what others think? We'll be a team."

This challenge to convention seemed strange coming from her when just seconds before she was worried that a policeman made her feel cheap. I immediately chided myself for thinking that I knew exactly what she was feeling. She was normal. She was honest. Gabriele wanted a steadfast married life, a family of her own, a future that was stable and anchored to the love and trust of one person. I felt small for allowing myself a moment's cynicism about it. Gabriele was in turmoil and I'd brought it on. I was involuntarily put in the role of someone who wields the power in a relationship and then behaves cruelly: the powerful hypocrite with a desperate mistress. It wasn't who I wanted to be. I didn't like it. I didn't like what I'd done to Gabriele or what it was doing to me.

"Of course we'll be a team, but we'll just have to wait." This conversation was embarrassing for me. Had I been in other circumstances, had I been Rory Ferrall or even really been Alex Baumann, I wouldn't have been prevaricating and stalling. I continued. "I suppose you're right. But for the same reason you don't want to be thought cheap, I don't want to be thought a freeloader or a kept man."

I was playing for time. I really did love Gabriele, but I couldn't possibly marry her knowing I intended to abandon her some time in the future. Marrying her would be an obscene betrayal of her trust; but I wasn't prepared to let her go either. I hoped that somehow the future would mend all this. I should never have become involved with her. "Why don't we wait one month. We'll decide how we'll go about things then."

There was a prolonged silence at the other end. "All right. Let's wait a month. I'll still feel the same way then."

"So will I, Gabriele." I ran my fingers through my hair. "My time at the front, my capture, my escape, and now finding you—it's all so much, it's been so fast. It's wonderful, I'm happy. But waiting, it's just a way of making certain that we aren't acting impulsively. Let's just wait, one month, we'll decide then. Can we do that, please?"

Gabriele was a sturdy character. If she was disappointed in me, she didn't show it. We chatted for a few moments and I got up from the telephone desk with my head spinning. In the last twenty-four hours I had murdered a man and now I was playing Russian roulette with my life and the fate of the woman I loved. I went to the hotel bar ordered a large brandy and smoked several cigarettes. My eye, my hand, and my head ached. Life in the trenches may have been more trying and dangerous, but it was simpler than this. When I finally went to bed I was no more assured of what I was doing than I had been a month before.

✠

Over the next several days, Von Lignow fed me a steady stream of material to read and I began my daily ritual of sifting through transcripts of wireless transmissions from British Expeditionary Force headquarters in France. The broadcasts were picked up at the front and relayed to Berlin. American material came to us in irregular avalanches of information, and so for much of the time, by default, I spent several hours a day attached to the British desk as a secondary analyst. If you weren't German, the news was encouraging. On the western front, the war was going badly for Germany. In a suicidal offensive along the Somme, the British had inflicted heavy losses that couldn't be replaced; and on the eastern front, Romania had come in on Russia's side. The country was on the brink of starvation and that was a problem operational brilliance could do nothing to solve.

My days at the Red House were intensely busy and I quickly slipped into a routine. I was up well before six, breakfasted hurriedly, and was into the office by 6:30. I read the night's wireless transcripts, reviewed my notes from the previous day, prepared my briefing for Von Lignow; and then based on our discussions, prepared my written briefing for the chief of intelligence. The rest of the day I spent reading reports and transcripts and listening to the wireless.

Twice a day I travelled from the Red House to the Army Radio Signals Centre to listen to my share of the day's wireless broadcasts. I usually spent several hours there hunched over a crackling wireless speaker, but on many occasions I was dragged from a short sleep and ferried across the city to listen with a group of other officers to high-priority wireless broadcasts. We tried to put together a picture of what was about to happen based on scraps of fragmentary information. It was hard, wearisome work, and for my part I threw myself into it just as wholeheartedly as my legitimate German compatriots.

The American picture I put together never varied and was little different from what I had been given when I first arrived. American entry into the war would be an unqualified disaster for Germany. The policy of unrestricted submarine warfare was steadily tipping popular American opinion into believing Germany was an international menace. From what I could see, if Germany continued sinking ships on the high seas and persisted in its diplomatic blundering, America's participation was as good as guaranteed. You didn't have to be a strategic genius to see that without a miracle, if America chose to fight, in six months to a year after her declaration of war, Germany would be finished.

My "British" duties also kept me abreast of activities in the Canadian sector. The Canadian army was now believed to have increased in size to a full four division corps; and because of its formidable reputation, German intelligence regarded its movements as a key indicator of any impending British offensive. Late one night I listened to a long transmission from a Canadian Corps rear-area station that sent an un-encoded message that included a list of casualties from the Princess Patricia's. When I heard the unit name, I sat up as if a wasp stung me.

One of the signallers sitting next to me looked at me queerly. "You look like something has gone wrong, sir?"

I smiled. "Oh. No, its nothing at all, Gefreiter. When I was on the Belgian front near Ypres my platoon took a prisoner from that unit."

From the back of the room someone piped up. "Well, sir, too bad you and your platoon didn't get more of them; if they did, we could all be home in our beds instead of listening to the wireless at nights."

We all laughed and someone else said, "From their casualty list, it looks like someone has finished up where your platoon left off." They all roared with laughter and I shook my head trying to smile.

The list went on for a depressingly long time, but I didn't recognize any of the names. Later, in the grey twilight before dawn, I walked back through the cold empty streets to the Red House thinking that now I'd probably be a stranger in my own unit. It wasn't entirely depressing. I was consoled by the thought that the odds of my being caught were increasingly getting smaller. There would be similar casualty levels in Alex Baumann's old battalion.

My confidence was premature. Just a week later Detective Sergeant Hulseimer loomed up in front of me like a snake slithering unexpectedly out from a tree branch. One moment I was absorbed in the analysis of a transcript of a two-week-old *Chicago Tribune* editorial on the need to keep America out of Europe's war and the next, I was looking up into Hulseimer's unsmiling face. Behind Hulseimer stood a sheepish-looking clerk.

"I have two questions for you, Oberleutnant. Did you know your hotel was not far from the spot Kleer was murdered?" Hulseimer said flatly. "And, has anyone here in Berlin identified you positively as Oberleutnant Baumann?"

I was taken aback. "Yes, of course. Several. Why are you asking? Your friend Kleer went to great lengths to contact my old unit and my identity was exhaustively confirmed by members of Ninth Landwehr Divisional Staff."

I took a breath and then began my counter attack. "I'm fed up with this foolish line of questioning. I've no idea where Kleer died. Detective Sergeant, I might ask a question of you. What permission have you been given to be on this floor? I'm certain you realize you are in a restricted location. Who gave you permission to be here and why have you chosen to sneak up here unannounced? I'm sure you know of the sensitive work we do here?"

"I am a police officer in the course of a criminal investigation and I was let into the building by the military police." He started off confidently, but when he finished he looked uncertain of himself.

"Hulseimer, it's a serious offence to trespass in sensitive military areas, areas where secret information is routinely discussed. What business could you possibly have that would allow you to sneak into a restricted area?" The policeman made to speak but I interrupted him. "You're to leave this floor immediately and we shall take this intrusion up with the military police. Unless there's a damn good reason for you to be here, your head and the head of the sentry who let you into the building are going to roll." I turned to the clerk "Escort this man out of here. Have him detained by the military police sergeant in charge of the sentry post."

I snarled at Hulseimer, "Consider yourself under military arrest. We'll deal with the rest of these stupid inquiries after we deal with your security breach."

As Hulseimer and the clerk went downstairs, I sat alone in my office. It was as if someone told me I was going to be shot in the next hour. This must have been how prisoners in the dock felt when they were condemned. My world went into slow motion and I felt numb. I suppose it was some kind of reaction to fear. Nothing was real. I'd only felt this way once before, when I was put under anaesthetic after Sanctuary Wood. Both times I sensed impending death, but as told myself then, I survived that.

I tried to clear my mind. Hulseimer suspected something was wrong with my story. How strong were his suspicions? If they were serious, I should run. If they were minor ones, I might be able to bluff my way through it. I didn't know how serious it was, though. Perhaps there was something of Kleer's he'd recently come across that incriminated me. In my gut I knew it could only be a matter of time until I was caught in this deadly pretension. I reached out gingerly and without thinking picked the telephone up from its cradle. I put the speaker to my ear and lifted the candlestick microphone as if it was a fragile piece of glass. The operator instantly came on the line.

"Yes, sir? Can I help you?"

"Give me the military police sergeant, immediately. It's an emergency."

"At once, sir." The line crackled and I could hear the operator shout, "Military police duty NCO, take phone line two now, a staff officer has an emergency." In seconds a breathless voice came on the line. "Yes, mein herr, this is Gefreiter Potsmann."

I took a deep breath and spoke as calmly as I could. "Gefreiter, downstairs there is a civilian police officer. He's not authorized to be in this building and he's been upstairs on the second floor snooping around for some time. You are not to let him leave the building under any circumstances. He has probably seen documents of the most sensitive nature. I'll be down shortly. I have to estimate what the damage could potentially be and what it is he may have seen. Find out how he got up here and who let him in. Do you understand?"

"Yes, Oberleutnant." He dropped the phone and was off before

I could reply. I took a wooden match and lit one of my last cigarettes. My hand trembled. Slowly and deliberately I inhaled the
harsh ersatz tobacco smoke. Perhaps there was still a slender chance
I could bluff my way through this. I had two options; both were
risky. I could squeeze Hulseimer; for a time I had him over a barrel
for trespassing in the Red House; or, I could gamble and let him
go, make him indebted to me. I smoked the cigarette deliberately
savouring every second of it.

Downstairs there was quite a commotion in the lobby. My
attempts to become a grey man were in ruins. Hulseimer wasn't
taking things quietly. "You have no right to detain me. I am a state
policeman going about my duty in the course of a lawful investigation. Let go of me!" The military policeman pushed Hulseimer
forward and gave him a brutal smash to the ribs with the butt of his
rifle. Hulseimer groaned and slumped against the wall.

"Gefreiter, Hulseimer, stop this foolishness! We'll talk in the
guardroom office," I barked at the two of them. "Thank you, Gefreiter. Stay outside please; I'll deal with this. Hulseimer, take a seat."

Hulseimer gasped for a few seconds and straightened his tunic,
smoothing the dignity back into his character. I motioned for him
to sit. He paused for a second and sat down slowly fixing me with a
nervous glance before complying.

I stood back and folded my arms. "What the hell do you think
you're doing, Hulseimer? If you want to talk to me all you have to
do is call and an appointment can be arranged. Now you've got
yourself involved in a serious security infringement." He wasn't
looking at me and I softened my tone.

"Is it the loss of your comrade, Vizefeldwebel Kleer? We've all
endured losses. His death was a senseless one; but tell me, why did
you push your way into a restricted area? If there isn't a good reason,
they'll punish you severely."

He sniffed and turned up his nose like a wilful child. "I came
here because I wanted to catch you unawares. You are having an
affair with a radical socialist, someone from a family of radicals,
people who have been recorded as having expressed seditious com-

ments about the Kaiser. One of our police officers who was investigating you has been murdered and both you and your socialist girlfriend were together that night not more than a couple of miles from the scene of his death. I have every reason to be conducting an investigation. It is you, Oberleutnant, who should be answering my questions."

"Hulseimer, I'm perfectly aware of where I stand with regard to the law, and my loyalty to Germany is more than a matter of record." I paused for a second. "I don't think you can make the same claim. But you, you're avoiding my question. You either give me a satisfactory answer or you go straight to the Berlin Garrison Military Prison. You can tell them your story. There's a war on and I'm not playing games. You haven't answered my question. Why here, why did you choose to surprise me in this restricted area? If you really think I'm some sort of subversive, that I was involved in Kleer's death or even that Gabriele killed Kleer or that she's plotting the overthrow of the Kaiser, why commit a serious crime to confront me?"

Hulseimer fidgeted in his chair. He said nothing.

My bluff wasn't working. "Fine. You won't talk to me; you can talk to the authorities at the military prison. Gefreiter! In here please! Hulseimer, I haven't got time to deal with lunatics." The military policeman burst into the room. "Gefreiter, this man is to be held at the Garrison Prison. He refuses to co-operate."

The gefreiter yanked him from his chair.

"I only wanted to find out the truth about Vizefeldwebel Kleer's murder. That's all!" Hulseimer shouted.

I motioned for the gefreiter to leave him be. "Hulseimer, you're an idiot. You're wasting my time and the gefreiter's time and you've trespassed onto a forbidden site. If I let you go, I never want to hear from you or see your stupid, pig-headed face again. If you persist in this lunacy, I'll throw you into the Berlin stockade and the world will never see your half-witted face again. Now, Gefreiter, see this man to the street; if he so much as shows his face near here again, arrest him. And, Gefreiter, find out who let this idiot upstairs and

ensure it never happens again, or you'll find yourself in a punishment battalion. Do I make myself clear?"

For a second the gefreiter stiffened. "Yes, Oberleutnant." He
grabbed Hulseimer by the collar and manhandled him through the
doorway.

✠

Several days after this incident, late in the evening a haggard-look-
ing Von Lignow appeared at my office doorway. He ran his fingers
through his hair in a tired sort of gesture. "Alex, it seems that at last
we've made our point; we're leaving Berlin tomorrow. We've both
been transferred to Headquarters Seventeenth Army." He waved a
sheet of flimsy message paper at me. "They know we can't beat the
Americans. They're finally listening to our reports. So, we're going
on the offensive. We're going to beat the French and British before
the Americans arrive. You and I, we're going to be a part of it. Don't
you wish we did this two years ago?"

I was stunned. Von Lignow looked slightly drunk. I'd never seen
him that way before. But that's not what bothered me. Since Hulseimer's visit, my nerves were strung to the point of snapping. Every
sideways glance from Von Lignow I saw as suspicion. Every footfall in the hallway was someone coming to arrest me. Now he was
telling me I was going to get out of this place and the news hit me
like an unexpected stay of execution to a condemned man. My first
thoughts were that I was going to survive for a little while longer. It
wasn't until a few moments later I began to think about my mission
to uncover Germany's strategic intentions. Only later, I felt intense
sorrow and shame for my deceit and having to leave Gabriele.

I smiled and tried to look puzzled. "What exactly have you got
there, sir?"

"Come down to my office, Alex. I'll tell you."

I followed dutifully behind him down the worn wooden floors
of the corridor. Major Von Lignow was thinner than when I first

met him. Tonight the energy, the determination in his step, and the vigour he once had was drained out of him. In a few months he'd become visibly older and thinner; his shoulders were stooped and his thick brown hair was like straw. When he stood still, he looked like someone in the final stages of a terminal illness.

"Close the door. We should celebrate." He pulled a bottle of German brandy from his desk drawer and poured healthy measures into heavy china mugs. "It's not often these days that we have victories we can celebrate, but our work, both yours and mine, has at long last convinced the Kaiser and Ludendorff that we can't possibly win if America comes in. So, do you know what we are going to do? We're going to win before America comes into the war." He looked at me with a half-smile. "I'm serious. This is a kind of pre-victory victory celebration. Do you know several of us have spent weeks arguing our recommendations to senior staff officers? I couldn't say anything to you, but yesterday I was told the senior members of the staff are now strongly of the same opinion." He smiled and raised his glass. "Of course they knew we were right all along. No one would admit it because we didn't have a sensible plan that allowed us to act on that information. Now, we have a plan, and so we can officially acknowledge the fact that if we are ever going to win, victory has a definite deadline tied to it."

I said nothing. He handed me a mug half-filled with German brandy. It was excellent. Wolfgang Von Lignow was forever coming up with scarce luxuries. In turn I offered him one of the stale old wartime-issue cigarettes.

"You don't look excited, Alex? Aren't you pleased?"

"I suppose I should be. You tell me we have a plan to win the war before the Americans get over here. I'm happy to hear that, but sir, I'm suspicious."

Von Lignow laughed. "Your problem, Alex, is you have a bloodless engineer's mind. You're too matter of fact. The staff has been working for a long time on the problems facing us." He took a long, thoughtful sip of his drink. "Let me describe it to you this way. The problem's been that we have been deadlocked; but you know, we've never really been stalemated. Stalemate's just a word that hides the fact that both sides have run out of ideas." He sat back and swirled the brandy in his mug.

"You see, Alex, you either win a war by manoeuvre or you win by attrition. Those are the only two ways you can win. You can get in around your enemy and hit him faster than he can react, or you can beat him by grinding him down. That's all there is to it, really. There's no such thing as stalemate. Stalemate just means you can't get in close to hit him and you haven't finished grinding him down. In the autumn of 1914, we tried to win by manoeuvre and that didn't work, so then we tried to win by attrition. For years now we've tried to win by attrition and that certainly hasn't worked. So, now, we're going to out-manoeuvre them." Von Lignow became serious. "But this time it's going to work. I'm convinced of that."

I wasn't sure what to say and tried to sound non-committal. "So what are we going to do?"

"Several things. We now have far more troops available to us than we had even two months ago. Serbia and Russia are for all purposes out of the war. So, with the divisions we transfer from the East we can field sufficient troops to make a difference. But we won't waste our troops like we did before. The first thing we're going to have to do is change the way we attack. Instead of attacking in one long rigid line behind a fixed artillery barrage, we're going to attack like water running down a hill. When we encounter a rock, we flow around it. Our troops are going to provide their own fire support. Instead of attacking in battalions, regiments, and divisions in one long line, we're going to attack in the smallest groups possible, three- and four-man teams covering themselves forward with their own light machine-guns and grenades. They will be following up closely behind a co-ordinated barrage. Our infantry will go around and behind strong points. Take them out from behind and from the flanks while the others keep going, driving deep into their rear areas, destroying their artillery and eventually their lines of supply. We'll have better communications with the artillery, better communications with our aeroplanes; the artillery will move forward in smaller groups. The enemy won't have the time to regroup and counter attack. It'll work, Alex. If we do this in a large enough offensive, we can break the Allied will to fight in thirty days."

I raised my eyebrows. "You know, sir, the tactics are a bit different; but I've heard that kind of enthusiastic talk before I was captured. How do we know this won't be just another bloodbath?"

"Oh, they'll work all right; we've already tested these tactics against the Italians. They work. I've read the reports and listened to the officers who ran the operation. That's where I've been the last three days."

"It'd be nice if we could end the war. You're right, maybe two years ago if we'd done something like this we might have..." My voice trailed off. "You really think this will work?"

"Yes, I do. You'll see, Alex. Tomorrow we take the evening train to Seventeenth Army Headquarters. We'll see a training demonstration and we'll be given a series of lectures by the planning staff explaining the details—all the co-ordination measures, all the training measures, all the logistic planning, all the deception planning, the movement planning—all of it. This one is going to work. Believe me, this is the one that's going to put an end to this endless slaughter once and for all."

I didn't say anything. I was becoming obsessive about being caught and my mind wandered. Was Von Lignow involved in some kind of elaborate trap?

"Alex, don't look so disbelieving. For now, we're being temporarily relieved of our American duties. You and I will be part of the team that maps out the British line. We have to determine where their army, corps, and division boundaries are. Then we work with the artillery and the planning staffs selecting specific targets. It's the English we're going to knock out. The French will sue for peace right after that; believe me. And when that happens, you and I come back here to work on the American desk again." He said nothing for a while and then, in a matter of seconds, he seemed to deflate. He looked at me morosely and poured more brandy. There was something more than the war on his mind.

"You know, Alex, this comes too late for me; but you, you may have some kind of life when it's all over."

"I'm sorry, sir, I don't know what you're talking about."

"Your life, outside the army, beyond the war you have to have a life. You have one. I don't. Not any more."

He was drunker than I thought. "What are talking about, sir?"

"Your girlfriend, Gabriele. I know about her." He swung his feet up onto his desk. "I know about her and I know about the police and I know all about their ridiculous suspicions. The police have been badgering me too. She's a harmless small-time socialist. She's not a violent radical. The police are afraid she's a Red anarchist and she's corrupting an officer who is working for the General Staff. Tell me this. Who isn't going to be a socialist when this war's over? Oh don't worry; your Gabriele's harmless, mostly harmless. You know I don't approve of you two going off like that together. You're not married. It's immoral. But I suppose you justify it because of the war. You'd have been thrown off the staff for that kind of thing before the war. You had to be careful with your indiscretions then. Now, we just pretend to ignore it." He stopped and lit another cigarette, blowing smoke noisily up at the ceiling. "You know without killing me or wounding me, the war's ruined my life. My wife has asked me to move out. We aren't going to live together as husband and wife any more."

The room grew silent. "I'm sorry to hear that, sir." I meant it.

"It's been a long time coming."

Neither of us spoke for a minute.

"You know this offensive may end the war in time for you and Gabriele to have a life together. My Lucy and I will never be the same though. She says I've changed. She says I'm angry and tense whenever I'm at home, which is not too often. That's funny. She thinks because I'm in Berlin I should be home more of the time. She says I've neglected her for too long. She says she can't stand it any more, and she doesn't love me. I suppose she'll eventually ask for a divorce."

He pulled his feet off the table. "I don't know why I'm telling you all this, Alex; probably because I don't have any other friends. Do you believe this? I'm telling my marriage problems to my staff oberleutnant. I should at least make you a hauptmann, Alex." He forced a laugh. "I've given my life to the army and what've I gotten for it. I'm a major on the Greater German General Staff, a key planner in the greatest fucking man-made disaster in all of history, and I can't even keep my wife, let alone plan the biggest war of all time."

"Let's finish our drinks, sir," I said as kindly as I could. "I think it's time we called it a night."

He pulled himself upright and straightened his tunic. The action seemed to put new life into him. "You're probably right, Alex; but don't give me any of this shit that things will be better in the morning."

"I promise, I won't."

18

GABRIELE worked the next day and I stole an hour from my duties at the Red House to call around at her hospital. She met me in the lobby. The sight of her worried me. She was showing the pallor of the chronically undernourished and there were traces of the dark circles growing beneath her eyes. You saw that on so many Berliners then.

"I don't know when I'm going to be back. I can't tell you anything about it just now; but you're not to worry. Believe me, unless I'm run over by a wagon team, I won't be anywhere near where I can be hurt." Gabriele choked back tears and nodded bravely. She didn't believe me. So many other young men had told their loved ones the same story.

I wanted to say more, to tell her that no matter what happened, I'd be back someday to find her but I couldn't think of a tactful way to express myself without making things worse, so I played out my charade and told her I loved her and that we'd get married when I had my next leave. I wished it could be true. I left feeling utterly dispirited and more like a traitor than at any other time in my life.

✠

The night train to Seventeenth Army headquarters was uneventful. Von Lignow and I carried our possessions in cloth staff officers' valises. Again I felt conspicuous amongst my fellow passengers in the officers' compartment. All the other officers we met carried the grey canvas and leather knapsacks issued to field soldiers. Von Lignow with his red tabs and scarlet striped trousers of the Greater General Staff drew deferential stares; and, although I didn't want to admit to it, I felt conspicuous dressed in my clean new coat and not carrying field gear. Once again I regarded myself as inadequate around those fighting men. It was a stupid way to feel. I knew that. It was evident I'd been seriously wounded, but I felt insecure anyway. It was one of those moments when your fears and worries override your intellect and you are incapable of doing anything about it. I kept my coat open keeping the ribbon of my Iron Cross visible. Just before the train came chuffing into sight Von Lignow saw me shiver. He looked me up and down and spoke sharply. "For God sakes, Alex, do up your jacket. What do you care what anybody thinks? You're a decorated German officer. You're not an American engineering student any longer."

We arrived at the town of Lougement in the dark. An elderly gefreiter manned the railway station's Army Movements Desk. His face and hands were red and purple with horrific burn scars. He sat dutifully at his desk in an unheated wooden cubicle shuffling his papers under a weak light. He ordered our transport and gave us forms and a printed map directing us to our billets and to the Seventeenth Army's headquarters buildings. When he handed me the papers I noticed he was missing the same fingers on his right hand that I'd lost on my left.

An open-topped grey touring car drove us through the town and dropped us at our billet. The house was one of the large three-storey brick buildings, not much different than every other house in that town.

A hideous-looking lady with an unlit clay pipe clenched between the stumps of her teeth muttered away in French when she answered the door. As she climbed the stairs in front of me, I could hear her grumbling. "You German officers never arrive in the daytime, do you? I'll be glad to see the end of all this, then we can all go back to living our own lives in our own houses."

When she reached our rooms she spoke much louder and smiled, showing stained teeth and white gums. "This is the oberleutnant's room and, Herr Major, you are here in the big room across the hall. There will be hot water in the morning."

My French, which I officially didn't speak, was passable enough to understand the old girl and I had to resist the urge to wish her good night. Von Lignow merely grunted at her and took the key from her hand.

It was dark and raining when we left the boarding house to go to Seventeenth Army headquarters. I stood in the cobblestoned street. Cold rain driven by a bitter wind drove into my face. The rainwater pattered on the bare stems of the vines on the houses opposite me and the wind shook its windowpanes. Von Lignow took his time coming out. I pulled my coat tight around me and turned the collar up.

I was certain Von Lignow was drunk again that morning. In the hallway he looked unsteady on his feet and there was something about the way he held his head. The controlled athletic grace of the fencing champion was gone. That morning out on the street he was ordinary and ungainly. The rain drummed down relentlessly and in the morning's grey light, and his face looked coarser and more worn than I'd ever seen it. His hair, normally so luxuriant and thick, was stiff like the hair on a wet corpse. He was white and had red patches the colour of scraped veal high on his cheeks. He said nothing to me until after we had walked for several minutes.

Suddenly he turned and stopped. "So, Herr Oberleutnant, what will you do if we win this war? Eh? What do you have planned?" He didn't allow me to reply. "You better hope we win this now. If the Americans come in and we lose, what will happen to you?"

I shrugged. "Herr Major, I'm a German now. America wasn't in this war when I joined, so I can't be responsible for what happens years later. If we lose, I'll go back to Berlin and marry Gabriele.

And if we win, I'll do the same thing." I looked at him for a second. "What will you do?"

"You are cheeky with your superiors, Alex. You know, you are pushing your luck. Me, if we win, I go back to Berlin and plan for the next war, and if we lose, I go back to Berlin and plan even harder for the next war. The difference between you and me is that you go back to Berlin to begin a marriage and I go back to end one."

He lapsed into silence having said his piece. He looked dejected as if the air had been let out of him. His head slumped down into his shoulders and his body drooped.

"I'm sorry about you and Lucy, sir."

"Yes, I am too. I never thought I'd be sorry for myself, ever. Now I will have to come and ask permission to visit my children. They won't like me when they get older. People will shake their heads and snicker when I leave a room. I'd never have guessed it. General Staff officers don't get divorced. Chorus girls, artists, politicians— they get divorced, not me." He walked for a time with his hands behind his back, head upright but his body looked deflated. The rain dripped from his pickelhaube and ran down his face. "You're younger and you still trust people. You're still wet behind the ears, do you know that?"

I said nothing in reply for a few moments. He didn't want an answer. The only woman I had ever really grown to trust that way was Gabriele. And unlike my drunken superior, who by the sounds of things had virtue on his side by being a victim, I was about to desecrate the confidence of the person I loved. Poor old Wolfgang Von Lignow, I should have had more sympathy for him than I did. I didn't particularly like him when he was drunk. To make matters worse, in these last few days he had lost his aura of genius and power; and the truth was, I didn't like him for that too. He was a bit like one of those explorers who the natives realize isn't an emissary from the gods.

On one level I believed that I liked him less because he seemed to have lost his stature. At least I certainly wanted to believe that—but I knew that Von Lignow was none of those things really. He was

just a man in intense pain, but I was preparing myself psychologically to betray him as well. You can't do those things cold-bloodedly
to decent people who you like and have helped you and offered you
kindness. You can't like a person before you destroy him. Perhaps
some people could. I certainly couldn't. You need a reason, so you
change them into different people than they are. You belittle them.
You make them responsible for your actions. I didn't think of any of
that at the time, though. I wasn't thinking deeply about my motives.
There was no time for that. For now Von Lignow was self-pitying
and dangerous, someone I had to defeat. "You must continue to
trust people, Herr Major," I said virtuously. "I can only imagine
what you're feeling, but it's probably like anything else, sooner or
later there's an end to it."

"I suppose you're right, Alex. You have to trust people. That's
probably the only thing that keeps us all sane."

We said nothing until we reached the headquarters. The rain
increased from a steady patter to a downpour and we walked officer-
like with our hands clasped behind our backs and our heads bent
into the wind.

Seventeenth Army headquarters was spread out in dozens of
buildings in central Lougement. The chief of staff of Western Army
Group Field Intelligence was putting on our briefing. His group
had commandeered a small hotel in the Seventeenth Army area. It
was recognizable by bundles of telephone wires running into the
upstairs windows. Two helmeted guards with rifles over their shoulders stood watching us cautiously behind rolls of rusty barbed wire.
Their black jackboots were rooted solidly in the street's pavement,
but their eyes tracked us steadily. The rain pattered on their helmets
and ran down in rivulets onto their rubber rain capes. Inside, a fat
cheery cavalry lieutenant colonel greeted us at the door as if we had
dropped by for Christmas drinks. "Welcome, gentlemen. Welcome.
I'm glad you could come," he said, rubbing his hands in delight.
"We're planning the campaign to end the war and I'm very pleased
you are here to be a part of it. Please put your wet coats away in the

room to your left and go on into the briefing room. We have some good hot army coffee to take the chill out of your bones."

He shepherded us into a large room in what must have been in better days an elegant hotel dining room. The parquet floor was badly scraped and scuffed, and instead of smart dining tables, it was covered with rows of folding wooden chairs. The gilt wallpaper was peeling. What had was once been a corner bandstand was now simply a platform covered with a series of easels each holding a large-scale map.

The maps showed the German front line, the rear area, and what must have been the communications zone. There was another large-scale map of the entire British sector running from the Channel to somewhere west of the French positions near Metz. There wasn't any doubt that whatever operations were intended, the emphasis would be heavily weighted against the British sector. Somewhere in that confusion of map pins and coloured paper was the Canadian Corps and whatever was left of my old battalion. It was strange to be looking at our own lines as seen on a map from inside a German army headquarters. I tried to appear as nonchalant as possible and took my seat beside Von Lignow in the second row of chairs. The first row was, in the German army as it was in our own, reserved for senior officers; no one in the room sat there. Like the few others present, Von Lignow and I smoked in silence and flicked our ashes into little tin cans that were liberally distributed throughout the room. In a few minutes, ten or fifteen officers drifted in and took their seats.

I looked sideways at Von Lignow. If I hadn't known better I would have sworn that he was now as sober as a judge. No signs of heavy drinking, fatigue, or undue strain. It was an act of the will. His face looked a little more flushed than usual, but apart from that he looked fine. It was there in the briefing room for the first time it crossed my mind that Von Lignow may in fact have been a secret drinker all the time I'd known him. That might have been the biggest problem between him and Lucy.

I didn't know much about that kind of thing in those days. I had never really personally known anybody who successfully drank in secret, although I'd heard about it. Whatever lay behind the drinking may have helped explain his motives for latching onto me. Apart from seeing in Alex Baumann qualities of courage and audacity, he also saw the opportunity to gain a friend.

There was nothing untoward about this. He needed someone he could have confidence in, someone who was a kindred spirit. The General Staff wasn't like the rest of the army; it didn't offer comradeship. If you worked hard and finished early, they gave you more work. It was a perverse friendless organization that prided itself on working its members to the point of collapse.

His need for some kind of friendly contact would have explained the responsible job he gave me right off, the encouragement, sharing his coffee and chocolate, and sending me off to his parents' house on my leave. He was just a decent and civilized man trying to live up to some impossibly bizarre standard. He was incredibly lonely, isolated by his work and his status, alienated from his family. He was someone who had been worked almost past the point of mental exhaustion; now his family life was coming apart, and since I had gone off with Gabriele he was probably offended at what he must have seen as my lack of morality. He was much more wretched than I ever imagined. Despite the intellect, the inflexible sense of honour, and the super-human capacity for work, Major Wolfgang Von Lignow was really nothing more than an ordinary man pushed beyond the breaking point. Now he was starting to crack.

The briefing began at seven sharp.

"Thank you for coming, gentlemen. My name is Lieutenant Colonel Ernst Von Litzengen," said the fat cheery cavalry officer. "We are all here to participate in planning the campaign to end the war. Germany has suffered enough—and with your help, we will put an end to these dark days. You have all been pulled from other headquarters and other jobs to help us here. All of you gentlemen have a background in intelligence collection and analysis, and now—" He took a great gulp of air. "Now we need these skills. Before I describe

exactly how we are going to do this, I want you to introduce yourselves to one another."

In turn we stood, gave our names, and described what our
employment had been before today. Most of the other officers had
been culled from corps and divisional staffs that had been freed
from the Russian front, although a few were English-speaking regimental officers pulled from divisions serving on the western front.
Von Lignow and I were the only officers from Berlin. We were
selected because of our English language skills as well as our strategic intelligence experience. As Lieutenant Colonel Von Litzengen
said with unconcealed enthusiasm, "Gentlemen your task is two-
fold. Half of you will put together the intelligence plan and the
other half will create and direct the counter-intelligence plan for
Operation Michael."

He read a list of names and then, as if we were school children,
he had us get up and change our seats to sit in our two groupings.
"Those of you who are in the Intelligence group on my right will
collect and analyze all the information to help us plan the operation
in detail. Those of you on my left will be the Counter Intelligence
team and you will create the plans to deny the enemy information
about our activities and to deceive him as to our true intentions.
Operation Michael will be the final destruction of the British Expeditionary Force. No details as to where the offensive will take place
have been decided upon as of yet." He beamed beatifically at us.
"We need your advice to determine that."

Stepping back, he steepled his fingers and said, "You gentlemen have critical tasks before you. We believe the British are in the
process of extending their line southward in order to provide some
relief to the French. To cover this extended frontage, we believe the
British have had to weaken all of their divisions. Thus, the weakened British front provides us a wonderful opportunity. When we
break through the British, we will roll up their rear areas and march
behind their backs to the North Sea. We can knock Britain out of
the war in two weeks. A second army will push forward into the
heart of the undefended French rear. In doing this, we will shorten

our line and threaten the western approaches to Paris. Believe me, oh yes, the French will sue for peace when that happens.

"We expect we can accomplish all of this in three weeks from the commencement of the operation. Now, please don't ask how we intend to do that when we have spent the last three years locked in static trench warfare. I know you have heard rumours, but I won't explain it to you now on a map. I want to show you in the field. Only then, when you have seen with your own eyes, will you truly believe me.

"There is an omnibus waiting outside for you. The mayor of Lougement has kindly lent it to us for the duration of the war." Colonel Von Litzengen paused, beaming at his wit. "You can pick up your breakfast as you go out. Believe me, you won't be disappointed with your morning." As we filed out the front door an attractive young Belgian woman in a cloth apron handed us each a paper package of dry sandwiches made from some kind mysterious brittle sausage cut into razor-thin strips.

Our bus drove us out of Lougement and through the countryside for almost an hour. The rain began to let up, but the sky remained overcast. I could not tell which direction we were heading, but I presumed it was north. The ground turned from flat, dreary plain to more pleasant rolling hills with a few lightly wooded areas. The fields were ploughed and bare. We pulled off a gravel road into an area guarded by a pair of smartly turned-out cavalrymen on horseback. The two horsemen gave crisp salutes with their lances as we drove past. The parking lot, such as it was, had off on one side several lancers brushing and grooming their mounts—beautiful, massive, chestnut-coloured horses. There were a dozen civilian and military trucks. We got out from our omnibus and one of the horsemen dismounted and led us forward on foot for ten minutes. We stopped at a rise in the ground where a small area had been carefully blocked off by an old length of rope pegged into the ground.

Lieutenant Colonel Von Litzengen became more cheerful by the minute. "This, gentlemen, is the site of your demonstration. What you will witness today is a demonstration of our tactical plan to break the deadlock. You will see something we all wish we had discovered several years ago. Now, if you allow me to explain how we have set things up here for you: three hundred metres in front of you, both to your left and to your right, you will see two parallel country roads. The coils of barbed wire you see running alongside these roads have been laid alongside two rather deep ditches. These ditches represent our trench line on the right and the enemy's trench line on the left." A few officers were studying the demonstration area with field glasses and muttering to themselves.

"Now, in a just a few minutes you will see a detachment of cavalry appear. These men will represent for you the forward edge of our friendly barrage. Wherever these men go, imagine a heavy weight of artillery falling." Seconds later a half-dozen lancers on horseback came thundering up the hill behind us, galloped onto the field and broke from single file into a long extended line just in front of the enemy trench.

"These lancers, gentlemen, represent the forward line of a hurricane barrage. Three hours of hell: high explosive and gas shells raining down on pre-selected portions of the enemy's front line." The horsemen closed up to the enemy wire and Von Litzengen raised his arm, at which point heavy small arms and machine-gun fire erupted from the German "trenches." At the same time that the shooting broke out, forty or fifty soldiers emerged from the trenches and ran forward twenty yards, and then flopped onto the ground and immediately began firing. No sooner had the line of soldiers begun firing than a second line of skirmishers charged up from the German trenches and ran twenty yards beyond the first line.

"You will see gentlemen that each line supports the next one. There is no point when our troops are crossing exposed ground that they will not have a heavy volume of covering rifle and machine-gun fire to protect them. Each section has been broken into two and given a light machine-gun. They will support one another in groups of four or five men. No more long lines of troops walking across no man's land without covering fire." He pointed to the horsemen. "Now look if you will, you will see the barrage has moved on past the first

enemy trench line and it is neutralizing a depth position. We will
have artillery spotters forward with field phones to co-ordinate our
artillery, and we will also use radio-controlled aeroplanes to direct
the fire of our artillery. These men before you will not find themselves caught out in the open without covering artillery to protect
them."

The two lines of infantry had by now closed up to the enemy
wire and while one group continued to pour fire into the trenches,
the second prepared grenades. "Watch carefully, those men are preparing real grenades. To protect the cavalry we use blank rifle and
machine-gun ammunition; but we are using real grenades in the
final assault. We take this training very seriously and I have enormous confidence in these troops." Seconds later a series of explosions erupted from all along the friendly trench line and drifting
clouds of grey black smoke rose from the ditch. "A major difference
between this form of attack and what you have been accustomed to
is that no group will wait until the troops beside them have caught
up. This new form of attack is not linear; it is more like a torrent of
water flowing forward and around any opposition it encounters.

"Watch now," he continued. "The assault troops will push through
their first objective and clear the next line of reserve trenches and
strong points. You will notice the barrage markers have moved forward at the same rate as the infantry advance. Now, look to your
right, you will see the next key element of this offensive." From the
right-hand ditch crews were manhandling a field gun and a large
trench mortar forward. The gun had wooden sleds attached to its
wheels so that it could be dragged across rough ground. The gun
and mortar teams were followed by groups of men pulling sleds
with wooden ammunition boxes fastened to the top.

"What you are seeing now is how we will keep our forward assault
troops protected by indirect fire. Field guns and trench mortars will
move forward with the infantry and will be able to provide a steady
rain of high explosive on any depth positions. I also want to point
out that the enemy intends to use tanks to seal off and break up
any penetrations we make. Our field guns will be right up with the

advancing infantry to take care of that. They will be able to destroy any tanks that move forward. Neither the English nor the French will be expecting that, and we shall hammer them as soon as they show their noses.

"We expect we can get our troops to advance at least two kilometres in the first wave. The second wave will be rushed in behind and we hope to make penetrations of up to thirty kilometres in one day. Once we are through the first two lines of defence, we will be able to bypass any pockets of resistance and keep going. We expect to push forward night and day for three weeks. In the first two weeks we will completely encircle the British army; we will push deep into their rear areas and then drive westward to the North Sea. We will then turn on the French, and with their left flank exposed and the loss of their only major ally, the French will sue for peace." Von Litzengen waved his right arm in the air and shouted to one of the Lancers behind us. "Tell them to knock off for the day. Give my compliments to the company commander; if he does half as well on the first morning of the operation, we'll all soon be having our dinners in Paris." Turning to us, Von Litzengen asked, "Are there any questions?"

At first, I think all of us were a bit stunned. It was all so simple; yet laid out in front of us it was entirely believable. Von Lignow had explained it to me a few days earlier; but here, it was utterly convincing, so relentlessly mechanical and straightforward. I had no doubt it was going to work. The first officer to speak, a Thuringian Grenadier captain, said laughingly, "This looks so easy, tell me Herr Colonel, why didn't any of us think of this three years ago?"

"A very good question, Captain. Sometimes the simplest things are staring us in the face and we refuse to see them. We spent all our time concentrating on gas and zeppelins and new kinds of aeroplanes; we also wasted a lot of effort thinking that if we just pushed hard enough at precisely the right point we could crack open the front. Who would have thought the answer would be in a simple change of infantry and artillery tactics? By the way, did you gentlemen know that all of these innovations came from men like your-

selves? Veterans. Captains and majors, men such as yourselves who
have lived through life at the front." Von Litzengen clapped his
hands behind his back. "The genius of our army is that it's a practical organization. Nothing fancy. Simple common sense, ruthlessly
exploited." He stared at us for effect. "Now, is there anyone here
who does not believe this will work? If there are, I want to hear
from you."

　　None of us answered.

✠

That afternoon, back in the town of Lougement, I was given the
details of my new assignment. Not surprisingly, I found myself
working again for Wolfgang Von Lignow, who was given responsibility for the intelligence mapping of the entire British sector. Along
with two other officers, I was tasked to put together the intelligence
picture for half the British front from La Fere to Arras. Our directions were simple. We were to map all major formations and units
as well as put together a detailed appraisal of their order of battle,
their boundaries, their strengths, the location of their reserves, and
assess their morale. In order to be closer to a key wireless intercept
station, we were moved by truck nearer to the front, to the farm
hamlet of Carréfour, which was a half-dozen battered farm buildings just out of range of British artillery. We were given the run of a
large Belgian farmhouse. A divisional supply and transport staff had
occupied the house before us, and from them we inherited several
of their orderlies, signallers, and clerks to help us manage our planning rooms.

　　I tried not to think much about Gabriele during those days, and
that bothered me. I was deliberately trying to keep her out of mind.
There was nothing I could do about the situation, and thinking
about her depressed me. I repeatedly had to make do, telling myself
that somehow, when it was all over, I'd resolve all this. I'd find the
right words. It was a practicable delusion.

Something else in me changed during that time, something quite unexpected. I knew I shouldn't have looked forward to my work quite as much as I did, but there was an indefinable element about operational intelligence that fascinated me. Compared to what I was doing in Berlin, my new employment was enthralling. When I was in Berlin, I read old newspapers and made academic estimates as to the potential strength of a newly mobilized American army. Everything in Berlin seemed distant and irrelevant. In Belgium, I was working with fresh information about real troop deployments. Operational intelligence was addictive: the immediate importance of the work, the sense of exhilaration, and the privileged and exclusive sense of understanding.

Here in Belgium, I had to figure out what a real enemy looked like, what he was up to and what his intentions were. It was intellectually fascinating. In a perverse way, I was completely enthralled by it, and for a week I fell to my new duties with a surprising vigour. Several times that week I had to remind myself that it was all a façade. Late on the sixth night at Carréfour, as we sat smoking and drinking ersatz coffee, discussing a problem in the farmhouse kitchen, I stopped and looked about me; it was time to put an end to all this fantasy. My illusion, so painstakingly developed, now had to be destroyed. I'd discovered what I'd come to Germany to find and I couldn't put things off any longer. It was time to go back.

During that week, Von Lignow wasn't making things easier for me. After that first night in Lougement, he seemed to have left his drunken anger and self-absorption behind and reverted to being a charming old-world gentleman. Much as I didn't want to, I liked him again. As we sat in the farmhouse kitchen he asked me, "What's bothering you, Alex? You seem a bit down in the mouth. Isn't this what we've all been waiting for after all these years?" He fished out his cigarettes and offered me one.

I accepted. "No, no, sir; not at all. I'm thrilled at the plan really. It's high time we had some tactical thinking to match the troops' courage." I was scrambling to hide my real thoughts. "My eye's bothering me, that's all." Von Lignow winced and nodded with genuine sympathy. His concern for my well-being told me how I was going to escape.

19

FOR THE NEXT TWO DAYS, I made an obvious pretence of taking off my eye patch and rubbing the edges of my socket as if I was in great pain. In fact, at the time, my eye hardly bothered me at all. One of the other oberleutnants on our team, a guards artillery officer who had seen a great deal of action in Russia, seemed to think my discomfort was funny and was forever making jokes about the fact that since I only had one eye, I was probably reading half as many intelligence reports as the rest of them and therefore I should stay on the job twice as long as the rest. He was a nice enough fellow, but had a painfully wooden sense of humour. I played along with him. He was good for my cover.

On the third day after making my decision, I was up early and met Major Von Lignow before breakfast. "Good morning, sir, if it's all right with you, I want to drop around to the nearest field hospital and get someone to look at this eye. I won't be long. It's been hurting like hell for days now and I'm sure someone with the right kind of ointment can make it better."

I quickly changed the subject before he could answer. "Oh, another thing, sir, I was thinking about that problem with the boundary between the British Fourteenth and Thirty-sixth divisions. Yesterday we had a wireless intercept describing their new artillery groupings. If we get back those aerial photos of their gun lines today, we'll be able to determine where their medium and heavy artillery units are located. I think we can match them to determine their forward boundaries; and once we pinpoint their ammunition supply points, I think we should be able to make some accurate predictions as to where their new rear-area boundaries are."

Von Lignow raised a hand. He sounded tired. "You're probably right, Alex. But it's not going to work, not today. It's a good idea, but the pilot you tasked to take these photographs, he didn't come back yesterday. He's dead. I agree with your approach. So go back, put in your request again. You're right, we need the information. If you brief someone else on our requirements, maybe we can get another flight tomorrow. But we won't get one today, not with this cloud cover. As for your eye, by all means go get someone to look at it."

I was shocked by the news of the pilot. I'd briefed the man personally. I sent him up, but I never expected him to die. Without being conscious of it, I'd come to see myself as a bystander, a kind of ghost. I hadn't expected anyone following my instructions to die. I liked the man. He was a quiet fellow, not much more than twenty years old; he was thick-set, with blond hair, an easy smile, and an open trustworthy face. Now he was dead and his remains lay smashed and burned somewhere to the west. I was thankful I wasn't sending anyone else to complete the mission.

In the farm kitchen, I breakfasted hastily on onion and potato soup, black bread, and ersatz coffee, and then went to the orderly room in search of a travel form. When I told Private Steiger, our clerk, he cheerfully told me, "Oh, don't worry, sir, if you're only going to the field hospital, you have no need of a travel warrant. There's a field hospital just ten kilometres from here and you'll be fine going there and back." He was a spirited and bright young man, but I didn't want his help today.

"Thanks. If I'm not treated at the field hospital I'll go back to the Corps General Hospital and get someone to look at it." I cut him short; Steiger was about to tell me that as a staff officer I didn't need a pass or travel warrant for that either. "I'm not taking any chances, and as you're not a doctor, Private Steiger, and neither of us know exactly where I'm going, I want you to keep your nose out of things. Now, just give me a blank travel warrant and stamp it. In fact give me two of them. If I need one for the General Hospital then I'll have that too. I'll fill them out at the field hospital." I smiled at him. I didn't want this man telling anyone I'd gone off taking travel warrants with me.

I began to improvise. "When you're finished that, I want you to ensure that you're free later today. I want you to put your talents together and gather materials to build a rough plaster or clay model of the entire British VI Corps sector for us. I'll need it this afternoon when I get back. I want something about the size of a door. I'll need it for briefings and discussions. I don't know where you'll find the materials. Use your head; surprise me. Dig for clay if you have to, but put your mind to it. I want something solid. I'll see you later this afternoon and I'll show you then what I want you to do with your materials. Don't start trying to build anything until I get back. Just make your plans."

It was that simple. Five minutes later I found a driver and lorry to take me to the hospital. Things seemed to be going well. In my pocket, I had two blank travel warrants; I was certain that either one, with no questions asked, could take me wherever I pleased in Germany. Despite several months as a spy, I was still very credulous.

✚

The field hospital was billeted in a forbidding grey stone building that had once been a large private school. As the lorry bounced over the curb onto the grounds, I thought that the old school's stone walls now enclosed far more pain and misery than they ever did when they held homesick students. The hospital was a ramshackle complex with faded tents and wooden temporary buildings tacked onto it.

When my truck pulled into the transport compound, I dismissed the driver. "I'll get someone here to take me back. No use in you hanging around all day waiting for me." Rather officiously, I added, "And make sure you report to the vizefeldwebel as soon as you arrive." I didn't want him available to answer questions when someone noticed my absence. With luck, the Transport vizefeldwebel would task him off on another detail the minute he reached headquarters.

As I watched the truck lurch through the mud of the compound and turn back down the road to Seventeenth Army headquarters, I was of two minds as to whether I should actually report into the field hospital. When inquiries were made as to my absence, the fact that I'd actually gone to see a doctor would probably buy me a few hours. I made a point of identifying myself and asking as many people as I could where one could go to get someone to look at my eye. I finally badgered a tired surgeon's assistant into giving me a small jar of some kind of ointment.

With the jar in hand, I stopped at a vacant desk near a side entrance and reviewed my travel warrant. I hadn't filled it in yet. According to that piece of paper, I had authority to go wherever I chose; but in reality I had only the vaguest notion of how I was going to get out of Germany.

Prior to being transferred to Belgium, I had been working on the assumption that I would escape the same way I came in, through the North. Sweden or Denmark seemed a natural route because their frontiers were furthest from any fighting and the least likely to be heavily guarded. My plan had been to make it to the Danish border and slip across at night, or conversely, get to a port and bribe someone to stow me away. Now unfortunately, here in Belgium, all the maps I had worked with were relatively small-scale and their detail showed only the immediate front and operational rear areas. On top of this, my memory of the border between Belgium, Holland, and Germany was indistinct at best.

To make matters worse, I knew I had other more immediate practical problems that, until now, for want of any obvious solutions, I had unwisely pushed out of my mind. I had no real idea what the train schedules were, or worse still, what the actual military process was to get a ticket. I was certain that in the Imperial German Army's Western Front Communications Zone, I could not simply stroll up to a wicket and say, "Ticket please, anywhere close to the Dutch border will be fine." I pocketed the travel warrants and decided to bluff my way through it.

I strode briskly through the transport compound and headed towards the railhead. Showing a confidence I didn't feel, I did my best to look purposeful. Once inside the station, without knocking or waiting at the front desk I pushed through the doors marked "Verbotten" and marched directly into the Rail Movements Office. The grey-headed unteroffizier behind the Movements Desk looked up in surprise from his papers. He pulled off his spectacles and tugged at his goatee. He said nothing.

"Unteroffizier, I have to go to a general hospital to have my eye looked at by a specialist. Where is the closest general hospital and when is the next train leaving here to get there?"

"You can't just get on a train, sir. We ship patients for recuperation from here. You need a travel warrant signed by a medical officer and you have to be put on the hospital's transfer manifest. I am sorry, sir." He shook his head slowly from side to side.

"Unteroffizier, I have just come from the field hospital. I am on General Von Below's staff and I have to get my eye treated. I have to be back for an important conference by this time tomorrow. I can't get my eye treated here and I do have a movement warrant. You must tell me what is the best way of going about this and please don't waste my time."

The old clerk looked hurt. "Yes, Oberleutnant. May I see your warrant please?"

I handed it over impatiently. He studied it carefully, turning it over repeatedly in his hand and then looked at me worriedly. "This is a Seventeenth Army headquarters warrant. I suppose it will do, but you have not filled in a destination, sir."

"I know that, Unteroffizier. I need you to tell me how I can I get out of here quickly, where is the nearest general hospital in the evacuation chain? I want to be back in time for my conference tomorrow."

He wasn't one to be rushed. He stroked his goatee and stood up slowly. "Yes, sir, well, you can do several things. I can give you two alternatives, I think." He paused and it took every ounce of self-control for me not to grab him by the lapels and shake the answer out of him. "Late this afternoon, there is a train leaving the Zotobeeken supply point, which is ten kilometres from here, and it will take you to Cologne. It will be empty and does not have any rail priority. It will be very slow as there will be many stops. Also, I don't know if there is a hospital such as you want in Cologne, and there are not such good return connections from Cologne, you know?

"Or, you can get the casualty train here." He allowed himself a half-smile. "There is no officers' car on it—but there is going to be some room and it is leaving in ten minutes. It's a much longer trip, it goes all the way to Berlin but there are no stops and there are several general hospitals there. Also, from Berlin you will have a much better chance of getting a direct night train to get you back here for tomorrow morning."

He looked at me with cheerful sparkling eyes, rubbing his beard as if to say. "You see? We railway unteroffiziers are not so stupid as a rude young staff oberleutnant might think, eh?"

I thanked him with as much warmth as an arrogant junior Staff officer would properly muster and the old man personally escorted me onto the hospital car. Not for the first or the last time I asked myself why we were fighting these people.

The hospital car was fitted with stretchers three deep on either side of the aisles. Only about a third of them seemed to be occupied. The smell of those dingy railway cars was the first thing I noticed. At first it was a strong whiff of disinfectant, but underneath it there was a sickly and persistent rotten odour. As we moved forward, the sounds were the same in each car: men in pain inhaling raggedly through their teeth and exhaling noisily. The unteroffizier took me to the forward car and saw to it that I had a bench seat to myself up amongst the walking wounded. I thanked him once again, but this time with quiet sincerity; he merely nodded and patted my shoulder as he left.

A few minutes after we chugged out of Seventeenth Army's rear area, I was watching the countryside roll by when a thickset blonde nursing sister with steel-framed glasses and coarse grey skin leaned over me. "Oberleutnant, I did not have you on my manifest?"

"No, Sister. The railway clerk got me a seat at the last moment. I have to see a doctor in Berlin and get back to duty tomorrow morning."

"Are you in need of anything?"

"No, thank you. When I get to Berlin I just need someone to look at my eye. But compared to these men, I'm fine."

She asked me to help her with some of the stretchers. It took two sets of hands to lash some of them in securely. I was taken aback by what I saw. There was no morphine for the wounded, and many of the bandages were nothing more than wads of paper. Several of the wounded men in stretchers suffered from seriously infected wounds. They were being shipped home to die near friends and family.

When I returned to my seat, the nursing sister followed and sat down next to me. She shrugged resignedly and whispered, "So many more of them die now. Each month it gets worse. With the blockade, we don't have proper drugs or linens like we used to. There's nothing left. Nothing. Do you suppose this war will ever end?" She sighed, and reached across me to lower the window. "You have cigarettes? Yes? It's hard for us to get even the ersatz ones. It's my only pleasure these days."

I was taken aback by her candour. When I offered her a cigarette, she took the packet, got up, and walked down the isle and passed them round to each of the half-dozen silent walking wounded soldiers seated near the back. Such liberties and informality were previously unheard of in the German army.

"I know you wouldn't mind," she whispered, returning to our bench. "These boys have no comforts whatsoever and some of them will be going back to the front in a few weeks."

I insisted she keep what was left of the package but I smoked my cigarette hurriedly. She had a heart of gold with a character to match; but I didn't want to get involved in any long discussions today. I spent the rest of the trip dozing and feigning sleep.

The shadows were lengthening when our train pulled into Berlin's Zoologischer Garten Station. I still hadn't come to any conclusions as to precisely what I would do that evening. I hoped to use my remaining travel warrant to get a train that would take me to the Danish border or a Baltic port. A part of me wanted to go and see Gabriele, but deeper survival instincts told me we'd enjoyed our last wartime meeting. I couldn't risk it. Sometime tonight I'd also have to do something about replacing my uniform. My absence would have been discovered by six or seven that evening; and by morning I reckoned the Germany army would be frantically combing the country for a missing German-American officer with a detailed knowledge of their most important wartime secret. Even considering the German army's legendary efficiency, at the earliest I didn't think they would begin to react much before midnight. I still had several hours of relative safety ahead of me. I wasn't certain what trains left from Zoologischer Garten, but with luck, I could be on the coast or even in Denmark by morning.

The walking wounded in the car began to move about, readying themselves to get off the train. I stared vacantly in front of me. I'd been in the Zoo Garten in happier times. Gabriele and I had spent an evening walking through the zoo's halls and enclosures. We were happy just being together that night. As usual, she was animated and laughed easily. But in a curious way, the night also had a few thoroughly depressing notes. The animals staring balefully out at us from their cages looked as hungry and shabby as the rest of Berlin's population.

The train juddered to a stop and I wondered if I would ever see Gabriele after the war. Would she ever understand what I had done? Perhaps we could both live in Canada when the war ended? Germany was out of the question for me, but if Gabriele could ever understand why I did what I did, she would surely be plucky enough to try life in Canada. I was feeling optimistic. It was just seconds before I alighted from the train when something caught my eye and made me take a step backward. There were police and armed soldiers at the exits to the platform. I'd been on enough German trains to realize this was an unlikely arrival party for a trainload of invalids.

✶

I pulled myself backwards up the train car's steps, knocking violently into the crutches of the soldier behind me. The nursing sister started to say something, but I pushed past her and shook open the door on the opposite side of the car. The sound of confused jostling, cursing, and angry voices followed me. I let myself down onto the tracks and ran back along the line of cars away from the station platform. I ran hard down the tracks for a hundred yards and scrambled between two dirty box cars over onto the next set of tracks.

I wanted to run but I forced myself to take a few deep breaths and looked around me. There were at least a dozen separate tracks in the station; all of them led behind me to the covered platform. In the opposite direction, away from the station, the tracks led out from under the canopy for a hundred yards and then split off running to the left and right into the distance. Were I to run for it out there, every soldier on the platform would have a clean shot at me. I couldn't go to my right. That way led back to the platform and the soldiers. To my left, smoke-stained factories and warehouses lined the rail yard. The buildings were separated from the tracks by high fences. There was nothing to decide. Getting over one of the fences was the only way out.

I ran forward, climbing through train couplings and stumbling over tracks to get to the fence line. The fence was an imposing barrier; it was eight feet high and made with massive brick posts with vertical steel rails on top that split into artfully fleur-de-lis-shaped sharpened spikes. Off on the platforms behind me I could I hear shrill police whistles and shouting. With my good hand I grabbed one of the vertical iron rails and began to haul myself upwards. My boots scraped frantically for a footing on the brickwork. The effort of hauling myself up with my right hand was excruciating. I pulled furiously with my right arm and could hear a grating sound as my arm strained in its socket. There was a commotion behind me near the train car. My breath came in ragged gasps. I managed to get a leg up to the top of the brick fence post and after much struggling and turning, got a knee onto the top of the fence post. I was frightened that I'd impale or slash myself on the curved metal spikes. My trousers tore and my knee scraped against brick. I stood up precariously for a second. Along the platform I could see helmets and field-grey uniforms running towards me. Someone behind me shouted. I turned to see a soldier a hundred yards away raise his rifle. I jumped upwards and out. As I did so, the loud crack and zing of a near miss ricocheted off a steel spike beside me. I don't remember hitting the ground, but the next moment I was running as hard as I could, hatless and desperate to make it to the safety of the corner in front of me. Several wild shots cracked past me, shattering bricks on the wall opposite me. As I rounded the corner of the building, whistles blew and men shouted orders.

I was in a cobblestoned lane with dirty red bricks on either side. There was no one about. I was probably in a back alley behind a factory complex. I wanted to run, anywhere, to get as far from the train station as possible and I had to make myself inconspicuous. My knee hurt, I'd torn my clothes, and I'd lost my pickelhaube. A limping, hatless officer walking the streets in a ripped and stained uniform would have caught the attention of the most unobservant Berliner. I continued to run for another minute and stopped. It was obvious I was running along a series of access lanes at the back and sides of an industrial complex. Behind me I could hear my pursuers shouting. Ahead of me was a glimpse of traffic and the sounds of a busy street. I looked frantically about for a door to get me out of the lane; there was nothing.

I ran forward for twenty seconds and turned into a recessed loading bay. The main door was locked and opened only from the interior, but on the walls on one side, about ten feet off the ground, was a line of what looked like eighteen-inch-square ventilation windows. Some of the windows were open, others were broken or cracked; one of them had a flimsy wire screen hanging across it to keep out birds. The windows were too high to climb into. Near the corner of the lane was a pile of rubbish: old wooden boxes, small cracked barrels, odds and ends of what might have been pieces of a builder's scaffold. I dragged the stoutest piece of lumber from the pile, a rough post, about six feet long and five inches in diameter. I laid it at a forty-five-degree angle to the wall and scrambled up onto it so one of my feet rested on the end nearest the wall. I balanced myself by leaning in to the wall. In this position I could grasp the window frame and with my left hand tore away the wire screen covering one of the windows. I threw the screen into the building and began another acrobatic struggle; hauling myself upwards I squirmed and wriggled my head and shoulders into the window. My foot lifted off the pole and the lumber fell behind me onto the pavement with a clatter. I now had nothing to push against.

The window was tiny and I struggled painfully, inching and heaving my body forward over the window ledge for several seconds before I was balanced. With my head and most of my torso inside the building I could see only shadows in front of me. Three feet beneath me was some kind of shelving. It was broad and made of thick planks. I reached down. It seemed sturdy enough. I wriggled forward, inching my hands ahead of me trying to grasp the sides of the shelf; and then, just when I thought I could pull the rest of my body through the opening, my leather belt and pistol holster caught in the window frame. I became excited and clawed and heaved wildly. I made a terrible racket as I tugged and tore to get free of the window frame. Eventually I pulled my legs through the opening and crawled sideways onto the shelf. There in the shadows, I crouched on all fours.

My eye patch was hanging around my chin, my ribs and sides were scraped, my heart was pounding, and my hands were bleeding. I was scratched and torn in a dozen places, but I was free and alive.

I lay still for several seconds. My good eye gradually became accustomed to the light. I was in some kind warehouse for building construction or public works. I could see stacks of bricks and tiles, bags of cement, a mixing machine, and piles of boards. The metal screen was digging into my cut knee and I had the good sense to stick it back onto the window frame as best I could. Then I lay still.

Except for my breathing there was no sound within the building; but as I lay there I heard running feet out in the lane. A pair of jackboots clumped past my window and then returned. Whoever it was stood just on the other side of the wall from me for I heard him kick at the scaffolding pole as if he was frustrated, and shout, "He must have gotten out into the main street." From a distance someone else shouted, "Not down here," and then a third voice shouted, "Keep going, this way!" Feet ran past the window and the lane went quiet.

I slipped off the shelf and eased myself onto the ground. I was wrenched and torn and bruised, but I was sure nothing was broken or dislocated. I rubbed my wrists.

The room was some sort of central storage area. On the main street side of the building was a series of cubby-hole offices and what looked like a rest area for the men who were employed there. There was a small gas stove, a bench and table, old newspapers, and to my great good fortune, at the back of the rest area was a small change room. It was obvious this was where the workers changed from their street clothes into their work clothing. On pegs around the walls I found, amongst other things, a pair of welder's goggles, a leather protective apron, several navy blue workman's canvas smocks, leather work gloves, old towels, a stained woollen flat cap, and a tin lunch bucket with a broken hinge. I wasted no time in getting out of my officer's tunic and dressed myself as a construction worker. No one could look too closely at me. I wouldn't stand up to prolonged scrutiny.

I put on the flat cap, which was too large, but to make up for that I clapped it down onto my head by strapping on a set of goggles above the brim of my cap. I found one of the dark blue canvas smocks that fit reasonably well and on top of that I wore the leather work apron. I draped one of the towels around my neck like a scarf. My torn trousers and scuffed jack boots were not at all out of place in this get-up. I put on the work gloves, which covered my left hand nicely, and in my right hand I carried the broken lunch bucket. My pistol I kept fastened on my belt beneath my smock, although I was certain that if I had to use it, I'd be dead or captured before I could ever get it out. In the toilet adjacent to the change room there was an old tin mirror. My reflection was distorted and veiled by dents and dust. At a glance I could pass on the street as a labourer; although what sort of working man would ever go out dressed as I was I had no idea.

My plan was to stay put until it was well and truly dark, and judging by the light from the windows, darkness wasn't more than a half-hour away. I was exhausted, shaky, and thirsty, but there was nothing to drink and no evidence of a tap anywhere. I sat down and rubbed my forehead, took a few long slow breaths, and forced myself to relax a bit, to try to think things through. I pulled out my billfold to count my money. I was flush. I still had the three hundred marks from Kleer as well as what was left of my own pay. As I counted the bills, tucked amongst them I found a small sheet of paper and written on it in a very precise hand was the name and address of Major Herr Doctor Gehlen, the medical officer who tried to engage me in conversation on the train back from Bialystock. I'd taken his address with the promise of looking him up if I was ever in Berlin. I sat back and exhaled noisily.

I stuffed my tunic behind a pile of cracked roofing tiles in the main storage area and to complete my masquerade went over to a tool rack to select something to carry over my shoulder. I was tempted to take a large street broom with me. It almost certainly would have made more sense at that time of night. Instead, I chose a small spade with a sharp edge. If the need arose, it would make a deadlier weapon than a broom.

The front door of the building was just to the side of the main vehicle entrance. I wished to God there had been a truck parked there, but superstitiously, I decided not to dwell on it. I didn't want to jinx myself. My luck had been strong so far and I wasn't tempting fate by feeling sorry for myself. I can remember my throat feeling incredibly dry. The front door had a spring-loaded latch so if I ran into trouble when I left the building, there'd be no going back. I straightened my cap, tucked the towel around my neck, took a deep breath, and stepped outside. As soon as the door shut behind me a sceptical, controlled voice beside me said, "How long have you been in there?"

I turned to find myself face to face with a tall, sour-faced Berlin policeman. He wore the angular green leather policeman's cap of the state police and a green leather trench coat. Behind him, further down the street, were three soldiers with steel helmets and rifles.

"I've been here since four, like every night. Those other bastards always leave me to do the clean up. None of them are veterans either. Too old, too sick, flat feet, and bad stomachs they claim." I began to cough as convincingly as I could. I wiped my mouth with the edge of my towel. "I have to do the clean-up every night. Me! With a lungful of gas and a gut full of shrapnel from the French at Verdun! What do I get for it? Junior man on a shit job and a bed at the veterans pensione." I did my best to look boorish and aggrieved.

The policeman stared steadily at me. My stomach began to churn. I coughed again, this time not as intensely. I made a face, pretending my lungs hurt. "So what do you want from me?"

"Have you seen anyone here in the last forty minutes?"

"No. When the day's over, the rest of them clear out like the place has the plague. I'm the last. I'm always the last."

"Open the door, I want to have a look in there."

"Fat chance of that." I shifted my towel and spat. "They don't even trust me with a key. There's only one key and His Royal Highness Herr Bartz keeps that. It's his way of showing who's boss. If it's raining here in the morning, I have to wait outside to be let in. You'd think I was the family cat." I coughed and wiped my mouth on the towel again. "Are there any jobs in the police? You must have people away in the army?"

The policeman looked distractedly down the street. He'd lost interest in me. "Go. We have a job to do. If you see anybody unusual around here, tell the police." He dismissed me with just the faintest nod of his head and a contemptuous flick of the eyes. As I trudged down the street I hoped to hell he didn't stop to think about why I was leaving work with a shovel over my shoulder.

20

I LIMPED ALONG for fifteen minutes putting as much distance between the train station and myself as I possibly could without running. The look on the policeman's face forcibly reminded me that if I didn't survive by my wits, I'd end up staring at a firing squad commanded by someone like him. The evening was cold and the whole area was alive with police and soldiers dressed in great-coats. They had obviously taken my absence seriously. I underestimated how quickly they could react. I should have been terrified, but I was distant and composed. Now, I wasn't as edgy. I felt collected, almost smug. I'd escaped from Belgium, I'd escaped from the train, and I'd given them the slip in the lane; and I'd bluffed my way past the policeman. I wasn't cocky, but I knew in my gut I could win. To this day I've no idea where the performance in front of the policeman came from, but I was thrilled with it. It gave me confidence.

I shifted my spade to the other shoulder and did my best to trudge wearily down the street. I told myself I was looking for an address; I was some kind of road repairman, harmless, badly wounded, mildly deranged, a likeable simple-minded man with his own purpose, definitely headed somewhere specific. I limped along dutifully saying hello in a slightly lunatic sort of way to anyone who met my gaze. Few people did. Not many people are willing to meet the stare of the lame or the mentally ill when they meet them on the street. Fewer still will ever try to speak to them. I wanted to get to somewhere safe as soon as I possibly could, so I stopped and wiped my forehead with the towel and tried to get my bearings. I'd no idea where I was going.

After I had shuffled along for a half an hour an elderly woman dressed in black, wearing a shawl and with a small dachshund on a leash, came tottering down the sidewalk towards me. "Excuse me, mother," I said in my best country dialect, "can you help a wounded soldier? I've been told there's work to be had helping with the gas line repairs in the Windscheldstrasse district. Can you tell me how I get there? I think I've lost my way and they told me at the veterans' pensione I have to get there before eight if they're going to give me any work tonight."

She looked at me sympathetically. "You're a long way from there. Windscheldstrasse is more than an hour's walk from here." She reached into her purse and handed me five pfennigs. "Take this. There's a tramline two blocks south of here. Take it and ask to be let off at Charlottenburg. You'll make it in time that way." She patted my hand and clucked caringly. "Gruss Gott."

I thanked her profusely, bowing slightly and tugging at my cap. I walked two streets down and stood dutifully at the trolley stop. Within ten minutes, I was sitting in a half-empty trolley car that whisked me from central Berlin to the northern suburbs. Before I got off I asked the driver, "Bitte, where can I find Windscheld-strasse? The gas line there needs to be repaired, can you help me?" He wasn't sure, but thought it was six or seven blocks away and pointed me in the right direction.

I shuffled on. It was more like fifteen blocks away; but I found Herr Major Doctor Gehlen's house and the downstairs lights were on. The street was empty. I wrestled my pistol out from under my smock and tucked it behind my apron. Nobody was looking out any windows. I crossed the street.

Major Gehlen lived in an expensive-looking three-storey brick townhouse. From our meeting on the train, I knew that he was a talkative congenial sort of man. I expected him to have company. At the very least someone of his stature would have a housekeeper. I'd have to deal with that. I was certain Gehlen's chatter on the train with a total stranger about how hard he worked and never having time for a wife was a guarded way of advertising a secret life. He looked to me like the sort who might appreciate young men showing up unannounced—not that I knew much about those things then. But an older, single man like that, I thought, might just be more vulnerable to someone intent on breaking in.

I stopped on the doorstep and listened for a few moments before knocking. There was no sound from inside. I lifted the ring on a large iron door knocker that was in the shape of a young man's head; I rapped aggressively. Several moments later Gehlen himself pulled the door open. He was dressed in an open-necked shirt and something that looked like a cross between a silk dressing gown and a smoking jacket. He stared at me angrily. "What do you want?"

"Dr. Gehlen?" I asked tentatively.

"Yes, what do you want?"

He didn't recognize me. I pulled the Luger out from my apron and flashed it once in front of his nose. Gehlen's face went white. "Inside, now! Don't make a sound." I stepped into the doorway, pushing him backward with my left hand. He was co-operative and didn't say a word. I closed the door behind me. "Who's here with you? Just the truth." I waved the pistol menacingly.

"Just one person, in the dining room. Please. Leave me alone, I'll give you whatever you want, please." His hands shook.

"Quiet. Lie down, face down." I pulled him forward and Gehlen dropped to his knees, settling himself carefully on the floor beside the stairs. I pulled his arms behind his back. With the silk belt from his dressing gown I tied his hands tightly behind his back. I whispered, "Stay on the floor, face down. If you move or make a sound, I'll kill you." I could hear a gramophone playing waltz music towards the back of the house.

I stood up and moved to the sound of the music. I walked quietly over oriental carpets through a well-appointed parlour and opened a large wooden door. My jaw dropped. Half a dozen candles burned around the dining room. The table was laid with crystal, silver, and starched linen. Sitting at the head of a table set for two was a petite blonde woman of about nineteen or twenty. She was sipping wine and toying distractedly with a silver bracelet on her wrist. Her hair was piled in curls on her head, and draped about her shoulders was a bright red silk shawl. Apart from that, she was nude. She was gorgeous, and for a moment, I simply stared.

Startled, she looked up at me and inhaled sharply. She began to choke on her wine. I waved the Luger. "Don't make a sound. Your friend's tied up in the hall. Stand up and put your hands up, slowly." Her eyes were as wide as saucers.

"I—I don't belong here. I'm just here for tonight, really. Please don't hurt me. I don't live here." I grabbed her by the wrist and towed her into the hall. She had a perfect figure.

"Take off his shoes and take out the shoe laces."

The young woman did precisely as she was told. Like an obedient retriever, Gehlen lay quietly and expectantly on his stomach. When the woman finished I ordered her to lie down beside Gehlen. I cinched her hands behind her back and then re-tied Gehlen's wrists with the second shoe lace.

When I finished, I said, "You don't keep this place up by yourself. Where are the maids?"

"There's only one. She returns tomorrow at nine. When I'm entertaining she goes to her sister's."

The gramophone record began to skip. "If the two of you behave yourselves and do as I say, you'll be alive to meet the maid." I reached down and grabbed Gehlen by the hair on the back of his head, pulling him to his feet. "Get up. What's your friend's name?"

"Anna, she's called Anna." Gehlen's bald head hung limply. I got the impression he was as mortified at being discovered in his indiscretions, as he was frightened. "Stand up, Anna." I grabbed her by the arm to steady her and then marched the two of them upstairs, making them lie face down on beds in separate rooms. I tied both of their feet with laces taken from shoes in Gehlen's closet and I stuffed socks in their mouths and gagged them with neckties.

I should have, but I didn't feel badly cinching the necktie tightly around Gehlen's head. It pulled his cheeks back, and although he didn't say anything, I could see from his eyes he was in pain. I looked down on him. He could still breathe. I'd wildly misjudged this man once already. If I did it again, it might be my undoing. For all I knew, Gehlen may have had more fight in him than was evident. I thought about it for a second and decided to tie his feet to the bedpost to stop him should he attempt to squirm free. Tied the way he was he couldn't shout, roll over, or squirm free.

In the next room, with Anna, I felt like a criminal. She was beautiful with thick shiny blonde curls falling over her neck, a long smooth muscular back, perfectly proportioned buttocks, and lean muscular legs. Sexy and alluring as she was, the whole situation was indecent. She whispered, tremulously, "Please, don't kill me. Please." She looked helpless and delicate, but in this situation, despite her beauty I found nothing erotic in her obvious terror. She was frightened for her life and in that room the thrill wasn't the same as when I discovered her.

"Just stay quiet for tonight. I'll be gone in the morning. Be still and you'll be alive tomorrow." I stuffed several socks in her mouth and cinched the tie tightly. She whimpered. I was of two minds to loosen the gag, but settled for a brief, "I'm sorry, I have to do this," and tightened it again. The worst that would happen to her would be a bruised cheek. If she struggled free or started screaming, I'd be shot for a spy.

I tied her feet to the bed frame just as I had Gehlen's and covered her with a sheet and blanket; and then, feeling like a cad, did the same for the old doctor. He hadn't done anything to hurt me. No matter what kind of a man he was, I couldn't leave him needlessly shivering through the night. As it was, they were both going to be cramped and miserable. I wasn't very good at being cruel; if either one of them called my bluff earlier, I don't know if I would have pulled the trigger.

When I was convinced Gehlen and Anna were not going to be a threat to me, I went downstairs. The gramophone was still skipping, stuck monotonously on its insane two-note cycle. I took the record off and carefully put it in its brown paper sleeve. I went to the front room, turned out the lights, and locked the door. I then explored the house looking for I don't know what. As Gehlen said, there was no one else in the building. I checked on my prisoners; they hadn't moved. I laid a hand gently on Anna's shoulder and whispered, "Don't worry, stay quiet and you'll be safe." I went back downstairs.

The meal on the table was sumptuous by wartime standards: roast chicken breasts in a mushroom sauce, fresh carrots and peas, fresh crusty white bread, two bottles of a chilled white Riesling, and a cheese tray. There was real, freshly ground coffee in the kitchen. Gehlen had connections somewhere to get this kind of food, but then half of Berlin was involved in some kind of black market racketeering. Few of them could afford this. I ate both their meals, telling myself I'd need the nourishment. I also drank the better part of a bottle of Riesling—I smiled at the thought: me, a wartime Goldilocks.

I desperately wanted to sleep. The day's anxiety had probably drained me of more energy than I knew, but I had to think things through. I'd love to say I knew exactly what my next steps should be, but I didn't. I'd no idea what I was going to do. I made a pot of coffee and helped myself to one of the small cigars Gehlen kept in a thermidor in his study. The man clearly enjoyed life.

I sat back with my cigar. Somehow, I still couldn't relax. I took a long swallow of the Riesling and thought that I'd like to enjoy life for a change. In a normal world, I'd like to marry Gabriele and go to the theatre and wake up together and discuss the million and one things people talk about in life. I blew cigar smoke noisily at the ceiling. I was ashamed of myself for worrying about my troubles just then. I was still free and when this was over, I wouldn't be ruined. I couldn't say the same thing for Gabriele or her family.

I didn't want to think about what was almost certainly happening now with Gabriele and the Richters. By this time they would have been arrested by the police and held in custody as dangerous enemies of the state. They would eventually be released, but only if they could prove beyond a doubt that they were innocent bystanders and that might not be the simplest thing to do.

But this was Germany, not Russia. There was a strong tradition of rule of law here. Germany had a constitutional government. They wouldn't be shot on the grounds of suspicion. I had a sinking feeling in my stomach the police would be threatening them with all kinds of dire consequences—and they would believe them because in wartime these things might be possible. The army had taken over the country in the last year. The stakes were desperate ones. Gabriele's safety wasn't a sure thing. She'd be in fear for her life now. She'd have to explain over and over again what went on the night I killed Vizefeldwebel Kleer, how she met me. Peacetime rules didn't apply now. I hoped to God her parents hadn't belonged to some sort of peace movement that at some point advocated an armistice with Britain and France. Wolfgang Von Lignow would also be sitting in a miserable military cell tonight, another one of the benefits of my friendship. I couldn't dwell on these things.

My question now was what to do. I was safe for tonight. I had nine or ten hours before the maid arrived.

I went upstairs and looked in Gehlen's clothes closet. He was about my height but heavier set. His clothes were expensively tailored and conservative in an old-fashioned, strongly Germanic way. The kind of thing one expected of a Berlin surgeon. I took a shirt and good flannel trousers, socks, a necktie, a sweater, a tweed jacket, and flat cap and laid them out. His shoes were far too big for me, but that would pose no problem. Without looking too out of place, my officer's boots could be worn under civilian trousers. I ran a hot tub, shaved off my beard, bathed, and put on my new clothes. In Gehlen's bedroom I found his billfold and flipped through it. Apart from a hundred marks there was nothing I could use. In one of his drawers he had a pair of stylish tortoise-shell reading glasses that I thought might come in handy.

During my wanderings throughout the rooms, I said nothing to my two prisoners. I'm sure they thought I was a madman who had arbitrarily taken up residence in this house and that I would unexpectedly go berserk and gruesomely murder them during the night. I went downstairs and drank another cup of coffee.

In Gehlen's hall closet, I found a nicely tailored blue overcoat, a dark wool scarf, and a pair of good leather gloves. The coat must have been an old one of his; Gehlen was now much heavier and it fit me reasonably well. In a closet off his study I found a very good quality leather doctor's portmanteau, which I filled with the remainder of the cheese, two loaves of bread, a bottle of brandy, a bottle of wine, a spare shirt, and a shaving kit that I made up from Gehlen's things. For good measure I added five or six cigars from his cache. Some bizarre sense of propriety stopped me from taking the entire box. I was a soldier on the run, not a criminal. I would only take what I needed. The lock made a satisfying click as I snapped it closed. I was ready to go if I had to bolt at a moment's notice.

My plan was to stay until morning. It wasn't yet midnight and I didn't want to be stopped suspiciously wandering Berlin's streets in the dark. I went into the front room, drew the curtains, and stretched out on the couch. I knew I'd need to be rested, but I slept fitfully for only five hours. I kept waking, worried that I'd overslept.

When I got up it was still dark; the house was cold and still. I checked on my prisoners. They were both awake and very much alive. I felt guilty. They were obviously uncomfortable. I rubbed Anna's wrists to get the circulation going in them and reluctantly did the same for Gehlen. I don't know why I disliked the man. Whatever kind of sexual appetites he may have had, he'd done nothing to harm me. I had less trouble understanding my sympathy for Anna. I went downstairs and heated the remainder of Dr. Gehlen's excellent coffee and ate some bread and cheese. The last thing I did was to put in my false eye. I hoped I wouldn't have to wear it for long. It was getting grey in the east when I slipped out the back door. I had a train to catch at dawn.

21

AS I LEFT GEHLEN'S HOUSE, a light snow was falling. Most of Berlin was still fast asleep, but at the tram stop I was joined by a half-dozen men and women who by their appearances were heading off to labouring jobs in the city's centre. My clothing made me conspicuous amongst them. I'd chosen much too fine a coat from Herr Major Doctor Gehlen's closet. As I waited for the tram to arrive, a grey-bearded man in scruffy clothes looked at me curiously and with his glance my confidence began to unravel again. I felt threatened, certain he sensed something wrong with me. I stared back at him coolly and turned away with a touch of hauteur, immediately censuring myself. Snubbing him was the wrong approach. Being anonymous meant I had to generate indifference, not hostility.

I took the electric tram back to the city centre. From my vantage point on a torn leather seat at the back of the trolley there was nothing abnormal about the numbers of police and soldiers on the streets. The other passengers ignored me. Except for the light snowfall, Berlin looked as it always did just before dawn in winter: faceless early risers scurried through the streets to get to their jobs; a handful of horse-drawn wagons plodded through the snow hauling their goods before the city awakened. With petrol rationing in effect, there were few motorized vehicles. The snowfall muffled the normal sounds of the city and drifting snow in front of sooty grey buildings made everything look like a black-and-white film. I got off at Rauch Strasse, and walked toward the train station. I approached the station from the north, the opposite side from where I'd fled the night before. Down the street, the zoo gate was closed and only a few early travellers struggled with luggage and parcels towards the station. Everything appeared normal. However, at the last second, I decided to give the train station a quick once-over before attempting to go in to buy my ticket. I crossed the street away from the train station and stopped opposite the front door. Bending down as if something was bothering my foot, I fidgeted with the cuff of my trouser and as the glass doors swung open, inside I could see the grey and green uniforms of soldiers and police stopping everyone who entered. I stood up and walked on. The station was being watched.

I decided to continue walking and try to think my way clear of this predicament. They were still searching intensely for me here in Berlin. My description was bound to have been passed on to the police and the army. Missing one eye and with only half my left hand, I certainly simplified their identification problems. I stopped and fished out Gehlen's glasses. When I put them on the world was slightly blurred and my good eye strained. The discomfort was better than the alternative. I walked on.

Trains were the only public system of transport in the country, and now, they were no longer an option. How long they'd continue to watch the railway stations I could only guess. The police and the army would probably keep searching until they caught me or were convinced I was beyond their reach. There had to be some other means of getting to one of the frontiers. As I walked along past the fence of the zoo gardens, a two-hundred-weight truck turned slowly around the corner. In the back, hanging onto the frame, stood half a dozen cold and miserable-looking steel-helmeted infantrymen with rifles slung and greatcoat collars turned up against the wet snow. They stared blankly at me as they drove by and I did my best to give them a cheery nod.

I walked for an hour. The fresh air was invigorating; and when the sun was well and truly up, with no reason to be self-assured and despite my quandary, I once again found myself cheerful and confident. I was going to get out of Germany safely. I was convinced of that. Near the Herrfurth Platz, I stopped at a large café, the Grünsteiner. It had a large copper samovar in the window with the morning's newspapers arranged neatly in a rack on reading sticks. I picked up the *Berliner Zeitung*. The café was smoky and poorly lit and there were more than thirty or so tables arranged in long lines. A dozen people, mostly middle-aged and elderly, sat quietly in the gloom. I was the only male of military age. I took a seat in a corner near the back and away from the windows. When the waitress came I ordered the breakfast special, the only thing on the menu: ersatz coffee, black bread, and turnip jam. The newspaper on a stick seemed an ideal cover for me. I held it up to conceal my face from the other customers.

Before the war, the *Berliner Zeitung* was a thick daily with several sections and hundreds of articles. Paper shortages now meant it was reduced to eight flimsy pages. I took off Gehlen's glasses and opened the paper in the middle. It was dull reading, an endless account of a report on the distribution plan for rationing livestock forage. The insides of the paper were filled with bleak wartime reports: casualty lists, rationing measures, and ceaselessly depressing details from the front. Two Iron Crosses were issued to soldiers from the Ninth Corps after counter-attacking and destroying British tanks at Cambrai. The Austrians were attacking but running into stiff resistance at Caparetto. The only cheerful article was a column on how to grow window box herbs to liven up Berliners' restricted diets.

I took a chance, closed the paper, and read the front page. I should have expected it; but I was stunned nevertheless. The main article was a report on the intensive search for Oberleutnant Alex Baumann who was believed to be at large in the Berlin area. There was a fairly accurate sketch of me in the centre of the page. I was in uniform and had my goatee. The article detailed how I was wanted for questioning in a recent murder case involving a Berlin policeman as well as probable treasonous links involving an Allied spy ring operating in Germany. Baumann, it said, was believed to be armed and dangerous. The article continued: "He has proven to be adept at disguise and bluff. He is in his early twenties, has an artificial left eye, missing three lower fingers on his left hand and has clear skin, fair colouring, curly brown hair, and brown eyes. The State police have announced that a senior staff officer and several radical social- ists have been detained for questioning in the case. Anyone know- ing of this man's whereabouts or sighting anyone who matches his description should advise the police immediately."

I immediately re-opened the paper and put on Gehlen's glasses. I couldn't conceal my left hand so I hastily replaced my glove and dropped my hand into my lap. The sense of buoyancy and poise that had propelled me along minutes before was gone and I had that hollow feeling in my stomach. I no longer wanted breakfast.

Minutes later the waitress, thin-faced and worried-looking, brought my order. She stopped, and motioning toward the leather portmanteau I had put beside my chair, asked, "Are you a doctor?"

I was at a loss for words and merely nodded.

"It's so hard to find a doctor now. After you eat, could you look at my daughter? She's upstairs. She's been violently ill for two days now. Please?"

If she thought I was someone other than Alex Baumann I wasn't going to change her mind. I looked at her gravely as if I'd been put upon. "I've been up all night; but yes, I can do that."

I swallowed my bread whole and drank down the scalding acorn coffee almost at a gulp. I picked up my bag and nodded to the woman. She dropped her dish towel and immediately led me back through the kitchen and up a narrow set of stairs to a small apart- ment at the back of the building. In a tiny bedroom, a pale girl with black rings around her eyes lay in bed staring at the ceiling. She was no more than seven years old. She coughed weakly. I knelt down. The little girl coughed again.

"Describe her symptoms for me."

"Monika complained of a headache three days ago; she then

became feverish and started to throw up. Her coughing has become much less violent, but she's had a fever and she does not eat so much."

I slipped off my glove and took her pulse. It was weak and fluttery. "How do you feel now, Monika?"

"Not good." Her voice was on the verge of tears. "My head aches and I hurt all over." I looked at her eyes and then had her watch my finger move up and down and across her line of vision. "Does it hurt your eyes to do that?"

"No," she said faintly.

"Good. How does your stomach feel? Does it ache?" She nodded. I looked at her hands carefully and then felt under her ears for swelling. I pulled the covers back and gently prodded her sides asking if it hurt anywhere. I nodded and looked as if I was in deep thought. Without a stethoscope to use, I'd exhausted my bogus repertoire of methods to examine her. The child was obviously very sick and I didn't have the slightest idea what could have been the matter with her. I stood up and motioned for the woman to leave the room with me.

"It's hard to tell what's wrong with her. It could be several things. It may just be a bad case of the flu; but to be certain, you must take her into the hospital in the next few hours. In the meantime, make sure she drinks plenty of hot fluids."

The mother looked at me chewing her lower lip. "There's no one else to watch the café and I have no money to pay for a hospital bed if she has to stay."

I said nothing, but then impulsively reached into my pocket and took out my billfold. "I spent last night with a wealthy patient. Take this. He paid me more than I deserve." I pressed fifty marks into her hand. For her it was a small fortune. "Take your child to the hospital. I think she'll be fine, but don't take any chances. Now, I really must go." I collected my bag and beat a hurried retreat out through the café and onto the street.

It was getting warmer and the snow stopped falling. The cloud cover thinned and a watery sunshine began to turn the sidewalks to slush. In another hour, Gehlen's housekeeper would find him, and after that, I could no longer safely walk the streets carrying his medical bag and wearing his clothes. It was time to change my plan.

I walked as purposefully as I could due east through the Neukölln section of Berlin. Here the streets were meaner. The people of Neukölln looked worn out. Their faces were pinched and had a look of despondency about them. Yellowed sheets hung in many of the windows in place of curtains. This was the industrial face of Germany, a view I had never really seen up close before. My summers in Germany didn't include trips to these neighbourhoods. The roads were narrower and were lined with squalid-looking four- and five-storey brick apartments, ugly blocks built to house the cheap labour that moved from the countryside in the manufacturing boom in the middle of the last century. The war did nothing to make this section of Berlin look better. After about twenty minutes, I slowed down. A dishevelled looking man with crutches, long hair, and a tobacco-stained beard struggled toward me. One of his trouser legs was pinned up well past the knee. His face looked pained.

"Excuse me, sir," I said. "I'm looking for the veterans' pensione near here. Can you help me? I think I've been given poor directions."

He looked at me vacantly and pointed down the street. "A kilometre from here, at St. Adolphe's Church. It's not a real pensione. They have cots laid out at night and a little soup and bread before bed. Like I said, it's not a real pensione. You have to have money and a real job to get into one of those. Do you have something you could spare for a veteran, sir?"

I gave him fifty pfennigs, thanked him, and walked off in the direction he indicated. St. Adolphe's was an old stone church. It looked like it had been here several centuries before Germany's industrial revolution spawned these depressing tenement blocks. Several men were leaving the church hall as I drew near. I slowed down and followed a small group. They were talking to themselves but I couldn't make out what they were saying. Two blocks from the church I called out.

"Excuse me, gentlemen, I'm looking for someone. Can you help me find him please?"

They stopped and turned. Three hollow, broken faces stared at me.

"The man I'm looking for, Horst Schreiber: very tall, blond hair, coughs a lot, and missing his left arm. I've heard he's drinking heavily now. He was in the Seventeenth Division and was badly wounded at Verdun. I've been told I could find him near here. He's my brother-in-law. If you can help me find him I'd be grateful."

They shook their heads and looked away.

"I believe he's living hard, on the streets; he's behaving strangely. Do you know where I should look then?"

The tallest man forced a laugh. "We're all living hard here. I don't know anyone by that name."

"But please, can you tell me where I should look for him. I've heard he's living in this section of Berlin. He's not well."

"There are a lot of men like that in Berlin. Try down by the Alsenbrücke Bridge. It's about a kilometre and a half from here." He pointed to the south. "You'll find some people who meet that sort description down there."

"Thank you, gentlemen. I'm sure you've been a big help." I gave them each fifty pfennigs. They looked at me with impassive faces.

✠

The ground around the Alsenbrücke bridge was as depressing a piece of overgrown industrial urban landscape as one could find. Empty wooden coal sheds were propped up against brick foundries; a central brick building with boarded windows and a large disused kiln stood at the centre of the riverside lot. The river was cold and black with clumps of ragged bushes growing alongside it. The Alsenbrücke area had been built up in the prosperous decade prior to the turn of the century, but whatever workshops had once operated here were now closed. The plants' workers had been shuttled off to the army or a score of other higher-priority wartime industries.

Across the River Spree, the high ground was still tidy farmland with scattered woodlots, a patch of old Berlin's trading area bravely holding out against its inevitable transformation into one of the sprawling new industrial suburbs. I sniffed disagreeably; there was a faint sickly chemical smell in the air. The bridge dominated the district; it was a hideous rusting monument to nineteenth-century railway engineering. It was obvious why they pointed me here. The area was an ideal spot for the hopelessly destitute, the mentally ill, and the criminally vagrant. It was exactly what I hoped to find.

I headed across the field toward the main building. The snow on the long grass was heavy and wet; before I had gone twenty yards, my boots were soaked. From the side of the factory that faced the road there was nobody in sight. I rounded the corner of the main factory building and there, a half-dozen men sat out of the wind hunched against the brick wall. Only the man closest to me looked up. His face was vacant, drained of all resolve. I walked down the row of huddled figures. At the very end of the wall I stopped in front of a young man. He was dark, unshaven with wild greasy hair, in a dirty grey overcoat. Something about his eyes told me he wasn't suffering the same inner turmoil as the others. I stopped in front of him and spoke quietly. "I have to get to Denmark. I can't take the train to get there. I'll pay well if you help me."

"What makes you think I can help you?" He looked at me suspiciously.

"You don't look like the rest of them here. My guess is you're on the run, the same as me. I can help you if you help me."

He grunted and looked past me. "How do I know you're not the police?"

"If I was from the police, I'd club you on the head, drag you off, and charge you with vagrancy and evasion of military service. Then I might tell you what I wanted." He laughed and said nothing.

I didn't know what to say. I hadn't expected to be ignored. I stared at him for several moments and when he continued to gaze out at nothing I walked on. I got about thirty paces away and he got up and followed me. This was not how I had planned things. I expected to be in charge.

"You look too well-dressed to be a deserter, my friend," he said, "and you're obviously not crazy, so what brings you out here?"

"I have to get to Denmark. The police are after me. Why are you here?"

"No. You tell me why the police want you. If I trust you, I may help you. Why are you here?"

I looked around me. My back was to the river. There was no easy way to get past this man. It was a stupid idea trying to get help in this way. "I beat a man half to death two nights ago. He was a colonel. I was staying with his family, recovering from wounds, and I was foolish enough to have an affair with his wife. He tried to shoot me and now I'm on the run from the army and the police. There's nothing heroic about it. I'm not a conscientious objector or a famous jewel thief or even one of the Kaiser's enemies. They say I tried to murder him and now they're looking for me at all the train stations. I don't know where to go."

He laughed again, a dry, hollow, raspy laugh. "Bourgeois decadence and scandal." He looked scornful. "At least you have a woman in your story. I had too much to drink, punched a military policeman in a gasthaus before I was supposed to go back to the front. I ran away and missed my train. I over-extended my furlough. Now, I'm considered a deserter, and even if I turn myself in, I'll end up in a punishment battalion. I've got nothing to lose." He kicked at the snow. "How do you intend to get to Denmark?"

"I was hoping you could tell me how to do that. I can't get out of Berlin. If you help me out of Berlin, I'll find a way to get us into Denmark."

"What would we do in Denmark? The Danes may be neutral but they'd turn us back, you know."

"I've thought of that. From Denmark we have to make our way to Norway. The Norwegians will keep us until the war is over. After that, we both go where we please."

"It's possible. I've been on the loose for three months. I tried to get to Holland, but the border is guarded. I'm sure the Danish border is too."

"Get us out of Berlin safely, I'll get us into Denmark," I said again with a confidence I didn't feel.

He offered me his hand. "I have nothing to lose. If I stay in Germany much longer I'm dead. They catch you sooner or later. The Feldenclaus, they're always looking for us. They're very efficient; nobody escapes their net for long: deserters, draft dodgers, people feigning illnesses. Once they catch you, you're a dead man. Three months in a punishment battalion is a death sentence by a different name. If people like me get away, they're afraid the whole army will fall apart. They're probably right too. That's why they search so hard."

I liked him. I don't know why, but I also trusted him. Looking back, I had no choice. We walked on for several miles trailing along the roads and trails on the northern side of the River Spree under a blustery early winter sky. He told me his name was Willy Stenhauser, the son of a bricklayer. Before the war, he was a baker's apprentice from a Berlin slum. Willy had been a patriot and now wasn't sure what he was. In a roundabout way he told me his story several times that day. He had served in the artillery on the eastern front since January 1915 and was hospitalized once for pneumonia and slightly wounded twice. He got in trouble on his only furlough in two years, overstayed his leave, and now he was running for his life. It wouldn't have been much different in my army. I remember being amazed hearing about the harsh sentences given for that kind of thing, but then, the Canadian army had no such thing as a punishment battalion. I wasn't too shocked; they were, after all, desperate times for Germany.

We walked on until we came to a bend in the river with rising ground on both sides. Stenhauser stopped and pointed at the hill on our side of the river bank. "I've been over that hill twice. The town of Rüderswalde is on the other side. Before the war it was nothing; now it's become the administrative and repair railhead for the army's northern rolling stock. This is the central control point for all trains going into Russia, Belgium, and northern Germany. It's not guarded. There's nothing to guard there but empty freight cars. Most of the trains despatched from Rüderswalde go to Berlin or the Ruhr to be filled and from there they go to the front to shuttle materiel. I'll bet some of them leave empty to go Denmark to be filled with food."

"How do you know this?" I asked.

"My father helped build the control buildings here when the war started. Since I left the army, I've been here twice before and stolen a ride in empty cars trying to get to the Dutch frontier. It's the best place to get a train. I've watched this area. It's not hard to figure out what the army does. They're very methodical, and besides, they've no reason to hide what they're doing this far from the front. They chalk the destination on each of the freight cars. The problem's getting across the frontier. It's guarded on both sides."

I shared my cheese, bread, and wine with Stenhauser. We hid for the final hours of the day in a hollow in a wooded area two kilometres from town. It was hard to feel concealed in a German forest. To the Germans, woods and forests aren't wilderness areas, they're crops that mature in fifty years. In our forest the undergrowth had all been carefully cut away. It was a lot like trying to hide under the trees in one of Montreal's municipal parks.

Well after sunset, we left the woods. We walked through the town, a densely built quarter mile of stucco and timber-frame houses and shuttered shops. The town was true to its frugal rural traditions. After ten the electricity was turned off. The sprawling rail yards and the station stood apart from the town on its northern edge. The station was a busy one, with trains constantly shunting back and forth, great puffs of steam and smoke venting upwards with the squealing, slamming, and clanging metallic sounds of freight cars being hooked and re-hooked.

Stenhauser seemed to trust me implicitly. He had no real education but he was tough, perceptive, and enterprising. He had been on his own since his desertion and he was starved for companionship. He talked almost non-stop. There was nothing criminal about him. He was a good man with deeply ingrained survival skills. He'd probably been a good soldier. "You see, Alex," he said, "we walk past the rail yards and come back on them from the other side. Each train and each car has the destination chalked on its side. You see that one? It's going to Düsseldorf and then on to Brussels. The load destination is written on top, the final destination is the one on the bottom. It's not hard getting into the right train. None of the cars are locked. They're all empty here. Our problem will be finding a train going to Denmark."

I nodded. "In that case we might get one going to Schleswig-Holstein. I imagine they regularly bring fodder and produce out from there and then ship it to the front or elsewhere in Germany. That would get us close to where we want to be. We should be looking for cars marked for Kiel or Flensburg. I wonder what the chances of finding those would be?"

"Good," Stenhauser said cheerfully. "The chances are good. If any empty freight trains are going north, they go north from here."

We walked past the freight yards and then headed north, crossing several sets of tracks. We decided that any trains heading north would presumably be marshalled on the north side of the yard. The freight yard was pitch black. The only lights in the marshalling yard came from the engine headlamps and the hurricane lanterns of the signallers and the men marking the freight cars. There weren't many of them about and we could see them hundreds of yards away so it was a simple matter to stay out of their sight. We were right about the northern trains. All the cars on the northern tracks were marked initially for Hamburg, Hanover, or Bremen and secondarily to points west of that. None of them were going to Schleswig-Holstein. Shortly before dawn we decided to take our chances and get a train heading to Hamburg. It would get us closer to where we wanted to go.

Stenhauser pulled back the heavy sliding door of a railway wagon at the end of a long line of freshly chalked freight cars and we climbed in. We sat in the dark and waited. It was cold sitting on the wooden floorboards of that wagon. We agreed not to talk while we were still in the freight yard. It made it hard to hear the approach of a signaller. Our wagon had previously been used to haul forage and there were several inches of loose straw left on the floor. We swept it up into a corner. It made a nice pile about three feet deep and we burrowed into it to stay warm. If anyone looked in, in that dim light the straw would also give us a degree of concealment. We flipped a coin to see who would stay awake and act as a sentry should anyone approach. Ten minutes into my turn to sleep, Stenhauser shook me awake. One of the train engineers was moving up our line of cars tapping the wheels with a hammer. He tapped our car and moved on. Twenty minutes later we were rudely jolted by an engine hooking up to our line of wagons. Shortly after that we were moving out of the freight yard. I was ecstatic but Stenhauser looked completely unruffled. He clapped me on the shoulder. "This is the easy part, believe me."

I snapped open my case and passed Stenhauser the brandy bottle. "That's fine. It still calls for a toast, not much though, it's the only nourishment we have left."

With the warming glow of Gehlen's good brandy in my belly, I figured that our train would do just under forty miles per hour and given that our route would likely take us through several smaller cities and towns, we would have about five hours of travel to get to Hamburg. We tried to sleep, but spent most of the trip sitting up discussing what we should do once we got to Hamburg. We agreed we had no idea what the station would be like, and waiting to get off at Hamburg was too risky. We decided to jump out at the first available opportunity any time past four and a half hours of travel. I'd never jumped out of a moving train before, but Stenhauser didn't look too worried by the prospect.

I checked the fob watch Von Lignow gave me. At ten o'clock we began to screw up our courage. The train was moving along at a good clip across gently rolling farmlands. On the long turns we could see there was no caboose and the train was about twenty cars in length. If we jumped on a concealed left-hand curve, no one would be any the wiser of our presence.

At 10:45, our train was still puffing along on a straight course across fields dotted with small farming villages and woodlots. To my reckoning we should have been approaching the heavily built-up areas surrounding Hamburg. I began to get nervous. Stenhauser looked composed. "We've either been going slower than we reckoned or the route has been more meandering than we expected," he shouted in my ear. I nodded in agreement.

At 11:00, I said, "I think we should jump at the first available opportunity; it's better than waiting. We may find ourselves suddenly in the city." Stenhauser merely nodded. "Okay, we can always walk a little farther."

No sooner had I said it than the train followed a long left curve and began to slow perceptibly. "This is as good a spot as any, Willy. Let's go. Good luck."

Stenhauser in mock gallantry motioned for me to go first. I looked up the track. It was sunny: ploughed winter fallow fields, a village and woods off in the distance, but no one in sight. A brisk wind blew in my face. No spot looked better than any other. I pitched my bag and jumped. Stenhauser followed.

I hit the ground hard and rolled twice. My left elbow and my hip hurt; I hit the ground where the butt of my Luger was tucked under my belt. I stood up gingerly; nothing was broken. I was thankful the pistol hadn't gone off and felt stupid that I hadn't checked the safety. Stenhauser picked himself up off the ground muttering and cursing under his breath. He promptly fell and picked himself off the ground a second time. He began to limp. His teeth were clenched.

"I'll be all right. It's not broken. It's not broken. I won't slow you down." He sounded as if he was desperate more than in pain.

"Don't worry Willy, even if it's broken, no one's leaving you here." He began to curse under his breath even more vehemently and sat down.

"Damn it! Damn it! Why now? Jesus! I think I turned on it when I landed." He winced and prodded at his ankle.

The train chugged off into the distance rounding its long curve. "Give it a few moments," I said. "These things hurt more in the first few seconds."

I looked about us; we were on some kind of small plateau in a large series of geometrically ploughed fields. It was typical North German Plain. A mile or so in three directions were small villages: one behind us, a larger one off to our left, and the tops of some buildings crested a hill to our right rear. Running up the side of a hill forward of us in the distance was a good-sized woodlot made up of mature pines. The sky was sunny but the wind was fresh with a cold bite.

"You think you can walk?"

Stenhauser going lame would put a huge crimp in my plans; but I couldn't abandon him, not after he got me out of Berlin. He was a fellow fugitive and I owed him not only my allegiance but probably my life.

"I'll be okay in a few minutes. I'm sure I just wrenched it."

A few minutes later he was still in agony, so without much discussion we decided to head for the woods ahead of us. We'd find a place there to shelter us and make plans. Stenhauser leaned against me and we struggled forward.

The woods were much larger than they appeared when we jumped off the train. We soon found a prominent trail, and putting my portmanteau down, I left Stenhauser perched just off the trail beside a large tree. I gave him a good stiff drink of brandy, told him not to take any more of it, and promised to return in an hour or so. I struck off to reconnoitre our whereabouts.

22

I WALKED for twenty minutes. The wooded area spread out on the other side of the hill. By European standards it was a substantial forest. I reckoned it covered several square miles. The forest was well looked after, which is to say it had little undergrowth and was intersected by numerous well-maintained tracks. I soon picked up what appeared to be the main trail and followed it for a further five minutes.

At the crest of a small rise I came upon an old wooden cottage. The cottage was a tiny two-room building with a slate roof; behind it was an outhouse and a large woodshed. Smoke curled from the stone chimney. An isolated dwelling like this could only be a forest-meister's house. Every substantial German forest was tended by a forest-meister. I went straight up and knocked on the door but no one answered. This was odd, for there was obviously a fire in the hearth and it would unlikely have been left unattended.

I walked around to the back of the cottage and could hear children faintly singing in the woodshed. The shed door was ajar and there before me were two very small children and a sturdy blonde woman in her late twenties. The woman was as tall as me, with sharp blue eyes and a broad angular face. She was dressed in a faded loden green skirt, a green blouse, and a leather work apron. Both she and the children were completely oblivious to me. The woman turned her back to the door and continued to lead the children in a song while she butchered a side of venison hanging from the hut's rafters.

I knocked gently and said, "Excuse me, bitte, I've been travelling through these woods with my companion and we've come upon some trouble. I'm hoping you will help us."

The woman gasped and stepped back holding the knife handle in front of her open mouth. She was terrified. It was obvious why. I'd caught the forest-meister's wife slaughtering a poached deer.

"Please, don't be afraid. I have no intention of reporting you. These are difficult times and you have small children. I understand completely. But I need help, there's been an accident. Is your husband around?"

Her eyes darted from me to her children. "No. What do you want?"

The child nearest me seemed unaffected by her mother's fear and blurted out, "Papa's gone away to the army." The woman blushed.

I did my best to reassure her. "Please, madam, I know the situation you are in. I won't tell anyone, but you must help me. My companion and I are travelling. He's taken a fall and sprained his ankle. He's a kilometre or so from here. We won't harm you, but we need a place to stay for the night. Please, can we stay here, here in the shed? We'll be off as soon as possible and we won't interfere with anything, I promise."

The poor woman was in no position to refuse me. I doubled back to Stenhauser and in an hour we were sitting in the shed with bowls of steaming venison stew on our laps. I'm sure the forest-meister's wife must have understood there was something not quite right about the two of us, but she asked no questions. Despite her care in not asking after us, she was a talkative soul. Her name was Brigitte Klausen and her husband, a landwehr gefreiter, had gone off in the first reserve call-up of the intake of 1887. Eighteen months ago, she received a call from the local Lutheran pastor with a telegram telling her that her husband was missing in action and presumed dead in the fighting in the Battle for Soissons.

Brigitte told us that, despite our reckoning, we were not south of Hamburg, but fifteen kilometres north of the city. The rail line we were following must have been a north-easterly spur designed to enter the city after servicing its northern towns and villages. After further questioning, Brigitte told me that although she had never in her life been farther from home than Hamburg, and then only twice, she was sure we could walk to Kiel in two days, three at the most.

I spent two days living in the woodshed with Willy Stenhauser. It was evident his ankle was sprained and not broken. The swelling receded and the bruising wasn't as bad as it might have been. That first evening he was hobbling around on a makeshift crutch. In the two and a half days I stayed there, Willy and Brigitte talked incessantly. The children seemed to have a fascination with Willy, and in turn, he carved small toys for them from scraps of softwood. For a boy from the slums of Berlin, Willy took an enormous interest in anything that had to do with the forest. I wasn't surprised to find that when I suggested it was time for me to go that Willy and Brigitte had agreed between themselves that he should stay on for a while longer, until he was stronger. I gave them fifty marks and in turn accepted a loaf of heavy black bread, two pounds of dried spicy venison, a bottle of spring water, and their good wishes. Willy had his arm around Brigitte's shoulders as they waved goodbye. Brigitte never commented on the fact that I was leaving just before dark.

✠

I walked all that night. I took the main track north out of the forest and kept to country roads, heading generally in a northerly direction. For the first two hours I kept my direction by keeping the glow on the horizon from what I guessed were the lights of Hamburg over my left shoulder. The city's glow faded not long after eight and by ten the night sky was completely clouded over. I was making good time. However, I was never sure that I was always headed in the right direction; this was despite the fact that the German countryside is extremely well signed.

I've come to believe that northern Europeans are fixated with signage, probably because they have so many villages. North Americans build their houses, barns, and outbuildings dispersed out on their fields. German farmers, in a tradition that started in the Dark Ages, live with their animals clustered centrally in villages. As a result, the German countryside is a spider's web of villages, fields, roads, and woodlots. The crossroads at every farmer's field has a picket with signposts indicating the distance to each tiny hamlet and village. Unfortunately, only the main roads indicate the progress one is making towards the larger cities and towns; and, without a map, a series of signs indicating that I was progressively getting closer to the villages of Bad Todberg or Heresdörf wasn't much help to me. I kept away from the main roads.

Throughout the night I met nobody. It's hard now to imagine everybody in such a heavily populated countryside staying indoors at night. But in those small villages nobody owned an automobile, and at the end of a day's toil, the farthest anybody roamed from home was for a brief trip down the street to the village gasthaus. By ten, every light in every village was out. My one good eye soon became accustomed to the blackness. I chose my route forward carefully in a series of bounds gauging each bound so that I continued north but avoided having to go through any villages.

By midnight, a wind came up and rain began to blow into my face. I assumed the wind was blowing in from the Baltic Sea and I was going in the right direction. Near three, I came across the intersection of what appeared to be a main road, with a sign indicating that Kiel was forty-three kilometres away. My instincts were right. I'd probably walked upwards of twenty-one miles, not a record-breaking distance; but good progress considering my route was so crooked.

Just before six, the sky began to turn grey. The cloud layer made it difficult to judge exactly where east was. I pushed on and at six o'clock I noticed lights showing in some of the buildings in a hamlet off to my right front. I needed a spot to lie up for the day. The ground was flat and there were no wooded areas in sight. I gambled and headed for Tumuring, the village with the lights.

The village of Tumuring was typical of nearly every German farm community in those days. It had less than twenty buildings: a church, a gasthaus, half a dozen stone-and-timber barns, and several two- and three-storey houses, some of which had their barns on the ground floor. Apart from a faded wooden sign creaking in the wind in front of the gasthof, there wasn't a commercial sign in sight. The village probably hadn't changed much since Napoleon's cavalry sacked the area searching for grain, livestock, and forage. I did notice one discreet improvement. Tumuring had electrical wires running along a series of poles into each of the houses and I had to assume there would be a telephone installed somewhere in the village.

There was no movement from any of the buildings or down the main street. I selected one of three large barns near the southern edge of town. The barns were tall thin buildings. The door of the barn I chose was barred from the outside with a heavy sliding wooden bar. I couldn't replace it once I was inside. I tugged at the bar. There was sufficient give in the door to allow me to slip inside over the lintel stone. Inside the barn was a black steam tractor with huge cleated metal wheels. At the back was an enormous hayloft that was only half-full; from stalls along the outer wall two cows turned and stared blankly at me. I remember wondering just how many generations it took for humans to breed the intelligence completely out of these animals. There was an assortment of small wagons and tools neatly hanging from the inner wall.

I climbed into the hayloft and tunnelled three feet into the hay by the back wall. The loft was warm and dry with a comforting smell. I opened my portmanteau and broke off a chunk of thick dry black bread. I wasn't hungry and forced myself to eat. I was shivering and slightly feverish, but I sipped at my water and tore off a piece of the rubbery peppered venison and chewed patiently on that. Before I'd finished my meal, a dog began to bark and scratch excitedly in front of the barn. A second later the wooden bar was slid free. I could hear a farmer shushing the dog. An old voice rasped, "What are you doing, barking at mice? Get out, get out of here, you'll put the cows off their milk." The dog continued to bark just below me and the farmer banged his milk pails together and chased the dog out. "Out! Out! Now! Outside!" The dog must have obeyed; it stopped barking, but I could hear it growl periodically from the street.

I slept that day until near three in the afternoon. When I awoke, my chills and fever were gone, and to my surprise, my clothes were completely dry. The dry hay acted like a sponge absorbing every bit of dampness. I had a dull headache and my throat was parched. Through a crack in the barn board I could see the sky was clear, the shadows were long and well-defined, and to the west the sun was dropping in a blaze of pink and orange. It seemed like the wrong kind of day to be at war. I thought for a time as to how Gabriele was doing. How long would she have been detained? Had they ransacked her house looking for evidence that didn't exist? Was she more hurt or angry? Had they mistreated her or her parents? There was no point on dwelling on it.

The sun dropped below the horizon by 5:30 and I slipped down from my loft. I'd noticed a pail hanging from the wall by the cow stall. I slipped it off its peg and tried my best to milk one of the cows. I was mostly unsuccessful. I was a city boy to my roots and I'd never done it before. The cow was bad tempered and tried to kick me and push me into the wall of the stall. I finally gave up. The little milk I coaxed out of the animal was warm and thick and I didn't like the taste. It was a humbling experience. I realized I was of a generation that was removed from the land and from an urban class for whom milk came cold out of the icebox in bottles or thick and sweet in tins. I put the pail back and slipped out under the door. The night air was cool and bracing. I may not have been much of countryman, but I was an infantryman and knew how to do a forced march.

I slogged along uneventfully that night. I had stars to give me my direction and I made good time heading generally northeast. By nine I could see the lights of Kiel. By one in the morning I was nearing the city's outskirts. I wanted to get to Denmark, which I reckoned was thirty to fifty miles to the north. Alternatively, I had vague plans of catching a ferry to one of the neutral Baltic ports, but the closer I got to the city, the more I realized I didn't want to meet anyone, and catching a ferry meant rubbing shoulders with people.

I pushed north again in hopes that my new route was taking me parallel to Schleswig-Holstein's Baltic coast. I walked that night until five in the morning, when I found myself outside another village, called Löttensdorf. Löttensdorf was approximately twice the size of the village I'd spent the previous day in. I estimated I must be ten miles north of Kiel and likely thirty miles south of the Danish-German frontier. Löttensdorf was overlooked by a small hill with a pine copse surmounting it. I ruled out trying to hide in the copse; this area was much more heavily populated and the woods were small. The more I studied the village, the more I realized that despite its size, Löttensdorf looked less like a farming community and more like a commercial centre. The village had two streetlights burning on the main road and while I watched, I saw a truck drive out from it. To have a truck in the village when fuel was so closely rationed had to mean that there was some kind of military connection to the place.

I pushed on and by sunrise found myself still on the road. I must have been more tired than I knew, because moving by day in open farm country was a dangerous thing to do. I walked for an hour past sunrise and finally discovered a small wooded area with some untidy bits of undergrowth in which to hole up for the day. I tried sleeping, but each time I began to nod off I was wakened by the cold.

By three o'clock in the afternoon I had to get up and move about. I was shivering uncontrollably. No sooner had I gotten up and moved onto the forest trail than I heard someone shout to me from behind. I couldn't quite make it out, but when I turned around there was a man in his mid to late sixties approaching me. He was dressed in an expensive tweed shooting jacket, a Tyrolean cap, stout walking boots, and was carrying a blackthorn walking stick: the perfect image of the wealthy German country squire. Fit-looking, he was red-faced, with duelling scars on both cheeks and an unpleasantly inquisitive look about him. I gave him my lunatic smile and chose to bluff it out.

"Good afternoon, sir. If these are your woods I hope you won't mind if I use them for today. I'm on my way to Schleswig to get a job in the new ammunition plant. I've been promised a job as a supervisor there. I was just passing through when I had, well you know, I had to nip into the woods to answer nature's call. How far do I still have to go to get to Schleswig?"

He tilted his head back disdainfully. "I own these woods and as long as you aren't cutting anything or poaching, I don't mind you passing through. But what's this nonsense about a new ammunition plant in Schleswig? There's no ammunition plant in Schleswig."

My insides began to turn to ice water. "Oh yes, of course there is." I lowered my voice conspiratorially. "When I left the veterans' pensione in Hanover my cousin and his friends told me I would have a good job there. They said I would be paid handsomely for the trip too. There are a great many men who would like to get such a job. But because I was a wounded veteran and I paid my cousin twenty marks, he made the call for me, and now I have a good job waiting when I get there."

The man in tweed looked at me for a moment. "I've lived here all my life and I know this area well. There is no ammunition plant, nor will there be one built in Schleswig. Whoever took your money cheated you."

"Oh no, sir, my cousin wouldn't cheat me. When I got out of the army hospital I could find no work. Then I ran into my cousin, Helmut; he told me he has made several deals like this for his friends. He knows a lot of the right people." This charade was going on far longer than I liked and the man in front of me was obviously no fool.

"How did you get here? And what are you doing in these woods if you are going to Schleswig?"

I hung my head in mock shame. "I was in Kiel last night. On my way to Schleswig I had a few glasses of beer." I looked up at him deeply embarrassed. "I don't normally drink, sir, but it was cold and I had no place to go. When I went outside the gasthaus, several sailors robbed me. They took my luggage and my wallet. I walked here and stopped because I was tired. But things will be all right when I get to Schleswig."

"There is no ammunition plant in Schleswig. Come with me." He looked at me sternly. "I'll see what I can do to help you."

I was sorely tempted to shoot the man then and there and run for it. He was obviously someone of wealth and influence and my half-baked story wasn't going to last for long in front of him. For all I knew, he may have already recognized me from a newspaper description. If I shot him here, there would be no witnesses. I gave it one more try. "If there is no ammunition plant in Schleswig, where will I work? I have to send money home to my mother in Hanover. She's a widow."

The man spoke softly. "You've been cheated, my friend. Come with me. I may have a job for you on my estate. All my men are off in the army. Now follow me. We'll see what we can do."

We walked in silence back down off the hill and down the other side. I followed dutifully like a well-trained spaniel. Five hundred yards away from the woods sat a large three-storey stone country house with stables, a fruit-tree orchard, and several farm sheds. The low-cut yew hedge was going wild and the gardens were overgrown. The place looked like it had seen better days. He took me to the rear of the house and we entered into a hallway. He shouted out, "Oskar, Oskar," and moments later an elderly man in slippers with a long grey moustache shuffled up from the cellar stairs.

"Yes, sir?"

"Oskar, this man needs a job. Try him for a few days. See if he's useful. If he is, we'll give him a place on the staff. If he's a fool or a scoundrel, we'll send him on his way. Give him Claus's old room for now."

The country gentleman marched off somewhere inside the house and I was left with the elderly Oskar. Oskar looked me up and down and I had to go through my half-witted routine again. Oskar clucked understandingly, made me get into some old dry clothes, and took me into the kitchen where he stoked an iron stove and heated up a pot of thick vegetable soup and sat down with me while I ate. The food and the warmth made me incredibly sleepy, but I forced myself to play the part and did my best to stay alert.

Oskar's story was a tale of woe. He was the only servant left in the house. His wife of forty years died the year before and all the other servants were either conscripted into the army or sent off to factories for essential war work by General Ludendorff's labour board. Oskar ran his bony fingers through his thinning grey hair. "Now there is no one to work this estate. It's falling into ruin. I've been here for forty-eight years and never have I seen a great house like this in such disarray, such bad times."

Oskar explained to me that the country gentleman was Baron Von Huttinger. "Yes, yes, you know the family, the famous Huttinger brewers and one of the largest land owners in all Schleswig-Holstein. He is the last of the family." The baron's only two sons had gone off to war in 1914. One was killed on the Russian front; the other was blind and a permanent invalid in an army hospital in the city of Schleswig. As for the baroness, Oskar lowered his eyes at this point. He ran his fingers over his scalp and down his cheek. He exhaled noisily. "We didn't know how good things were in 1914. We just didn't know. The poor woman rarely leaves her room now." There was much, I thought, that was left unsaid about this family.

Von Huttinger, I gathered, was a decent man, a true gentleman of the old school. His station in life was so far above mine he didn't find it necessary to introduce himself. This wasn't rudeness. In his world, servants did that for him. When Oskar finished his introductions of the Von Huttinger family, he got out a pen and a bottle of ink and began to scratch away at a list of the things that needed doing in the house and on the grounds. He had me move some furniture in an empty salon upstairs; and after, he asked me if I would please go out to the small barn and on the back seat of the touring car, which was parked there, there was a box of books; the baron needed them in the morning.

The "small barn" was a splendid stone building. It had electric lighting and the walls were lined with expensive riding tack. There were at least a dozen horse stalls, all empty. Over by the far wall sat a massive gleaming black Daimler touring car. It was a beauty: solidly built with hand-crafted wooden spokes, soft black leather upholstery, and a mahogany dashboard. I'd never seen anything quite like it. An automobile like that was certain to have nothing less than a sixty-horsepower engine under its hood. The baron could give up his prize horses, but an engineering masterpiece like his Daimler, it was clearly was beyond patriotism. It was a shame. I couldn't imagine the baron spent much time driving it about in those days of tight fuel rationing. The books, a dozen expensive leather-bound volumes, were in a small wooden crate on the back seat.

On a hunch, I opened the front passenger door and in the glove box, as I hoped, was a neatly folded large-scale ordinance survey map of Schleswig-Holstein. I studied it thoroughly. The woods nearby, along with "Schloss Huttinger" and the major outbuildings, were all precisely illustrated in carefully sketched detail. I was delighted. Nobody makes maps as superbly as the Germans. It must come from the same part of their national psyche that places road signs everywhere. Maps are essential to armies, and with maps, as with all their tools of war, the Germans take infinite pains. The baron's map was perfect for my needs. I was forty miles from the border, ten miles from Schleswig, and depending upon my route, I was probably seven miles from the Baltic coast. I re-folded the map and put it in my pocket.

For the rest of the evening, Oskar had me do a number of small chores in the kitchen as well as sweep the carpets in the library and the front parlour. Before we retired for the night, we had another bowl of vegetable soup and Oskar began to probe me about my background. I was friendly but not forthcoming.

For my war experiences, I simply changed my rank to private and filled in the details for Alex Baumann's Ninth Landwehr Division. I was an only child, my father was dead, my mother was an invalid, and I was bitterly disheartened with my cousin Helmut's fraud.

I asked him, "Will I be able to send money home to my mother?"

Oskar merely nodded and said, "Yes, yes. Some money, not a lot."

I grew quiet and thanked him for his hospitality and retired to Claus's room in the old servant's wing behind the kitchen.

I went to bed but didn't sleep. Shortly after midnight I got dressed in my dry clothes and slipped out, gently shutting the massive kitchen door behind me. The moon was full and in the frosty air I could see my shadow and my breath. The house was in darkness when I crossed the vegetable garden, but as I looked back upon reaching the woods at the top of the hill, several of the downstairs lights were turned on. My flight had been noticed.

23

I HAD TO ASSUME Von Huttinger would immediately report my suspicious behaviour and it wouldn't be long until someone connected me to the description of Alex Baumann. If that were the case, the police and the army would be beating every bush in the province for me. My very presence in this part of the country indicated where I was headed; and knowing that, the army and police would waste no time sealing the border. That meant that any chance of slipping unnoticed into Denmark was now gone. My prospects for going back into central Germany were equally bleak. Going back would mean a long cross-country trek and now that they had located me, the police would put a twenty- or thirty-mile ring around my last known location and then they'd search inside that circle until they found me. I'd have done that if I were in their shoes.

I was thoroughly disheartened and had an overwhelming urge then and there to quit, to sit down and wait for them to find me. I was more tired than I knew. I hadn't slept more than a few minutes the night before and I'd had little to eat for days. Physically I was weak and shaky. I wasn't much better mentally. I'd been as tense as a coiled spring for days and it was taking its toll. My energy was gone. For a quarter of an hour I was close to being overwhelmed. My pace slowed and I wandered along the trail half-heartedly looking for a place to sit down. I don't know why, but in fifteen or twenty minutes my despair passed and I went from being dispirited and sluggish to vigorous and lucid. I was determined to get out of this alive.

I pulled out the map and in the moonlight studied the route to take me to Gelting, a small village on the Baltic coast. As the crow flies, Gelting was just under nine miles away and if I forced myself, going across country I estimated I could get there easily in three hours.

I alternated running and walking. I was soon out of the woods and paralleled a country road for almost four miles. It was hard trying to make good time across ploughed frozen fields, but I did it. I ran most of the way. The furrows were deep and more than once I stumbled and fell, skinning my knees and hands on the icy ridges of turned earth. I was sweating heavily. When I walked I began to shiver and when I ran I became winded and tired.

Despite this, I made good time. The road I followed was mostly on a gentle downhill gradient; and when it veered southward, marking the end of the first leg of my cross-country march, I stopped to check my progress. Behind me, silhouetted in the moonlight and dominating the skyline, was Von Huttinger's hill. But my elation at making a clean break was suddenly deflated. Coming round the hill from the direction of Schloss Huttinger and running diagonally away from me in a north-westerly direction were two sets of head-lamps driving steadily up the north-south road. After a minute, as if to confer, they stopped and joined. Then, one after the other, they both headed north again. I'd made the right decision changing my objective and my route. The vehicles had to be a party sent out to search for me.

I ran on for three miles heading northeast across open fields, threading my way in between a series of small farming hamlets and lastly paralleling the road leading in to Gelting. The village was in complete darkness. Gelting must have had about thirty house-holds. I guessed from the number of fishing nets set out to dry that half the population were farmers and the other half were fishermen. Gelting's buildings were similar in design to most of the farming communities in the area, a picturesque Germanic collection of stucco and timbered buildings with red-tiled roofs. I was pleased with one thing: there were no electrical or telephone lines running into the village. With no telephone lines it was unlikely that Gelting had been alerted about me. If whoever was searching for me still thought I was travelling straight north, I was safe here for a while.

The breeze blowing down the village's main street made me shiver, but a breeze was exactly what I needed. I ran down the main road, and as I hoped, in the centre of town, built behind a stone breakwater, was a cement pier with a dozen small boats floating alongside. Ten of the boats were broad-beamed fishing vessels, thirty- and forty-foot wooden boats that bobbed and creaked in the night's swell. They were bigger than what I wanted. The wind was raw and damp, and it smelt of salt water and seaweed. Except for a flock of squabbling sea gulls, no one was about. I thought it odd that in the dead of night these sea birds would be wrangling so energetically. Lodged at the far end of the pier were two much smaller vessels. One was a rotting rowboat, its oars stashed neatly with two inches of scummy water covering its ribs. The other was a small trim-looking dinghy with a seven-foot mast and furled canvas. The rowboat was lashed to the jetty with rope but an iron ring with a thin steel chain secured the dinghy. I wrenched on the chain. It was solid.

I was livid. I'd come so far and was so close. I heaved a deep sigh and plunged my hands deep into my coat pockets and my right hand involuntarily grasped my Luger. In a flash of insight, I'd found the key to my problem. I loaded the oars from the smaller rowboat, placing them into the dinghy's oarlocks. The oars were too small, but they'd have to do in a pinch. I checked that the dinghy's canvas was useable and then wrapped my coat several times around the action of my Luger; at the same time I pulled the boat's chain tight against the muzzle. I leaned over the dinghy's side and held the chain and muzzle just slightly under the water in hopes of further muffling the sound. A quick glance up at the main street confirmed Gelting remained in darkness. I closed my eyes and squeezed the trigger. Against the wind and the waves, the pistol made a dull smacking sound, like someone slapping a wet towel on water. The chain slid away freely in two parts.

Minutes later, as I rowed around the breakwater with my short oars making shallow strokes, my last glimpse of Gelting was of a sleeping village. No lights were burning and I felt like cheering.

*

Beyond the breakwater the wind was raw and it drove me back towards shore. I struggled with the sail and it flapped about for several minutes before I got it raised. Then I set about reefing it tight. The sail fluttered momentarily and then snapped briskly as the wind caught it, scooping my little boat and driving it parallel to the coast. It took me twenty or thirty minutes to get a feel for the boat and to feel confident enough to run with a full sail.

I hadn't been in a sailboat since my second year of high school, when over four weekends one May and June my father insisted that I take a course at the Montreal Yacht and Canoe Club on Lac St. Louis south of the Island of Montreal. At the time, I resented the course as an infringement on my spare time. Amongst other things, a basic knowledge of sailing was one of the things my father believed essential in the practical education of a gentleman. He had no idea how right he was or how appreciative I was for that training. I may have been grateful for it, but that night I was also very conscious that my sail training was about as elementary as it could be.

My dinghy was a solidly built craft, twelve feet long with a three-foot removable centreboard keel, a beautifully made oak rudder, and a tiny locker for spare tackle under the bow. I was grateful that whoever owned it was so fastidious. He'd miss his boat.

I checked my watch. At 3 a.m., the winds seemed to be coming at me from all directions. I wasn't making much headway. It was bitterly cold and I pulled my coat around me but couldn't stop shivering. I crawled forward into the sail locker and wrapped myself in a spare sail. That worked for a time, keeping me both warm and dry. By 3:30, the wind began to settle down and began blowing steadily from the south. I reckoned I was making four or five knots; and, if I could keep it up, I'd make landfall on Danish soil sometime before the late afternoon the next day.

By four, the moon had set, and judging by the stars, I was confident I was making excellent easterly progress. Once sunrise came, my plan was to use the sun as a reference point as it would be low in the southern sky. By keeping track of the time I'd have a general idea as to where north was. As long as I kept the sun to my back I'd be fine. By five I began to worry. Fewer stars were visible and a high cloud formation was blowing in from the south. I didn't know much about winter conditions on the Baltic, but I assumed that like any similar body of water, it could be treacherous in winter. So far, I had been lucky. The wind was brisk but the waves were small with only a slight chop.

Dawn broke some time between six and seven. It was hard to tell exactly when the sun came up, for with the high clouds, the sky gradually became lighter. By eight, the cloud ceiling lowered and I began to worry, as I had no idea which way north was. The wind gradually increased in strength and I guessed that it was still blowing from the south because I'd not had to make any major changes to my sails. Nonetheless I was worried. I didn't really know what I was doing; and for all I knew, I could have been sailing in a big circle. My spirits weren't helped at all by the weather. My hands had a blue tinge to them, and even though I was wrapped in the spare sail, I was chilled to the bone and spent much of the time and almost all my energy flexing my arm muscles to keep warm.

By ten, the sky was grey and threatening and the waves were steeper, with whitecaps breaking on their tops. By 10:30, I was alarmed. The wind steadily increased and rain began to fall. I was rapidly becoming both wet and cold, and the waves, although they'd be no problem to a big ship, were frightening if you were an inexperienced sailor in a small boat. Worse still, to the south of me I could hear the intermittent drone of an aircraft.

The fact that the sound was intermittent indicated to me that someone was out searching in a grid pattern and it would only be a matter of time before they discovered me. Then it would be a simple task for the pilot to make a leisurely pass and confirm who I was. If he machine-gunned my little boat, Germany's most threatening security problem would be solved. My only consolation was that the cloud cover was getting lower by the minute. Anyone searching for me would have to fly through rain at a very low altitude and the lower the altitude, the slower would be his search.

By eleven, the sea was very rough and I had almost capsized twice. I wasn't entirely displeased with the storm. I reduced sail so that I carried only a wisp of canvas, just enough to keep me stable. Although I'd never had to do it on Lac St. Louis, I'd read about what sailors did in rough weather and I "heaved to," manoeuvring my little boat so it was facing into the wind and riding the waves face on. As the weather worsened, my fears began to subside. Perhaps I was so cold that I couldn't expend any mental energy thinking about my safety. I should have been terrified but I wasn't. I knew the storm actually increased my chances of survival. If the weather had been clear, a German aeroplane would have caught up with me and killed me before the morning was out.

I hadn't really thought about aeroplanes when I stole the boat. As it was, my grey boat with only a shred of sail showing would be hard to see; and with luck, soon the weather would be too rough for canvas aircraft flying beneath the clouds. I lay shivering for six hours curled up and wrapped in my spare foresail praying for the storm to hold until nightfall.

Darkness brought no change in the weather, and in addition to being wet and cold, I became thirsty. The wind blew all night, dropping slightly around five in the morning. With no reference points, I was no longer sure what direction the wind was coming from. For all I knew, I was drifting back onto the German shore.

Dawn broke and although the wind continued to ease off, low cloud banks scudded across the sky. At eight, I checked my watch and made the decision to raise my sail and follow the wind, wherever it might take me. I was so cold and weary I knew that if I stayed another night out in that open boat, I'd be dead from exposure. That afternoon my superstitions gave me confidence. The wind rose and my boat skimmed along on a steady breeze for several hours. It had to be a good omen. By four, the sky began to break.

I was ecstatic. From time to time I could see the sun as it dropped and it was always sinking lower off my port side. I was zooming north by northeast. By six it was dark, with broken cloud cover. I had trouble seeing the stars, but the wind held steady and just after seven I sat up as if an electric current went through me. Ahead of me I could hear the booming and crashing of waves breaking on a darkened shore line. I swung the boat round so that I ran parallel to the coast, although to be truthful, sailing so neatly along the shoreline was more luck than skill. In the dark I had trouble estimating my distance from land and only when it seemed to me that the breaking waves were much smaller did I turn the boat and make a run for the beach. I pulled up the keel and the boat surfed in beautifully, grinding to a halt three feet out from a gravel beach. I was alive and I'd arrived. But I had no idea where I was.

I clambered out of the boat and stumbled up the beach. I was too weak and cold to consider dragging the boat safely up the shore. Fifty feet ahead of me on a small rise were clumps of grass. I reached the rise on wobbly legs. There was nothing in sight but scrubby pine trees and tufts of blowing grass. On the beach, moonlight broke through the clouds. My boat turned gently on the crest of a breaking wave and began to drift back out to sea. I may have had no idea where I was, but I had no intention of going back to rescue her.

Exhausted, I kept moving. I only wanted to lie down and sleep but I still had the wits to realize if I lay down, I wouldn't be getting up again. A hundred yards inland I came to a web of cow tracks and began to follow one of them. The track led over rocky undulating ground to a wire fence, which I followed and soon I came to a set of darkened farm buildings. I knocked at the farmhouse.

A tall man in his mid-thirties with a candle lantern came to the door. I began to jabber at him in German, saying I'd just washed up on shore and needed shelter. He was sceptical but opened the door to me. Although I was on the point of exhaustion, Ewen Crossley's advice rang in my ears, "When unsure of yourself, say little."

I asked the man with the candle, "Do you speak German?"

He looked at me steadily before replying, "Ja," in a measured tone.

I prayed my disappointment didn't show. I must have sailed back to Schleswig-Holstein; the game was up.

"A very little, I speak," he added in a lilting voice.

My knees turned to water. I don't remember much of what happened after that. I was dangerously hypothermic, shattered by cold and fatigue, and I wasn't thinking clearly. The man and his wife gave me a hot drink, some kind of chicken broth, and led me to an attic to sleep.

When I awoke, the shadows were long and my head ached. I was thirsty, and my lips and hands were cracked and dry from the cold and salt water. All I knew for certain was that I was alive and somewhere in Denmark. I was lying on a thick straw palliasse under a goose-down quilt. My dried clothes were neatly folded beside me. Placed with obvious care beside my clothes were my damp billfold and my Luger. I'd been a soldier long enough to wince at the sight of my pistol—the action had a fine layer of rust covering it. I cleaned the pistol as best I could, dressed, and went downstairs.

The man of the house was waiting for me. Behind him sat his wife, a plain-faced, much younger, brown-haired scowling woman. She held a swaddled baby in her arms. I thanked them in German, but it was obvious they didn't understand. I spoke more slowly. "Is this Denmark?"

"Yes," he nodded.

"I have to get to Copenhagen, very soon. It's very important. How can I get there?"

They both stared back, incomprehension on their faces. The husband spoke. "My German, not so good."

I gambled. "Do you speak English?"

Again, there was no sign of understanding. I tried again. "Copenhagen?"

"Ah København, København! Ja, Jahvol. Ja, København."

The woman gave a thin smile at the thought of me leaving them for Copenhagen. It was obvious she'd rather have a family of poisonous snakes infesting her house than have to endure my visit any longer. I pulled out my billfold and offered them fifty marks, repeating the word "København."

They both smiled broadly. The man nodded vigorously and said, "One moment, one moment." He returned with an old copy of what must have been the Danish equivalent of a local farmer's almanac. On the inside cover he pointed to a map. "København here, København here. We here, Avernakø." He was indicating that we were on Avernakø, a tiny island off the larger Danish island of Fyn. I nodded. By the looks of things, in the dark I'd sailed past several other small islands.

After much gesturing and misunderstanding, we agreed he would take me to the ferry for the island of Fyn the next morning and from there I could get transport to Copenhagen. I ate an uncomfortable but appetizing meal of potatoes, eggs, cheese, and bread. I was uncomfortable because both the Danish farmer and his wife stared suspiciously at me throughout the meal. The two of them sat there, humourless and surly, watching me like a dangerous animal in their midst. Not that I blame them. They did after all have an anonymous, filthy, half-dead, unshaven armed man force himself upon them in the middle of the night.

The next morning just after sunrise we set off with the farmer's horse and buggy for the ferry to Fyn. I waved cheerily to his wife but she only frowned and gave me a relieved nod as her husband jerked the reins and we lurched forward.

Later that morning, one of the fishermen from Avernakø sailed me over to Fyn in his small boat. It was a much briefer and more pleasant ride than what I had recently endured. At the small dock on Fyn, I was left to wait for an hour amongst drying fish nets and salt barrels while a calico cat glowered at me from its perch on one of the sheds.

I was eventually greeted by a tall overbearing man who spoke excellent German. He browbeat me into overpaying for a wagon ride on a farmer's vegetable cart that would take me to the Zeeland ferry in Odense. I was in no position to argue strenuously or negotiate. The farmer who drove me was a jolly sort—he'd good reason to be happy; he was probably delirious with joy over his take on the price of my ride. He had long blond sideburns and an enormous pipe. He smiled a lot, but as he spoke no German, we both eventually gave up trying to communicate and we jolted along over Fyn's dirt roads like travelling monks. We sat companionably in utter silence through miles of flat but picturesque farm country.

I crossed over on the late afternoon ferry to Zeeland without incident. The ship was immaculately kept and efficiently run, and no one paid me the slightest bit of attention. At the town of Halsskov, I bought a train ticket to Copenhagen. At the wicket, I simply grunted "København," and pushed over four German marks. The man behind the screen didn't bat an eye and gave me several Danish coins in change. My train ride to Copenhagen was equally uneventful but I was constantly on the alert out for signs of being watched.

When I got off the train in Copenhagen, I chose to walk about the city for a spell. I wasn't sightseeing. If I ran into trouble at the embassy and had to flee, I wanted to know something about my surroundings. I was close to bringing my escape to an end and now was no time to let down my guard. In the trenches, one of the most dangerous times for a patrol was when you brought it back to your own lines. You always sensed an enormous feeling of relief and some people became careless. In the larger patches of no man's land it was the perfect opportunity for the enemy to ambush you. I was dealing with the same enemy. I had to work out some means of getting safely into the British Embassy. If I was a German counter-intelligence agent, I'd watch the embassy and I wouldn't stand by and let my quarry saunter cheerfully through the front door.

I strolled through central Copenhagen for half an hour. It was a

beautiful city, crammed with glorious architecture, dramatic statues, magnificent cobblestoned streets, and populated by pretty but
solemn-looking women. I suppose I was being thick-headed, but
until that moment I had come to the conclusion that the Danes
were unfriendly. Nobody greeted you with a smile or a friendly nod.
But then I caught sight of myself in a bakery window and only then
did I realize that were I to meet a dishevelled-looking thug like the
one staring back at me, I'd ignore him too. He'd probably be violent and likely be carrying concealed weapons, someone sensible
people took pains to avoid. I shrugged and walked on; the Danes
were right.

Returning to the area by the train station, I found a small café.
There were no customers inside. The proprietor, a middle-aged man
with wispy grey hair and a sparkling white apron, looked at me
aloofly. It was a tiny place: crisp linen napkins, fresh flowers, and
reeking of understated elegance. No doubt, I was scruffier than his
regular customers. He accepted my order for beer, a plate of herring
fillets, and rolls. After paying him for the meal, I discreetly waved a
ten-mark note over the table. "May I please use your telephone?" I
said quietly. "I have to make two calls, here in town."

He looked at me, then at the money and nodded reluctantly. "It's
in the back," he said in perfect German.

The phone was an original wall-mounted affair with a hand
crank. I turned the handle vigorously and a woman's voice came
on the line. "The British Embassy please," I said slowly in German.
In reply, I got an earful of incomprehensible Danish. I held up the
phone's earpiece and shrugged at the proprietor who stood a short
distance away. He raised his eyebrows ever so slightly and took the
hand piece from me and spoke briskly. A few moments later he
handed the telephone back and with a frown on his face folded his
arms and leaned against the counter.

A man's voice was on the line; he was speaking in Danish. "Hello,
is this the British Embassy?" I said in English. The café proprietor
looked perplexed and annoyed.

""Yes, yes, who is speaking please?" said a crisp English public school voice.

"Please listen carefully. I want you to tell the military attaché that 'Landslide' is coming to the embassy. I want you to tell him to be prepared to let me in within the next hour."

"I'm afraid, sir, you aren't making any sense at all. The embassy offices are closed for the day and we don't respond to asinine games."

I tried to sound as reasonable as possible. "Please, do as I say. Just find the attaché and tell him Landslide is on his way and to be prepared to let him in when he arrives."

"The military attaché is gone for the night. Call back tomorrow. You can talk to someone on his staff then."

"Listen, please—" The line went dead in my ear.

I handed the proprietor the earpiece and quickly left the café.

I couldn't risk attempting to get into the embassy at night. If German agents were watching the place, I wasn't going to risk a scene. I still had over a hundred marks left, a fair amount to be carrying around in your wallet in those days, so I walked for an hour in search of somewhere to stay. Copenhagen looked relatively unaffected by the war. People were well-fed and well-dressed, and were shopping and dining as if the world was a normal place. There was one difference: there were far more horse-drawn vehicles than automobiles on the streets, and I suspected petrol rationing was in effect here as well. Just after seven I found a not-so-prosperous-looking small hotel. From the street, the Hotel Kierensgaade looked respectable and suitably nondescript. Anything larger or more luxurious would have invited suspicion. As it was, the place was spotlessly clean and when I asked the night manager to send me a razor, soap, and fresh towels, he simply said, "Immediately, sir."

In the morning, I went downstairs, breakfasted on real coffee and pastry, and at the front desk attempted to contact the British military attaché on the telephone. The residency's telephone operator gave me the same exasperating answer, although this time I got the embassy's address before he hung up. I asked the manager to call me a cab, and much to my surprise, five minutes later a horse and hansom cab appeared in front of the hotel.

✖

The morning was cloudy, cold, and damp. Bitter enough to chill you, but not cold enough for snow. The British Embassy was discreetly located in a fashionable district: heavily treed, large private homes with extensive gardens and lawns hidden behind well-manicured hedges. Unlike the other homes in the area, the embassy had a coat of arms hanging triumphantly from black steel gates at the mouth of the driveway. My cab pulled up in front of the gates. The horse, anxious to be off, pawed impatiently, snorting, jingling, and bobbing his head as I paid the driver. No one was in sight either on the grounds or in the street. I pushed the electric buzzer beside the gate and waited, watching as my cab trotted off. Nothing happened. I pushed the buzzer again and a fit looking man in late middle age with a dark suit, a grey handle bar moustache, and some kind of regimental tie came out and spoke to me through the gate.

"'Ello sir, and what can we do for you today?" He was barrel-chested, and had his hands behind his back and a confident air about him that screamed regular army senior non-commissioned officer.

As he spoke, I noticed movement from a driveway several doors down on the opposite side of the street. A man in a homburg and tan trench coat with his hands deep in his pockets was hurrying towards us. "Listen, I absolutely have to see the military attaché. I'm a Canadian officer. My code name's Landslide and that man's a German agent who's about to try to kill me, so please, let me in!"

"Yes, sir," smirked the man behind the gate. He clapped his hands in front of him, "and since we're both such very good friends, I'll tell you, I'm the Duke of Wellington, and that man, 'e's Napoleon, 'e is. Now, why don't you just run along now, eh? We 'ave serious business 'ere, sir."

The figure in the homburg was now fifty yards away and pulled a pistol out of his pocket. He began to run with it raised, waiting until he was in range. I immediately pulled the Luger from my pocket and fired twice, missing him by a country mile. The German dove for cover, firing back without aiming. From behind me, another shot cracked much closer over my head. I turned. Far behind me was another running figure in a grey coat.

"For the love of Jesus, sir, why didn't tell me you were serious?"

"Open the gates, now!" I fired again, once in each direction.

"I am, sir, I am."

The gates swung open. I slipped through and they clanged shut. We ran through the front door with wild shots tearing through the hedge behind us.

24

INSIDE THE EMBASSY, I was treated well. The attaché, a naval officer, Captain Walker-Clitheroe, apologized profusely. I sat in a leather armchair in the ambassador's office with a glass of brandy and a cigarette in my hand.

"Ferrall, how awful! It was one of those things, I suppose. Nobody really expected you to show up. Here, I mean. You know, so much going on and I suppose we thought you'd escape through Holland or some such. You're the only one to do it. If there are any others out there, none of 'em have come in. A really splendid show, actually. That's one for our side, isn't it? Now, if you'll excuse me please, I'm going to encode a message and cable London. Well done, Ferrall, well done."

They only kept me in Copenhagen long enough to get a reply from Whitehall Court in London. The next night I was smuggled out of the embassy via the tradesmen's entrance and into a waiting lorry. We roared through Copenhagen's deserted streets down to the harbour front. From there I was loaded onto a powerful civilian motor launch that took me well out into the Kattegat, the sea separating Sweden from Denmark. There, in the midst of a misty heaving grey nothingness, we rendezvoused with Her Majesty's Submarine *J2*, and four days later, I was put ashore at the Edinburgh dockyard. The Royal Navy gave me new clothes: an officer's duffel coat and a submariner's white turtle-neck sweater, but I refused to part with my handmade German officer's jack boots. The submarine's Scottish skipper was appalled. "You're not a bloody pirate, Ferrall, you'll wear a proper uniform." I smiled and quietly agreed with him, but I ignored his orders anyway.

From the Edinburgh docks, I was driven south of town and put into the back seat of one of the new Handley-Page long-range bombers. It was the first time I'd ever been in an aeroplane and I was temporarily given a unique view of the world. I'd seen pictures taken from high in the air before, but for a few moments, until we got to our cruising altitude, the new perspective made me feel insignificant. Except for the bits around the takeoff and landing, the flight was mostly cold and cloudy and not as interesting as I'd hoped it would be.

Cumming was waiting at the sides of a deserted airstrip outside London, swotting impatiently with his sword cane at frozen tufts of grass. Standing behind him was Lance Corporal Reagan.

✲

In the back seat of his car, Cumming grinned and shook his head. "I knew you'd do it. I knew it. I had a feeling about you, Rory. Tell me everything, from the beginning."

Over the next several days I lived a closely chaperoned existence, restricted to my tiny room and the offices in Whitehall Court. In the evenings, I dined with Cumming in his club. With the exception of several cuts and scratches, I was pronounced fit by an army doctor. I began to put on weight and Mrs. Chaver resentfully made an appointment for me to get me a new set of uniforms. Over the course of that week I told my story to four different people: Cumming; a brigadier, who, I was later to learn, was John Charteris, Field Marshal Haig's chief of staff for Intelligence; and two lieutenant colonels, both from Field Marshall Haig's headquarters in France.

Cumming was the most enthusiastic of all my interrogators. In characteristic fashion, throughout my debriefings Cumming would make his entrance after the meeting was well under way. He'd always take a seat away from the table, leaning on his cane, thumping the floor and interrupting things when he felt a point needed emphasis. As much as I liked him and appreciated his support, I thought he looked ridiculous. His late entrance was his way of showing Charteris that he was maintaining some semblance of control over the proceedings. It was apparent he was championing his organization's credibility in the face of the British Expeditionary Force's disbelief.

Cumming looked much less sophisticated than I remembered. The brigadier, a tired, pensive-looking man, didn't inspire me either. He was very tall, with a slow, measured manner and a commanding voice. I thought it a shame such magnificent vocal chords weren't connected to his brain. For just under an hour and a half on the first day, the brigadier made a superficial pretence of listening to my story. After thirty minutes, he became restless and began to sneak frequent glances at his fob watch. He seemed completely indifferent to my warnings about Operation Michael. When I tried to explain to him the importance of the Seventeenth Army's planning efforts and the implications of the tactical demonstration that I'd witnessed, he became irritable and switched the subject.

At one point he waved his hand dismissively, "Yes, yes Ferrall, we've heard these kinds of reports before. Just tell us what you've seen. We'll assess the significance of it. That's a good fellow now."

He showed a spark of interest in German intelligence collection and analysis techniques and he sat forward in his chair when I described day-to-day life in Germany. Things like ration scales and whatever information I could provide on the state of morale and Germany's industrial situation stirred some enthusiasm in him. But these were two subjects I wasn't really qualified to express any kind of an opinion on. Early in the afternoon he attempted a tight grimace in lieu of a smile, thanked me for my time and effort, and then excused himself to return to British army headquarters in France.

The two other staff officers exchanged knowing looks. Both of these men were from the cavalry. One, a Territorial officer from the Oxfordshire Yeomanry, was a lawyer in civil life. He was a short aggressive-looking man with a perpetual five o'clock shadow. The other, a balding and brusque regular from the Scots Greys, smoked a pipe constantly. They both took reams of notes and questioned me in wearisome detail.

At the end of my last day of questioning, as the two colonels gathered their papers, the Yeomanry officer leaned across the table and said in a confidential tone, "What you've done, it's amazing, really Ferrall. You know, and I'm allowed to tell you this, Cumming has swung a Distinguished Service Order and a promotion to major for you. You deserve both the medal and the promotion, believe me. Damn fine bit of work, no question. We never thought Cumming's organization was capable of this sort of thing. Hats off to you."

He paused, chewing his lower lip. "But you know, I must tell you, we don't believe the Germans will use these new tactics the way you've described. They're too risky. Oh, we believe they're developing something, several things as a matter of fact. And we believe every detail of your account; but this offensive, it isn't the big one. Jerry doesn't put all his eggs in one basket, much too crafty for that."

I began to protest, but the tall Scots Grey colonel waved a hand to silence me. "Steady now, Ferrall. You've given us a tremendous amount of information, useable information, valuable information. We haven't been able to get this kind of detail elsewhere, Rory. What you've told us about their views on America's entrance to the war; you've confirmed the effects of our naval blockade; you support most of our views on how the Hun thinks and in this respect you're dead to rights. But this offensive, it's not going to be their big push, we just can't come to the same conclusion as you on this one. We believe, and again much of what you've said confirms our view, they just don't have the strength for this kind of an operation."

"Colonel, respectfully sir, that's crazy." My voice was rising. "Sir, I was there. I helped draw up the intelligence picture in the British sector. I saw their preparations in the rear area. I saw their demonstration team. I saw their training plans. What do you mean they aren't going to implement this plan? With all respect, sir! How can you possibly come to this conclusion? If they come at us with this offensive and we're not ready for it, they'll knock us out of the war. Everything we've done up to now, everything we've sacrificed ... it'll be for nothing."

"I sympathize with how you feel, Ferrall." The bald regular soldier ran his hand over the top of his head as he spoke. "But, really, you are much too close to this to be objective. And two other things: if we get this wrong, just as you say, everything we've sacrificed to date may be imperilled, especially if we go off chasing shadows in the night. We can't be caught flat-footed."

"Secondly, Rory, you've got to take the wider view," said the swarthy yeomanry officer. "We see the big picture. You aren't our only source of intelligence and we've a responsibility to advise Field Marshall Haig as to how we interpret things. We can't be filling his head with imaginings. He has a lot to think about as it is." He pulled out a silver cigarette case and offered me one of the new fancy American cigarettes with a brown cotton filter on the end. He exhaled loudly, as if he were explaining things for the ninth time to a dull-witted child.

"And frankly, we have a duty to keep strategic planning on a steady footing. If we had Field Marshall Haig reacting to every conflicting report, we'd have lost this war years ago. No, we have a duty to present only the most compelling and sensible arguments. What you say doesn't make sense. You've seen the state the Bosche is in. Germany's holding out for the best peace terms they can get. The Kaiser's losing his nerve, the country's on the brink of starvation. They've seen what happens in Russia when you push things too far. The Germans aren't fools. They know they're at the end of their rope. We know that. Think about it, Ferrall, everything you tell us indicates that. They're not going to risk this one."

The Scots Grey officer nodded his head and sat back gently tapping his pipe against his lower teeth. "There's another angle to all this, Rory. What if the Germans are trying to deceive us? Have you thought about that?"

"Absolutely not!" I was shouting. "Why would they have tried to kill me right up to the time I got into the embassy? They weren't try-

ing to deceive us. They were trying to kill me. Why would they…"
I was dumbfounded, completely at a loss for words.

"Perhaps they just wanted to make a show of trying to kill you.
You were after all an enemy spy in possession of valuable information. If they really wanted to get you, why didn't they have a sniper
cover the embassy gate?"

"Rory, we had to examine that angle," interrupted the barrister.
"Frankly, we believe you. It's a possibility that the whole chase thing
was staged; but for our part, we really do think the Germans would've
shot you dead if they could. We went down that road and we ruled it
out. I'm sorry we had to raise it with you." He sat back and folded his
arms. "But you see it's just that, at the end of the day, we don't interpret things quite the same way you do. Germany's finished, believe
me. That doesn't make what you did any less gallant. I'm personally
very impressed. What you've done wasn't a waste of effort."

"Now, Rory," said the bald cavalryman, "this is going to be hard,
but you can never tell anyone about this. Never. There are a lot of
very good reasons why this has to stay 'most secret'—forever. Lives
are at stake. Things you don't know about and can never know. You
just have to trust us. You can never talk about your clandestine activities. Never. It's the way these things must be done. If you ever go
public with any of this, the authorities will deny everything and then
quietly lock you up and throw the key away, or worse." He stopped
and stared at me pausing for emphasis as well as intimidation. "We
feel guilty telling you this, Rory. After all you've done, we know you
aren't the type who is going to talk, but I'm sure you realize this is a
necessary formality. You understand the stakes involved."

"That means you cannot try to contact Gabriele," said the bald
officer. "Not now, and not after the war, which we fully expect to be
over in the next few months. Captain Cumming is aware of all this.
This is Field Marshall Haig's policy and we've briefed Captain Cumming. He's developing a cover story for you as to how you spent
your time in East Africa. I realize that more than anything else you
will want to get in touch with Miss Richter. Its completely under-
standable." The barrister shook his head. "Can't be done, Rory.

"For one thing, if you did that, the Germans might well have a case against you, and possibly against her as well. For murder. This Kleer business, who knows what might happen after the war when civil rule is imposed on the world? We could protect you, but we can't extend that to Miss Richter. I agree with what you did. I'd like to think I'd have the courage myself to have done that sort of thing if I had to, but this part of your life, as far as anyone else is concerned, it never happened."

✠

I spent the next twelve weeks working for Cumming in Whitehall Court. I was lucky in some respects. Cumming advised me of a little flat that had become available not far away, and I jumped at the chance and moved out of my cupboard on Whitehall Court and leased a small set of furnished rooms in an old building off Baker Street. At work, things weren't much different than they had been in Germany. Just like Von Lignow, Cumming had piles of cable transcripts and reports that had to be read and assessed as to their possible intelligence value. British intelligence seemed much less well organized and less systematic than the work that went on in the Red House. But in London, conclusions were generally considered on their own merits.

In Berlin, as with the army on the continent, intelligence assessments were judged more favourably the higher up the military hierarchy they were formed. But for me it didn't matter much. Most of the material that passed through my hands was useless routine commercial traffic. During that time I was also tasked as part of a three-man economics team. It was a foolish project dreamt up by a frail old Oxford economist who was trying to devise a mathematical model to predict when Germany would sue for peace based on the size of the country's food supply. It was a frustrating task and we had no means of determining what Germany was producing so we changed all our numbers on a daily basis.

March 21 was a day I remember well. Just after lunch, I was

working at my desk reading transcripts of diplomatic cables when Cumming came and stood at my door. His face was the colour of last night's fireplace ash and he was chewing furiously on the end of his cigarette holder.

"A word with you, Rory?" I followed him down the hall to his office and he closed the door carefully and sat behind his desk.

"So, it appears you were right," he whispered. "For the last two weeks, all across our front, the Germans have been frantically busy. We thought it was some kind of diversionary activity, that they were going to make a last conventional push against the French. Our people only became convinced that the Germans were actually moving against us in the last forty-eight hours. By that time it was too late. Just last week I spoke to Haig's new chief of intelligence. Even then they still disbelieved us. They said the Germans were bluffing." He shook his head sadly.

"The Germans launched their offensive at dawn this morning. We've lost contact with numerous frontline divisions. In some locations large numbers of German infantry are appearing up to twelve and thirteen miles deep in our rear areas. We might not be able to stabilize the situation. Our reserves are tiny. We may have lost the war today, Rory." Cumming licked his lips and ran a finger around his collar. He was obviously distressed. He looked much older.

I had nothing to say. I didn't feel vindicated. I didn't feel smug but I wished I could have kicked those two cavalry colonels down the street.

"We're moving French and British reserve divisions to try and seal off the penetrations, but we won't know how successful those have been for several hours yet. We're spread so thinly nobody's even talking about launching a counter-attack. If we had the troops..." He stopped and banged his fists on the table. "It doesn't matter, we don't even know where to counter-attack. We have holes everywhere." He got up and walked to the window. "Rory, no matter what happens, you can't breathe a word of what you know about this. The people who disregarded your information will move savagely to protect themselves."

"I realize that, sir." There was a long uncomfortable pause.

"Don't you have anything more to say?"

"No, sir. I really don't know what to say." Privately, I was think-ing that if this meant the end of the war, perhaps it wasn't such a bad thing. Maybe we deserved to lose. This, as ugly a possibility as it was, might at least be an end to it all. "How frequently are we receiving reports from the front, sir?"

"Every two or three hours. I'll call you when I hear anything. I thought you'd want to know."

"I appreciate that. Thank you, sir." I went back to my desk and for the next thirty-six hours listened to a stream of gloomy reports as to how the Germans had made major penetrations east of the towns of Bapaume and Ham. London was in shock. My economist stopped calculating how long the German food supply would last. Conversations in the pubs were held in whispers. For a brief period people walked about on the streets as if in a trance. Everything they had suffered and sacrificed for was in danger of collapse. By the morning of the twenty-eighth, the tone of the news from the front began to change. The Germans had been contained. Our front line had stabilized.

Cumming dropped round to my office again that day. He was sombre and restrained. "We think it's over, Rory. They've shot their bolt. The Germans have begun to consolidate. All offensive activity has ceased and they've gone over to the defensive. They're putting up wire and digging again. It was close, very close."

"Why did they stop, sir? It seemed two days ago they had us on the run."

"It would seem the entire German army just ran out of steam. They got through the hard part all right. They pushed right through us, but they can't muster the strength for the second phase. There are stories of German troops across large areas of our front, they've just given up. Our own troops who've escaped back into our lines report whole German battalions have run amok looting our rear areas. They're half-starved. They don't have the energy to march north and we're hanging on by our fingernails and can't counter-attack, not yet anyway. Amazing really. This time I really think they've shot their bolt. It's a matter of time now. They get weaker, and as the Americans arrive, we get stronger. They can't hang on."

✠

Despite everyone's predictions to the contrary, the war had a further eight months to run. The German army reorganized and went onto the defensive. Aside from the temporary breakdown in discipline at the end of Operation Michael, they never did crack. I spent my time working in that strange block of apartments in Whitehall Court reading transcripts and despatches and re-juggling the starvation numbers. When the end finally came, I applied for a three-day leave. This time no one was surprised. We were advised of Germany's peace overtures early on.

Without explaining why, on November 9 I asked for a few days away from the office. I didn't want to be in London when the armistice was announced. I had nowhere particular to go so I took a train to Portsmouth and went for long walks by the sea. I'd heard about the diplomatic proposals and the secret planning to allow the Kaiser to abdicate and go quietly off to Holland.

I was sure that as McLeish, Redvers, and Von Lignow had all predicted, the terms of the peace treaty were going to be harsh. I was no psychic, but I knew things weren't settled. In the pubs and shops, just as in Cumming's club, they were all talking the same way. The Hun would have to pay. I'd just come back from walking along the beachfront in Portsmouth watching the November breakers roll in when I heard the whooping and shouting. People were banging on pots, church bells rang out, and there was euphoria everywhere as the news raced up and down the streets. It was over, but unlike everyone else, I was strangely indifferent to it all.

✠

I received my demobilization orders three months after the armistice. The Canadian army headquarters in London sent me a small sheaf of yellow flimsy papers advising me when I could board a ship to take me home and where I was to report in Montreal so that I could make my return to civilian life official. While I waited for my demob orders, I continued to work at Whitehall Court translating German newspaper reports, writing assessments, and working on a new economic model to predict how the Germans would feed themselves over the next year.

Over those months, I gradually came back to something like my old self. I went out at nights, I went to the theatres and cinemas, I read books, and twice Cumming invited me down for weekends at his country house in Hampshire. Old Cumming tried to interest me in some pretty young English girls, but I wasn't in the mood for romance, not then. I was still feeling like a cad and I was sorely tempted to send Gabriele a letter through Switzerland. I never did; and my inaction left me feeling hollow and angry.

On March 3, 1919, I left London and found myself in Liverpool sitting amongst a hundred other Canadian officers in the Cunard Shipping Line's waiting room. I suppose when I looked back on it all, I'd been successful. But like so many other successes in one's life, it didn't seem to matter much. Like a small stick vainly trying to make its way onto the beach in a surging tide, events swept my moment of truth back into the ocean. I looked up at the clock on the wall and watched the second hand fly around the dial. I'd given a lot and I'd done my best; but I'd also survived when so many good men didn't. I was thankful to be alive. For now, there was a boat to catch and I sat quietly in a leather chair until the boarding call at ten o'clock. While I was waiting the rain stopped. When the porter announced the gangplanks were down, I shouldered my kit bag and cloth valise and pushed my way out through a revolving door onto a crowded wharf. I was going home and had a new life to build.

✠ ✠ ✠

EPILOGUE

MANY PEOPLE go to great lengths to maintain contact with old acquaintances. I freely admit, I'm one of them. As through most of my long life, I have been able to keep track of many of the people I knew in the Great War. I have always kept up a vigorous correspondence and I confess that over the years I have also developed a certain professional skill at keeping tabs on people. I returned to Germany on several occasions after the Great War: in the late 1930s, during the Second World War, and again in the early years of the Cold War.

Of those people of historical importance who I encountered in my war years, my information is readily verifiable and detailed information on their lives is a matter of public record. Those who have been recorded in the annals of history, I have identified with an asterisk. On all the others I have personally verified the information. As far as I know, like myself, their faint mark on history has never been recorded outside these memoirs.

Jeanine Dupuis was happily married. I was a very distant friend for life. Her husband eventually became a judge on the Quebec Superior Court. Jeanine raised a large family and was actively involved in the community and charitable works. She remained an example of grace and dignity until her death in 1977. I last spoke to her when I attended her husband's funeral in 1964. She is survived by numerous children and grandchildren.

Mr. and Mrs. Ferrall—My parents lived together but followed very separate lives. My father never retired and died at his desk of heart failure in 1943. Mother lived to a vigorous old age and died peacefully in 1959. She was to the end an ardent Canadian and was active in numerous charities.

Agar Adamson*—My old company commander stayed on with the regiment throughout the war. When I knew him, he was a courageous, magnanimous, and gracious man. Clearly, the war and his long gruelling service in the trenches changed him. He returned very different from the man he once was. His character changed abruptly, he cruelly ignored his wife to whom he had once been utterly devoted, and he took to reckless gambling and heavy drinking. He died from complications related to an entirely preventable airplane accident over the Irish Sea in 1929. (Editor's Note—Ferrall is largely correct in his notes on Adamson. Subsequent to the author's death, Adamson's letters and diaries were published and have become a frequently cited original source for historians of the period. See *The Letters of Agar Adamson*, edited by N.M. Christie, CEF Books, 1997.)

Hamilton Gault* survived the grave wounds he received at Sanctuary Wood. He refused to be repatriated and went on to serve out the war as a staff officer. At the war's end, with one leg, he was placed in temporary command of his beloved regiment and brought it home to Canada. After the war, he moved to England and became a country gentleman and a Conservative MP holding a safe riding for many years. He was a major benefactor of McGill University. He died in 1958.

Lance Corporal George Mullin* was one of several truly exceptional soldiers I had the honour of serving with. He was a tough, resilient, and humane man, one of those very rare individuals who thrive and are seemingly unaffected by calamitous circumstances. While I recuperated in hospital, George Mullin was deservedly awarded the Military Medal for his actions at Sanctuary Wood. Later in the war, at the Battle of Passchendaele, as a sergeant he was awarded the Victoria Cross. After the war, he returned to Canada and lived a quiet life. He died in Regina, Saskatchewan, in 1964.

Private Geoffrey Hendricks, the divinity student who helped carry me out of the line at Sanctuary Wood, survived the war and went on to play a minor role in forming the United Church of Canada from the Canadian Methodist and Presbyterian churches. Hendricks became a social activist and later in life was a driving force behind the creation of the Cooperative Commonwealth Federation, a forerunner of Canada's principal socialist party. I last saw him in person when I had dinner with his family at his rural parish in Alberta in 1933.

Mansfield Cumming* was the first head of MI5. He served in that capacity from 1909 to 1923. He was a naval officer who proved to be unfit for sea duties because of seasickness. He proved to be a gifted practitioner of the intelligence trade. Although I did not know it at the time, he established a useful surveillance ring based on civilian train watchers in Belgium and the occupied areas of France and he was instrumental in breaking the German submarine codes used in the Great War. He was a mild eccentric, and despite his documented penchant for dressing up in disguises and building secret passageways in his house, in the pre-war years he kept British intelligence alive in the face of great opposition from the Foreign Office, the army, and the Royal Navy. His greatest legacy was the establishment of one of the world's first professional intelligence services. Cumming died of natural causes in 1923. (Author's note— Throughout the Great War, George Bernard Shaw lived for several years at Whitehall Court in a flat directly beneath Cumming's. By all accounts, Shaw never suspected who he was.)

Professor Bronau—I never saw or heard from Professor Bronau again. I have been told he returned to a quiet scholarly life at Cambridge after the war. He was one of the first of many scholars and academics to become involved in intelligence activities. He died of natural causes in 1943.

Major General Sir Sam Hughes*—Canada's notoriously energetic but pig-headed minister of the militia, he was despised by the troops and although my run-in with him was never recorded, he had previously been at the heart of numerous well-documented public embarrassments. The most famous incident took place at Camp Borden, Ontario, where he was booed from the podium by angry troops who had been left waiting his arrival for two hours in the heat and dust. Upon his return from England, Hughes was viewed as a political liability and dumped from the federal cabinet. He died in 1921.

Mrs. Chaver—Although I could never prove it, I believe she was the precursor of Mrs. Moneypenney. Ian Fleming, the author of the James Bond novels, portrayed Mrs. Moneypenney as a Canadian. Her predecessor was in fact excruciatingly English, but she was by no means typical of that high-spirited race. I lost track of her. No doubt she died as cantankerously as she lived.

*John Charteris**—was Field Marshall Haig's chief of staff. Just days after my briefing, Charteris was fired from his position for entirely unrelated political indiscretions. Over the next several weeks after our meeting, Charteris became convinced that a German offensive was imminent. Unfortunately, he had lost his position of influence and few of those in authority took him seriously until it was all but too late. Charteris retired from the army in 1922 and served for a time in Parliament. He died in 1946.

Ewen Crossley—I met up with Ewen briefly in the early days of World War II. He remained in secret intelligence between the wars and characteristically volunteered for duty in occupied France. As a member of one of SOE's compromised resistance networks he was parachuted into France where he was captured, endured terrible tortures, and was murdered by the Gestapo.

*General Groener**—When I went to Germany, Major General Wilhelm Groener was the General Staff officer tasked with guaranteeing the country's food supply. He was a remarkable man with an intellectual range that embraced liberal social views and oppressive militaristic insularity. Just after I went to work for Von Lignow, Groener was posted to command the Supreme War Bureau, a position from which he assumed responsibility for the entire German economy. Characteristically, he made himself unpopular with his military superiors and was demoted to command a division in France, and shortly after that was sent off to supervise the economic exploitation of the Ukraine. In the last months of the war, he was recalled to provide advice to a faltering High Command in Berlin. In November 1918, Groener was the man who convinced the Kaiser to abdicate. After the war, Groener held numerous cabinet-level positions in post-war governments. He was opposed to the Nazis but failed in his efforts to prevent their infiltration in the army's leadership. He died in 1939.

Alex Baumann was repatriated, along with tens of thousands of other POWs, to Germany at the end of the war. In the chaos of post-war Germany, it is unlikely, that as one of Europe's millions of displaced persons, Alex was ever officially connected to the man I impersonated. I ran several discreet checks on him during my later career but I was never able to find him. There are no records of him ever returning to America.

Unteroffizier Brickner—I was unable to find any information about this man.

Captain Ebersbach became a Nazi in the earliest days of the movement. His name crossed my desk in the Second World War in an intelligence report relating to incidents that took place in 1934. Ebersbach was a member of Ernst Rohm's SA and was dragged from his bed and shot during the Nazi Party's murderous Night of Long Knives.

Jacob Lazarowicz—After the war, Jacob Lazarowicz once again became a highly successful businessman in Bialystock. Unfortunately, this gallant little man was financially ruined in the 1930s by racially oppressive trade laws imposed by the Polish government against that nation's Jews. A nephew who emigrated to Israel in the early 1930s believes that Jacob was murdered in the Holocaust along with over four million fellow Jews from the Pale of Settlement.

Princess Patricia's Canadian Light Infantry*—Because it was a celebrated national unit, as opposed to a locally recruited unit, the PPCLI was designated as one of Canada's three regular army infantry regiments after the war. Many of its officers went on to become senior leaders in the Canadian army. The regiment exists today and has seen extensive service in the Second World War and Korea. (Editor's note—Since this memoir was written, the PPCLI has served with distinction on numerous UN peacekeeping missions, with NATO as well as in Bosnia, Kosovo, and Afghanistan. Numerous histories of the regiment are in print.)

Arne and Peder Knudson—Peder died in the 1920s. Arne was later in life crippled by rheumatoid arthritis. Despite this, he was an active anti-Nazi in Norwegian politics. He played a minor role in the resistance and died of natural causes in the late 1960s. His descendants still live in southern Norway.

Dr. Gehlen—My first impressions about Dr. Gehlen were not unfounded. He achieved notoriety as a member of Berlin's underground counterculture. In the early 1920s, he was involved in a very public scandal involving sordid sexual activities at a Berlin nightclub. As a result, he was forced to go into private practice for a time. His trail goes cold in the late 1920s. In his professional life he pioneered techniques in the surgical treatment of trauma casualties. Despite his brilliance as a surgeon, it is unlikely he survived the Nazis.

Willy Stenhauser—I went to the forest-meister's cottage in 1938. The old man who lived there knew only vaguely of Brigitte and Willy. Apparently they lived out the war together and moved on after the war. Their trail ends in 1918.

Baron Von Huttinger—Died in 1919 in the Spanish Influenza epidemic. His property and businesses were broken up and sold.

Alex Von Lignow—Alex predictably became a scapegoat, and was tried by court martial and found guilty of the relatively minor charge of negligence. Reduced in rank and officially disgraced, he served as the officer commanding a company in a punishment battalion and, despite all this, was for his courage and skill awarded an Iron Cross Second Class in Operation Michael.

Promoted back to the rank of major, in September of 1918, he was again seriously wounded leading his battalion in the battle that has become known in Allied history as "The Battles of the Last Hundred Days."

He survived the war, with his health but not his spirit impaired. Upon his return to Berlin he was for a time reconciled with his wife, Sophie, but they went their separate ways within the year. He left the army in 1919 and for eight years ran a successful import business but was cheated and bankrupted by a partner. He later turned to journalism and was a prominent anti-Nazi. He disappeared one night in 1934. Officially listed as a missing person, he was almost certainly murdered by Nazi thugs.

Gabriele Richter—I disobeyed the orders of the two staff officers. In 1920 I wrote to Gabriele. For a year I received no answer, but she eventually came to terms with me, the war, and all it entailed. She wrote me a long letter in 1921. Although we never met again, we preserved enormous friendship and respect for one another; but clearly, the spark from our relationship was gone. We kept up an intermittent but clandestine correspondence until 1925, at which point we mutually agreed to cease communication when she became engaged to be married.

Along with her parents, Gabriele was held for intensive questioning for a month after my escape. All three were released without charges in January. In early 1921, she sat the entrance exams for medical school and that same year, after receiving the highest marks, was the only woman accepted into the University of Berlin's prestigious medical program. Her husband, Axel Heimler, was a fellow student. They separated in 1930. There were no children. Gabriele continued to practise medicine until shortly before her death from cancer in East Germany in 1966.

MICHAEL GOODSPEED has had careers in business and in the army as an infantry officer. He has lived and worked across the Americas, Europe, the Middle East and Africa. He has degrees in English literature, business administration and strategic studies.

The author of numerous articles and newspaper columns, Goodspeed wrote a major 2002 non-fiction work, *When Reason Fails: Portraits of Armies at War*. Michael and his wife, Shannon, have three grown children and live in an old farmhouse in the Eastern Ontario countryside. His hobbies include reading, music, fitness, writing, travel, sailing and skiing.

WHAT'S AHEAD? Goodspeed's next novel from Blue Butterfly Books will pick up the career of Rory Ferrall, protagonist of *Three to a Loaf*, at a very different stage of his career in military espionage during the early years of Nazi Germany's occupation of The Netherlands.

AUTHOR INTERVIEW

Your first novel is just coming out but I understand your author's tour will be rather dramatically curtailed.

MICHAEL GOODSPEED: Yes, I'm about to depart Canada for Afghanistan, as part of the Canadian Forces mission there. I'll be stationed in Kabul for a year at least.

For someone so immersed in current events at the front line, how did you become a fan of "historical fiction"?

GOODSPEED: I've always been interested in history and grew up reading historical novels. We try to make sense of our own world through the experiences of others. That's probably true for stories in general, but historical novels bring the circumstances and problems of a bygone period to life. They provide an explanation and context for important events that shaped our lives today. Coupled with this, I think we have an instinctive need to have the world explained to us in stories. It's in our DNA. It was probably as true for cavemen hunched around their fires as it is in modern novels, films or television.

Does the point of view or perspective in historical fiction correspond to an interpretation of history, then?

GOODSPEED: I think it was E.H. Carr who said. "History isn't a collection of facts, history is an argument." This should certainly be true for historical novels. They should generally have a purpose beyond simply the entertainment and the problems provided by their narrative and their characters. By their nature historical novels provide a distinct interpretation of history, and because novels are usually a lengthy accounting of a period, we can be exposed to numerous ideas and shades of meaning within that interpretation. So I think, in addition to being a good story, good historical novels should serve as a highly nuanced form of historical argument.

How has being a lieutenant colonel with many years service affected your writing?

GOODSPEED: Because I've been able to travel extensively I've had a lot of unusual experiences in some out of the way and distressed places. During my time in the army and to a lesser extent when I was in industry I met thousands of different people in highly diverse circumstances in many corners of the world. Those experiences are bound to have shaped my view of mankind.

I think an individual's outlook on the world is what ultimately informs his or her writing. Jane Austen lived her life in a village in Hampshire and wrote brilliant miniature portraits, while someone well travelled like Joseph Conrad worked with equal effect on a much larger canvas. The larger worldview doesn't necessarily guarantee one's writing will be any more perceptive or point of view more compelling, but I think worldview has an influence on what intellectual focal length an author chooses.

 *Conducting your research, reading through so many letters, diaries and unit records, what struck you most about the people and times you treat in* Three to a Loaf?

GOODSPEED: Human nature has certain constants, but different societies, just as different people, exhibit diverse traits. In the case of the First World War, one thing that jumps right out is people's capacity and willingness to endure hardship. It was much different than our era. And in this sense, I'd also include their resourcefulness, their sense of tolerance, their staying power and their commitment.

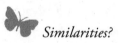 *Anything else?*

GOODSPEED: They had a slightly different sense of humour, they had a simpler and maybe even a more profound sense of enjoyment of life; and they had a greater degree of trust in what they perceived to be the natural order of things. With regard to this last one, the effects of World Wars One and Two in particular had a lot to do with changing our views of the natural order of things. Those wars also probably helped stimulate a more aggressive sense of inquiry in our societies.

Similarities?

GOODSPEED: Despite all the differences, First World War veterans were also very identifiable in terms of their fears and hopes and ambitions. It sounds corny, but in answering your question I can't help but think of the Canadian poet soldier John McRae: they "lived, felt dawn, saw sunset glow, loved and were loved…" They were as ordinary as the people around you on the bus.

Turning to your book, which—congratulations!—has been receiving high praise in advance of publication, how did you come up with the idea of the story's hero Rory Ferrall being on both sides during the First World War?

GOODSPEED: I've been interested in that war since I was a boy, you know. The ideas and the outlook of the generation that fought the First World War have always intrigued me.

When I was in grade school I met several veterans of the war and I've always been in awe of them for what they had been through. The war was one of those disastrous watersheds in history, a war that should never have happened. But they did their best in appalling circumstances that weren't of their making.

But still, you developed an unusual plot here.

GOODSPEED: That's because a few years ago I came across one of those little known facts: the war had placed a terrible strain on recent German immigrants to North America. As a result, large numbers of them, from both Canada and the United States, went back to the old country to join up with the Kaiser's Army, many to fulfill their reserve obligations. Reading about this certainly made for some plausible "what-if?" scenarios.

The idea for the novel came to me when I was living in Calgary with access to the Princess Patricia's Regimental archives. I spent many afternoons in a room in the Regimental Museum studying original letters and first hand accounts of the war. In reading the letters and studying photographs of the time, many of the voices and personalities became very real to me. In a sense I felt that I knew many of them.

In this way the character of Rory Ferrall and his predicament emerged. And having been a soldier, it was natural for me to think: "What would I have done if I had discovered someone like Rory Ferrall?" If I was in the intelligence world and faced as desperate a situation as the Allies found themselves in, I would have sent Ferrall into Germany to discover what they were planning to do to win the war. And because of that Rory Ferrall finds himself in Germany.

The memoir you've created makes clear that the interpretation of military intelligence was as problematic during World War One as it has been for the Americans and British in Iraq nearly a century later. Why is this?

GOODSPEED: The field of intelligence has unique problems and always will. When you are gathering, assessing and analyzing information, the technical means of collection is always going to be only of equal importance to the human factors. It is a mistake to believe that technology gives you an absolute advantage. Technology is important, but no matter how you gather information, whether it's by broadband satellite intercepts or untrained partisans probing the flanks of a deployed force, your opponent is always trying to deceive you as to his strengths and his intentions. In any human conflict you will always have to contend with that other brain, and he or she wants you to misread the situation.

But you give an insider's stunning portrait of a far more complex challenge than just that.

GOODSPEED: That's because the other great obstacle to intelligence is an internal one. Humans have a hard-wired predisposition to believe what we want to believe. Many errors in intelligence are made because people misinterpret information by being unable to overcome their own biases. You see it everyday in the stock market, in political campaigns and more catastrophically in war.

In World War I the Allies thought the Germans would rely on a technical invention to break the deadlock on the Western Front.

In World War II the Germans thought the Allies would land at the Pas de Calais rather than Normandy. The Israelis didn't believe the Egyptians could get over the Suez Canal in 1973.

History will provide an endlessly fascinating list of intelligence blunders. It's in our make-up.

If television cameras had been in the trenches of the First World War and the public been aware of the atrocious conditions described in Three to a Loaf, *do you think that would have caused the war to end more quickly?*

GOODSPEED: Any answer to that has to be speculative, but I would guess it's very likely that television would have accelerated the movement of some of the political issues of the day. We probably would have seen national will erode faster than it did.

Remember that in countries like Canada and Britain casualties in previous conflicts had been, in relative terms, quite low. So the war really was an enormous shock. That wasn't true later on for the Americans when they came into the war. Not too long before they had endured one of the bloodiest civil wars in history and they had almost four years to witness the carnage.

On the other hand, it's also important to remember that the war's high casualty rates were very obvious within the society. We tend to forget that. Modern media gets the message home faster, but the scale and impact of personal tragedy remained the same. People draped black crepe on their houses; newspapers and posters had long casualty lists prominently displayed in black borders. Letters from the front were passed around. Wounded veterans returned home. I think people understood how terrible the war was.

There's also a dark side to your question, you know. Television can be controlled. It's probable that the governments of the day would have used the media as a means of deliberately shaping opinions. So in that respect, the technology probably isn't as important as would have been the controls that would have been imposed on it.

The human dramas may remain the same, but what has changed in the Canadian Forces between Rory Ferrall's era and 2008?

GOODSPEED: That's a tough question. It was one of the things I had to come to grips with in order not to simply superimpose my impressions and preconceptions on the reader. It was important to understand the similarities and differences in the generations and the institutions.

In some respects things have changed dramatically, and as a society those who lived through the First World War had radically different views on many issues. But equally, military life was in many ways similar to what it is now. If we ignore the obvious things like clothing, food, weapons and tactics, many of the certainties of army life are the same. It's a hierarchy, you live and work in close-knit teams, there is a heavy emphasis on strength of character and you need to develop strong bonds of trust. Those kinds of basic things are probably very similar.

Having said that, I think institutionally we are now considerably more attuned to the subtleties of personal and institutional leadership. People can't be taken for granted as they once were; and equally, some of the key measures that the army uses have evolved.

For instance?

GOODSPEED: The whole concept of "character" has progressed, for example. We've whittled down the constituent elements of "character" from what it was in 1915. Back then, stress disorders were seen as character problems, not medical conditions. Other elements that fall into that category would be social distinctions, the role of individual rights, attitudes to authority, attitudes to sacrifice and death, racial tolerance, the role of women, our belief in political symbols such as the king and the nation. All of these have changed substantially over the last ninety years. I think too the rhythms of everyday life are probably more intense.

Yet for all of this, you can't escape the similarities. They remain the same: honesty, fairness, integrity, intelligence, creativity, compassion, and courage—both moral and physical. These things really determine the quality of an army, and a society for that matter, and they're timeless.

One difference between the First World War and today is that book clubs and readers of Three to a Loaf *will be able to keep in touch with you in Afghanistan through the Blue Butterfly website* while you're on the other side of the globe in Kabul.*

GOODSPEED: No question, that's certainly a huge difference. It'll be interesting to hear from them.

Good luck.

GOODSPEED: Thanks.

*www.bluebutterflybooks.ca

ORDERING INFORMATION
for Blue Butterfly Books

Trade Distribution (Canada)

White Knight Book Distribution
Warehouse/fulfilment by Georgetown Terminal Warehouse
34 Armstrong Avenue, Georgetown, Ontario L7G 4R9
Tel 1-800-485-5556   Fax 1-800-485-6665

Trade Distribution (U.S.A.)

Hushion House Publishing Inc.
Warehouse/fulfilment by APG Books
7344 Cockrill Bond Boulevard, Nashville, Tennessee 37209
Tel 1-800-275-2606   Fax 1-800-510-3650

On-line Purchase (world wide)

www.bluebutterflybooks.ca

ABOUT THIS BOOK

Rory Ferrall, a young Canadian officer of Anglo-German descent, is wounded and disfigured at the battle of Ypres during the First World War. After he's shipped back to a convalescent hospital in Britain, his night terrors in German catch the attention of British Military Intelligence. Rory's German-speaking North American background is invaluable to war planners desperate to discover Germany's plans.

When the Allies capture a German-American officer, one of many who had left the U.S. to fight for the Fatherland, Rory is trained to impersonate him. He then "escapes" back to Germany to infiltrate the German General Staff and discover their top-secret plan to break the stalemate on the Western Front. In Germany, however, Ferrall's mission is jeopardized when his identity become suspect, then further complicated when he becomes involved with an intelligent and free-thinking German nurse.

Suspense, moral and personal quandaries, and historical detail are all woven together with a realism that resonates as sharply today as it did nearly a century ago. The context of *Three to a Loaf* has been meticulously researched with original material drawn from regimental, national and archived intelligence sources.

More than a page-turning novel of war and espionage, *Three to a Loaf* vividly portrays societies and individuals pushed to the breaking point. Goodspeed artfully blends the tension of a thriller with period detail and the detached commentary of a nitty-gritty travelogue. As an experienced soldier himself, the author tops it all with psychological understanding of a harried man facing soul-destroying ethical decisions.

From the participants' eyes we glimpse the harrowing fate awaiting the losers of the world's first total war. Goodspeed's book is as much an explanation of how and why the world was driven to embrace the 20th century's most brutal ideologies as it is a tale of how one man preserves his spirit and dignity in hopeless times.

In tracing the folly and desperation of a flailing civilization that has spun horribly out of control, the central theme of *Three to a Loaf* will strike a responsive chord in a readership today wrenched once more by polar tensions of security and morality.